THEIR *Fairy* PRINCESS

OFFICE INTRIGUE, 7

BECAUSE NAUGHTY CAN BE OH SO NICE®

NE LTD

By Nicole Edwards

ALLURING INDULGENCE
Kaleb
Zane
Travis
Holidays with The Walker Brothers
Ethan
Braydon
Sawyer
Brendon

THE WALKERS OF COYOTE RIDGE
Curtis
Jared
Hard to Hold
Hard to Handle
Beau
Rex
A Coyote Ridge Christmas
Mack

AUSTIN ARROWS
Rush
Kaufman

CLUB DESTINY
Conviction
Temptation
Addicted
Seduction
Infatuation
Captivated
Devotion
Perception
Entrusted
Adored
Distraction

DEAD HEAT RANCH
Boots Optional
Betting on Grace
Overnight Love

DEVIL'S BEND
Chasing Dreams
Vanishing Dreams

MISPLACED HALOS
Protected in Darkness
Salvation in Darkness

OFFICE INTRIGUE
Office Intrigue
Intrigued Out of The Office
Their Rebellious Submissive
Their Famous Dominant
Their Ruthless Sadist
Their Naughty Student
Their Fairy Princess

PIER 70
Reckless
Fearless
Speechless
Harmless
Clueless

SNIPER 1 SECURITY
Wait for Morning
Never Say Never
Tomorrow's Too Late

SOUTHERN BOY MAFIA/DEVIL'S PLAYGROUND
Beautifully Brutal
Without Regret
Beautifully Loyal
Without Restraint

Author: Nicole Edwards
Title: Their Fairy Princess
Office Intrigue, 7

Cover Details:
Image: © Irina Kharchenko (75558354)| 123rf.com
Design: © Nicole Edwards Limited

Interior Details:
Formatting: Nicole Edwards Limited
Editing: Blue Otter Editing | BlueOtterEditing.com

Identifiers: ISBN: 978-1-64418-016-7 (ebook); ISBN: 978-1-64418-017-4 (paperback); ISBN: 978-1-64418-018-1 (audio)

Subjects: BISAC: FICTION / Romance / General

THEIR *Fairy* PRINCESS

OFFICE INTRIGUE, 7

NICOLE EDWARDS

Prologue

IAN STOKES

Tuesday, November 13, 2018

WHEN IT CAME TO DICHOTOMY, I WASN'T much into the training aspect, but I had to admit, it had been an honor when Gregory Edge requested us for this session. More so when he requested our assistance with an experiment he was having his submissive undergo, which meant, the sweet Jamie Lautner was checking out the action from a discrete location. Likely on the other side of that two-way mirror.

Initially, I'd had some ideas of how a casual session could play out, then Master Edge outlined his intention in the hopes that my twin brother and I would help him out.

Who could say no to Gregory Edge?

Certainly not me.

So, here we were, role-playing in what was, in my humble opinion, a rather lackluster theme room. Since I had a living room at my own house, I didn't really see the appeal. As far as scenes went, a leather sofa and a throw rug weren't exactly my idea of a good time. However, it was requested we use it, so we would be using it.

At least it was nice. Elegant, comfortable. Trent Ramsey's decorators knew how to spruce up a space with the expensive art deco on the walls, the various knick-knacks tucked in for accent. Luckily for us, they'd spared no expense for comfort, either.

Granted, my brother was the only comfortable one at the moment. I was in the pretend kitchen that was nothing but a door leading out of the theme room, and Isaac was sitting in a leather chair, one ankle propped over the opposite knee, giving great attention to what appeared to be a bondage equipment magazine. He was likely bored out of his mind.

"You're up," I cued Everly Hughes, the sweet little submissive we were assigned to tonight.

"Thank you, Master Ian."

From the moment I saw her, I'd been … well, to be fair, I'd been slightly hesitant. Had I met her anywhere else, I would've thought someone was trying to punk me. She looked all of eighteen on a good day. So sweet and pure it was a wonder her parents had ever let her out of her house when she had been a teenager.

Yet I knew she was twenty-four years old, fresh-faced, and rather eager for this training class as it would give her grand entry into one of the most sought-after fetish clubs in the BDSM community.

I watched as she practically danced across the room, all light and sunshine, while my brother pretended not to notice her.

Impossible.

No straight man could miss her. Certainly not in here.

She reminded me of a fictional fairy. All five feet of her. Between the delicate bone structure and the big blue eyes, she had captured my attention from the very beginning. Isaac's, too, although I was fairly certain my brother was still in denial.

The best part about this particular submissive-in-training: she wasn't built like someone had glued a bunch of toothpicks together. No, Everly Hughes was curvy in all the right places. From her narrow shoulders, her perfect-handful breasts, the cinch of her waist, the delectable flair of her hips. And those thighs … oh, yeah, I could easily envision those thighs wrapped firmly around my waist or better yet, cradling my head as I feasted between them.

As she pranced over to Isaac, her light brown hair swayed, tickling the small of her back, falling like fine silk almost to her pert little ass.

Isaac kept his attention on the magazine, following the makeshift script to a T. Our objective was to show Edge's submissive what a rigid household might look like. Two Doms, one submissive playing out a structured evening at home. It was exactly what Isaac and I had envisioned for ourselves one day.

As he was apt to do, Isaac left Everly waiting as she stood before him, patiently anticipating his instruction.

Of course, my twin was a stickler for self-restraint—for himself as well as the submissive he was engaged with—and it showed in the way he thumbed his way through those glossy pages, his head canting to the side every so often as though he was considering what that particular piece of equipment might look like in his bedroom.

Yawn.

I was growing bored when Isaac finally set the magazine down on the table beside him, dropped his foot to the floor, and tapped one finger on his knee.

Everly didn't miss a beat. She instantly danced toward him before easing herself into his lap, curling up in his arms.

That was the moment I saw it.

No one else in the world would've been able to detect the slight nuance, but I had. Isaac was my identical twin and we had a bond stronger than most.

And right there ... the moment the fairy princess curled up against him, my brother fell a little bit in love, even though I knew he would never admit it. Not even to himself.

While I stood around, pretending to be doing something in another part of the house, he started a conversation as his hands roamed easily over her, gliding up her thigh, never going too far.

"Did you finish the dishes?" Isaac asked, exactly as his character was supposed to.

"Yes, Sir," she said sweetly.

"Where's Ian?"

"He said he had a surprise for me. Told me to come into the living room and wait."

Yep. Surprise in hand, I was just waiting for my cue.

"I take it to mean you've been a good girl?"

"Yes, Sir. Very good."

And there it was.

Hefting her surprise in my arm, I carried it into the room.

The small sex machine, which we referred to as a saddle, was roughly thirteen inches long and twelve inches wide. It stood approximately eight inches tall. The best way to describe it was as a half of a barrel laid on its side with a padded leather cushion across the center of it. Nothing particularly fancy unless you had a sweet submissive straddling it.

Which we would. And not soon enough.

"Do you think you've been good enough for this?" Isaac asked Everly.

She lifted her head, glanced at the machine I'd set on the floor. I carried the plug over to the wall, slid it into the electrical socket.

"Yes, Sir."

Good or not, I was excited about watching her ride the damn thing.

Isaac lifted her off his lap, steadying her on her feet as I took my seat on the plastic-covered sofa.

"Present," Isaac commanded.

I watched the show the beautiful fairy put on for us, moving a few steps away, angling herself so that she was facing both of us before she slipped off the silk tank she wore, revealing her small, pert breasts with their dusky pink nipples. Her tiny skirt was the next to go, unveiling a hairless mound at the apex of those soft, smooth legs.

Neither of us had to say anything because Everly knew the drill, lowering herself to the floor, her movements fluid, elegant. She rolled herself out flat, legs wide, toes pointed, that pretty pink pussy on display, practically beckoning my tongue to tease it. Her chest arched upward, arms stretching over her head, hands resting elegantly on the floor.

Beautiful. Absolutely stunning.

I pretended to be relaxed and comfortable, admiring her sweet, lithe body, while my cock thickened with a greed that quite honestly surprised me. "Very nice, fairy princess. Now ass position."

As though she'd practiced a million times, Everly curled up, rolled over, and propped herself on hands and knees, her sweet little ass facing us at all times. As her chest lowered to the floor, she spread her knees wide, putting all her private parts on display.

She did have a very pretty pussy, one I was hoping we had the pleasure of teasing at some point in the future.

"What did you have in store for her?" Isaac asked, his question directed at me.

"Since she's been a good girl, I thought I'd let her perform for us."

While Everly remained perfectly positioned, I took the opportunity to tease her a bit. Ensuring I didn't block anyone's view from the window behind me, I walked over, bent down, and slid my fingers along her slit.

I figured she deserved some praise for doing so well, so I fondled her clit, loving her soft moans of pleasure.

"Wait pose, fairy princess," I instructed as I forced myself to stop before I took it too far, returning to my place, using a cloth to wipe my hands.

Everly repositioned onto her knees, pivoting to face us, toes pressed against the floor, butt resting on her heels as she clasped her hands behind her back, her eyes on me as she waited for my next instruction.

"Did you enjoy that, little fairy?" Isaac asked.

I glanced over at him, wondering if he realized his Irish was showing, the brogue thicker than usual, the pet name tumbling from his lips as though it was natural to refer to a submissive in training in such a manner.

He didn't look my way, so I turned my attention back to Everly, smirked. If she'd been surprised, she hid it well.

"Yes, Sir, I did. Very much." Those pretty brown eyes shifted to me. "Thank you, Master Ian."

"You're very welcome, princess." I held out the bottle of lubricant, nodding toward the machine. "Prepare the toy."

"May I stand, Master Ian? Or shall I remain on my knees?"

"Knees."

I had to admit, I was rather impressed. She hadn't missed a beat. I wondered if this was how she would handle being at home with us. Would she sit in the middle of our living room, awaiting her instruction? Or would she sit on the sofa, secretly hoping for some playtime?

I could see it going either way, the more I thought about it. The strangest part was that I was now thinking about it, taking sweet Everly home with us, indulging whenever we wanted.

Everly took the bottle, drawing me out of my wayward thoughts, thanking me as I passed it to her.

She surprised me again, seductively stroking the fake dick, slicking it, preparing it for her pussy. When she handed me the bottle, I took the liberty of wiping her hands, my gaze dropping to her pretty nipples as they puckered sweetly.

Yeah. This one was going to be damn hard to resist.

"Mount the toy, little fairy," Isaac commanded.

"Yes, Master Isaac."

Still smiling sweetly, as though this was the only place she wanted to be, Everly positioned herself over the dildo before easing down on it. Her pleasure was obvious from the second that fake dick began sliding inside her. Her mouth opened, eyes hooded, nipples pulling tightly as the sensations coursed through her.

So fucking sweet.

Now it was my turn to have a little fun. I retrieved the remote from my pocket, relaxed into the sofa, and pressed the buttons to bring the saddle to life.

"I expect to hear your pleasure," Isaac told her. "And you are not allowed to come until I give you permission. If you do, you will be punished."

"Yes, Master Isaac."

We'd never played with Everly before. I hoped she knew how very serious Isaac was about that rule.

With my eyes on her, the remote in my hand, I thoroughly enjoyed myself, using the vibrating toy to work her into a frenzy while Isaac and I alternated our commands, having her shift positions for both her pleasure and ours.

Figuring I might as well have a little fun, I turned the vibrations up.

"Masters"—Everly's head tipped back, her hands cupping her breasts as Isaac had instructed—"I'm going to come. Oh, God. It's too much."

"Not enough," Isaac growled.

I pushed another button. Everly cried out, a startled scream ripping from her throat as the sweet fairy princess came right there before us, her body taut as she came apart.

At this point, my brother wasn't the only one who had fallen for the fairy princess. I'd fallen a little in love with her myself.

"What did I tell you?" Isaac questioned when her body had relaxed somewhat.

"You instructed me not to come, Master Isaac," she whispered, remorse ringing every word.

Although I'd seen some submissives come without permission on purpose, I heard genuine remorse in Everly's tone. She was disappointed in herself for failing him.

"And did you come?"

"Yes, Sir."

"Come here, little fairy," he ordered.

Her legs were wobbly, but Everly managed to get to her feet, then straightened her spine, thrust her chest forward, and gracefully pranced toward Isaac.

My brother shifted seconds before Every draped herself over his thighs, her palms pressing against the floor as she held herself over his lap.

"Five," Isaac warned seconds before he smacked her ass. Hard.

That sweet fairy princess moaned.

She fucking moaned and I think I fell a little more.

Isaac smacked her ass again and again. Everly whimpered, her ass red where his hand had lanced. I envisioned my hand on her ass, her little body tightening over my thighs as she took the punishment without complaint. That tingling sensation in my palm … oh, yeah, I could so get behind this.

When he finished the punishment, Isaac helped her to her feet.

"Now you may retire to your bedroom for the evening. Ian or I will inform you where you will be sleeping in a little while."

She slowly turned toward my brother, a single tear sliding down her cheek, proof that she had endured. "Thank you, Master Isaac." She turned to face me. "Thank you, Master Ian."

Yeah. It was safe to say we were both in deep, deep shit.

One

ISAAC STOKES

Saturday, May 25, 2019

"Everly." Staring down at the fairy princess who had graced more than one of my theme rooms over the past few months, I kept my voice low, even. "I need you to tell me who attacked you."

"I don't know him," she said softly, firmly, her eyes lowered.

Even now, a good half hour after she'd stepped through the front door of Zeke Lautner's house sporting a black eye and a puffy lip, I could feel her anguish, her pain. I couldn't explain it, wasn't sure I even cared to, but I wanted to know what motherfucker had battered her pretty face so I could beat him to death with my bare hands.

"But he knows your roommate? Heaven?"

"No," she said insistently. "I asked Heaven. She doesn't know him."

Similar to the way Zeke's sister had earlier, I crouched down in front of Everly. "Look at me."

Her cornflower-blue eyes shot to mine. While she appeared fragile and broken, I could see the strength behind the fear and pain, beyond the splotchy bruising on her porcelain skin. The sight of her marred by someone's hand made my fists clench, my teeth grind together. There was no denying my past had hardened me, left me bent on vengeance. But never in my thirty-one years had I ever laid a hand on a woman out of anger or violence. Nor would I ever.

Doing my best to stay on subject, I held her gaze, thinking back to her revelation of events.

I was in the kitchen, had my earbuds in. Didn't hear him come in. He came up behind me. Covered my mouth and dragged me out of the kitchen. Threw me on the floor. When I tried to fight him off, he punched me. I kicked and screamed. Heaven came home. He ran. Must've been scared ... Kept saying, "I've got you now, sweet Heaven. You're not my first choice, but you'll do."

"Why did he threaten Heaven if he doesn't know her?"

Everly shrugged.

I sighed, stood tall, and paced the room, my mind going through various options in regard to getting the answers necessary to resolve this for her. That was what I did, who I was. And right now, I'd never been more inclined to resolve an issue, whatever it took to ensure no one harmed this woman again.

"I'm sorry," she said quickly. "I don't want to upset you."

When I pivoted back around, Everly was standing, a pleading look wrinkling her forehead, making her appear sweet, innocent. So fucking sweet and innocent.

Only she wasn't. Sure, on the outside. Like a fairy princess. But inside ... deep down there was a sexy spitfire, a submissive who knew exactly what she needed. A strong, independent woman who accepted who she was even when others didn't understand her. That was one of the many reasons I'd enjoyed scenes with her over the past few months, all of them carefully designed and carried out at the club we belonged to.

I frowned, moved closer, then grazed her smooth cheek with my knuckles. "You didn't upset me, sweetheart."

When Everly plastered herself to me, her arms wrapping around my waist, the air rushed out of my lungs in surprise. I cupped her head, holding her against me, the urge to keep her there forever stronger than it ever had been.

Not for the first time, I noticed the drastic differences in our sizes. She was so small, the top of her head barely reaching the middle of my chest, so delicate. From the first time I'd scened with her at the club, back in that ridiculous living room setup, I'd found myself coming back for more. Ian and I had a fondness for the fairy princess—as we'd come to think of her—but try as we might, the woman had managed to keep her distance.

I held her, secretly loving the way she fit so perfectly against me. More so the fact that she was clinging to me, clearly not worried I would hurt her. I wouldn't. Not ever.

"You're safe, Everly," I whispered, sliding my hand over her silky hair. "I won't let anyone hurt you."

It was a promise I fully intended to keep.

The door opened and I glanced over to see my brother, a frown on his face. He missed nothing, his attention to detail honed better than mine.

"I think there's more to this story," he said, nodding toward her.

I didn't release Everly and she made no move to separate.

"Did you talk to the roommate?" I returned my attention to the sweet woman in my arms, sliding my hand slowly over the long fall of her hair.

"Yeah. Heaven's only *one* of her roommates. There's another one."

I tilted Everly's head back, met her gaze. "Is that true?"

"Yes, Sir. Dante." Her eyes widened as though something had just clicked. "Oh, my God."

When she pulled away, I felt the loss but kept myself from reaching for her again.

"Dante?" Ian muttered. "You live with a man?"

I bit back a smile at the barely restrained accusation in his tone.

"It's not like that," she said quickly. "He's... We're ... It's not like that."

I found people tended to not be quite so defensive when that really was the case. There was certainly more to the story, but it was clear she wasn't in any condition to lay it out for us. And we weren't really in a position to inquire.

Yet.

"What's his last name?" I asked.

"Novak," she mumbled, her thoughts obviously elsewhere. "But that makes sense. That guy ... he's trying to hurt Dante."

"By hurting you and Heaven?"

"Yes." Everly wiped her eyes, squared her shoulders. "I need to call him. To tell him not to go home."

I nodded.

She patted her pockets, her butt. "I don't have my phone," she sobbed. "I must've left it at my house."

Ian produced his phone, passed it to her.

Everly swallowed hard, then focused on dialing. I took a step back, standing shoulder to shoulder with my twin as she made her call.

Her tormented gaze shot to mine. "He's not answering." There was silence before she spoke again. "Dante, when you get this message, I need you to call me. Don't go home. Please. Just call me." Her eyes shot to Ian's. "Can he call this number?"

Ian nodded.

"Just call this number back," she said quickly. "I'll tell you what's going on when you do. Please don't go home."

She disconnected, stared at the phone for long seconds before passing it back to Ian.

"I'll be all right," she said softly, wiping the tears from her face with the backs of her hands, flinching when she pressed on her bruised skin. "I didn't mean to crash the party. I just... I didn't know where else to go. I was coming here anyway, figured..."

I had no idea what she figured, but it didn't matter. I was glad she'd come, grateful that Ian and I had been here.

18

Everly's eyes darted between the two of us. "Is Heaven still here?"

Ian shook his head. "She went to her sister's."

Everly nodded, as though that made sense. "She was staying with her this weekend. Came back to grab something." A sob tore free. "She wasn't supposed to be home."

Thank God she had come back. Otherwise…

I shrugged off the thought, not willing to go there.

"You're safe," I repeated. "Everly. Look at me."

Her eyes jerked up to my face, another tear dripping down her smooth cheek.

"You made the right decision," I told her.

"Heaven wants you to call her when you can," Ian added.

"I will." She furiously wiped at the tears as though she was angry they were there.

"You want to go back downstairs?" Ian offered, probably feeling as helpless as I was.

Everly took a deep breath, exhaled slowly. When she looked up again, her eyes were clearer, her defenses back in place. "Yeah."

My brother opened the door, stepped out into the hall as though ensuring she knew she had space.

Not wanting to make her feel trapped, I obliged, motioning toward the bathroom across the hall. "Splash some water on your face. We'll wait for you here."

When she had secured herself inside, I turned to Ian.

"Heaven told me she hasn't been their roommate for long," he explained. "That she didn't know who this guy was or what he might want."

"Did she mention Dante?"

"No." His eyes hardened.

"Find out everything you can about him," I instructed. "And when he calls back, I want you to talk to him. Explain what happened."

"Sure. What're you thinking?"

19

I peered back at the closed bathroom door. "I'm thinking she's not safe at that house, and I'm not sure her roommates are, either."

"Doesn't sound like it. She have somewhere to go?"

I met his eyes again and I didn't bother to explain. The man already knew what I was thinking.

"It's a risk. "

"I know."

"I don't mind, but…"

I waited, needing him to finish that sentence.

"We need to get more answers," he finally said. "If she's willing to stay with us, she can. Otherwise, you'll have to let her go, Isaac."

He was right. Although I wanted that woman with a passion I didn't understand, I certainly wouldn't force her to stay with us.

Then again, I wasn't beyond using a little Dominant persuasion, either.

Everly Hughes

I SPLASHED COLD WATER ON MY FACE like Isaac had instructed, my hands shaking.

When I got a good look at the damage, the black eye forming, the puffy lip, I shuddered, remembering the way that man had dragged me by my hair, rough and mean. I could still feel the searing pain in my scalp, the fear that had closed my throat when I'd thought of what he might do to me.

I've got you now, Heaven. You're not my priority, but you'll do for now.

His voice, high-pitched and frantic, rang in my head. I'd been so shocked by his appearance, I hadn't been able to react in time to defend myself.

Where's Everly? Huh? Maybe she'll come back. Join us.

He had thought I was Heaven, though I wasn't sure why. I'd never met him before, and if he'd actually met Heaven, he would've known I wasn't her. We had similar characteristics, dark hair, light skin, close to the same height, but that was where the similarities ended.

I'll show you what it's like to be dominated. That's what you like, right? Rough, hard. Someone to slap you around?

His rambling had confused me because he had me and Heaven completely mixed up. Heaven wasn't a submissive, didn't know anything about the lifestyle aside from what Dante and I had told her. In fact, Heaven was pretty vanilla. She would be the first to say she didn't understand at all what our fascination was with BDSM. Not that I held it against her, but for someone to get the two of us mixed up like that … it made me think he didn't know Dante all that well, either.

He'll learn. He'll know who he belongs to, that he can't ignore me because of a couple of sluts. I'll show him. But first, I'll show you.

The *he* had to be Dante. The guy wanted Dante, and if I wasn't mistaken, this man thought he was a Dominant.

Key word being *thought*. In no way, shape or form did he resemble any true Dominant I'd come in contact. He'd been brutal and mean, which was not the same thing. Not by a long shot.

God. I needed to talk to Dante.

Shaking it off, I reached for the hand towel, patted my face dry, wincing when I touched the sensitive swollen skin under my eye.

"You shouldn't have come here," I told the woman in the mirror. "Now they'll all think you're fragile and breakable."

It had been the same thing I'd repeated over and over in my head as Heaven drove me to Zeke's at my request. I'd been invited and so excited to attend right up until… I'd been tidying up the house, wanting Dante to come home to a clean place. Then … that asshole had ruined it.

Now that I'd left that message, I knew Dante would be worried about me. He always was.

21

I took a deep breath, exhaled.

I knew exactly why I'd chosen to come. It was to feel safe. Not because of Ian and Isaac. Not entirely, anyway. Yeah, they made me feel safe, but so did everyone at the club. When I was there, I didn't have to worry about anything like this. So rather than find some hole to hide in, I'd begged Heaven to bring me here even though she'd wanted me to go to the police.

A soft knock sounded on the door.

I opened it, not sure how long I'd been in there. "I'm sorry. I didn't mean to take so long."

Isaac tipped my chin back, urging me to look up at him. "Stop apologizing."

It wasn't a request, it was a command. Something I'd gotten quite familiar with from these two. The few times we'd played together had been the most intense of my entire life. I craved them like a drug, which was the very reason I had managed to keep my distance. Ian and Isaac Stokes weren't the sort who were going to take a club submissive as their own and I knew that. I'd met them during the submissive training class months ago, which probably, based on some archaic D/s rule, meant I was off-limits on a permanent basis, and I had reminded myself of that over and over again.

Yet I still longed for those discreet glances they shot my way from time to time, secretly enjoying when they asked me to scene with them. The way they looked at me... No man had ever looked at me like that.

Well, that wasn't entirely true. Dante looked at me like that. But he wasn't a Dominant. Not even a switch. No, he was pure submissive, and he knew what I needed, what I craved because he was looking for the same. Hence the reason we were only friends. Close friends, yeah. Probably closer than we should've been, but I couldn't help it. Dante made me feel cherished, as though I mattered. And when he would hold me in his arms, curled up on the sofa to watch television, I couldn't seem to come up with an excuse as to why it was wrong.

"Do you need to call someone?" Ian asked as we moved toward the stairs. "Parents? Brother, sister?"

I shook my head. "No. Only child. My dad died when I was ten, my mom … she does her own thing. Haven't heard from her in a while." A really, *really* long while but I figured now wasn't the time to go into that.

"How long's a while?" Ian probed.

Or maybe it was. "Five years."

Isaac grunted but I couldn't translate the gruff sound.

"And you live with Dante?" Ian asked.

"Yes. And Heaven. We're roommates. There's … um … there's nothing going on between any of us."

I wasn't sure why I was vomiting up my personal information, but I couldn't help myself. When it came to them, I found myself willing to tell them anything, even the most private things.

"Let's join the others," Isaac said, his hand splaying across my back, gently guiding me to follow Ian down the stairs.

Going back to the party gave me the distraction I needed. For the next couple of hours, I mingled as much as I could, assured Jamie Lautner, Zeke's younger sister, I was fine several times. She was sweet and I could tell she was worried, but I didn't want her to be. I was a big girl, I could hold my own.

Isaac was always close by, not leaving me alone for a second. He had someone bring me drinks—fruit punch, not alcohol—and continued to watch me as though I might shatter into a million pieces. I couldn't deny I was probably going to have nightmares, but for those couple of hours, I felt more at ease.

I would've felt a million times better if Dante would've called.

Two hours later, the party started to wind down, a few people still milling about, most having left already when Isaac and Ian offered to take me home. Without any other options, I accepted.

"Thanks for coming," Zeke told Isaac, shaking his hand as we stood at the door. "And thanks for agreeing to help my sister."

By help, I assumed Zeke was referring to everyone's willingness to open up to Jamie about their lifestyle. Apparently, Jamie was working on her thesis and convincing everyone to let her dig into their psyche had been Edge and Cav's way of helping out their submissive.

"Thanks for inviting us," Isaac told the giant Sadist.

Isaac and Ian couldn't have been more different from Zeke Lautner, at least in a physical sense. Although they were tall, Zeke seemed to dwarf them. I was only five one, so perhaps it was my own height challenges I used as a ruler. Ian and Isaac surpassed me by at least a foot, but the Sadist was several inches taller than they were. Where Ian and Isaac were pretty-boy handsome with their dark hair, chiseled features and deep emerald eyes, Zeke was … intimidating. He wasn't attractive in the conventional sense. No, more like unique but there was something appealing about him, though I couldn't quite put my finger on it.

"Everly?"

Realizing I'd been staring, not at all hearing the exchange between them, I jerked my attention away, forcing my eyes downward. "I'm sorry."

A deep rumble sounded in Isaac's chest as his arm slid around me, crossing my chest as he pulled me back against him. It was a protective gesture but also a dominant one. It wasn't the first time he'd held me like that, either, and I'd fantasized about it on more than one occasion.

"We're going to have a chat about the apologies," he said, leaning down close to my ear.

"You ready?" Ian asked, his gaze skimming over me, taking in the way Isaac's arm crossed over my chest, his hand curled around my arm.

"Come on," Isaac said. "We'll stop by your house, grab your cell phone and some clothes."

With his arm securely around me, he steered me toward the black Escalade parked on the side of the driveway. Most of the other vehicles were gone, the party having died off.

"I can afford a hotel," I told him when he opened the back door, helped me inside.

He leaned in, tipped my chin up. "Is that what you want?"

I couldn't look away and found myself shaking my head. It would've been smart to separate myself from him, yeah, but not what I wanted. And when it came to lying to either of them, I was not going to do that. It wasn't to my benefit to withhold the truth.

He nodded. "You'll stay with us, then."

I could tell he was trying to read my expression, ensuring I wasn't opposed to the idea. I wanted to be, only because I knew he alone was capable of breaking my heart into a million pieces. That didn't take into account the damage his brother could do, but I also didn't want to be alone right now.

The door closed and Isaac climbed in the driver's side, Ian getting in the passenger seat.

I clicked my seat belt into place, then leaned my head back and closed my eyes. I was so tired. The adrenaline that had flooded me earlier was long gone.

"What's your address?" Ian asked.

I rattled it off as he entered it into the navigation.

"Relax for a little while," Ian said softly, staring back at me, concern evident in his expression. "You're safe."

My body, maybe.

My heart was another story entirely.

Two

IAN STOKES

I HAD KNOWN FROM THE VERY FIRST scene we had with Everly Hughes that she wasn't going to be easy to get out of the system. I was right. My brother was in deep. The kind of deep that made a man ignore logic and sense, his only objective to acquire what he longed for most. She'd become his obsession, even if he had done a damn fine job of pretending otherwise.

Isaac wasn't the sort to deny it, either, but I had yet to broach the subject. Mainly because the woman had made it apparent she wanted little to do with us. When we asked her to scene, she was always game, but outside of the intimate club interaction, she held herself at a distance.

That didn't seem to be the case today.

Then again, scening with her was the furthest thing from my mind at the moment. No, I preferred to encase her in a protective bubble and stand guard to ensure no one got close. Seeing the damage to her face was like a punch in the gut every fucking time.

From the instant she stepped through Zeke Lautner's door, I'd felt it. I couldn't pinpoint what *it* was exactly. Could've been my brother's feelings for her, his innate need to protect her, or it could've been something she was projecting. Either way, it felt important, as though I needed to pay attention because it ultimately would change the course of my life.

Enter Dante Novak.

I hadn't told Everly that roommate number two had called back. I figured she would realize that soon enough. I also hadn't told her that I'd done some digging on Dante while the others had mingled at the party. A few database searches on my smartphone had given me more details than I'd expected.

Dante Novak had been born on Leap Day, 1992. Twenty-seven years old, in the foster care system from the time he was twelve. No details on either parent. Started out working at McDonald's at the age of sixteen, stayed there until he was twenty, kicked fast food and moved into the restaurant business, where he'd been for the past seven years, moving up in the ranks, now an assistant manager of some fancy steakhouse downtown. He owned a three-bedroom house—the one he shared with Everly and Heaven—for going on four years now. He didn't have a criminal record, not so much as a speeding ticket. Which was a wonder considering he owned a brand-new Camaro, though there was no record of him ever buying one.

Based on my search, he didn't do a lot on social media, aside from post pictures when he spent time out with Everly, and never did he even mention his affiliation with the BDSM club known as Inferno, a place he'd apparently been a member of for the past three years.

As for Heaven Whitley, Dante didn't appear to be close to her in any way. In fact, I couldn't tie the two of them together at all, except that they slept under the same roof, which was why I'd done a little digging on the brunette who'd been far too eager to disappear after learning Everly would be fine. Aside from a couple of speeding tickets when she was younger, Heaven's record was also squeaky clean. She worked full-time at a chain bookstore while taking night classes to obtain her bachelor's degree in art and literature of all things. She had a long-term boyfriend, Danny Spielburg, who looked like an uptight douchebag based on their social media pictures. If her Instagram account was anything to go by, those two had been riding the breakup train for a while now.

"Did Dante call back?" Everly asked after a few minutes of silence.

I peered over my shoulder. "Yeah. He's meeting us at your house."

While I hadn't intended to keep it a secret from her, there had been something in Dante's reaction to what had happened that concerned me. But it was his voice, the sound of it, the distinct submission in his tone that had intrigued me. Everly hadn't explained her relationship with Dante, but I got the feeling it was somewhat complicated in nature. Especially if he was as submissive as I believed him to be.

I was nothing if not astute.

"When we get there, I want you to pack a bag," Isaac instructed. "Grab whatever you might need for a few days."

Looked as though we were definitely doing this.

"Yes, Sir."

I liked that she didn't feel the need to argue. Perhaps that was because of the incident from earlier, her need for protection, but I didn't think that was entirely the case.

When Isaac parked the Escalade in front of the small redbrick house, I climbed out, glanced around the neighborhood. The street was quiet, older. The mature trees filled the manicured yards, hung over the sidewalk, made it feel homey. It was well-kept, a nice area with probably minimal crime. That made me feel marginally better.

Well, except for the fact some asshole had broken into this very house and attacked a female he clearly didn't know.

My eyes shifted to the white Camaro parked on the street. It had leaves scattered over the top and hood that told me it hadn't been moved in a while. If ever.

As I waited for Isaac and Everly to grab her things from inside, I stood on the porch. It wasn't long before a four-door older-model Camry pulled up behind the Camaro on the street.

So, he drove a beat-up piece of shit that needed a new passenger door at best, four new tires at worst, instead of the brand-new sports car. Interesting.

The man who stepped out wasn't at all what I'd expected. His pictures had mostly been selfies with Everly, which hadn't done this man justice whatsoever. He was tall and thin, rangy was a good way to describe him. Also ridiculously attractive with his shaggy blond hair, squared jaw, and lean features. He moved with purpose, not swagger. He wasn't a showoff and he carried himself well.

If appearances were all I based my sexual encounters on, I would've been all over the man in a heartbeat.

When his eyes lifted to mine as I stood over him on the porch, I saw what I'd suspected just from hearing his voice. A glint of submission, along with a healthy dose of ambivalence in his midnight-blue eyes.

"Dante?"

"Yes, Sir."

Most definitely submissive.

Heat simmered beneath my skin. I felt an instant connection, but I knew without asking that it was one-sided. Dante regarded me with hesitance, as though I was a viper getting ready to strike.

It was the curiosity, not the fear, that attracted me to him.

Yeah. I was bisexual, so was my brother, but we rarely played with male submissives. Every now and again, it would be an entertaining endeavor, but I had yet to be knocked off my feet by a man, wasn't sure it was in the cards. Didn't mean I wasn't keeping my options open.

I took the steps down until we were on even ground, scanned Dante's handsome face briefly. He was a few inches shorter than I was. At six four, I pegged him closer to six, maybe six one. "Who would want to hurt you?"

That spark of fear ignited into an inferno before he managed to mask it.

Interesting.

I waited to hear what lie he would try to feed me.

Dante swallowed hard but didn't say anything. I wasn't sure how I felt about that. Either he wasn't forthcoming with details, he didn't know anything, or I intimidated him enough for him to keep his mouth shut. If it was the latter, we'd have to work on that.

"PB!" Everly yelled, barreling out of the screen door and running right into his arms.

PB? What the hell was PB? I glanced at Isaac when he stepped outside to join us.

In a protective manner, Dante wrapped Everly in tight, enveloping her tiny body in his. His body language reflected his desire to keep her safe, but there was something else, too. Love? Lust? Both?

"I'm okay," he assured her.

When she tried to keep her face buried in his chest, he forced her head back, stared down. His forehead wrinkled, his breaths ragged when his thumb ghosted over the bruise on her eye.

"You can't stay here," she mumbled.

"He hit you."

She shrugged him off. "It's fine. I'm fine. I promise." Her quivering voice hardened. "You can't stay here."

"I know. I'll find a place."

"Everly's staying with us," I told him when his eyes lifted to mine again. "We've got plenty of space."

I wasn't sure he realized it was an invitation. Since I hadn't phrased it as a question or a command, he seemed to wait for something more.

All the more intriguing.

"Please?" Everly begged. "Stay with us. At least until they figure out who did this."

Dante glanced down at her, back to me.

"You'll stay with us," I decided for him, keeping my tone firm.

"Yes, Sir," he said softly, releasing Everly when she took a step back. "What about Heaven? Is she okay?"

"She went to her sister's," Everly informed him.

He nodded, as though satisfied.

"Was it Danny?" he asked, his eyes imploring her. It was clear he was hoping for a specific answer.

"What?"

He motioned toward her face.

"No. God, no. Danny's a douche, but he wouldn't hit *me*."

"Is there something wrong with Heaven's boyfriend? You think he's behind this?"

Dante's eyes narrowed and I suspected he was curious as to how I knew Danny was their roommate's boyfriend.

"No. I don't," he declared, tearing his gaze from mine.

I watched the pair as Dante stepped to Everly once more, his fingertips gentle as they brushed over the bruise. I could see the anger behind the mask. He knew something.

"Pack a bag," I instructed, then nodded toward his car. "You can follow us back to our place."

"Yes, Sir."

Everly held on to his arm, following him into the house. They passed Isaac on the way and I watched my brother's eyes rake over Dante. When they met mine, there was the same interest I felt reflecting back at me.

"Submissive," he stated as though it was written across Dante's forehead.

"Very much so."

"Not a member of Dichotomy."

"Nope," I agreed.

"She cares about him," Isaac muttered. "Perhaps loves him."

Based on his tone, that wasn't necessarily a bad thing.

Isaac looked at me. I held his stare, an entire conversation taking place without a word being spoken. We were on the same page. Whatever was happening here, it was as though it was meant to play out this way.

Not that I cared for the circumstances. Any man who put his hands on a woman in anger deserved a beat down of the most heinous kind.

No doubt, we would find him, and he would get what he deserved.

I only hoped it was before that bastard hurt anyone else.

Dante Novak

HEARING EVERLY'S VOICEMAIL HAD PUT ME ON high alert, fear and anger coalescing into a dangerous concoction. I'd returned her call immediately, only to be told by the gruff voice that answered that she was fine, and I needed to meet them at my house. He hadn't gone into detail, hadn't shared with me the story Everly just outlined as I rummaged through my room for the essentials.

"Do you know who it was?" Everly asked, her concern evident as she sat on the edge of my bed while I packed a few things into a duffle bag.

"I'm not sure," I lied. "Could be … a few people."

"Who wants to hurt you?" she asked, her voice edging toward hysterical.

I shrugged, but it was another untruth. I knew exactly who wanted to hurt me. His name was Roger Cherlish, a Sadist at Inferno, a man I wanted nothing to do with but had little choice under the circumstances.

"We'll figure this out," Everly said sweetly, her hand covering mine.

I nodded, pulled away.

Her touch was painful. It made me want things I knew I couldn't have. How I'd fallen in love with the woman, I would never know, but it had happened, and try as I might, I couldn't seem to move past it. I knew there would never be anything between me and Everly, besides a mutual love and friendship. We were too alike for it to work in our favor, so I had never pursued her, choosing to be friends so that I could keep her in my life.

"How do you tell them apart?" I asked Everly, hoping to change the subject as I marched to my closet.

"Aside from the fact they're night and day as far as personalities?" Her smile was sweet.

"Yes." Since I'd yet to interact much with either of them, that wasn't a distinction I was aware of.

"Isaac has a small birthmark on the back of his right hand, between thumb and forefinger."

Ah. Well, that made sense. Otherwise, I suspected they were identical. Their faces certainly were. Both had dark brown hair, cut short on the sides with distinguishable sideburns, top slightly longer, combed to the right. They were clean-cut, handsome in the traditional sense. But it was the eyes that did it. Sparkling emeralds full of heat and light and...

Of course, the voice was a nice touch. Deep, low, with a distinct accent. Irish, perhaps Scottish. Wasn't sure I'd be able to tell the difference. It held a lilt that sparked things inside me.

Yeah. Okay. Going a little too far.

I had no business fantasizing about the twin Doms. They belonged to Everly, or so I figured they would eventually. That was the way it always worked for me. I couldn't seem to nail down one of my own. Not because I wasn't attractive or obedient. I was. In spades.

However, I was also unconventional in what I wanted. People rarely understood my needs, so I didn't share them often. I figured these two would come and go from my life long before any of that would ever even matter.

"Ready?" the deep voice sounded from the doorway.

I slipped into the bathroom, tossed in shampoo, body wash, shaving cream, razor. It would do for now. At least until I could come back here. If it weren't for Everly, I wouldn't be leaving, but I wasn't willing to be without her. She needed me. Perhaps not in the same way she needed those Doms, but she did need me. Of that I was positive.

When I stepped out of the bathroom, one of the twins was standing there. I knew without looking at his hand that it was Ian, the one I'd spoken to on the phone and interacted with outside. He might've been identical in appearance to his brother, but there was something in his eyes that helped me differentiate.

"Yes, Sir," I said simply, showing the respect this man commanded with a simple look.

While I wasn't prone to calling all Doms by their respectful honorifics, I sensed something here. And I wanted to. Not out of obligation, but out of … desire. He was the type of man I'd longed for, the one I wanted to kneel before, to submit to on the deepest, most basic level. How I knew, I couldn't explain.

"Come on, panda bear," he directed.

I started to pass, then jerked my head to him. "Panda Bear? Really?"

He smirked. "PB, right?"

"Yeah." But that was Everly's pet name for me. No one else referred to me that way, thank God. "How did you know?"

"Wild guess." He gestured for me to lead the way.

I hoisted the bag over my shoulder, gave the room a quick once-over before stepping in front of him and heading down the hall.

"I've checked the doors, windows. All's secure," Ian said. "You should consider getting an alarm."

I nodded. I would. Once this was over. Everly had been attacked in this house. You'd bet your ass I would be ensuring her safety from here on out.

"Hand me your phone," he instructed.

I paused by the door, dug my phone out of my pocket, unlocked with the passcode, and passed it over.

With skilled fingers, he found what he was looking for and typed something in, handed it back.

"Address entered in your maps app. Added my contact information, too."

"Thank you, Sir," I said, meeting his brilliant green gaze.

He stepped forward, tipped my chin with a brush of his finger. "I do like hearing you call me that."

There was something in that tone. A promise, perhaps. It could've been wishful thinking on my part, but I didn't think so. This man wanted something from me.

And I could only hope it was what I so desperately found myself wanting to give him.

Heaven Whitley

"I THOUGHT..." I LET THE WORDS HANG, listening to Danny breathe on the other end of the line.

My boyfriend of three years was cheating on me. I knew it just as sure as I knew my own name. However, he continued to deny it even though his actions spoke far louder than his words.

"Sorry, babe," he said simply. "Got plans tonight. Can't make it by there."

I'd been hearing that more frequently as of late. In the past three months, I'd seen Danny three times. All three had been on weekdays when he'd come over late in the evening. It wasn't only in my head that the man was treating me like I was a booty call.

And it was high time I did something about it.

"No worries," I told him sweetly.

"I knew you'd understand, babe. We'll get together next week sometime. I promise."

"You know what, Danny?"

"What's that, babe?"

He referred to me like that always, and I was starting to think he'd forgotten my name.

"I think it's time we called it quits."

He was silent for a beat. "You don't mean that, Heaven. Look, I'm sorry. I've got a lot of shit going on right now. I've been busy. No need to be a bitch about it."

"It's cool." There was no heat in my words, no anger. I was simply done. And breaking up with him left me feeling freer than I had in a long time. "I've got a life, too. I'll get on with mine, while you get on with yours."

"Whatever, Heaven," he snarled. "I don't have time for your passive-aggressive bullshit right now."

I laughed. "Okay, Danny. I'll let you go."

Disconnecting the call, I took a deep breath, exhaled slowly. Yep. Free. That was the feeling that fluttered inside me.

"Everything okay?"

I looked up to see my sister standing in the doorway, wiping her hand on a kitchen towel.

"Peachy," I said with a smile. "I dumped Danny. Feel much better."

That familiar line appeared in her forehead, a sure sign that Honor was worried about me. Before she could launch into a spiel about love and life and happily ever after, I shot to my feet.

"I just remembered..." I shuffled around the room, snatching my overnight bag and my purse. "I've got a paper due next week." I pretended to look for something in my bag. "Forgot my book."

"Heaven," Honor said softly. "Please don't go."

"It's fine," I assured her. "I'll stop by later in the week. We can have lunch."

When I looked up, Honor was staring at me, that motherly look on her face. I hated that she felt the need to take care of me. I was a grown woman, had been taking care of myself for a while now. Ever since our mother died, Honor had taken on the role of surrogate and she seemed to forget the fact that I was twenty-five.

"You can't go home," she said firmly. "What if that guy comes back? Attacks *you* this time?"

Pain lanced through my insides. Everly had been attacked and whoever had done it thought she was me. I'd been the target, yet I had no idea why. It had been dumb luck that I'd forgotten my phone and had gone back to get it. If I hadn't...

I shook off the thought because I was not about to think about the possible outcome if I'd had my phone or decided I didn't need it.

"I'll be fine," I assured her. "I'll lock the doors. He won't come back this soon." At least I hoped he wouldn't.

Fifteen minutes later, I was pulling up to the redbrick house I lived in with Dante and Everly, parking beside a black Escalade. I climbed out just as the hot twins from that party were getting into the SUV.

The man on the passenger side paused, stared over at me. "What are you doing here?"

My eyebrows shot to my hairline. "I live here?"

"I thought you were staying with your sister."

I shrugged. "Change of plans." I leaned back into the car, dragged my overnight bag over the center console. "Broke up with my boyfriend," I continued, "don't care to be around anyone right now."

"You can't stay here," he said simply when I turned back to face him.

"I'd beg to differ." I held up my keys. "I've got a key. I signed a lease. I think it's a fair assumption I *can* stay here." I gave him a sassy smirk. "And I will. You guys have fun."

Just as I was about to walk toward the house, the back passenger window rolled down, the soft whirring sound drawing my attention.

"Everly." I dropped my bag, moved over to her. "Are you okay?"

The bruise on her face had already formed, the skin swollen and red, with black rimming the bump. There was a small scratch over her eyebrow and another on her puffy lower lip.

"I'm fine." Her hand settled over mine on the door. "You broke up with Danny?"

"Yeah. No biggie." I glanced around the interior of the SUV, not looking at the driver for too long. "Where're you going?"

"To stay with Isaac and Ian for a couple of days." She motioned toward the house with a slight tilt of her head. "You know. Just in case he comes back."

"Ah." I stood tall, pulled my hand from beneath hers. "Dante going, too?"

"Yes."

Well, then. Looked as though I was on my own.

Not that it mattered. I was familiar with being by myself.

In fact, it seemed to be the story of my life.

ISAAC

FROM THE DRIVER'S SEAT, I WATCHED THE interaction between Everly and Heaven. When I wasn't observing them, I was watching my brother. Ian was standing outside the Escalade, his full attention on Everly.

I found it interesting, especially since he liked to give me shit about how I was head over heels for her. Right there in front of him was a very attractive brunette he should've been charming, yet his attention was snagged by the one woman who had changed my entire world simply by breathing. If my hunch was right, Ian was trying to figure out how to protect her and I didn't need the twin bond to know that. He looked pained, almost at a loss, and it made me curious.

His eyes shot to mine. I nodded.

"We need to get out of here," Ian told the girls. "Why don't you come stay at our house for a couple of days? Just until we've had time to figure out who this guy is, what he wants. We've got plenty of room."

Heaven pushed away from the back window, disappearing into the blind spot between the doors. I glanced at Everly because I couldn't seem to stop looking at her.

"I don't want to impose." That sassy voice floated in through the open window.

This woman had an edge to her. Very standoffish, almost volatile. I wondered what had prompted the behavior. More importantly, I wondered how two obvious submissives had ended up with a friend who was, for lack of a better term, dominant. And I wasn't referring to her sexual desires. Heaven just seemed like the type who wanted to be in control of her decisions.

"You aren't," Everly and Ian said at the same time, making me smile.

Heaven reappeared outside Everly's door. "Are you sure?"

"Yes," she said quickly. "Please. Come with me. I'll feel better knowing you're safe."

With far less argument than I'd expected, Heaven nodded. Before she could reach for her bag, Ian was hefting it toward the back of the SUV.

"What about my car?" she asked, her gaze swinging around.

"We'll bring you back here when it's safe," Ian said absently.

I reached back and tapped Everly's knee. "Sit up front."

Her eyes met mine. "Yes, Sir."

Passing a look to Heaven, she opened the door. They traded places, Everly relocating to the front passenger seat. She buckled herself in while Ian got into the back behind me.

It had taken far longer than it should have, but a minute later, we were on the road, the Camry behind us.

"Whose Camaro is that?" Ian asked.

"Dante's," Heaven offered. "But he didn't drive it. Said he hates that car."

I glanced at Everly to see if she had something to contribute, but she was staring down at her hands.

Ian and I lived roughly forty-five minutes outside of Chicago in a rambling ranch house in the middle of a subdivision parsed into narrow, five-acre tracts. We'd bought it a decade ago, rehabbed the interior over the course of a couple of years to turn it into exactly what we wanted. Five bedrooms, six bathrooms, formal dining and living room, workout space, along with a huge den, where we spent most of our time. On one end of the house was a guest suite, complete with separate living area and spa bathroom, though no one had ever stayed in that space. The basement had been converted to our office, the attic into what would pass as a fairly decent library.

Although we were rarely home these days, I still loved that house, longed to be there for longer than a couple of days at a time. Having taken jobs with Ransom Bishop and the security division he was running for Trent Ramsey's talent agency, we found most of our time spent these days with A-listers who were in need of personal protection. This was supposed to be our downtime, after having spent the past two months in Los Angeles, and to ensure that happened, I'd cornered Ransom back at Zeke's, informing him of what was going down. He'd agreed to keep us out of the rotation for as long as he could, or until we found the fucker who'd attacked Everly.

Which meant we had roughly two weeks to get the job done.

"Wow. This is impressive," Heaven said from the backseat as I pulled down the long dirt drive leading to the garage.

The big metal door opened when the sensor hit the answering one on the front of the Escalade. My cell phone buzzed, notifying me when the motion was detected. I didn't release Everly's hand, simply waited a moment before pulling into one space. Ian exited first, motioning for Dante to pull into the only other empty space in the five-bay building.

"A Stingray?" Heaven asked.

Ian was the one to respond. "My baby."

Heaven chuckled. "Doesn't surprise me. Boys and their toys."

I could've told the woman there wasn't a boy amongst her, but I refrained. Not to mention, our toys came in the human form, not vehicle.

I didn't think she'd care to hear that, either.

I glanced over at Everly. "I'll get your bag. You sit there until I get your door."

"Yes, Sir."

If I hadn't known Everly, hadn't interacted with her so much at the club, I wouldn't have been quite so demanding with her. Not this early in a relationship, anyhow. But I'd gotten to know her, and I wanted to think I understood her needs. She craved dominance, appreciated it even. That was evident in every Dom she interacted with at Dichotomy, male or female. From what I'd seen, she gravitated toward those who didn't waffle, leaving the passive ones in her wake. Perhaps because her needs aligned with my own, every second I'd spent with her over the past six months, I'd done so with the intention of connecting on a different level from anyone she'd ever known. And I had never been the sort to let a perfect opportunity pass me by. I wasn't about to do so now.

Ian took Heaven's bag while he waited for Dante to join us. I grabbed Everly's, then moved around to the passenger side, opening her door. I did my best to ignore the bruise that had turned an ugly purple over the course of the past few hours. It pained me to see her hurt, made me want to rip someone's throat out. I fought back the anger, knew it wasn't necessary right now.

I led the way into the house, set Everly's bag on the kitchen island. "Anyone hungry?"

"Starving," my brother noted.

Not surprising. He was always hungry.

I glanced at Everly, warmth filling me when she smiled. "I could eat."

"I'll cook," Heaven offered.

Four sets of eyes turned to her.

"What?" she asked, glancing between us. "I like to cook."

"Is that true?" Ian asked, looking to Dante for the answer.

"Yes, Sir. She loves to cook." He smiled. "And she's quite good at it, too."

"You do much cooking for five?" I asked.

"From time to time. I'm sure I can make it work."

"Let me show you your room first," Ian said. "Then the kitchen's all yours."

I watched as Heaven's eyes tracked Ian when he moved. I could see her interest and it made me curious. While I knew Everly was a submissive and I highly suspected Dante was, I didn't get the same vibe from Heaven. However, the way she looked at my brother told me there was a spark there.

This just might take a turn not even I could've seen.

Everly

WHEN ISAAC TOOK MY HAND, I FOLLOWED him through the door separating the garage from the house, into the elaborate kitchen, past the stainless-steel appliances, the miles of glossy countertops, the large island that stood proudly in the center, then beyond to a series of floor-to-ceiling windows and bifold glass doors. We passed through a large den, complete with oversized furniture and a wall dedicated to the entertainment system, including what was likely an eighty-inch television.

We ended up in a long, narrow hallway that branched off to the left and to the right with doors down one side as well as one on each end. Isaac went to the left, while Ian and Heaven went to the right.

The sexy man holding my hand stopped at the first door we came to, opening it into what appeared to be a guest room.

"This is all yours," he said, stepping back so I could go in.

As I entered the beautiful space, the first word that came to mind was soft. Not quite feminine, but not masculine by any means.

The walls were what I'd describe as a light apricot, the color carried throughout the decor in varied tones. The king-sized bed with its large headboard and four thick posts sat along one wall, flanked by two tall windows with vintage night tables in front of them. At the end of the bed was a bench as wide as the footboard and topped with a cushion slightly darker than the walls. The wall to the right of the bed had two doors and a squatty four-drawer dresser between them. A tall chest stood catty-corner on the farthest end of that wall. One door led to what I could see to be a bathroom; the other I assumed was a closet.

On the left side of the room was a single door and a fancy canvas painting of some mosaic design that covered a large area on the otherwise empty wall. The furniture was a distressed white, French country by design. It all matched, including the nine-drawer dresser with the large mirror on the wall opposite the bed.

"This is beautiful," I whispered as I turned back to Isaac.

"Bathroom." He motioned to the far side of the room, then shifted to the right. "Closet." His arm swung toward the door beside the painting. "My bedroom."

I smiled. "It's connected?"

"It is." He stepped closer, tilted my chin up. "Do you wonder why that might be?"

Heat curled deep inside me. "It's so you have access to your submissive at all times."

He smiled and I thought my knees would buckle.

Although nerves stirred in my belly, they had nothing to do with fear and everything to do with my craving for this man. It sometimes shocked me with its intensity. During the drive to their house, Isaac had held my hand the entire time, making me feel as though I belonged to him in some way. I found myself craving that feeling, eager to explore what it might possibly mean. I tried not to think too long or hard on that, though. For one, I'd spent months attempting to keep myself distant from them and in the matter of a few hours, I was already looking forward to more.

"Thank you for letting us stay here," I told him, keeping my eyes on his.

His thumb brushed the sensitive skin beneath my bruised eye. "I'm glad you're here. Sorry it's under these circumstances."

Yeah, I was, too. The last thing I wanted was his pity.

"Why don't you take a shower, get comfortable. Come back to the kitchen when you're ready."

Although I wished he would, Isaac didn't kiss me. He merely smiled, then walked back out into the hall, closing the door behind him. I forced my feet to move, grabbing my bag on the way to the bathroom. The space was about five times the size of the one I shared with Heaven at Dante's. Plus this one was updated. The mirror over the sink matched the furniture in the bedroom. The glass doors on the shower were so clear they were almost invisible.

"Shower," I muttered to myself, setting the bag on the vanity table beside the sink.

I managed to pass a good thirty minutes while I cleaned up. I changed into a T-shirt and shorts, leaving my feet bare. After unpacking the few things I'd brought, tucking the clothes into the dresser rather than the enormous closet, I couldn't resist taking a peek in Isaac's room.

It was probably an invasion of privacy, but I found it intriguing that he'd had the forethought to connect the two rooms. As though he'd always anticipated having a submissive in his home. Perhaps he had. I knew from the rumors around the club that the Stokes twins were looking for two submissives they could share between them. When the stories were told, no one ever mentioned whether they were looking for a male and a female, simply two.

Since the rooms connected, did that mean he intended to have a submissive who wouldn't sleep in his bedroom? But still be accessible?

While some would've thought it off-putting, I didn't. In fact, I purposely made no judgments on others. It wasn't my place. I preferred they didn't judge me, so knew I had to offer the same in return.

I opened the door and stepped from my room into Isaac's. The difference between the two was drastic. There was nothing soft about this room. Light furniture and dark blue walls gave it a masculine vibe. The ceiling was brilliant white, far taller than the one in the room I was staying in.

The bed was the centerpiece. The headboard was a rectangle comprised of many single pieces of wood woven together but not quite connecting. The footboard was even with the mattress and thick. I'd seen something similar on one of the HGTV shows. I was pretty sure there would be a television that rose out of it.

The nightstands were chests with three drawers, a lamp and clock on one and nothing on the other. The wall to the right of the bed was floor-to-ceiling windows with doors that appeared to open all the way back. The navy curtains were open, revealing the concrete porch that led to the shimmering swimming pool and the circular hot tub, a bit higher and connected, the water pouring out of it into the pool.

There was a click behind me, and I turned in time to see Isaac coming out of what I assumed was his bathroom, a towel wrapped around his lean hips, another he used to dry his hair.

He smiled. "Taking a tour, I presume."

"Yes, Sir. I'm sorry. I didn't mean to invade your privacy."

"No apology necessary. You're welcome anywhere in my home."

My gaze traveled over him slowly, taking in the long, lean lines of his body. He was utter perfection. Bronze skin covering dense muscle. I'd touched that body before, but only once. During my scenes with Ian and Isaac, they kept it mostly about me and I had yet to have sex with either of them, but not because I didn't want to.

I most definitely did.

When it came to my sexuality, I wasn't shy about it, didn't feel the need to hide my desires. I was a highly sexual creature and I'd long ago accepted that about myself. It was the very reason I'd ventured into the realm of BDSM. I felt a sense of peace knowing there were others just like me, people who were open and honest about what they were looking for.

As for Ian and Isaac … I wasn't quite sure what their true desires were. There was no denying they were a different breed. While many of the Dominants at the club were eager to fuck the submissives they played with, the identical twin Doms weren't. Their scenes were well thought out and, honestly, some of the most intriguing I'd participated in.

"Look your fill," Isaac said.

My gaze shot to his face when I realized I'd been ogling his chest.

"While you're here, I want you to feel at home."

"Thank you, Sir."

He set down the towel he'd been using to dry his hair before he stalked toward me. I couldn't seem to move, my feet rooted in place. My nerves jangled loudly, my body going soft with the need for him to touch me.

My head tilted back naturally as he moved into my personal space.

"I have a single request, fairy princess."

My heart thumped hopefully against my chest. "Anything, Sir."

His eyes scanned my face briefly. "I prefer you to call me anything except Master or Sir."

I blinked twice, trying to process what he'd just said.

He apparently picked up on my confusion, because he cupped my face in his big hands, held my gaze. "Something to show respect, just not either of those things."

Unsure what to say, I nodded. "Of course."

My hands were trembling, and he must have noticed, because he dropped his hands from my face, took my hands in his, then backed up until he was sitting on the bed. He tugged me closer, between his thighs.

"I'm not a man to pretend." His voice was soft, sincere. "Not when it comes to what I want."

I couldn't look away, trapped by the intensity registering on his face.

"I want you. Have since the first day I met you. I won't deny it. I also think this doesn't surprise you. In the same regard, I'm a man who knows when to approach and when not to."

My brain processed the words but couldn't find the meaning.

His attention shifted to my mouth briefly before his eyes met mine once more.

"When you're ready to take what I want to give you, Everly, you'll make the first move."

I frowned and his hand rose, his thumb brushing over the line in my forehead.

"That's a directive," he clarified. "And if you never want me, I won't hold it against you."

For whatever reason, I leaned in. "I do, Isaac. I do want you."

He smiled, his hand sliding over my cheek once again. "I know you do. That's why I'm willing to wait."

I exhaled, grateful he understood me. I'd wanted him and Ian since the first night I was in their company. However, they scared me. Not simply because I knew they could break my heart, but I knew if I gave myself to them, they'd expect everything from me. And while that was what I wanted more than anything, to find a Dominant I could give my whole being to, I wasn't sure I could follow through.

Mainly because of Dante. He was a part of my life I wasn't willing to let go of. And until I found someone who understood that, was willing to accept the fact that I was in love with a man I knew I would never be with, hope was the only thing I had.

"So, when you're ready, you'll let me know. But it won't be tonight."

I nodded, my voice a raspy whisper when I said, "How will I let you know?"

"Trust me. I'll know."

It was then that I fell a little bit in love with the man.

It wouldn't be long before a little turned into a lot, I knew.

Four

IAN

"Not bad considering what you had to work with," I told Heaven when I joined her in the kitchen after I'd taken care of business in my bedroom, washing up, emptying my pockets, locking up my weapons.

When we'd come inside, I had showed Heaven to the room attached to my bedroom. The entire time I was showing her around, I'd noticed Dante's shoulders working their way closer and closer to his ears. The man was stressed, and it seemed he didn't do that well when in confined spaces. Which was the reason I opted to give him the guest suite on the opposite end of the house. It offered more privacy, more breathing room for him.

In all the time Isaac and I had lived here, the extra rooms had never been used. Strange how quickly things could shift and turn, flipping your normal world on its ear. This afternoon, when we'd ventured out for the evening, I hadn't expected that by the time night fell, all the rooms in this house would have occupants.

But I wasn't questioning what was happening here. That wasn't my style. I was more the go-with-the-flow sort. Whatever was meant to happen would.

"Smells good." I watched the pretty brunette as she put the finishing touches on her entrees.

"Thanks," Heaven said in that chipper tone that I knew was a facade.

"I'll set the table," I offered.

"I've already done it, Sir."

I glanced over at Dante. He was standing in the doorway that separated the formal dining room from the kitchen. He had taken a shower, pulled on black jeans and a black T-shirt. His blond hair was a shaggy mess that somehow looked good on him.

"Thank you."

"You're welcome, Sir."

"I still don't understand all the formality," Heaven stated. "I mean, I get that it's part of the whole BDSM thing, but it's odd to hear so many sirs being passed around."

I looked back at Dante, saw the only thing I needed to see. He preferred high protocol and that was all that mattered.

"To each his own," I told her. "What works for one won't necessarily work for you."

"Don't I know it," she continued. "I've heard their stories." Heaven shook her head. "So totally not my thing, but they seem pretty happy."

"Then you know it's not your place to judge." I didn't say the words with heat, it was merely an acknowledgement.

"No judging." She smiled back at me as she headed to pull something out of the oven. "How old are you, anyway?"

Not quite sure what that had to do with anything, I answered anyway. "Thirty-one."

I watched her work, admiring the way she all but pranced around the large space. She was cute. Small, brunette. Reminded me a lot of Everly, though she lacked the sweet innocence I saw in Everly, something that had attracted me to her from the beginning.

But Heaven had a vibrance about her. She was fun, carefree. Or so that was what she wanted me to see, anyway.

"Thirty-one," she mused. "Not too old." A mischievous grin formed on her cupid's-bow lips. "Then again, not that young, either."

I couldn't help but smile.

She was something. Not at all what I usually encountered.

Probably due to my brother's reputation, most submissives believed they had to follow high protocol when they were with us. Sir this, Master that. Formality, mostly. And while I tended to cater to the needs of submissives I interacted with, it was interesting to keep company with someone who wasn't into the lifestyle. She had no clue the transgressions I would've pointed out if she had been a submissive.

Perhaps that was what I liked about her. She wasn't a submissive. It meant she was safe for me. There would be no mistaking any chemistry for something more. As for why I was making that delineation, I wasn't quite sure. Had it been any other day, any other encounter, I probably would've flirted with Heaven, talked her right out of her clothes. She was physically attractive, seemed to find me equally so, and sometimes that was all that mattered.

Only, there was someone else on my mind, had been since the moment she'd walked into Zeke's house.

The object of my affections appeared in the kitchen and my full attention shifted to her.

Everly looked so young, so pure. I figured that was one of the things I liked most about her. I had the overwhelming urge to dirty her, to peel back all those innocent layers and free the sexy spitfire underneath. I'd spent plenty of time thinking about her, quite a bit interacting with her in the past six months or so. Craving her in a way I didn't quite understand. It wasn't like me.

However, I wasn't the sort of man to question my desires. At my core, I was laid-back when it came to emotions. They passed freely through me without much consideration. I countered that with the hardcore dominance I pursued. It was a perfect balance.

For whatever reason, I felt the need to touch Everly, something I'd refrained from doing since she arrived at Zeke's earlier in the day. Her eyes were focused on me as I approached, and when I pulled her in for a hug, she relaxed, her hands fisting in the back of my shirt as though she didn't want me to let her go.

If I wasn't mistaken, she had needed that. Needed me to acknowledge her.

I looked up when Isaac appeared. Immediately I saw the relief, recognized it even. He'd been waiting for me to connect, to show him that I was on the same page as he was when it came to her.

I was. I most definitely was.

But right now, Everly scared me. She seemed brittle and the last thing I wanted was to hurt her.

Leaning down, I kissed the top of her head. "You're safe with us."

She pulled back, smiled up at me. "I know."

The fact that she didn't call me Sir pleased me. I hated that term. Master, too. They were overused, in my opinion. Sure, some Doms preferred them. To each his own and all that. I wanted a submissive to call me something that would connect us on a deeper level, something that meant something to both of us.

"None of that mushy stuff," Heaven said. "Let's eat."

Releasing Everly, I allowed them to go into the dining room while my brother hung back, pulling out a couple of Guinness while I grabbed chilled mugs from the freezer.

"Everything all right?" I asked, setting the mugs on the island.

He nodded. "It will be. When we find this bastard."

Yeah. I hadn't been talking about that, but whatever. If that was where my brother's head was at, I'd be shocked. But for some reason, he felt the need to remain on neutral ground.

So neutral ground we would remain on.

For now.

I grabbed a mug and followed my brother into the dining room. As I planted my ass in the cushioned chair, I took a moment to look at the table. We'd never sat at it before, tending to utilize the island as seating for the rare meals we ate here. It felt almost foreign.

Then again, having Everly in my house wasn't normal for us, either.

Since I figured I could certainly get used to her presence, I figured I could do the same with the table.

Perhaps I could get more familiar with both.

At the same time.

The salacious thought made me smile.

Dante

"SO, HOW'D YOU TWO MEET?" IAN PROMPTED when the five of us sat down at the dining room table.

His gaze darted toward me, his fork motioning toward Everly. Not sure which he was wanting to answer, I waited to see if she would respond. My stomach was growling, and Heaven had outdone herself with the meal. Beef tips and egg noodles had obviously been her intentional main dish, but since I was vegan, she knew I would never eat it. However, the salad she had piled together with more vegetables than I had in my own kitchen would definitely hit the spot.

"Since no one else wants to talk," Heaven said with a smile in her voice, "I'll be happy to give you the rundown."

"Please," Ian urged, his eyes skimming over her with apparent interest.

Initially, when we'd come into the house, Ian had regarded Heaven as though she was on the outside looking in. The puzzle piece that didn't quite fit. However, their conversation in the kitchen had seemed to lighten his mood. I wasn't quite sure what was happening, but I felt as though I was in some sort of alternate universe where strangers were pulled into an intimate setting and forced to interact. Then again, that was sort of what happened.

And now it was a matter of finding where all the pieces belonged on the board.

Isaac was the easiest to decipher being that he couldn't take his eyes off Everly. Ian was shooting his own longing looks in her direction, but he also seemed rather intrigued by Heaven. Of course, there was the interested looks I'd received from both men. Those quick perusals meant to gauge and assess. Add to that the fact that Everly was here with me and it all seemed to come together to form everything I'd ever dreamed of. A smorgasbord of options specifically selected to meet my own unique needs.

Or the more likely case: it was happenstance.

"Dante and Everly met at the library," Heaven said between bites.

"The grocery store," Everly corrected.

"Right." Heaven pointed her fork as though recalling the event. "Grocery store. They'd been in the bakery."

"Produce section," I mumbled.

Heaven laughed. "Why don't I let *them* tell it?"

Isaac's mesmerizing gaze met mine and I saw the curiosity there. As though he was inside my head, tossing the words directly into my mouth, I began rambling. "I met Everly at the grocery store. Produce section." I glanced over at her, smiled. "She'd been looking for an eggplant, of all things."

"Yeah?" Ian's curiosity shone like a beacon. "Eggplant?"

"For the record," Everly said, "turns out I hate eggplant."

"Keep going," Isaac urged, his eyes still locked on me.

"She asked about the shirt I was wearing," I explained. "It was one I'd gotten from a club I belong to."

"Inferno?" Ian asked.

I paused, a feeling of dread trickling through me, as though I'd been caught doing something I shouldn't.

"Go on."

I swallowed, nodded. "Everly asked about it. The shirt. Said she'd be interested in going. We started talking. Turned out, we had a lot in common."

"Mostly submission," Everly added. "And as the saying goes, the rest is history. I asked for his number so I could get more details about the club." Her head lifted and she met Ian's gaze, then Isaac's. "For the record, I never went to Inferno. Dante said it wasn't the right place for me."

"He looks out for you," Isaac mused, his attention on the food in front of him.

"I do," I agreed. "I'd just started to check out the club, went a couple of times just to get a feel for it. I wasn't going that often back then, so I didn't feel right giving her details. We talked on the phone, texted a lot. Became really good friends. We got on the subject of where we lived. I told her I'd found a three-bedroom house for a steal, but I was thinking about selling it so I could get something smaller. Everly mentioned her rent was about to go up on her apartment, I suggested she rent a room from me. She did."

"Then I came along," Heaven added, "about a year ago."

"Now we're one big happy family," Everly said sweetly, patting my arm.

"Like brother and sisters?" Isaac asked.

Knowing what he was hinting at, I opted for full disclosure. "Definitely not." I cast a sideways glance at Everly. "I care about them, but I don't look at either as though they were my sister."

"We think he's hot," Heaven offered. "And vice versa."

Heaven had a way of simplifying things. Plus, she lacked a filter most of us had been born with. Despite that, or perhaps because of that, I liked her. A lot.

However, the attraction was on a base level. A man admiring a woman on a sexual level, knowing he would never give in to the urge.

"Has there ever been anything intimate between you?" Ian asked.

"Get right to the point, why don't ya?" Heaven teased. "But no. Well, not between me and Everly or me and Dante."

"Interesting way of laying that out there," Ian said, his eyes on her. "Are you bisexual?"

I could feel the heat emanating off the man. He was curious, and now that the question was out there, so was I.

When Heaven didn't answer, I glanced down the table to see she was blushing and Everly had taken a keen interest in one of the noodles on her plate, which was the only thing she was eating due to the fact she was a vegetarian.

"Less about us," Heaven said quickly. "Let's talk about you two."

"The answer is yes," Isaac said before sipping his beer. "We're bisexual."

I grinned, dipping my head to hide it. For whatever reason, that acknowledgement pleased me greatly.

Ian appeared captivated by Heaven. "What else do you want to know?"

"You're twins."

"And you must be a rocket scientist."

"Touché." She giggled. "You're identical."

This time he simply smiled.

"Thirty-one years old."

When Isaac peered over at Ian, he smirked. "She asked. I answered."

"You're both Dominants and you want Everly to be your submissive."

Both men's eyes instantly shot to Everly as though they were admitting as much.

"But there's more to that, isn't there?"

All eyes moved back to Heaven, mine included.

I got the feeling that whatever came out of her mouth at this point was going to lay the foundation for what was to come.

And who better than the filterless female to rocket them into whatever happenstance had in store for them next.

Heaven

I LIKED THEM.

All of them.

It was fun to be around a group of people and not have to worry that they were sitting there judging you. That was the way I felt when I was with my sister, or even with Danny. As though I was going to be called out for doing something wrong at any moment. Perhaps that was why I enjoyed spending so much time with my roommates, even if I didn't quite understand their … lifestyle.

Okay, so maybe that wasn't quite accurate. I understood. To a degree. From what I'd ascertained, they were extremely sexual in nature and this lifestyle they gravitated toward was heavily based on intimate sexual desires. Not exactly difficult to figure out.

But there was a unique dynamic, one I clearly didn't fit into.

Not that I was trying. I had no desire to be bossed around the way Everly and Dante enjoyed. A submissive, I was not. But I did find it all very interesting. The intimidation factor was evident. Isaac and Ian were quite competent when it came to snapping their fingers and getting the desired result. Hell, it was a wonder Everly and Dante weren't kneeling at their feet while the two men alternated between feeding them and eating.

But the most interesting was the way everyone was looking at me, likely wondering what was going to come out of my mouth next.

"And how do you see the story going?" Ian prompted.

I smiled, chewed, swallowed. "It's clear you've both got a thing for Everly." I glanced over at her. "Not that I blame you. I do, too. But not like that. Or rather, nothing I'd ever act on, anyway. But whatever." I pointed my fork at them, shifted it between them. "You're interested in a male and a female submissive."

"Good guess," Ian stated, grinned. "We admitted we were bisexual."

"That's not what I mean," I told him. "I deduced it based on the way you interact with them."

"Quite perceptive considering it's only been what? A couple of hours?" Isaac commented.

"Time is irrelevant. I see the way you look at them. Like you want them to strip naked and kneel at your feet." I felt the heat wash over me. While I was trying to keep this light, it was affecting me in a way I didn't expect. "So, I'd say you're Dominants who've always wanted to have two submissives who you could share between you. A male and a female." I met Ian's gaze. "Am I close?"

"Close," he acknowledged.

"Where'd I miss the mark?"

"What about you?" Isaac asked, redirecting before his twin could respond.

"What about me?"

"You seem to have left yourself out of this story. How do you fit?"

I waved him off with my fork. "I'm just a fifth wheel. Not even necessary."

It was clear he didn't like my response, but I blew right on by, pretending not to notice.

"I'm not a submissive," I told him. "Plus, I'm bisexual, curious, and only recently single, so sowing my wild oats is about all I'm good for these days."

"You seem rather focused on Dominants and submissives," Isaac stated.

"They've told me all about it."

"And it doesn't intrigue you at all?" Ian questioned before he took a long pull on his beer.

I watched his throat work, admired the column of his neck. He was ridiculously attractive, there was no denying that. But I figured that was the wild oats speaking.

"I didn't say that," I admitted, feeling the need to tell him the truth, though why that was, I didn't know. "Based on what they've told me, I find it fascinating. How one person could possibly want to be owned by another."

"It's a little more complex than that," Isaac noted, his distaste for my response evident.

"What does that mean?" I put my fork down.

He took a swig from his beer. "We can discuss later."

Was that a threat or a promise? And why did he care what I thought about his lifestyle? It wasn't like he was going to ask me to join in their little orgy, was he?

Wow. Heat bloomed in my core.

Wait.

No.

That wasn't why I was here. These two belonged to Everly. The last thing I would ever do was overstep like that. She was my friend. And though she spent more time with Dante than I did, I considered him a friend, too.

"What's wrong?" Everly asked, her pretty eyes locked on me.

"Nothing." I shrugged it off. "I just…" I glanced at my plate. "I think I'll get seconds."

I launched to my feet, grabbed my plate, and made a beeline for the kitchen. I was piling on more noodles when I heard footsteps behind me.

I knew without looking that it was Ian.

Warm hands curled over my shoulders. "Are you okay?"

I relaxed a little but subtly sidestepped his touch. "Yeah. I'm just an idiot."

He took the plate, set it aside before turning me to face him. I had to tilt my head back to see his face, and when our eyes met, I noticed the lust burning in his gaze.

"Why're you an idiot?"

I laughed, but it wasn't funny. "I really am the third wheel," I told him. "Fifth in this case. But I've gotten used to that. I'm always the outsider, the one tagging along."

His eyes narrowed, his hand curling over my cheek. "In case you haven't noticed, there's no inside or outside here."

"Really?" *Was he blind?* "I've seen the way you look at Everly. I know she's the one you and your brother want. And Dante..." I threw up my hands but, due to our proximity, ended up swiping across his chest. "Sorry."

Ian took my wrists, held my hands to his chest. "What about Dante?"

I could hardly breathe with him touching me like that. The way his thumb brushed over my pulse point, it had my body heating and my knees turning to Jell-O.

"I was right, wasn't I?" I asked, my voice far softer than I intended it to be.

"About?"

"You and your brother. You want two submissives to share."

"You're right, yes."

"And now you've found them."

"Have we?" His eyes implored me, urged me to continue.

I could hardly swallow past the lump in my throat, much less form words, so I continued to stare at him, not sure where this was going.

"How about I tell you how I see this situation?" he prompted.

"Okay."

"Isaac and I invited the three of you here so we can keep you safe, figure out who's after you, who attacked Everly and why." He shifted his head, studying me as he spoke. "There's no plan here, Heaven. We haven't abducted you, brought you back here so we can have our wicked way with the three of you."

"But you'd like to?" I muttered, not meaning for it to come out as a question.

"There's chemistry. Is there not?"

I swallowed hard. "Yeah."

"So why don't we chill, see how it plays out. No expectations."

I nodded.

After all, what else was I going to do?

Five

ISAAC

Sunday, May 26, 2019

I HEARD THE SCREAM, JOLTED UP OUT of my bed, my gun in my hand before I realized what I was doing, where I was.

Home. Not on the job. There was no threat here.

Setting it back on my nightstand, I glanced at the clock. Three a.m.

Taking a deep breath, I calmed myself, willing my heart to slow. As I did, I stepped out into the hall, listened for the noise that had awoken me, and when I heard it again, I glanced at the door to Everly's room.

My shoulders loosened as my surroundings became apparent, my adrenaline waning because there was no threat to tackle.

But there had been a scream and it had come from Everly's room.

Standing just outside her bedroom, I heard her whimper. Not wanting to intrude, I rapped on the door. When she didn't answer, I opened it, peeked in. Another soft whimper came, and I made the decision to go in, screw her privacy.

"No, don't," she cried out, her words distorted from the dream that had her trapped within it. More than likely, she was reliving the traumatic events from yesterday.

Placing a gentle hand on her arm, I nudged her. "Everly, wake up. You're dreaming. Wake up."

Everly squirmed, kicked at the blankets.

I shook her gently, saying her name over and over until she stilled.

Her eyes opened. Startled and out of breath from the terror of her dream, she sat up, swiping her hair back from her face. Her eyes were wild as they scanned the room, looking for a threat.

When her gaze swung back to me, the wildness I'd witnessed disappeared.

"It was a nightmare," I told her. "You're safe here, fairy princess. I won't let anyone hurt you ever again."

I cupped her face, lightly brushed beneath the bruise on her face, hating that I could do nothing to heal her.

She nodded.

"Go back to sleep," I ordered, helping her to lie down before pulling the blankets over her.

She didn't close her eyes, but she didn't say anything, either.

"You want some water?" I offered, not sure why I didn't just return to my own bedroom and go back to sleep.

"No. I'm good."

I gave her a curt nod and made my way to the door before I did something stupid, like slip into bed with her. I'd told her yesterday that she would make the first move and I meant that. Hell, I *needed* that.

"Isaac?"

"Hmm?"

"Thank you."

"For what?"

"For letting me stay here."

Me. Not us. Last night, whenever she spoke, she always seemed to incorporate all three of them, as though they were a unit that couldn't be separated.

"Anytime."

Since it was too damn early to get up, I forced myself back into my bed, propped up on the pillows, then hit the button to pull the television out of the encasement at the foot of the bed. I was flipping through channels when the door that connected my room to Everly's opened. She slipped inside, closed it behind her.

"Something wrong?" I asked, not moving from my spot.

She came to stand on the far side of the bed. "May I watch TV with you for a while?"

Saying yes was as natural as breathing, even though there was a slight niggling in my head that said this was a mistake. If I let her in my bed, there was a good chance I would never want her to leave.

"Please, my Liege."

My eyes shot to her, my heart slamming into my sternum. Not Sir. Not Master.

My Liege.

It sounded right coming from her.

"Come here, fairy princess." I yanked the blankets back enough for her to climb under them.

As though she had been made just for me, Everly curled up against my side, her head on my shoulder. I doubted she had a good view of the television from her position, but if she didn't care, neither did I.

While I flipped through the channels with my right hand, I kept my left arm curled around her, playing with her hair. There was nothing sexual about our interaction, yet it felt more intimate than anything I'd experienced before.

We remained like that for the rest of the night. At some point, I drifted off, waking only when I felt her stir beside me.

Not wanting her to slip away, I pulled her in tight to me. We'd shifted positions and I was spooned up against her, her head on my left arm, my right draped over her, her ass pressed intimately against my erection.

"Good morning," I whispered softly.

"Good morning, my Liege." Her hand clasped onto my wrist, squeezing gently as though she didn't want to let me go.

"I'm glad you're here," I told her.

"Me, too."

This woman…

She was everything I'd ever wanted and more than I knew I deserved, yet I had this strange connection to her, as though I'd known her my entire life, not merely for six months during which we'd only had minimal interactions. Then again, I'd seen her in the throes of orgasm, completely vulnerable in every way. And every time I witnessed it, I'd wanted her, ached for her. Now that she was here, I felt this overwhelming need to keep her close.

Sort of like the fairy tale. The Beast had been locked up for so long, without the intimacy he needed. Then she walked in and all was lost. My entire world had slowly started to center on her.

But she was vulnerable, and I had to remember that. What had happened yesterday had set this in motion, and I knew I couldn't take advantage of the situation. She was a guest in my house, here for her own protection, not because she'd agreed to sleep in my bed.

Though my logical, rational brain knew all of this, I was having a hard time relaying that information to the rest of my body.

Most importantly, my heart.

Everly

I FELT ISAAC TENSE BEHIND ME. HIS bicep flexed beneath my cheek. I remembered what he told me yesterday, that I was to make the first move to show him that I wanted all that he was willing to give me.

I wanted to make that move.

It might seem impulsive. No, make that *was*. It was most definitely impulsive. So? I hadn't even been here twenty-four hours and I already wanted the sexy, brooding Dom to ravish me.

That was my hormones talking.

But my hormones had never been in charge of my decisions. They spurred my actions, but they weren't a result of accepting my fate. I was the sort of woman who knew right from wrong and nothing about Isaac and Ian felt wrong. And it wasn't like I didn't know them. I did. On an intimate level, sure. But more than that. We'd spent hours together over the past six months, not all of them while I was naked. Though mostly, yes. Still.

My desire for them wasn't spur-of-the-moment. It had built over time, growing into something that I hadn't been aware was quite this intense until I ran into them yesterday at Zeke's. Since then, I couldn't seem to justify why I couldn't explore this further, see what might happen.

However, something deep within told me now was not the right time. If I propositioned him, Isaac would think this was purely sexual in nature and I couldn't allow that to happen. Not after what he'd told me last night.

When his stomach rumbled, I couldn't help but laugh. "Are you hungry, my Liege?"

I didn't know why I got such great pleasure in calling him that. I'd seen his face when I first said it, recognized the warmth that had radiated from him upon acceptance. And it felt so right. My Liege, the man I wanted to serve for the rest of my days. I'd never felt for anyone the way I felt for him and Ian. But here in this room, Ian wasn't the one I was thinking about. Only Isaac. And there was something between us, a connection I knew had to be explored.

"Starving," he mumbled, his whiskers brushing against my cheek as he buried his face in my neck.

His warm breath fanned my skin, made my nipples pebble. My body ached for him, but I knew I couldn't advance this. Not yet.

I gave his arm a gentle squeeze, loving the way he'd kept me close to him all night.

"May I make you breakfast?" I offered.

He lifted his head, and I turned, staring up at him.

The smile he gifted me with hit me square in the chest.

"How about I make *you* breakfast?"

I smiled back. "Okay."

His eyes dropped to my lips but didn't remain there long before he was unwrapping himself from around me.

"While I get it started, why don't you get dressed? Meet me in the kitchen."

"Of course."

I watched as he grabbed a pair of shorts from the back of a chair, slipped them on over his boxer briefs before disappearing from the room.

I couldn't stop smiling, even as I raced to the bedroom I was supposed to be sleeping in. I exchanged my tank top and sleep shorts for the same T-shirt and shorts I'd had on last night, then brushed my teeth, my hair. I studied the ugly bruise on my face, gently poking at it. It hurt, but a lot of the swelling had gone down. It was definitely black and blue, but I was hopeful it would fade in the coming days.

By the time I made it to the kitchen, I could smell bacon.

I was temporarily rendered immobile when I came upon Ian and Isaac working side by side on the other side of the island. Isaac was cracking eggs into a bowl while Ian was flipping bacon on the stove.

They both looked up at once.

"There she is," Ian said with a sexy smirk. "Come over here, little fairy. Keep us company."

To my surprise, my legs worked as I moved toward them.

Ian patted the countertop on the center island.

Before I could try to hop up, he lifted me easily, setting me on the cold granite.

"Since you're vegetarian and not vegan, I'm making pancakes for you," Isaac stated as he turned to another bowl he was adding oil to.

"How did you know?" I asked, glancing between the two of them.

Ian was the one who answered. "You didn't have a problem with egg noodles, but you bypassed the beef tips last night. Educated guess, you could call it."

I laughed. "Good guess. I do eat eggs and dairy."

"I assume that makes Dante a vegan?" Ian asked.

Wow. They were far more perceptive than I'd given them credit for. "It does."

He smiled. "One of the reasons you call him panda bear, huh?"

I nodded. "PB for short. That and because he's beautiful, has such endearing qualities, and as far as I'm concerned, he's an endangered species. Not many as sweet as him in the world."

Isaac was staring at me. "You love him."

It wasn't a question, but I felt compelled to confirm. "Yes. I do."

Ian winked. "Good to know."

They worked side by side easily, picking up where the other left off multiple times. It was thrilling to see their unique dynamic. Though I'd known twins, I'd never seen two who were quite as connected as they were. It was almost eerie.

"Do I smell bacon? Please tell me I do." Heaven stumbled into the room, her hands working to pull her hair back.

"You definitely do," Ian said with a grin. "Sleep well?"

"Very. Thanks."

"Why don't you get plates and forks," Ian suggested.

"I... Yeah." Heaven's gaze slammed into mine, a hint of what could only be described as confusion reflected there.

As though breaking from her weird trance, Heaven began to hum, sliding between them to reach for plates and silverware. They worked around her, patting her ass when she moved by. A couple of times Heaven's eyes shot to mine and I could tell she wondered whether I had noticed.

Did it bother her?

Ian and Isaac didn't seem to notice. Every so often, one of them would brush against my leg, another's hand would slide over my thigh. As though this was a completely natural situation.

"Two minutes," Isaac said. "We'll eat on the back patio. Could one of you get the coffee? The other can go get Dante."

"Of course, my Liege," I said quickly.

Ian's gaze shot to mine and I smiled at the approval I saw there.

I hopped off the counter, then turned toward the coffeepot as Heaven did the same.

"I'll … uh… I'll go get Dante," she said quickly, before racing out of the room.

I stared after her, unsure what was going on.

IAN

"DANTE SAID HE'LL SKIP BREAKFAST," HEAVEN INFORMED us when she returned a couple of minutes later.

"I'll talk to him," Everly offered.

"No," I said firmly. "I will. You three go eat."

Isaac glanced my way briefly, nodded before helping the women carry the food outside.

I headed toward the wing of the house I'd put Dante in. When I'd chosen the room for him, I hadn't done it to separate him from the rest of us. I had sensed he'd needed space, time apart. And by doing so, I had given him some privacy. I had to wonder now whether that had been an ill choice.

His door was closed, so I rapped my knuckles on it but didn't bother waiting for a response before I stepped inside.

"Morning," I greeted.

He wasn't asleep, but he was sprawled on the bed, his gaze fixed on the ceiling, the sheet pulled up to his navel. "I'm not hungry."

"Good," I said, keeping my tone hard. "Because I didn't ask."

That got his attention.

Dark blue eyes shot toward me. In them was something I was used to seeing from true submissives, those who sought a full-time Dominant in their life. There was need there, a desire for something I suspected had been lacking from this man's life for far too long.

I moved across the room, took a seat in the chair in the corner.

"Come here," I ordered.

Dante got to his feet slowly, his hesitance evident. He hadn't shaved, the blond scruff on his face, along with the squared lines of his jaw, a good look for him.

"Now," I added, wanting to see the way his eyes dilated with pleasure.

When he approached, I pointed to the floor at my feet. "Kneel."

Without hesitation, he lowered himself to his knees. This man was eager to prove his obedience. That much was obvious.

"Do you know who I am?"

"Yes, Sir. I do."

"Who am I?"

"You're the Dominant Everly plays with at the club."

"One of them," I admitted. "What has Everly told you about us?"

"That she trusts you."

That revelation hit a spot inside me that took me by surprise.

I admired him for a moment, the way he kept his head lowered, hands resting on his thighs. He was wearing shorts and had yet to pull on a shirt, so I had the distinct pleasure of admiring his musculature. He was healthy, probably a runner if I had to guess. His muscles were defined but not bulky, and right now, every rigid line was visible, the tension coursing through him intense.

My gaze snagged on a few scars on his upper arms. They looked like burn marks. Like someone had put a cigarette out on him a time or two. I had to wonder what foster care had been like for him and how he'd ended up there. But that was a subject I would tackle at another time. Right now, I needed to get down to business.

"You don't have a Master."

"No, Sir."

"Have you ever?"

"No, Sir. Not a permanent one."

"You're a member of Inferno. For how long?"

"Three years."

"Is that where you met the man who wants to hurt you? Do *not* look at me," I barked when his head began to lift.

"Why do you think I know him?" Dante countered.

"Because you do. He's not interested in Everly or Heaven, but he's willing to hurt them in order to keep you in line. How am I doing so far?"

Silence.

"Am I correct, Dante?"

When he spoke, his words reflected a deeply disturbing remorse. "Yes, Sir."

I sat there for a moment, watching him. He was still as stone, his breaths slightly elevated. He seemed to know how to sit to please a Dominant, the appropriate reactions to show respect. But he was completely closed off. I could practically see the rope he'd lassoed around his emotions, pulling them in tight to himself to ensure no one got close.

"So you know who attacked Everly?"

"I suspect who it is, Sir," he said softly.

"Who is he to you?"

"No one."

"Seems kinda harsh to attack an innocent woman for no reason at all. Who is he to you, Dante?"

His muscles tensed but it was almost impossible to notice. Had I not been looking for it, I would've missed it.

"He's a Sadist at Inferno. I've refused to play with him, but he doesn't take no for an answer."

"Has he cornered you?"

"Yes, Sir," he said through gritted teeth.

"Forced you?"

"Yes, Sir."

The anger at his admission surprised me. It made me want to strangle the bastard with my bare hands. That was one thing I didn't tolerate. Consent was key. It was the only thing that mattered in my world.

"Why do you keep going back?"

"Because ... I need it," he said, his voice full of torment and self-loathing.

Yeah. That was a lie. Or at least not the complete truth. However, I decided to continue down the path he'd taken.

"You need him to force you?"

This time his eyes shot up, met mine. "No, Sir. I need to submit."

I knew that, but I'd wanted to hear him say it.

"And you understand this should not be forced upon you?" I asked.

"Yes, Sir." His gaze lowered, he sighed.

"How long has it been?"

"Three months. I haven't been back to Inferno in three months. Haven't been to any other clubs."

"Have you tried to go to Dichotomy?"

"No, Sir."

"Why not?"

He didn't answer right away, and when he finally did, it was on a frustrated exhale. "Because I don't want to go through a training class."

"Understood." It was a requirement at Dichotomy that all submissives who were new to the club attend the training class, unless they were accompanied by a Dominant who was already a member. I could see for an experienced submissive that might be off-putting.

Pushing to my feet, I moved to stand behind him, placing my hands on his shoulders, kneading the muscles there. He moaned softly and I could feel the friction beneath the skin. He was on edge.

"Stand up."

I kept my hands on his shoulders as he stood.

"Face me."

He slowly turned, his eyes meeting mine.

"I want this man's name."

"I need to talk to him first," he said in a rush.

"No." It was as simple as that.

His eyes widened, his mouth opening then closing.

I stepped closer, gripped his jaw firmly. "I'll talk to him. You'll do what I say. And everyone will be happy."

Dante's chest rose and fell, but he didn't move away from me.

"Give me his name and I'll look into him," I told him. "For a couple of days, you'll stay here, keep the bastard wondering where you disappeared to."

"It won't matter," Dante stated. "He'll find me. Or them."

"His name," I demanded.

"Roger Cherlish."

I locked the name away in my memory, staring at the sexy man before me. I wasn't sure what drew me to him, but I wasn't going to pretend I didn't have a deep-seated desire to dominate him, to give him what we both needed.

"Isaac and I will take care of it," I assured him. "In the meantime, I want you to stay here. Pretend it's not an option if you'd like."

His jaw flexed beneath my fingers when he replied with, "Why?"

I opted for the truth. "Because I want you here."

That seemed to settle him.

"I won't hurt you," I told him. I wasn't attempting to make him feel safe, I was being truthful. I wasn't a Sadist. Pain wasn't my thing. If he needed it, I wouldn't give it to him. Couldn't.

"I don't want you to."

"Good. Then we're on the same page." I released his jaw. "Call in to work. At least through tomorrow. We'll see where we are then."

"Yes, Sir."

"You'll come eat breakfast, then I want you to take a shower. And if you want to scene, I'll meet you in the basement at two o'clock. There's a rug in the TV area. You can kneel, wait for me."

His Adam's apple bobbed, his eyes flared, and when he said, "Yes, Sir," I knew exactly where I'd find him at two o'clock.

Dante

ALTHOUGH I'D WANTED TO HIDE OUT, I had followed Ian's instructions, joining them for breakfast.

Everly's expression had revealed her concern, and I made an attempt to shrug it off, then felt guilty for it. Not enough to break down and tell her everything, but enough that I'd spent the morning with her and Heaven, watching TV while Ian and Isaac went down to the basement to work.

At one forty-five, Isaac returned, his eyes scanning the three of us where we sat on the sofa, me on one end, Heaven on the other, Everly curled up between us, her head on my lap. It was a position familiar to us, one we gravitated toward at the house. When Heaven wasn't with us, I would often spoon behind Everly, resting my head on a pillow and watching TV over her while she snoozed. I think it was my instinctual need to protect her. What brought out that instinct, I didn't know, but it had always been there. Only with her, though.

"How long's she been asleep?" Isaac asked.

"An hour," I told him. "Maybe two."

He nodded, then, with minimal effort, slid his hands beneath her and lifted her up. He held her as though she was fragile, and it consoled me somewhat. He wasn't going to hurt her, I knew that much. He cared about her, and though Everly hadn't gone into detail about her relationship with Isaac or Ian, I knew they were important to her. She'd mentioned them a couple of times, told me about the scenes she'd done with them. I'd always noticed the wonder in her voice, as though she couldn't quite believe they were real. However, she had always used words to belittle what they had: temporary, fleeting, fun. There was more to this than that, I could already tell.

Isaac's eyes met mine before he turned. "Ian's waiting for you downstairs."

"Yes, Sir."

His gaze turned to Heaven, but he didn't say anything.

I wasn't sure what dynamic was forming here, but it was interesting, to say the least. These two Dominants were definitely interested in Everly, but their attraction to Heaven was evident, as though she was a bonus.

What their intentions were with me, I didn't know. But I certainly wanted to find out.

When Isaac left the room with Everly in his arms, I started to get up.

"Do you know who did this?" Heaven whispered. "Attacked Everly?"

I couldn't look her in the eye. "I don't know for sure."

"Why would someone think she was me?"

That was the million-dollar question, one I didn't have an answer for. Roger Cherlish only knew I had two roommates. I hadn't given him any details about either of them. So any information he had, he'd dug up on his own.

"Whoever he is, he's an asshole," she muttered.

I smiled, couldn't help myself. "He is."

"How do we stop him?"

I shrugged. It had been the same question I'd asked myself a few dozen times in the past year. Ever since that asshole showed his true colors.

Before I could slip out of the room, Isaac returned. "Heaven, come with me. I'd like to show you something."

"Sure." She popped to her feet, a hint of uncertainty in her tone.

Realizing I was only minutes away from being late to my scene with Ian, I hurried to the basement stairs, trotted down. He was sitting at a desk, his full attention on the laptop screen in front of him. With his instructions clear in my mind, I headed for the small seating area at the far end of the room.

The basement was decked out as nicely as the house. Furniture was expensive and plentiful. From the desk areas that were structured as an office, to the small kitchenette with stainless steel appliances. There was a game section with a pool table, dart board, and a high table with two chairs. The seating area had two plush leather sofas facing an enormous television mounted on the wall.

They spent a lot of time down here, obviously.

Not looking back at Ian, I went to the center of the rug, eased down to my knees, and waited for him to join me.

With every passing second, I could hear my heartbeats increase, anticipation building, making it easy to drift in my head. Dozens of questions appeared: Why was I here? What did I want from this guy? Would it even be possible to find a Dominant who would take on someone like me? If and when I did, would he understand me? Get that I only wanted to please in whatever way possible?

Ultimately, that was what I needed. Probably more than I needed love. I needed to serve, to feel appreciated. Maybe one day I'd feel loved in a way that mattered, but I didn't hold my breath thinking about it.

"Tell me something about yourself," Ian said when his feet came into my field of vision. "Something most people don't know."

"My mother was fifteen when she had me," I said easily. There were millions of secrets stored in my head. While I felt they were better left there, I didn't think Ian would agree.

"Fifteen, huh?"

I heard the familiar creak of leather when he took a seat on the sofa. "Our mother was nineteen. What about your father?"

"He was not fifteen."

"Ah. And how old was he?"

"Twenty-eight."

Which, yes, meant he had been having sex with a minor. That wasn't the worst of his transgressions, though. Not by a long shot.

"Did they get married?"

"No, Sir. My mother left me with him when I was two, said she was too young to have a baby or a husband. Or at least, that's what my father told me."

"Just you and him, then?"

"Yes, Sir."

"Do you love Everly?"

The question took me by surprise, but I hid it the best I could. "Yes, Sir."

"I can tell." He was quiet for a moment before he added, "She loves you, too."

It wasn't a question and I wouldn't have known how to respond if he'd asked it.

"She doesn't know how deep that love runs, does she?"

"No, Sir."

"Why haven't you told her?"

"Because … it's complicated," I admitted. "It wouldn't change things between us, so I figure it's better left unsaid."

"Complicated how?"

I should've known he was going to give me the third degree. "I'd rather not get into it."

"Fine." I could hear him moving. "You can go back upstairs then."

"No, wait," I blurted when he began walking toward his desk.

He stopped, pivoted.

When I looked up at him, I saw his disappointment. He wasn't angry, which didn't surprise me. The man was completely controlled.

"You're finished talking," he stated. "Seems like the conversation is over."

I didn't want it to be over and I told him as much.

Ian stepped closer until he was standing directly in front of me. I stared up at him and a tremor danced down my spine. It was an intimidating stance, one that generally put me on edge.

Unlike with most men I'd encountered in my life, I didn't feel threatened by him. It was such a strange feeling, I wasn't even sure how to process it. And because of that, I needed this, needed him. So, if he wanted to talk, I couldn't see any reason not to tell him everything he wanted to know.

"Stand up," he commanded.

I rolled to my feet, keeping my movements smooth.

"Strip."

Swallowing hard, I heeded the command, stripping off my shorts and T-shirt, setting them on the sofa cushion before resuming my spot in front of him.

"Turn around, face the sofa."

I did.

Ian moved around me, returning to the sofa and taking his seat.

I didn't fidget, didn't so much as flinch. I knew the purpose of being naked in front of a Dominant. It was my vulnerability he was after.

"Do you run?" he asked.

"Yes, Sir."

"Look at me, Dante."

I lifted my gaze to his face.

"Very nice. I like to see your eyes. I'm a runner also," he admitted. "Isaac and I usually do five miles each morning. Perhaps you'll join us."

"If you like, Sir."

"I'd like a lot of things from you."

His admission had warmth coursing through me.

"Now tell me how your relationship with Everly is complicated."

With my eyes locked with his, I decided to confess. "I love her. Have for a long time. But what she wants and what I want are too similar for it ever to work between us."

"And what do you both want?"

"To serve our Dominant, to find someone who would put us before all others."

"Do you lean more toward male or female Dominants?"

"Male."

"Why is that?"

"I don't want to serve a female."

He didn't say anything, but his eyes implored me, urged me to continue.

"Everly and I are friends," I told him. "Good friends."

"Have you fucked her?"

"No, Sir."

"But you want to?"

"Not fuck," I admitted. "Make love."

"You have something against fucking?"

"No, Sir. But that's not what I feel with Everly."

"You don't want to do dirty things to her?"

"No, Sir. I want to cherish her."

"Is that not what she wants?"

"No, Sir."

He seemed pleased by my response, but I wasn't sure why. I hadn't gotten explicit details from Everly as to their interactions, but I assumed he knew she wasn't nearly as sweet and innocent as she looked.

"And Heaven?"

"What about her?"

"Do you love her?"

I swallowed hard, fought the urge to look away. "No, Sir, I do not. I care about her. She's my roommate. But we're not close."

He smiled. "I appreciate honesty."

We remained like that for several minutes. Me, naked and standing before him. Ian, hiding nothing as his gaze raked over me from head to toe and back again.

"When you say you want to serve, do you not want to work?"

"Only if it pleases my Master," I admitted.

"If he wants you to stay home and take care of the house?"

"Then I want to stay home and take care of the house."

"Cook, clean, the whole nine yards?"

"Yes, Sir."

"And you want to be available to him twenty-four seven?"

"Yes, Sir."

"But you don't want to sleep in his bed."

It wasn't a question and the way he said it had my breath halting in my lungs. "No, Sir. I don't."

"But you're willing to be available to him? Your ass, your mouth, your cock?"

"Yes, Sir." Heat spiraled inside me, the blood redirecting south.

Ian smiled. "Your cock agrees."

"Yes, Sir."

His eyes moved back to my face. "So if I told you to bend over and give me your ass, what would you do?"

"I'd bend over and give you my ass."

He nodded, as though accepting my response. His eyes narrowed. "I'm not going to take your ass right now."

Disappointment replaced some of the anticipation.

"That bothers you."

I hated that I was compelled to tell him the truth. But that was the way it was with me. At least with Ian. I didn't feel the need to hide from him. Mostly.

"Have a seat," he ordered, motioning toward the sofa he was sitting on.

Ian shifted, moving toward the corner and twisting so that he was relaxed, one arm across the back cushion, one knee pulled up.

"Back to the arm," he instructed. "Feet flat on the cushion. Knees wide."

I joined him on the sofa, the position he'd directed making me feel incredibly vulnerable, which I knew would be part of the power play.

"Scoot your ass down, lean back." He met my eyes. "I want to see your asshole."

My cock jerked as I shifted, half-sitting, half-reclining.

"Very nice. Now stroke your cock."

Curling my hand around my cock, I began stroking slowly, leisurely.

"Have you fucked Heaven?"

"No, Sir."

"Do you want to?"

"No, Sir. I don't see her that way."

"In all the time you've lived with them, nothing's ever happened?"

"Not between me and them, no, Sir."

"Between them? Have they been intimate?"

"I don't know, Sir." That much was true. "Heaven's openly admitted she's bisexual, but I haven't witnessed anything."

I got the feeling Heaven wasn't opposed to the idea of being with Everly, but I wasn't sure how Everly felt about it. She'd never shown any interest in women.

He watched me for several minutes, observed me fisting my cock, the sensations intensifying as his gaze did. I liked him watching me, I decided. It was intimate, stimulating.

I kept my eyes on his face as he'd instructed, watching every expression, the way his emerald eyes hooded, his lust becoming more apparent. Sure, he hid it well, but it was in the lines around his mouth. He wanted me and that was a powerful feeling.

"I don't know what's going on here," Ian said softly, his attention redirecting to my face. "It piques my curiosity, though. It wasn't my intention." He motioned toward me. "For this. My brother and I invited the three of you here to keep you safe. We want to find the bastard who hurt Everly and ensure he doesn't hurt anyone else. But this…" His gaze swung back to my dick. "This intrigues me. Makes me want to explore."

My fist tightened at his admission.

"What's your take on it?" he asked.

"I want the same thing, Sir." My voice, usually deep and even, was now choppy.

"I usually take what I want," he said. "When I want."

I didn't say anything, but my hand began moving faster, my cock throbbing.

"But only from willing submissives, those who know what they want and don't have trouble expressing it."

I squeezed my cock, fearful I was going to come from that sexy Irish lilt alone.

"I think this might get interesting, Dante."

"I hope so, Sir."

His eyes locked on mine. "I want you to come."

"Yes, Sir." In an effort to give him what he wanted, I jerked my cock faster, harder. My legs fell open, my chest rising and falling as air became scarce.

"Let me hear you."

His encouragement was the tipping point. I groaned, unable to stifle the cries of pleasure that ripped from my throat as I watched him watching me.

"Now," he demanded, his tone so low, so deep, I was powerless against it.

My release slammed into me, draining the air from my lungs and the strength from my muscles. I aimed my cock at my chest, cum splashing on my skin.

"I'm going to enjoy you," he said softly, almost reverently. "You're unexpected. In a very good way."

Ian Stokes would never know how much I had needed to hear that.

Heaven

I HADN'T EXPECTED A LIBRARY IN THE attic.

Yet that was exactly where I found myself.

After Isaac had said he wanted to show me something, I'd followed him up a set of back stairs, ending up in this beautiful room full of books and history. It was gorgeous.

And when he'd left me here, telling me to make myself comfortable, I had. Grabbing a worn copy of *Pride and Prejudice*, I curled up in the huge leather recliner. At some point, I must've fallen asleep, because I woke to someone gently shaking me.

When I opened my eyes, it took a moment to acclimate to my surroundings, but I did so with a smile.

"You look comfortable," Ian said as he moved to the other chair, easing down into it.

"This is amazing." I was unable to hide the wonder in my voice.

"You like it, huh?"

"Books are my jam," I told him.

His soft chuckle warmed me. "Dinner's almost ready."

"Oh." I sat up, looked around for a clock. "What time is it?"

"Five thirty."

Wow. I'd slept for hours.

"Are you doing okay?" he asked, the concern on his face confusing me.

"Of course."

"Need anything?"

"Um… Not that I can think of."

He smiled again. "If you do, you only need to ask."

I nodded.

"In case you haven't noticed, I like to talk," Ian said. "My brother often says I talk too much."

"Do you?" I teased.

"Probably. But it works. It quells my curiosity. In my line of work, it pays to know all the details."

"What line of work is that?"

"Personal security."

I nodded, understanding. "You're a bodyguard."

"You could say that, sure."

"Do you enjoy it?"

"Mostly, yes. And you? Do you enjoy your job?"

I nodded, grinned. "Mostly, yes."

He chuckled. "Where do you work?"

"Barnes and Noble," I told him. "I take classes online."

"Do you need to call in to work?"

I frowned, confused. "I'm supposed to be there tomorrow at eight."

He nodded. "Do you plan to go to work?"

"Yes?" I wasn't sure why it came out as a question, but I got the feeling he was angling for something.

His smile widened. "Let me rephrase. Do you want to go to work tomorrow at eight?"

"I need the money," I admitted.

"Then I'll make sure you get there," he said simply. "And I'll have someone stay with you until you get off."

I frowned. "Why would you do that?"

He cocked his head to the side, a silent encouragement for me to answer that question myself.

"You think this guy's gonna come after me."

"I do."

I waved him off, got to my feet. "He won't come back. Not this soon."

"He's already been by the house twice today," he said.

I put the book back on the shelf, turned to face him. "How do you know that?"

He smiled, but this time it was roguish. "I have my ways."

I couldn't deny that the thought of that man coming back, doing what he did to Everly... It didn't sit well with me. Not because I was necessarily scared of him, but I definitely didn't want to risk Everly or Dante. I cared about them both and I hadn't realized just how much until I'd walked in to find some asshole attacking my friend.

The memory had my knees weakening, but I forced them to remain steady. "I can get a hotel for a few days."

"If that's what you want," he said simply.

Ian got to his feet, walked over to me. I forced myself to remain where I was.

"However, I know Everly and Dante would prefer you stay here."

"Do you want me here?"

He considered me for a moment. "If you're asking whether or not I'm attracted to you, Heaven, the answer is yes."

I blushed. "That's ... actually... Well, thank you. But that's not what I meant."

"No?"

"No. I mean, I just broke up with my boyfriend and all. I'm not looking for anything ... you know, serious."

He smiled and it almost reached his eyes. "I wasn't offering serious."

"Oh."

He chuckled, stepped closer until I was forced to look up at him. "Call in to work for a few days." Ian cupped my face, his pretty eyes linking with mine. "Stay with us. Think of it as a vacation of sorts."

"Okay." The word was out before I even realized I'd said it.

"Heaven?"

"Hmm?"

"I'm going to kiss you now."

I swallowed, the sound loud in the otherwise silent room.

When Ian leaned in, I closed my eyes, my lips tingling, eager to meet his. He hovered just out of reach, his hands cupping my face in a move that had my body warming. I liked the way he touched me, talked to me. I hadn't had that before. Certainly not with Danny the Dickhead.

"Was that too serious for you?" he whispered against my lips.

"No." Yup. That was me all breathless and needy.

"Good. And neither is this." His lips melded to mine in a kiss so soft it felt otherworldly. As though we were connected on another plane in another universe.

"Touch me," he urged. "Put your arms around me, Heaven."

As though I had needed his permission, my arms instantly snaked around his neck. I leaned into him, my lips parting, accepting him as his tongue slid against mine.

What started out sweet morphed into something else entirely. Ian's hand slid into my hair, fisting it as he claimed my mouth. In that moment, I wanted to give myself to him in every way. Sowing oats or whatever. I didn't care because mere mortal men did not kiss like this.

Certainly not Danny the Dickhead.

"Here with me," he ordered, pulling back, his hand still wrapped in my hair, forcing me to look at him. "When it's about pleasure, that's all it's about. Your mind stays in the moment, not wandering to other men."

I frowned. How did he know what I'd been thinking?

Ian's big hand engulfed mine, our fingers linking. "Come on. Let's get some food. Then we'll talk some more."

Confused as to why I still wanted to do anything this man wanted, I nodded.

Oh, crap.

I was so screwed.

even

ISAAC

"IS THE POOL WARM ENOUGH TO SWIM in?" Heaven asked as the five of us sat down for dinner, once more occupying the dining room Ian and I had never used before they'd come here.

"Probably not," Ian told her. "But it's worth trying."

"I'm game," Everly said, her gaze scanning the rest of us. "But I didn't bring a swimsuit."

"Well, then you'll be happy to know we don't allow clothing in the pool, anyway. You're all set," Ian stated, his tone so serious I almost would've believed him.

Heaven chuckled, and for the first time since she'd come down from the library, she seemed to relax. I wasn't sure what had happened between her and Ian earlier, but when they had appeared in the kitchen, they'd both been tense.

"Seems like a rule of convenience," Heaven added as she sipped her wine.

Ian laughed. "Well, my house, my convenience."

"Don't you mean your house, your rules?"

"That's a given," he told her between bites. "But I do like the convenience."

"So we can swim?" Everly asked, her gaze sliding to me.

"You can do whatever you'd like," I told her. "Whenever you'd like."

There was heat in those baby blues and it touched something deep inside me. I'd been holding back with her. Mostly because I didn't want her to misunderstand the reason we'd brought her here. She was free to go at any time, but I wanted her safe. But mostly, I wanted her here. With me. Because she wanted to be here.

And yes, I was offering the same protection to Heaven and Dante, but not for the same reasons. While Dante piqued my curiosity unexpectedly, the same couldn't be said for Heaven. She was an interesting woman, but not at all my type. While my twin would dally with women who weren't in the lifestyle, I rarely did. I knew what I wanted, knew what was required to make me happy. Pretending otherwise was simply a waste of valuable time all around.

"You should check out the library," Heaven told Everly. "It's amazing. I think they've got all the classics."

"There's a pool table and dart board downstairs," Ian said helpfully. "Tomorrow morning, I'm going for a run."

I nodded. "I'll join you."

"I will, too," Dante said, his tone not quite certain.

"Good." Ian glanced at the women. "And you two? You up for a run?"

"Absolutely," they said at the same time.

I frowned. "You run?"

Everly nodded, continued eating. I'd made her and Dante quinoa salad, wanting to ensure they had enough to eat. Not having known their dietary restrictions had been an issue since Ian and I being meat eaters had made things awkward last night. But I had rectified that this afternoon, slipping out while Everly napped, Heaven read, and Ian and Dante did their thing in the basement.

"I try to go with Dante at least three days a week," she said. "He's got far more energy than I do, though."

"And by three days, she means once every three weeks." Dante chuckled.

"Whatever," she said, smacking his arm playfully. Her gaze shifted back to me. "But I'd love to go for a run. Where do you go?"

"Through the neighborhood," Ian answered. "We've got a five-mile route mapped out."

"Perfect."

"Well, if it's all right with you, I'd really like to go for a swim after dinner," Heaven said, not committing to the run.

"Me, too," Everly added.

"Like I said," Ian teased, "no clothes allowed in the pool."

"I don't need clothes," Everly stated, drawing all eyes toward her. She grinned impishly. "What? I don't."

"What about you?" I asked Heaven directly.

"Naked doesn't bother me."

I grinned, turned my attention to my food.

"I think we might be onto something," Ian said in a conspiratorial whisper. "Anything else we should restrict clothing for?"

I looked up, met their gazes one at a time. "I can think of a lot of things."

Heat curled into the room, sliding between us. The chemistry was off the charts and I found it both interesting and a bit surprising. At the club, the sexual tension was generally the focus. Whether it was one submissive or a handful. But this... We were in the intimacy of my home and though I'd always intended to have a full-time submissive, I'd pretty much given up all hope.

Until I'd met Everly.

"There's only one problem with that." Heaven pointed with her fork.

"What's that?"

"I'm not a submissive."

"You're in luck. It's not a requirement."

Her eyes swung to me. "No?"

I sat up straight, took a swig of my beer. "No. Why would it be?"

"That's what you're looking for, right?"

"It is." I didn't mean for it to happen, but I found my hand sliding over to Everly's thigh, a protective gesture that was instinctual.

She surprised me, placing her hand over mine and holding on.

"So that's what it is," Heaven said. "I don't have to be because you've already got your submissive."

I didn't respond.

"See? I'm right. You've got your sights set on Everly."

I wasn't quite sure why she was so defensive, but I couldn't refrain from responding. "There are some things you shouldn't call me on, Miss Whitley."

"Testy," she snapped. "Are you denying it?"

"Denying what?"

"That you want them?"

"Not at all. Why would I deny what's true?" I told her, holding her stare, waiting to hear a rebuttal.

Not surprising, one didn't come.

"Dante, I'd like you to do the dishes," Ian said absently.

He didn't stop eating. "Yes, Sir."

"Naked."

The man didn't even flinch. "It would be my pleasure, Sir."

Heaven seemed to find her chicken to be interesting while Everly relaxed, as though some of the tension had drained out of her. I hoped by the end of the evening, they all would.

Half an hour later, we'd all deposited the dishes in the kitchen, where Dante took on the task of hand-washing every dish while buck naked. The dishwasher would've been faster, but where was the fun in that?

Everly and Heaven disappeared down the hall while Ian and I sat at the kitchen island, watching the man work. He certainly held my attention, moving with ease, quite comfortable in his own skin. Perhaps because he was vegan, Dante was quite lean. Then again, he had admitted to running, so it could very well be a rigorous exercise regimen. Whatever he did, it was working, and I couldn't deny, he had a delicious physique.

I did my best not to ogle the numerous scars that marred his back and arms, but I cataloged each one, wanting nothing more than to hurt whoever had put those on him.

"I'm gonna meet the owner of Inferno tomorrow," Ian told me, his voice low. "Want to get his take on this Roger Cherlish."

I nodded. "Want me to go with you?"

He shook his head. "Nah. The club's not open tomorrow. He said he'd meet with me at noon."

"What do you hope to gain from the meeting?"

"Explain to him what happened, see what actions he intends to take."

Nothing if I had to guess. It was unfortunate, but some of the BDSM clubs didn't care what their members did after hours. As long as they paid their dues and didn't cause issues at the club, they could overlook a lot of things. Of course, there were also clubs who turned a blind eye to what went on inside their walls. I hoped like hell Inferno wasn't one of those places.

"You get any more info on him?" I asked.

"Nope. I've called in a favor. Got someone digging. It's like the guy doesn't exist."

I took a long pull on my beer. "He clearly does since he's gone back to Dante's twice today. What's he up to?"

"Figure he's looking for this young stud."

I admired the flex of Dante's back muscles, my gaze drawn to a few faint lines on his back. They were scars that had been put there by either a whip or a flogger. Appeared to be rather old.

I nodded toward his back. "He mention anything about those?"

"Haven't asked. Yet."

I nodded. I'd had a conversation with Ian earlier regarding what had transpired down in the basement. He relayed the conversation they'd had, none of which surprised me. I'd known from the second Everly saw Dante yesterday that there was a connection there.

I was more interested to know the dynamic. They'd had plenty of opportunity to explore one another, see whether a relationship would work or not, yet they hadn't.

Then again, I hadn't gotten Everly's take on the situation either.

The sound of pattering feet on hardwood alerted me to Everly's and Heaven's return. They were practically skipping when they joined us in the kitchen, both wrapped in towels.

"Come here," I said, speaking directly to my fairy princess.

Her smile was brilliant as she fluttered over. "Yes, my Liege?"

I pulled her closer, widening my legs so she could stand between them. "Have you ever seen Dante naked?"

"Yes, my Liege," she said, her eyes scanning mine as though looking for something. "But it was by accident."

I nodded. "This isn't accidental. What do you think?"

I turned her in my arms, ensured her only focus was the man finishing up the dishes.

"He's beautiful, my Liege."

Dante's shoulder muscles tensed slightly.

"I agree."

The shoulders relaxed.

"What about you?" I asked Heaven, who had found her towel quite fascinating.

"No. I haven't seen him naked."

Ian got to his feet, walked over to Heaven, stopping to stand behind her.

She inhaled sharply when he put his hands on her shoulders. Ian turned her to face Dante. "What do you think?"

When she didn't respond right away, Ian pulled her hair back over her shoulders, teasing her skin with his fingertips as he leaned down close to her ear.

"Do you find him attractive?"

"Yes," she said, her tone clipped.

"Yes, what?"

"I don't know."

Ian lifted his head, met my gaze, and motioned toward the door.

"All right, you two," Ian announced. "Let's go for a swim."

I pulled Everly close before she could slip away. "You are to keep the towel on until I instruct you otherwise."

Her eyes glazed over, her excitement palpable. "Yes, my Liege."

Dante, realizing Ian was talking to him, too, shut off the water and turned, revealing his obvious approval of the conversation taking place around him. His thick cock bobbed proudly as he dried his hands, then followed Ian and Everly out the back door.

"Heaven, wait. You and I should talk."

She slowly pivoted to face me. "I'm sorry if I've offended someone," she said softly. "I just don't know how any of this stuff works."

"How do you want it to work?"

She shrugged. "I don't know the rules."

"There aren't any rules." I walked toward her, tilted her chin up, catching her gaze with mine. "Not yet, anyway."

"I'm not a submissive."

I grinned. "You keep saying that."

"Because it's true."

"Why does it matter so much to you?"

She shrugged.

"We're in the privacy of our own home, Heaven. We're all adults. Rules of proper etiquette are a given. Aside from that, I'm a firm believer in going with the flow. The one thing Ian and I will always be is honest with you."

"I'm not looking for anything serious," she blurted.

"I wasn't offering."

I could see a hint of disappointment flash in her eyes. While I hated that it was there, I wasn't going to lie to her. I found her attractive, interesting even, but there was no chemistry between her and me. Likely due to the fact that I couldn't see beyond Everly. Didn't want to.

However, I did want Heaven to feel comfortable while she was here. And I got the feeling Ian wasn't opposed to including her in a scene or two.

"What do you say we pretend for a little while?" I offered.

"Pretend?"

"Yes. Let's pretend we're all just normal people, hanging out."

"We are normal people," she countered.

"Then I don't see the problem. If you feel like joining in an activity that interests you, no one's going to stop you."

"You're talking about sex."

"Was I?"

She rolled her eyes, smiled.

"Do you have a problem with exploring your sexuality?"

"No."

"Then I say you pretend for a bit, see how it plays out. Who knows. You might end up enjoying yourself."

She nodded. "What do I have to do?"

"Enjoy yourself," I said softly. "That's the only rule for tonight."

"Why does Everly call you that? My Liege?"

"Because I'm her Dominant. It's her way of relaying her desire to submit to me."

"What am I supposed to call you?"

"Whatever you'd like."

"Can I call you Isaac?"

"If that turns your crank, sure."

She grinned, relaxed.

I took a step back. "Shall we join the others?"

She nodded, then skipped out through the back doors and onto the patio.

Not wanting to keep my fairy princess waiting, I grabbed two more beers, then joined them.

"Towel must go," Ian told Heaven when she eyed Dante getting into the water.

"Is it cold?" she asked.

He shook his head.

I smiled to myself.

"Sneaky Doms," Heaven teased. "It's heated, huh?"

It was. But it was more fun to let them believe otherwise.

"Lose the towel," Ian snapped, his gaze locked on her.

While they battled it out, I took Everly's hand, led her toward one of the tables. I took a seat in the tall chair.

"What's on your mind?"

She smiled sweetly, then, as gracefully as she did everything else, she unhooked the corner tucked in by her breast, then allowed the towel to slide to the ground. "This is me making the first move, my Liege."

I would forever remember that single moment in time because it was the very moment when I fell completely in love with Everly Hughes.

With my heart in my throat, I smiled. "Thank you, fairy princess."

"It's my pleasure, my Liege."

"Turn around for me."

She pivoted in a slow circle.

"Now come here."

Everly moved to stand between my legs and I couldn't resist touching her. My hands skimmed over her chest, her collarbone, her neck.

"You are so fucking beautiful," I whispered, not bothering to hide the way she made me feel. Looking at her robbed me of breath and sense, made me want things I'd never wanted before.

"Thank you, my Liege," she whispered.

Pulling her in closer, I lowered my head, grazing her lips with mine. I teased her tongue with my own, approval glowing inside me at the way she gave herself over freely.

"I want you to sleep in my bed tonight," I whispered when I drew back.

"I would love that, my Liege."

I smiled, ensuring she saw how happy she made me. "Now, go swim. Have fun."

"Will you join us?"

"Is that what you want?"

"Very much."

I nodded. "Give me a few minutes."

Her eyes glittered with hope, a warm smile on her face before she turned and headed for the pool, her cute little ass swaying sweetly.

"You're done for, brother," Ian said, joining me at the table.

There was no reason to confirm or deny. I was most certainly done for when it came to this woman.

Everly

"I COULD COME OUT HERE EVERY NIGHT," Heaven said, floating on her back, her bare breasts above water.

"Me, too." My gaze swung over to Isaac and Ian, deep in conversation at the table.

"Are you mad at me?" Heaven asked.

I jerked my head toward her, realized she was now standing, her shoulders beneath the water.

"What? Of course not. Why would I be mad?"

Her gaze shifted to Ian and Isaac, then back to me. "I see how you look at him."

I wasn't going to pretend I didn't know what she was talking about.

"Nothing happened," she said quickly, as though to reassure me.

"I wouldn't be mad if it did," I admitted, although that wasn't entirely the truth. When it came to Isaac, I knew exactly where I stood. With Ian, it was quite the opposite, as though he was keeping his distance for some reason.

And while I didn't have the same sense of belonging with Ian that I did with Isaac, I couldn't deny I wanted it. But it wasn't my place to make those decisions. If Ian was keeping me at arm's length, I had to believe he had a reason. Perhaps that reason was Heaven, but I didn't want to think too long or too hard on that.

"It's not weird?" Heaven asked.

"What?"

"The way they act. Like there's nothing wrong with one big orgy under their roof?"

"Is there?"

Heaven laughed. "Of course you wouldn't think so."

Dante swam by, continuing to do laps. He seemed lost, but that wasn't unusual for him. I'd gotten used to his moods over time, realized he needed his space more than most people.

"And him," Heaven added. "They're quite fascinated by him."

That they were. It allowed hope to bloom deep inside me, though I wasn't going to share that with Heaven.

"I'm getting the impression they want us equally," Heaven pondered.

No, not equally. I knew deep down, there was something powerful between me and Isaac. I felt it when he looked at me. Did I think he wanted Dante? Yes. Did that bother me? Oddly, no.

As for their intentions with Heaven, I couldn't quite pin them down. It was almost as though they were willing to include her in an effort to make her more comfortable. Then again, they were highly sexual creatures, so it was quite possible they were interested in letting it play out.

Truth be told, I didn't mind. I was also a highly sexual creature, and I'd never been the sort to refrain from exploring new things.

Perhaps it was because I'd been in the scene for so long, seen the traditional and untraditional interactions. Some Doms were extremely possessive of their submissive, couldn't imagine another Dom touching her or him. Ian and Isaac were different, though. At times, they seemed almost like one person, not two. As though their needs were so in tune, it was hard to figure out what it was they wanted to make them happy.

"It's not just sex, is it?" Heaven asked, her uncertainty clear in her words.

I turned my attention back to her. "No. It's never just about sex."

"Does it make me a bad person that I find it hot? That I don't care about all the Dom/sub stuff, but I wouldn't mind getting laid?"

I smiled. "Not at all. To each his own."

"What happens if they command you to sleep with Dante?"

Dante had slowed his pace, stopping a couple of feet away.

"Well, I doubt there would be much sleeping," I teased, finding it amusing that Heaven had such a difficult time talking about sex. She called me sweet and innocent.

The sound of a chair scraping on concrete had all three of us looking over. I had to work hard to keep my jaw from dropping as both men stripped, then made their way toward the water. They were an intimidating pair. So big, so powerful ... and the way they moved—a mixture of power and grace—had my mouth watering. I could've stared at them all night, but admittedly, my skin itched to feel their touch.

Isaac made his way over to me while Ian moved toward Heaven. As though their movements were choreographed, they stepped up behind us, Isaac pulling me against him. Skin to skin. His arm slipped over me in that protective gesture, crossing over my chest. He held me tight as he backed toward one of the concrete benches along the side. Ian did the same on the opposite side of the pool.

"Dante," Isaac called out. "Come here."

"Yes, Sir."

Isaac's head dipped beside mine, his mouth near my ear when he said, "Have you kissed him before, fairy princess?"

"No, my Liege." I was breathless as Dante approached.

"Do you want to?"

That was a tough question. To put it simply, yes. I'd wanted to kiss Dante for a long time. However, I also didn't want to do anything to jeopardize our friendship.

"Answer me," he growled in my ear.

"Yes, my Liege."

"Then I'll leave it up to him," Isaac said.

Dante stared into my eyes and I saw the battle brewing there. I knew how he felt about me. The same way I felt about him. Was it the same as what I felt for Isaac? No. Significantly different. But there was a connection between me and Dante, a love that had built from friendship, grown. We'd never crossed that line.

"Dante?" I whispered his name, wanting him to say something.

He stepped closer, the water warm and still between us.

His gaze shifted over my shoulder briefly.

"I can see it," Isaac said. "The chemistry between you. More than friendship, but not enough to where either of you acted on it."

"Yes, Sir," Dante whispered, his eyes meeting mine again. "It's always been that way."

"Then why don't you explore it?" Isaac suggested.

"I don't want to lose her," he said, his voice full of torment.

"You won't," I blurted, reaching for him without thinking. "You'll never lose me, Dante."

He moved closer, his hands sliding up my arms, over my shoulders, down my sides until they rested on my hips beneath the water. I was sitting on Isaac's lap, could feel the hard ridge of his erection against my back.

"You don't have to do this," I told him, hating the anguish I could see on his face.

"I want to. I've wanted to since the day I met you."

I swallowed, leaned into Isaac. For whatever reason, having him there made it all okay. As though he was my anchor and his approval made it all right. As though he would be able to keep me and Dante together, not let something like this come between us.

"It'll always be there. That need, that desire," Isaac whispered. "It won't go away. It's easier to accept it than fight it."

Dante's eyes locked on Isaac's face. "May I have your permission to kiss her, Sir?"

"You have my permission."

Dante leaned in, our mouths hovering for breathless seconds before he finally closed the distance, sealing his mouth to mine. I whimpered, emotion slamming into me as I slid my arms around his neck and let him feel everything I was feeling.

Isaac's hands slid over my ribs, holding me firmly as though he was grounding me, ensuring I knew he was there. Or perhaps he was simply ensuring he was part of it. Giving permission, keeping us close. He had the control we both eagerly wanted him to have.

"Everly," Dante whispered, changing the angle before plunging his tongue into my mouth.

I could taste his passion, his protectiveness. From the day I met him, Dante had watched over me, but he had always kept his distance. He wasn't now and I needed this, needed him. Although Heaven didn't seem to understand the dynamic here, I did. It felt right, as though it wasn't meant to be picked apart, piece by piece, and analyzed. It was simply meant to happen.

When we came up for air, Dante pressed his forehead to mine, cupped my neck with both hands.

"You're my angel," he whispered. "I can't lose you."

"Never," I promised.

He pulled back, slid deeper into the water once more, his gaze meeting Isaac's. "Thank you, Sir."

"No need to thank me," he said firmly. "I don't want anything coming between you. It's evident you're both worried about it."

Dante nodded, then turned when Ian called his name.

Isaac lowered himself back into the water as I turned in his arms, wrapping myself around him.

He brushed my wet hair back, stared in my face.

"I want you," he whispered, his voice rough. "Not just your body or your submission. I want all of you, Everly."

I could hardly breathe, his words washing over me, warmer than the water we were in.

"I figure it's best you know that now. No reason to pretend otherwise."

"No pretending," I agreed.

"It seems easy now, fairy princess. But I'm not an easy man." He nodded toward Ian. "He's the one who talks. I tend to hold it all in. But you'll always know where you stand with me. You're the most important to me."

I nodded.

"Even when I share you," he said, his tone shifting, garnering a dangerous edge.

"With Ian?"

Isaac swallowed. "Yes."

"How does he feel about it?"

"Ian has his own needs and wants. When he's ready to act on them, he will. And I'm sure you'll be the first to know when it's real for him."

I wasn't sure what that meant, but I didn't know how to get more information, either.

"Will you share me with anyone else?"

"Until today, that's never been something I considered."

"What changed?"

He nodded toward the side of the pool where Ian, Dante, and Heaven were. "Dante came along. Now I find the idea of watching you with him rather enlightening."

"And Heaven?" I prompted, needing to know his stance on it.

"For entertainment purposes, perhaps. No one else. No one else will ever touch you. But I need that as much as I need you."

"I understand, my Liege."

"Do you?"

I looked him directly in the eye. "Yes."

"You understand that I want Dante? That I want his submission as much as I want yours?"

Relief poured through me. "Yes, my Liege." This time I cupped his face, ensured he understood the truth in my words.

"But I want your love," he noted. "Only yours."

I wouldn't promise him my love because we both knew that wasn't necessary. It wasn't something that had to be said, it was felt. And though I didn't understand how it was possible, I knew I loved this man already. How it would play out would be up to the universe, but I knew I would come to love him with not only my heart but my soul as well.

I didn't realize we'd moved to the dark end of the pool, but it was our own little cocoon, like we were the only two people in the world.

Isaac backed up against the wall, his hand sliding between us.

"I need to feel you," he whispered. "I need to be inside you. Right now."

"Please, my Liege."

Within seconds, he had aligned our bodies, nothing between us, as he slid deep inside me. There were no conversations about protection because those were out in the open between us, everything maintained in our files at the club. I was on the pill and my blood tests were up to date, as were theirs. Which left only pleasure as our main concern.

"Eyes on mine," he ordered as he pulled my hips, plunging all the way inside me.

I moaned, gasped. He was huge, filling me, stretching me. It was pleasure and pain all at once. But it was the greatest feeling in the world, being this close to him. I'd wondered for so long how it would feel to have him inside me. Now I knew and it was … overwhelming. More than I'd bargained for. Perfect came to mind.

His hands slid up my back, fingers curling over my shoulders. Isaac tipped me backward, his fingers tightening over my shoulder as he moved his hips. Thrust, retreat, our eyes never straying. The buoyancy of the water kept me afloat, but it was Isaac who held me as he drove himself deep.

"It's not enough," he groaned. "Will never be enough. Arms around me."

Once more, he shifted our positions, his hands returning to my hips. I slid my arms around his neck, held on tight as he increased the rhythm of our bodies, driving into me again and again, displacing the water around us as he fought for more friction, as though he couldn't get close enough.

I tightened my legs around his waist, dug my ankles into his thighs, trying to bring him back from the edge.

"My Liege," I whispered, using my own strength to get closer to him.

"Christ," he groaned. "Yes. Just like that. Ah. Yes."

He relaxed his hold, allowed me to move, to impale myself on him again and again.

When he crushed his lips to mine, I could feel the tension, a rubber band about to snap.

"Come for me," he said, nibbling my lower lip. "Come all over my cock, fairy princess."

His hand snaked between us, his thumb finding my clit. My whimpers and moans grew louder, drifting in the humid air. I knew the others were still in the pool, but in this moment, they didn't matter. Only Isaac.

"I want to feel your pussy ripple on my cock," he groaned. "Come for me. Come all over me."

The way he filled me, the pressure he applied to my clit, and his words shot me over the edge. A strangled cry ripped from my throat as a glorious orgasm shattered me.

His hands came around, cupping my ass as he jerked me to him hard, his cock pulsing inside me as he breathed my name again and again.

When the world righted itself, Isaac buried his face in my neck, held me in the water, our bodies still joined. Only then did I hear the muted conversation taking place at the other end of the pool.

"My Liege," I whispered against his ear, my heart still thumping hard in my chest. "Don't ever let me go."

His arms tightened around me, a silent agreement between us.

Eight

IAN

I WATCHED MY BROTHER CARRY EVERLY OUT of the pool and directly into the house. He was holding on to her as though he would shatter if he let go.

Oddly, I sort of knew the feeling. I'd felt their connection when they'd been in the water, watched as their bodies came together in a desperate passion they'd ignored for so long. In that moment, I'd wanted to join them, to sink deep inside Everly at the same time as Isaac, to fill her completely, to take her between us, claim her together.

Only, that wasn't going to happen. I knew better than to think Isaac was on the same page I was. It wasn't in the stars, wasn't how we'd always envisioned our lives going. My brother and I had always intended to have two submissives, each having their own, sharing them between us.

Isaac had found his one love, the woman he would spend his nights sleeping beside.

And I was on the periphery, expected to align with my own submissive, to pave my own way so that we could meet in the middle at some point.

Needless to say, things were not going the way we'd planned.

"Sir?"

"Yeah?" I glanced over at Dante.

"May I please turn in for the evening?"

I nodded. "Of course. If you need anything … the house is as much yours as it is mine."

"Thank you, Sir."

I watched as he stepped out, his perfect ass ripe for the picking. While I wanted to explore him on a much deeper level, I figured he'd had enough for one day. Tomorrow … that was a different story.

I found myself smiling.

"Uh-oh." Heaven giggled. "That looks like a mischievous smile. Dirty thoughts about a particular male submissive?"

"Stand up," I said, keeping my tone cool, relaxed, the smile firmly in place.

"I am standing." She grinned. So coy, so sweet. I wasn't quite sure what to do with her yet. But I was glad we had a little time to explore alone. I wouldn't go so far as to say she was a substitute for Everly, but she was a worthy distraction.

"All the way up. Let me see those beautiful tits."

Heat swirled in the soft green of her eyes, giving her away. She'd given me the spiel about sowing wild oats, and initially, I'd thought she was placating me. Now, I got the sense she'd been telling the truth.

Which made her all the more appealing. I would never feel for Heaven what I felt for Everly, but I certainly didn't mind losing myself in her for a bit.

Heaven surprised me, standing tall and dropping her arms to her sides.

I found myself entranced by her in so many ways. Not only in her physical beauty, but that inner light I could see hidden beneath dark shadows.

"I'm thinking that boyfriend of yours didn't pay nearly enough attention to your tits." I met her gaze. "Hot or cold?"

"Hot," she said quickly.

"What did he pay attention to?" I asked, standing tall so that I towered over her. I moved closer.

"Other women," she said, a snarky bite to the words.

"Really?"

"Yes."

"How long were you with him?"

"Three years. On and off."

Well, that explained a lot of her insecurities. She'd spent the past three years with a douchebag who didn't realize the gift he'd been given.

I moved to stand behind her, not touching her. Not yet.

"Do I scare you, Heaven?"

"No."

"Good. May I touch you?"

"Uh … yes."

I eliminated the space between us, pressing my chest to her back, then pulled her back against me. "Good girl. Just let yourself go. It's about pleasure, nothing more."

"Only pleasure," she whispered, trembling.

"Let's move into deeper water. You're shivering."

She moved with me, allowing me to take her weight in my arms.

"Put your arms around my neck."

She did, lifting her arms behind her, then cupping my neck until her fingers touched. Considering the size difference, it wouldn't have worked if I hadn't had my knees bent, allowing her sweet little ass to press against me.

I trailed my fingers from her elbows downward until I ran my fingertips over her puckered nipples.

She moaned softly.

"Now tell me, why'd you stay with a man who didn't appreciate you?"

"I'm an idiot," she muttered.

I tweaked her nipples, making her squeal. "From this point forward, I don't want to hear another negative word about yourself. Understood?" I released the pressure.

"Yes."

I teased her nipples, giving pleasure where I'd just applied pain. She relaxed into me again.

"How'd you meet him?"

"At the bookstore. He came in one day. Started talking."

I cupped her breasts, squeezed gently, enjoying her soft moans.

"He took you out?"

"In the beginning."

"When did you know it was going south?"

"Three months in."

I stilled. "Three months? And you gave him three years?"

"Yes."

"Did you break up with him?"

"Several times."

"Did you go back to him? Or him to you?"

"He always came to me. Apologized, swore he'd never do it again. I took him back like an—"

I smiled, pressed my lips to the top of her head. "Good girl. Did he hit you?"

"No. Never. I wouldn't put up with that."

"But you let him screw around and you took him back."

"I always made him use a condom," she said defensively, as though that was the only problem with the scenario.

"Because you're smart. That doesn't mean he deserved you."

Heaven didn't say a word, her head resting back against my chest as I continued to tease her nipples. She shivered again and I knew it was time to give up the pool.

I took her wrists, lowered her arms, then turned her.

"Are you mad?" she asked, her voice soft, uncertain.

"Not at all." I tipped her chin up, pressed my lips to hers. "I'm taking you inside so I can warm you up."

Her eyes widened, and for a second, I thought she would run.

I gripped her chin more firmly, met her gaze. "Heaven, with me, it's always your choice. At any time. I don't assume anything. When you want to stop, say the word."

She nodded.

Regardless of what happened next, I knew I had to get her inside, warm her up. The night air was cool, and I didn't want to risk her catching a cold.

I hooked one arm under her legs, lifted her up, made her laugh. The sound loosened something inside me.

By the time I made it to her bedroom, her teeth were chattering.

"Shower with me?" I asked, ensuring she knew it was her choice.

"Yes."

I padded to the bathroom, set her down long enough to turn the water on. It heated instantly and I dragged her into the glass enclosure, pulling her against me as I let the hot water pour over us both.

"Did he force you?" I asked, needing to know the demons in her past.

"No. Never." She pulled back, looked up at me. "He just used sex against me. Accused me of only wanting him for sex."

"That's rich," I grumbled.

"He did it enough, I started to wonder if that was true."

"He was guilting you because of his own guilt," I told her.

"When I think about it rationally, I know that's true. It's just..."

I stepped back, grabbed the body wash, poured a generous amount in my hands. "Just what?" I made a spinning motion with my finger. "Turn around."

She faced away from me and I used my soapy hands on her skin, slicking her shoulders, her neck, massaging her as I went. I took my time, working down her back.

"I've always had a high sex drive."

"You make it sound like that's a bad thing," I said as I cupped her ass with my hands, squeezed.

"According to Danny, it was."

"Because he was getting it elsewhere," I said simply.

"Yeah. I know."

I got more soap, continued down one leg, then back up the other. On one knee, I told her to turn around. With her facing me, I worked my way up her body, paying special attention to her most private parts.

She was panting, her eyes closed, by the time I was finished. When I dropped my hands, her eyes shot open.

I grinned. "Your turn." I held out the body wash.

"My turn? Really?" She sounded intrigued by the idea.

"Yes." I chuckled. "But no playing. Not yet."

Her lower lip puffed out in a pout, but she didn't say a word as she began the same trail I'd made, only on my body this time.

"How tall *are* you?" she asked.

"Six four. You?"

"Five two."

"And I'm sure I outweigh you by a hundred pounds."

"I could stand to lose a few," she said absently.

My muscles tensed and I knew she could feel my disappointment. "What was that?"

"Nothing. I ... uh..." Her hands trailed up to my cock.

The instant her fingers curled around me, I grabbed her wrist. "What did I say?"

"I'm sorry." She sounded anything but. "It's a hard habit to break. The derogatory self-reflection, that is. I've spent so long thinking I was"—her eyes held mine—"not good enough."

"I can promise you, by the time this is over, I'll have proven to you just how untrue that is."

Something passed over her face, an emotion I couldn't place. "By the time this is over?"

I didn't look away. Couldn't.

"Does that mean there's a timer that's been set? Once that time's up…?"

Taking both her wrists in my hands, I backed her up against the tile wall. She never flinched, never looked away.

"Pleasure, Heaven. That's what this is about. Nothing more, nothing less," I told her. "You're here so we can keep you safe. Until the threat is eliminated. Why shouldn't we enjoy ourselves?"

I couldn't lie to her. What I really wanted was currently curled up in bed with my brother. It pained me not to have time with Everly, but I knew it would come. But what my brother needed was equally important to me.

Hence the reason I wasn't going to push.

"Is this what it's like to be into BDSM?" Heaven inquired.

I frowned.

"Sex with strangers?"

"I'd like to think you're not a stranger. You've slept under my roof. I don't extend that to strangers." I leaned in, my mouth hovering over hers. "What you need to do is remember sex doesn't equate to a relationship. You don't have to commit to someone to enjoy them. Separate yourself, Heaven."

"You're right," she whispered. "Pleasure. Nothing more, nothing less."

"Exactly," I said, sealing my lips to hers.

"May I finish washing you?" she asked, breathing roughly when I pulled back.

"Who am I to deny a beautiful woman?"

When I stepped back, Heaven reached for the body wash, poured more into her hands before gliding them over my chest. I could see the heat in her eyes as she focused on the action. That was the point, right?

This time, when she closed her fingers around my cock, I didn't stop her. When her eyes lifted to my face, I ensured she saw the danger in my gaze, the promise of what was to come if she continued down this path.

"Can I ask you something without pissing you off?"

My eyes narrowed. "Depends on what it is."

"Do you always share women with your brother?"

"Yes."

"Do women fall in love with both of you at the same time?"

"It's not about love," I explained.

Seemingly bothered by my response, she rinsed her hands.

I could feel the distance growing between us. Although she was willing to explore this, Heaven didn't understand how to keep sex and love separate. As was the case for many people, it was one and the same for her. But that wasn't how I saw things. I'd been in this lifestyle for so long I'd come to expect those I encountered to get it.

But Heaven wasn't a submissive. She didn't understand that playing was part of the game. A way for two souls to interact on an intimate level.

Perhaps by the time I was through with her, she'd realize there was more out there than falling in love.

I shut the water off, stepped out, and grabbed a towel. Rather than dry myself, I took my time running the cotton over her curves, drying every inch before wrapping her in it.

"I won't make promises I can't keep," I told her. "But I can give you pleasure unlike anything you've ever felt before."

She nodded, her green eyes glittering. "I know."

"Is that what you want? If it's not, I won't hold it against you."

I thought for a moment that she wasn't going to answer, but finally Heaven nodded. "It's what I want."

I smiled, ensured she saw my approval. "Good. Then get in the bed and wait for me."

I waited until she slipped out of the bathroom before I grabbed another towel, dried myself off. I caught a glimpse of my face in the mirror and paused there. I couldn't help but think about Everly. She understood this lifestyle, likely knew that what I wanted from Heaven was simply sex. But did she understand what I wanted from her? That I was willing to play a game with her friend if it meant I'd have the chance to spend time with her?

The last thing I wanted was to hurt anyone, but right now, I needed the distraction more than ever.

Dropping the towel, I marched into the bedroom, set my gaze on Heaven. "No clothing allowed in the bed, either. That includes towels."

Without hesitation, she stripped it off, tossed it to me before sliding beneath the blankets.

"No blankets, either," I informed her, grinning. "I want to see you."

"You're terrible."

I brushed her hair back from her face. "Baby, you have no idea."

Easing her back, I trailed my hands over her skin, touching every part of her. Neck, shoulders, arms. I glided my hands over her chest, watching her face for clues as to what she enjoyed most.

After teasing her breasts, I paused for a moment, snagged a condom from the nightstand. As I rolled it on, she stared at me, watching my every movement.

And when I joined her on the bed, she seemed to think I was going to sink inside her. I had to smile because it was obvious she'd been with the wrong men if she thought that was the only pleasure we were after. The condom was necessary because I had no intentions of stopping later and ruining the moment. However, I wasn't even close to fucking her with my cock. That would come. In time.

I easily shifted her on the bed, making my way between her thighs. With my hands on her knees, I stared down at her even as I began moving them toward her torso, effectively opening her pussy, giving me an unobstructed view of those glistening pink folds.

"You're wet for me."

She inhaled sharply but didn't reply.

Didn't matter. It wasn't a question. I could see the evidence of her arousal for myself.

"I'm going to eat your pussy," I informed her simply because I liked the verbal exchange. "Do you have a problem with that?"

"No."

I smiled at the rasp in her voice.

"And once I make you come with my tongue, I'm going to watch you ride my dick."

Her eyes widened, lips parted.

"Is that what you want?"

Heaven nodded.

"Say it aloud."

"Yes."

"Good girl." I met her gaze, held it. "But when I'm done, I'm going back to my bed. Alone. That's the only way this works."

She seemed surprised, whether from my honesty or the words themselves, I wasn't sure. Didn't matter. I would only be truthful with her. And something told me Heaven needed that.

"Do you understand?"

"Yes."

"And you still want this?"

Her eyes locked on mine. "I definitely want this."

It was then that I showed Heaven the hunger that lurked within. I wasn't gentle as I positioned her to my liking, bending her in half, diving between her legs like I was starved. I didn't rush, licking and sucking, thrusting, teasing. All the while I took my cues from her urgent pleas and the rough tug on my hair. It took far less time than I'd intended to give before she was coming, her back arching off the bed, thighs gripping my head as she came undone.

Before I could dive back in for a second helping of her lovely cunt, Heaven took the reins. I chuckled when she tried to flip me over, giving in to the pressure she applied to my torso and rolling to my back. I'd barely had time to get flat when she was on me, straddling my hips and guiding my cock to the heat of her.

I groaned, forcing my eyes to remain open, refusing to let my thoughts drift elsewhere. There was a part of me that wished she was Everly, but I refused to give it any attention because Heaven deserved better than that. I'd told her how this would work, and she had accepted it. The least I could do was stay right here with her.

"Ian!"

"Ride me," I growled. "Fuck me, Heaven. Take what you need."

Her movements were jerky as she rocked on my cock, attempting to gain a rhythm that seemed just out of reach. I assisted, gripping her hips and stilling her momentarily.

"Put your hands on my chest."

She did.

"Now lift and lower yourself on me. Take my cock as deep as you can."

Heaven closed her eyes, doing what I said. I moved my grip to her hands, holding them to my chest as she found a pace that worked for her. Before long, she was dropping down on my dick, driving me deep inside her. I could feel that tell-tale tingle as her warm pussy milked me, the warning that my orgasm wasn't far off. I held out, letting her take what she wanted.

"Come on my cock," I urged, feeling her way her pussy fluttered over me.

"Ian!"

Ah, yes. Just like that.

I remained beneath her as she rode the wave of her orgasm. Only when her upper body relaxed did I roll her beneath me and pound into her, taking my own pleasure from her body. But it wasn't all about me. I worked her right to the edge once more, driving her over with my thumb on her clit. When she came that time, it was with a strangled sigh.

Then … only then did I find my release.

I draped her knees over my forearms and held myself over her, pounding into her, filling her, stretching her. Her fingernails dug into my shoulders as she took every inch of me inside, her breaths being driven from her with every punishing thrust. But she took me like a champ, even if she remained far too quiet for my taste.

"Fuck … I'm—" Yep, I was coming.

My hips slammed forward one final time. As my cock jerked, I closed my eyes and imagined it was Everly's body I was coming deep inside.

Needless to say, I wasn't proud of that moment.

Nine

Dante

Monday, May 27, 2019

BY THE TIME EVERYONE STUMBLED OUT OF their hidey-holes the following morning, I was finished stretching, ready to hit the pavement.

Ian arrived first, Isaac close behind.

"The girls?" I asked, already knowing their answer.

"Asleep," they said at the same time.

I grinned. "You don't know how many times they offered to run with me and wouldn't get out of bed."

"Well, we'll keep you company." Ian smirked. "If you can keep up."

"I can hold my own."

"If you can make it back before us, you can cook breakfast."

I grinned. "Yeah?"

"Yup. And if we make it back first, you can cook breakfast naked."

"Hope you're not making bacon," Isaac said as he headed for the back door.

I fell into step as we walked up the hill to the road. From what I could tell, there was a relatively good amount of land allocated to each of the properties, but the houses were relatively close together considering.

"I feel at a disadvantage since I don't know the route," I admitted, glancing to my left, then my right.

"Keep up," Ian said, his eyes sliding over me. "Or don't. I happen to be quite fond of that ass. Don't mind ogling it a little before breakfast."

His comment sent a bolt of heat through me, both unexpected and welcome. While Ian and I had shared those few minutes in the basement yesterday, he hadn't made any advances since.

"Five miles," Isaac stated, pulling his leg back and stretching his quad. He motioned toward my watch. "Route's up to you if you can't keep up."

"Yes, Sir."

I made it back to the house in thirty-seven minutes, with five-point-one miles logged. A personal best, which had me smiling when I walked in through the back door, intending to have breakfast ready by the time the twin Doms arrived.

"You made it," Isaac said, downing a bottle of water as he stood at the kitchen island.

He was covered in sweat, his hair slicked back, his breaths returning to normal.

"What was your time?" I asked, glancing between them.

"Twenty-nine," Ian said with a shit-eating grin.

"No way."

He passed over his phone. There on the screen was the GPS of his route including the time and distance.

"Son of a bitch," I grumbled, curling over and placing my hands on my thighs.

"So you *have* met our mother?" Ian teased, but the look on his face said he wasn't really joking.

"Can I grab a shower, Sir?" I aimed the question at Ian.

"Of course. Just remember to leave the clothes behind when you return."

"Yes, Sir."

"I'm going to join you," Isaac said.

As I started toward the guest room, I learned he'd meant that literally. I thought he was going to do the same, only in his shower. A tremor of awareness skated down my spine, warming my already overheated body.

"Unless you have a problem with that," he stated as I slowed my pace.

"Not at all, Sir."

"Good."

He began stripping as soon as we stepped into the guest suite bathroom, which was more like some fancy spa. They'd gone all out in the house, from the rooms I'd seen. But mine especially. This entire side of the house was dedicated to a guest suite, complete with adjoining entertainment area.

While I fumbled to get out of my shorts, Isaac was in the shower, flipping on the water, then standing beneath it. Steam instantly started to flow up from the floor, hindering my view of all those sleek, toned muscles. The man was gorgeous, no doubt about that, but it was his control that appealed to me the most. Of both brothers, Isaac seemed to have himself on the shorter leash, revealing nothing.

As though he realized I didn't know what to expect here, Isaac stepped back, motioned for me to take a turn beneath the spray. The water was cooler than I'd anticipated, but it did little to bring down my body temperature. I figured that had a lot to do with the man now standing behind me.

When I turned, he stepped into my personal space, his eyes hot, fierce as they locked on my face. I knew he was going to kiss me before it happened, but the lip-lock still caught me off guard. He gave no quarter, his tongue thrusting into my mouth as he backed me up against the tile. I moved with him, my hands sliding over his slick skin. Warm, wet, it felt good to touch him, to be touched by him.

I'd had no physical intimacy with anyone in such a long time, it was easy to surrender to it. This was what I'd always fantasized about, a man who would use me, command me. And not abuse me in the process.

Isaac and I hadn't talked much since I arrived, but I got the feeling he wasn't a wealth of information on a good day. While Ian was the inquisitive type, Isaac was more the strong, silent type.

I had a penchant for both.

His hand slid behind my neck, holding me in place as he pulled back. "Did you enjoy kissing Everly last night?"

There was no heat in his words, just simple curiosity, as though he needed to know how I felt.

"Yes, Sir," I rasped. "I've wanted…"

"Tell me," he urged, his voice deep, assertive.

"I've wanted to taste her for so long." My breaths began to increase again. "I can't give her what she needs. That's the only reason I've refrained. But I can't deny I've wanted it."

His eyes scanned my face for a second before he crushed his mouth to mine again. I could taste his approval and it singed my insides. I burned for him, my entire body aflame with a need so intense I expected to be turned to ash. I didn't know what this was, what any of it was. I'd never found myself in a situation like this, but it wasn't awkward. In fact, in just the short time I'd been here, it felt more right than anything I'd ever experienced. I was given the space I so desperately needed, the silence that I rarely got to find in the normal world. Everly and Heaven had always respected it, but I'd seldom entered into a relationship where a guy understood I couldn't give him one hundred percent because I didn't have it to give.

Isaac bit my lower lip, dragging me from my thoughts. He didn't ask where I went, but I could see the question in his eyes.

"In the future, I'll demand what I want," he whispered. "For now, I want you to give me what you're willing to give."

The future. As in tomorrow or the next day. He wasn't intimating that this was going to be over soon, and I wondered about that, even as I slid my hand down, wrapped my fist around the long, hard length of him. The man was well-endowed, his large body hard, firm, his cock in direct proportion. His thick shaft was velvety smooth, pulsing in my hand.

"I'm willing to give you everything," I admitted, holding his stare.

I wasn't sure why I said it aloud, but his reaction told me it was what he'd hoped to hear.

He leaned in, nipped my lower lip again. "I want to feel your mouth on my cock."

A tsunami of heat slammed into me, my legs weakening even as his hand curled over my shoulder, guiding me down to my knees. His palms cupped my head, his eyes focused on me. Only me.

I licked the thick crest, lapping the pre-cum pooling there, drawing a moan from deep within him. The rough sounds spurred me on, had me leaning in, taking his cock into my mouth. I leaned in, took him deeper. I was keenly aware of the pressure his hands had on my head. They were firm yet gentle, the complete opposite of what I'd experienced as of late. There was a reverence to his touch, an intimacy. This wasn't merely about his ability to control me. He was enjoying this as much as I was.

"Suck me," Isaac ordered. "Don't worry about deep throating me yet. I just want to feel your lips on me."

His hands were gentle, cradling my head, guiding me forward and back as his cock tunneled past my lips. I moaned, knowing he would feel the vibrations in his balls.

Words rasped from Isaac's mouth, but I didn't recognize the language he spoke. It gave me pause.

Isaac smirked. "It's Irish. Means *good boy.* Your mouth feels so fucking good."

I took the praise, storing it deep in an effort to hang on to it forever.

His hands, still gentle, tightened around my head. He held me in place, his hips pumping, pushing his cock in deep. I hollowed out my cheeks, sucking him in an effort to send him over. The look on his face would be one I thought about endlessly. Wild need and pure adoration were the only way to describe it. It shocked me to the roots of my hair.

"Suck me … fuck … too good…" He growled, rough, coarse words following as though he couldn't quite let himself go. "Fuck … yes… Take all of me."

He drove his hips forward, his expression changed as his cock pulsed in my mouth. I swallowed him down, breathing through my nose when he buried his cock in the back of my throat, holding my head firmly in place. When he stumbled back, Isaac reached for my arm. I got to my feet, fell into him when he jerked me forward. His mouth fused to mine even as he fought for air. His hands slid over me, almost desperate.

The kiss turned from a rapid boil to a slow simmer, but Isaac didn't release me. He seemed content to touch me and I enjoyed the same.

A knock sounded on the door. "Breakfast won't cook itself."

Isaac pulled back, a small smile tipping the corners of his mouth. "He's right."

"Naked cooking," I mumbled, stepping beneath the spray. "My favorite."

"Get used to it," Isaac said as he stepped out, grabbed a towel. "My brother's not the only one who's fond of seeing you naked."

He left me staring after him, a huge smile on my face.

ISAAC

I SAT NEXT TO EVERLY AT BREAKFAST, feeling the need to be close to her. I wasn't the sort of man to make excuses for what I wanted, and I wanted her. To be close to her, touch her, feel her, taste her. She'd consumed my every sense and I craved more. Ever since she had slept in my bed, wrapped tightly in my arms.

I'd slept better than I ever had.

But even as I sat beside her, my mind drifted to the intimate moment I'd shared with Dante in his shower. Oh, how I'd wanted to sink deep inside him, to feel his ass gripping my cock, to hear those soft moans as I fucked him hard and deep. I'd refrained only because Dante needed that from me. There was a vulnerability to him that ran incredibly deep and before I could take things to the next level with him, we had to unearth them. Regardless of how much I wanted him, I wouldn't risk him in that way. He had triggers, of that I was certain. I had to know what they were to ensure I didn't hurt him unintentionally.

"I'm heading over to Inferno at noon," Ian reminded me as he pushed his empty plate back.

Dante's head snapped over, real fear on his face.

"To talk to the owner," Ian explained, his voice soft, as though speaking to a wounded animal. "Nothing to worry about right now."

That seemed to placate the man, because he nodded, downed the rest of his orange juice, then started to get to his feet. "I'll do the dishes."

"Actually," Ian interrupted. "The girls are going to do them."

Everly smiled at Ian. "Gladly, Sir." She glanced over at me. "May I be excused, my Liege?"

I pulled my arm from the back of her chair, took the kiss she offered before watching her flutter off into the other room.

"Goner," Ian muttered.

I didn't respond. Didn't need to. That woman had me so twisted up, any excuse would've come out as complete bullshit.

Heaven glanced between the two of us. "I guess that's my cue to help."

My brother grinned like a loon. "Unless you're keen on punishment."

"Yeah, no. Totally not my thing." She giggled. "You can save the spankings for those two. I get the feeling they'll need it more than me."

"Doubtful," Ian taunted. "You've got quite the mouth on you."

I had no idea what had transpired between the two last night, but I knew Ian hadn't taken Heaven to his bedroom. That told me more than anything. My twin was keeping his distance from her. Didn't mean he wouldn't fuck her, but it hinted at the lack of intimacy between them.

Quite frankly, I was a bit surprised. Heaven seemed exactly what tripped my brother's trigger. Well, aside from the fact she didn't seem the least bit submissive.

"May I be excused, Sir?" Dante asked.

I watched him for a moment. He intrigued me. There was something about him I didn't quite understand, and in the short time I'd known him, I was starting to realize he was hiding something. Oh, he was free with his body, but his emotions were in check, locked up tight. The only person he opened up to was Everly, but I hoped that would change in the coming days.

"Yes," Ian said, his blue eyes locked on Dante, trailing after him even when he disappeared.

"He likes to be alone," I mused.

"I noticed that. As though he craves the solitude."

"More like a polar bear than a panda," I surmised.

Ian laughed. "Hadn't thought about it, but yeah. Likes the solitude."

Just another reason this felt right to me. I wasn't sure what it was or how it even happened, but it was happening. I wasn't going to pretend otherwise.

"How was the shower?" Ian asked, and I knew he wasn't referring to the water temperature.

"He's tense."

"You think it's from what happened yesterday?"

I nodded. "Whoever came after the girls is doing it to punish him. Or at least he feels as though he is."

"I should ask the girls if they need me to pick up anything at their house," Ian said, pushing to his feet.

"We have to find this bastard," I told him. "Eliminate the threat."

"Aye. And we will."

While I didn't mind the excuse for Everly to be here under our roof, I couldn't keep her locked up like some princess in the castle. She needed to be able to come and go without me worrying about her. And I wanted her to be here because she wanted to, not because she had to.

I stared out the window, listening to Heaven and Everly chatter away in the kitchen while they washed dishes. I enjoyed the sound. It seemed I'd spent most of my life wanting this. And though I hadn't asked Ian's opinion on the matter, I had realized it wasn't necessary. We'd always been open with one another, on the same page in every aspect. We worked together, lived together, shared submissives. It was natural. I couldn't imagine it any other way. But we'd always expected to find a love of our own, to share our submissives in the physical sense but not emotionally. And while this situation seemed to fit the mold perfectly, I got the feeling it wasn't quite right.

"Can I get you anything, my Liege?" Everly asked, reappearing like the fairy princess she reminded me of.

I was pretty sure I'd found the love I'd been looking for.

"I'm good. Thank you."

"I'll be up in the library if you need me."

I nodded.

"Oh, would it be all right if I got on the internet?"

"Of course." I got to my feet, carried my glass into the kitchen, and rummaged through the junk drawer. When I located the piece of paper with the wireless passcode on it, I handed it over.

She went up on her toes, kissed my cheek, then headed for the stairs.

Figuring now would be a good time to catch up on a little light reading of my own, I headed down to the basement.

It only took a few clicks to pull up information on Dante Novak. It wasn't his personal information I was looking for. I already had all of that thanks to Ian's research. I was looking for incidents that might've involved him, something to explain his need for solitude. I spent a good hour scanning the Google results to no avail. Just when I was going to take a break, I came across an old newspaper article:

TWELVE-YEAR-OLD BOY FOUND LOCKED IN ATTIC.

I went on to read the details about the boy whose father had kept him locked in the attic from the time he was four until the authorities were called in after the new neighbors next door saw an emaciated boy staring out at them from the small circular window. According to the neighbor, they'd gotten concerned because in the two weeks they'd lived there, they had never seen anyone come or go from the house. The police found Dante padlocked in the attic with a mini-fridge that had a single bottle of water and the remains of a loaf of bread. The bread had been coated in mold. The story went on to note that Dante had been almost feral, malnourished, and hadn't had a bath in what they'd guessed to be six months or so.

I stared up the stairs, wondering what that sort of trauma did to a person. Dante seemed well put together, smart. Well, mostly. As far as brains went, he seemed to have them in spades, but his common sense was questionable. Based on the scars, some of them recent, I feared he'd gotten in over his head with the man Dante had told Ian about. I was hoping Ian would get a better feel for how a sadistic asshole had gotten his claws into Dante in the first place. He was a submissive, not a masochist.

I heard someone laughing, got to my feet, and went to the doors leading to the basement walkout. I peered up the hill to the swimming pool, where two very naked submissives were jumping into the pool. The sight had a smile forming.

To my surprise, Dante appeared, but he'd opted to wear shorts. Smart man. Probably didn't want to show the neighbors the family jewels in broad daylight. He jumped in, splashing Heaven and Everly. I stood there for a few minutes, watching the dynamic between the three. They talked, laughed, and it was obvious they were close. It still surprised me that nothing had transpired between Everly and Dante. Their desire for one another was palpable, as I'd witnessed in that kiss they shared.

The memory had my cock stirring.

I had this overwhelming desire to see the two of them together. Hell, I wanted to see Everly and Heaven together, but I wasn't quite sure Everly swung that way. Didn't stop me from fantasizing, because my kink ran deep. I was the sort of man who preferred to explore a submissive's desires, to push their boundaries. I knew deep down that Everly would do whatever I asked of her, but that wasn't my end game. Erotic encounters were only exciting if they played out naturally. Forced was not my style, nor would it ever be.

My cell phone rang. I snagged it from the desk, hit the answer button when I saw it was Ian.

"Yeah, I'm heading over to their house now. Got a list from the girls."

"Did you talk to the club owner?"

"Aye. He's a bigger dick than I expected. Tell you about it when I get there. Need anything while I'm out?"

"Nay." My attention turned back to the pool. "We're good for now."

I tucked my phone back into my pocket. I'd been hoping the club owner would be able and/or willing to give us some information on Roger Cherlish. We had done our own digging and come up completely empty.

Unfortunately, from what we could tell, the bastard didn't actually exist.

# Ten

Everly

"MY TURN TO COOK DINNER!" I YELLED so everyone would hear me wherever they were in the house.

I'd spent most of the day in the attic library, like a little kid in a candy store. I hadn't quite believed Heaven when she'd gushed about how amazing it was. That was an understatement. And while I'd intended to play solitaire to pass the time if I got bored, turned out I'd never touched my laptop or my phone, finding more than enough to keep me busy in the wide variety of books they had.

"Depends on what you're making, fairy princess," Isaac said when he appeared at the top of the basement stairs.

Oh, right. They were worried she'd deprive them of their precious meat.

She smiled. "Well, I thought we'd start with kale."

His eyebrows shot downward.

"I'm kidding. You don't have kale."

"Do you like it?"

"I do," I confirmed.

"Then by tomorrow, you'll have kale." He stopped in front of me, tipped my head back with a gentle finger beneath my chin.

"You don't have to do that."

"I'll give you anything you want, love."

As I drown in those emerald green depths, I was beginning to wonder if this man was too good to be true. From the moment I'd stepped foot in Zeke's house, Isaac had been right there with me. He took care of me as though I was the most important thing to him. And sure, he'd said as much, but hey, sometimes things were said in the heat of the moment. I wasn't naive enough to take every word muttered at face value.

Isaac pressed his lips to mine, then stepped back. "How can I help?"

"Well, I'd considered making an Irish meal, but then I learned that most of your meals are loaded with meat. So...I figured spaghetti would have to work."

He laughed. "Italian. Not quite Irish, but a good choice."

"I thought so."

"But not necessary," he said, pulling me back against him.

"What? You scared I can't cook?"

"Not at all. But I ordered out. It'll be delivered shortly."

"Is that why you asked if I had any food allergies earlier?" I turned in his arms.

His smile was wicked and guilty.

"Are we celebrating something?"

"Being alone."

I glanced around. "What do you mean alone? Where is everybody?"

"Ian took Dante and Heaven to dinner. Said he wanted to load up on fried food and he knows I'm not a fan."

"Well, then, I guess it's just the two of us."

"It is." He cupped my face. "And tonight, we'll have dinner my way."

I felt a shift in the air, a charge that had my insides tingling. "What way is that?" The words were said on a breathy sigh.

"With you naked, kneeling at my feet."

My skin felt two sizes too small. Desire pulsed through me. Not many Dominants were as observant as Isaac and Ian, but it seemed they were in tune with me. Or at least that was my experience when playing with them at the club.

Isaac's thumb brushed over my lower lips. "I'll feed you."

"Thank you, my Liege."

"My pleasure, fairy princess."

As though he'd timed it perfectly, the doorbell rang.

"I'll get that. I want you to put a pillow on the floor in the living room, strip, kneel, and wait for me."

"Yes, my Liege."

I hurried to the living room, listening as he spoke to the delivery person. I quickly removed my shorts and T-shirt, setting them neatly on the coffee table before grabbing one of the fluffy throw pillows from the sofa and placing it on the floor in the spot I felt most convenient for Isaac.

The sound of silverware and dishes clanging came from the kitchen as I kneeled in position. I drifted off into my head. The only way to describe it was a mental high. Some would probably say it was a form of subspace, but I didn't have a label for it. It was as though endorphins flooded my bloodstream, a feeling that wasn't easy for me to get to. Except when I'd played with Isaac and Ian. It had always come instantly when we were together.

The guttural sound of Isaac's voice alerted me to his presence, though I couldn't translate what he'd said. I had noticed Isaac's and Ian's Irish had come out more, including that ridiculously sexy accent they both sported, the longer I was around them. When I'd interacted with them at the club, it was usually masked. I wasn't sure if they relaxed more at home, hence the reason it came out more. Whatever it was, I loved hearing it, the lilt, the seduction in their voices.

"I'm going to blindfold you," he said simply, pulling out a black silk mask. He gently put it over my eyes, securing it behind my head. "Comfortable?"

"Yes, my Liege."

His footsteps faded momentarily, returning not long after. I heard the sound of a plate on the glass table, then another. He left again, returned. This time, he set more things down.

"Turn to your right," Isaac instructed.

I shifted in that direction.

"Spread your knees apart. I want to see that pretty pussy."

My nipples pebbled as I widened my knees, and I knew he could see my obvious appreciation of his words. He turned me on like nothing I'd ever experienced.

"You're beautiful," he whispered, the reverence in his tone causing goose bumps to cover my arms.

For the next twenty minutes, Isaac teased and tormented me with his words and subtle brushes of his fingers on my skin. He fed me, making me guess what I was eating. Considering he'd gotten me a portabella mushroom burger, it hadn't been an easy feat. But it was delicious.

After he had cleaned away all of the dishes, he returned, removing the blindfold.

"Do you want to know what I'm having for dessert?" he asked, holding out his hand to help me up.

"Hopefully it's me."

His smirk was sexy. "It definitely is. But I'll be eating the traditional way."

"How's that?"

The heat that flashed in his eyes made my heart rate spike. "On the dining room table."

My belly fluttered, like hitting the high point on a roller coaster and plummeting over the edge.

"Oh, and Ian's on his way back," he said passively, as though it was normal for his twin to walk in while he was feasting on me in the formal dining room.

Isaac didn't have me get on the table and spread out. No, he seduced me up there, pulling me against him, his big, warm hands sliding over me, heating me from the inside out even as he managed to get me right where he wanted me.

He positioned my feet so that they were flat on the table, my toes curling over the edge, knees spread wide, on full display for him. His fingers trailed over my mound, a teasing promise of what was to come.

I heard the sound of a door opening, then closing.

"Looks like we've got company," he said softly.

"Hey, you guys—Oh." Heaven stopped just inside the room, her eyes wide.

Dante was right behind her, Ian pulling up the rear.

"Just in time," Ian said, urging them farther into the room.

"In time for what?" Heaven asked, her breaths slightly erratic. She was definitely turned on seeing me there and I couldn't deny that it did something for me that she was watching.

Truth was, I wasn't bisexual, though there was a curiosity. I figured that had a lot to do with my exploration into BDSM. I'd given in to my darkest desires and promised myself I wouldn't hold back, even from things that intimidated me.

"For dessert," Ian whispered, his mouth brushing against Heaven's ear when he moved behind her. "She's not the only one we're going to feast on, though."

"Me, too?" Despite the surprise in her words, Heaven certainly didn't sound opposed to the idea.

"Absolutely." Ian glanced over at Dante. "Could you help her up onto that end of the table? Same position as this little fairy."

Ian's hand trailed over my right knee, Isaac's over my left, and I inhaled sharply, desire, hot and fierce, erupting, making me needy. The way they looked at me ... as though I was the most intriguing thing they'd ever seen... It was a heady feeling, that was for sure.

Isaac turned my chin, forcing me to look over at him. He studied my face momentarily, as though looking for something.

"Green, my Liege," I said softly, referring to the stoplight system we used at the club. Green meant I was completely on board with the idea.

When I felt Heaven's head nearly bump mine, I lifted my arm and reached for her. She moaned softly, then took my hand, then my other, linking our fingers. I honestly hadn't expected her to touch me, but found I enjoyed it. More so the scene the twin Doms were setting up.

"Dante," Isaac addressed him quietly. "The choice is yours. If you need to escape, feel free. If you'd like to stay and play, you're welcome to."

I couldn't see him, even when I tilted my head back. I wanted him to stay, wanted to feel his hands on me. I couldn't explain the need, but it was overwhelming. The way they looked at me… It wasn't objectifying like I'd experienced before. Perhaps that was because they continued to touch me, their hands gentle. As though they wanted the connection at all times.

"I'll stay, Sir."

My breath raced out, my lungs instantly filled. I was breathing harder than I should've been, anticipation overwhelming my system.

And then there was movement.

No words as Isaac leaned over, his lips grazing my knee, sliding down the inside of my thigh. He licked and kissed, tormenting me until I was practically begging. Heaven's hands were squeezing mine, soft moans escaping her. I wanted to see, but I couldn't. Not only because they weren't in my line of sight but also because I was blinded by the pleasure.

And when Isaac's tongue slid through my slit, I cried out, my back bowing off the table.

His warm hands settled on my hips, holding me in place as he feasted on me, flicking my clit, tonguing my pussy, driving me closer and closer to the edge before he slowed, bringing me back down.

Then Ian was between my legs, doing the same thing, his skillful tongue making me cry out, beg, plead.

It was the first time he'd given me any real attention since I arrived at their house and I couldn't help it, I nearly cried from the intensity. I'd wanted this for so long, wishing for something but not sure what. And here he was. Had it not been for Heaven holding my hands, I would've reached for his head, run my fingers through his soft hair, held him to me.

"Oh, God," Heaven hissed. "Please don't stop. Isaac … please!"

The thought of Isaac's tongue on Heaven's pussy had my insides quivering. I thought for a moment I would come, but Ian stopped just shy of sending me over. They certainly knew what they were doing.

I was panting, tears streaming out of my eyes, though I wasn't going to look too deep into why they were there. I was blaming it on the exquisite torture, the slow burn they were forcing me to endure.

"Please," I whimpered. "I need to come."

More movement, and then warm hands settled on my thighs, sliding lower. I watched as Dante's blond head shifted lower, his mouth trailing kisses over my skin.

"Dante … please…"

"Tell him, little fairy," Isaac urged, leaning over from the side of the table and pressing his lips to mine. "Tell him what you need."

"Dante, lick me…" I moaned when he trailed his tongue just shy of where I needed him.

He chuckled and I groaned.

And then I was completely lost. Dante's mouth was divine, his tongue doing wicked things, licking, suckling. He flicked my clit ruthlessly and I crested, my entire being soaring as the most exquisite orgasm of my life pummeled me.

Dante kissed the inside of my thigh before disappearing from view. Isaac helped me to my feet, but spun me around, allowing me to watch as Ian finished with Heaven, his head between her legs, his mouth feasting on her pussy as she writhed and moaned, Dante watching from the sidelines.

"You want him to make her come?" Isaac whispered.

I nodded, raptly watching as Ian worked his tongue over her pussy. There was a strange flicker inside me, something close to jealousy. I suddenly wished that was me, that Ian's head was between my legs, his full attention on making me come.

Heaven cried out Ian's name, her back bowed, muscles tightening. She was beautiful like that, in the throes of orgasm.

Ian helped Heaven to her feet, held her close. She was boneless, more so than I was.

"May I thank him, my Liege?" I asked, tilting my head back to look up at Isaac.

"Of course."

I walked over to Dante, went up on my toes, and pressed my lips to his. I could taste myself on his tongue as he kissed me back. I wrapped my arms around him, almost desperate to get closer. He was the one who held me back, his hands firmly on my hips.

"You're so sweet," he whispered, nuzzling my neck. "My sweet girl."

When he pulled away, I let him go. He glanced at Isaac, who nodded.

I stared after him when he darted out of the room, and I couldn't help but wonder whether that had just changed everything.

And not in the way I'd been hoping for.

Eleven

IAN

Wednesday, May 29, 2019

"HE'S IN THE WIND," I MUTTERED, UNABLE to keep the blistering frustration from my words.

It was ten o'clock and I'd been watching the feed from Inferno for the past three hours, waiting to see Roger Cherlish, or whatever the fuck his name was, appear.

As it was, we hadn't caught a trail of him since Sunday, when he went by Dante's house twice.

"Maybe he's lying low until the heat dies down," Isaac said, his face buried in his own laptop screen.

"What heat? He attacked a woman, and no one knows about it."

"He doesn't know that."

He probably did, but I didn't need to tell Isaac that. For most of the day, we'd been calling in favors, trying to figure out who this asshole was. I'd talked to Dante for a few minutes, tried to find out if he knew the guy by another name. When I brought him up, Dante seemed to shrink in on himself, which only pissed me off more.

Not at Dante. Never at him.

At this bastard who had hurt him.

I still didn't know the lengths to which he'd gone. I had managed to hack into Inferno's feed but had yet to locate their archived records. While Dichotomy respected the rights and privacy of its members, I'd already realized Inferno didn't operate with the same code of conduct.

"They can't keep calling in to work," I told Isaac.

He leaned back in his chair, sighed. "I know."

"How do we handle that? There's three of them, only two of us."

"Yeah." He leaned his head back, closed his eyes. "Everly works mornings, Heaven works morning and afternoon, Dante afternoon and evening."

"They overlap." Not that I thought we could sit around on our asses at their places of business. I doubted their employers would be keen on the idea. Not to mention, Isaac and I had jobs of our own and we'd asked for extended time off for a reason. Made more sense to solve the problem than babysit.

"I'm going to suggest Everly quit her job," Isaac stated, his eyes still closed.

I turned in my chair, facing him. "What? Seriously?"

"I want her here. With me."

"She's not Rapunzel, Isaac. You can't lock her away in the castle."

His head snapped up. "That's not what I'm doing."

"Are you sure about that?"

"Yes." He got to his feet.

Before he could fly past me, I grabbed his arm. "Let's talk this out."

He paused but turned back, flopped in his chair. He was hardheaded at times, stubborn always. And unlike me, Isaac didn't like to open up. He certainly wasn't fond of my constant interrogation. But this was serious.

I could see where he was coming from. Mostly. However, we'd never had a submissive we'd taken on full-time, much less a … what did we call Everly, anyway? Girlfriend? That seemed too vanilla. And yet, it suited the situation.

"I know we don't need her income," I said, keeping my voice low, reasonable. "But that's not the point. This is moving fast, Isaac. Even you can see that."

"Six months, Ian. I've been holding back for six months with her."

"I know."

I had been, too. Ever since the first night we scened with her at Dichotomy, we'd both been holding out. Me more than him, but that was due to my caution. I wasn't sure Isaac was prepared to know the depths of what I felt for the woman. We'd always intended to find a submissive of our own and I'd ruined that, falling for the same one my brother had.

"I'm ready for this," Isaac said, not looking me in the eye. "I want this. Her." He sighed, then spoke in our native tongue "*I'm falling for her. Fast.*"

Yep, that was what I was afraid of. He loved her even if he opted to say it in a different way.

And if I was being completely honest, I loved her, too.

"Does she feel the same?"

He shrugged.

"Have you told her?"

"Not in so many words, no."

"Don't you think this is a discussion you should have with her? Maybe before you waltz up there and ask her to quit her job and be a stay home submissive?"

My phone buzzed, Isaac's two seconds behind it. I grabbed mine off the desk. It was an alert. One of the motion-sensor cameras at Dante's house had been activated.

My fingers flew over the keyboard as I pulled up the image on my laptop.

"Who is *this* jackoff?" I muttered, watching as a guy walked into Dante's like he owned the place.

"Not Roger Cherlish," Isaac noted, leaning over my shoulder to watch the screen.

"No. Not him."

We watched as the familiar frat-boy moved through the house. I'd seen him somewhere, but I couldn't place him.

He went to the kitchen first, then down the hall.

"That's Heaven's room," I told him. I'd gone in there yesterday to grab a few of her things that she'd asked me to get.

The camera was only in the hall, so I couldn't see what he was doing in the bedroom. Since I hadn't expected anyone to be rummaging through her things, I hadn't bothered to wire her room. Only Dante's. In the hopes I'd catch the bastard coming back.

"Maybe the ex-boyfriend," Isaac mused.

"Aye." That was exactly who it was. The fucker who didn't deserve Heaven.

"He must have a key to the house."

I continued to watch the screen, waiting for the douchebag to come out of her room. A minute turned to two, then to thirty before worry started to set in.

"Keep an eye on that," I instructed my brother. "I need to talk to Heaven."

I took the stairs two at a time, stomping through the kitchen, the living room, then down the hall to the bedrooms. I found Heaven sitting on her bed, her laptop in front of her. She looked up, smiled.

"I was just watching a movie."

I skipped the pleasantries and went right for the heart of the matter. "Did you talk to your ex today?"

Her chin jutted out just slightly. "He … uh … he texted me. Why?"

"What did he say?"

She reached over to get her cell phone from the nightstand, typed in the code to unlock the phone, then passed it over to me.

Danny: *Hey, babe. I miss you. Wanted to come see you.*

She hadn't responded to the message.

Two hours later, another text came in.

Danny: *Heaven, don't do this, babe. You know it's stupid to pretend you don't love me.*

Again, she had ignored his text.

Danny: *Playing hard to get won't work this time, babe. I already know you like to put out. Since you haven't gotten your fill lately, I'm gonna stop by. Show you how much I love you.*

I looked up. "You didn't text him back."

She shrugged. "What exactly do I say to that shit?"

I grinned. She had a backbone, that was for sure.

"It's not like I'm home," she continued, "so he can go there all day and night for all I care."

"He's there now," I informed her.

"What?"

"Does he have a key?"

She shook her head, glowered. "No. I never gave him one. Respect for Dante and Everly."

"Hey, Ian!"

I tipped backward to peer out of the room, glanced down the hall to see Isaac jogging toward me. "We've got a problem."

He held up his phone to show he had transferred the video image to his mobile device.

"The Sadist just got there."

"Shit." No way could we make it to the house to catch the bastard. I went back in the room. "I need you to call your ex."

Heaven did not look happy about that. "Why?"

I passed her phone back to her. "Call him. Tell him if he's smart, he'll get out of there. Fast."

She was dialing, probably spurred on by my urgency.

"I called the police," Isaac said. "Anonymous. Told them I saw someone suspicious lurking around the house."

"Hey, Danny. No. Shut up. Listen to me. Get out of my house. Go. Now. Don't ask questions, just—"

Her eyes shot up to me, the phone still to her ear. The color drained from her face.

"He's there," she whispered.

I reached for the phone, but by the time I got it, the call had disconnected.

"What's he going to do?" Heaven asked, her voice trembling as she got to her knees.

Everly came into the room, her face soft from sleep. "What's wrong?"

Isaac pulled her to him, kissed the top of her head. "Nothing. Go back to sleep."

Clearly, she wasn't buying it, especially after she set her sights on the pale and trembling Heaven.

She slipped past me, crawled up into the bed with Heaven, knelt beside her. "What's wrong?"

"Danny ... he broke in. Now that ... that asshole's there."

Everly's gaze flew up, locking on me, then Isaac.

"The police are on the way," Isaac informed her.

"Do you think ..." Heaven gripped the comforter. "Will he hurt him?"

Probably. However, I didn't respond. Couldn't. I hated the pain and fear etched on her face, didn't want to add to it.

"The Sadist's leaving," Isaac muttered, his eyes glued to his phone. "Alone."

"*Foc.*" I grabbed my brother's arm, steered him out of the room. "Come on. Let's go."

Everly

"I DON'T KNOW WHAT JUST HAPPENED," HEAVEN whispered, her voice frantic even as I tried to calm her down.

When Ian and Isaac split, tearing out of there like their asses were on fire, I'd convinced Heaven to join me in the kitchen for a drink.

It was my thing. RumChata and Fireball had a way of soothing the most frantic of friends.

"Aren't you supposed to be force-feeding me warm milk?" she asked, though I could tell her mind was elsewhere.

I merely smiled. Sweetly. "Same difference. Only this really makes you feel better."

As we were sitting at the island, Dante walked in. He didn't appear as though he'd been asleep. Then again, he never did. The man would disappear into his room for what felt like days, but I never actually saw him sleep. Not unless he was curled up on the sofa with me. When he did that, he was usually out like a light though he rarely admitted it.

"Why're you up?" He glanced between us, then went to the cupboard and pulled out another glass. He passed it over to me, and I did the honors of making his nightcap, too. The man was vegan, so he passed on the RumChata and stuck with the Fireball.

"Danny's at the house," Heaven told him. "That Sadist guy … he must've seen someone go in. Probably thought it was you. Broke in."

I expected to see concern on his face, but there was … nothing. Absolutely nothing. As though he couldn't care less that the man who was hunting him had broken in.

"Ian put up cameras," Dante noted, sipping his drink and grimacing. He walked to the freezer, grabbed a few ice cubes, and dropped them in his glass. He pointed toward me with his glass. "I still don't understand how you can drink that."

"It does the trick."

He nodded, grimaced as he took another sip.

"He only put cameras in the main areas, the hallway, and your room. Danny went to my room," Heaven rambled.

"So did Roger?" Dante inquired.

Okay, there it was. That glimmer of fear I was familiar with. It flashed quickly in his eyes and I had the sudden urge to throw my arms around him. I didn't know what that asshole had done to Dante, but it had been bad.

"Yeah. Then Roger left. Danny hasn't come out."

"Are the police there?"

I nodded. "They called them, anyway."

I felt so useless. And though I wasn't Danny's biggest fan, thought he was a world-class dickhead, I didn't want some crazy bastard to hurt him. The concern on Heaven's face said she felt the same.

"I'm sure it's fine," Dante said, clearly trying to dismiss the situation, but not quite accomplishing that goal when his eyes wouldn't make contact with ours. "Probably realized Danny wasn't me, left."

I reached over, touched Dante's arm. "He knew I wasn't you."

Dante pulled away, his face crumbling as though the reminder ripped him to shreds.

"I'm so sorry," he whispered.

I shot to my feet, threw my arms around him. As I'd hoped he would, he set his glass down, enveloped me in his arms. I wasn't sure who got more comfort between us, but physical contact never failed to settle us both. I think it was how we'd gotten so close over the years, gravitating toward one another when there was no one else.

"Why don't we watch TV," I suggested as I unlatched the fierce grip I had on him. "I can make popcorn if you'd like."

"No popcorn," Dante muttered, his thumb brushing over the fading bruise under my eye.

147

"But you'll watch TV with me?"

"Of course."

"Come on." I reached for Heaven's arm as I passed.

Heaven tossed back what was left of her drink, grimaced, then followed us. She snagged two throw blankets from the storage ottoman and passed the remote over to Dante.

As we did at home, Dante took one end, sitting up. Heaven placed a throw pillow on the opposite end, propped up on it, her feet tucking behind Dante. I settled in front of her, my feet near her face. She pulled me into her, spooning so I wouldn't fall to the floor. Dante spread the blankets over us, his arm stretched out, hand on my hip.

I wasn't sure when we'd begun the tradition, but it had stuck. Most of the time it was me and Dante, him spooning behind me. I preferred those moments, but only because I cherished every minute I got to spend with Dante. But whenever Heaven was on the outs with Danny, this was how we spent our evenings, camped out like this in the living room. At some point, Dante would relax, but he didn't sleep. He only did that when it was the two of us.

Heaven reached up, clicked off the small table lamp.

Dante flipped through a few channels until he settled on *Rush Hour.*

The house was silent, the TV on low. I relaxed but couldn't sleep. Then again, I'd been asleep before everything happened.

"You're not tired?" Dante asked after a while.

"No. Want to be awake when Isaac gets home."

Dante's hand slipped beneath the blanket, smoothed over my side in a sweet gesture. I knew he wasn't copping a feel, just comforting me.

For whatever reason, memories of the other night flooded my brain. Being laid out on the dining room table, naked. Ian, Isaac, and Dante taking turns eating my pussy. I'd never done anything quite so taboo. I wasn't the sort who went through men. The most I'd ever played with was Ian and Isaac together, but even then, they rarely touched me. It was more about me performing for them, as though they were respecting the distance I'd needed. Now that I'd had all three of them, I wanted to explore more of it.

In fact, I was hoping for a repeat. Or maybe something equally exciting.

Since the first morning, I hadn't returned to the guest room. Instead, I'd been sleeping in Isaac's bed. I'd been hoping for some alone time with Ian, but I had yet to get any. I wasn't sure why that was, but I got the feeling Ian was keeping his distance from me, perhaps respecting Isaac?

And while I cherished every second with Isaac, Ian had invaded my thoughts numerous times. Every minute of the day I was thinking about one of them, sometimes both. While I had expected this to be one big orgy party after I realized what Ian and Isaac were interested in, turned out that wasn't the case. Even though I certainly wouldn't balk at the opportunity.

A door opened, closed. I waited until the footsteps drew closer, then turned my head, watched as Ian and Isaac walked through the kitchen and into the living room. Their keen eyes scanned the scene, taking it all in.

"Everything all right?" Dante asked.

I knew by the look on Ian's face that everything was most definitely not all right.

"Your ex is pretty beat up," Ian told Heaven, his accent thicker than usual. "But he's not dead."

"You ready for bed?" Isaac asked, his eyes on me.

I nodded, got to my feet. Isaac came over, picked me up, held me in his arms.

"May I go back to bed, Sir?" Dante asked, his full attention on Ian.

149

"Aye. See you in the morning. Still up for a run?"

"Absolutely, Sir."

Ian grinned and something passed between them. Obviously, an inside joke.

"I'll meet you both in here at seven," Isaac told them.

"We'll be waiting," Ian replied.

Then the big, beautiful Irishman was carrying me out of the room, down the hall. "You, my sweet, are coming with me."

"You won't get any argument from me."

He leaned his forehead against my head as he walked and I could feel the tension, knew there was something they'd been holding back.

"Was it bad?" I asked.

"Yeah. From what the ex said, Roger thought he was there for Dante. Ensured the ex knew that wasn't even an option."

"Oh, God."

He set me on the bed.

"Yeah. The ex is at the hospital."

I noticed he referred to Danny as the ex. Not by name. Simply, the ex.

"Did he hurt him that badly?"

"He beat on him," Isaac whispered. "But worse, he raped him."

I fell back onto my butt, staring up at Isaac. My hand was covering my mouth and I realized it was to hold in a sob.

"I'm sorry. According to the doctor, he'll be all right. Physically, anyway."

Yeah. Mentally was a different story. Especially after something as traumatic and horrific as being taken against your will.

"I can call and check with the hospital if you'd like," he said softly, his eyes narrowed on me.

I shook my head, hating that he misunderstood almost as much as I hated myself for not thinking about Heaven's ex-boyfriend at that moment.

"Do you think he … did that to Dante, too?"

Isaac's eyes cooled and I could tell he'd thought about that, too. "Yeah. I do."

He leaned over, kissed my cheek. "I'm going to shower. You better be naked when I get back."

I nodded, watched him disappear into the bathroom.

Slightly numb, I managed to strip off my pajamas before sliding under the covers. A few minutes later, the lights went off and Isaac climbed into the bed beside me.

"Come here, fairy princess," he growled softly.

I started to turn, thinking he meant so he could spoon behind me.

"Beneath me." His voice was rough, gravel and sand laced with need.

I reached for him, cupping his face as his lips covered mine.

Without fanfare, Isaac settled between my thighs, his body warm and heavy above me, his cock thick and hard as he pushed inside without preamble. Granted, nothing else was necessary because I was wet and aching for him already. I kicked off the blankets, wrapped my legs around his lean hips, my arms around his neck, and fused myself to him.

I gasped, rocking with him as he took me straight over the edge within seconds. It was unexpected and a serious rush for his ego, apparently.

"Ah, love," he mumbled against my neck. "Let's see how many times I can make you come."

I held on to him, falling just a little harder as he plunged in deep, retreated. Slow, easy. The man made love to me in a way I'd never experienced before. He drove me to the edge, gave me false hope that he'd let it build, then pushed me right over again and again.

When he slid one arm beneath my head, his other hand gripping the headboard, impaling me over and over, I was pretty sure I'd died and gone to heaven.

"Isaac," I whimpered. "I ... oh, God ... need ... my Liege."

A roar escaped him as soon as those last words were out of my mouth. It was like they were a trigger, unleashing the beast. His muscles flexed beneath my hands as he strained to get closer, deeper.

"Take all of me, Everly," he growled low in his throat.

"All of you," I whispered. "Everything."

With that, he launched us both right over the cliff into oblivion.

Twelve

Dante

Thursday, May 30, 2019

SITTING IN MY BED, I LISTENED TO the silence.

Unlike some, I didn't mind it. In fact, I found I needed it to calm the chaos in my head. Being around too many people was like being in a room with strobe lights and loud music. It overwhelmed my senses, made me anxious.

The shrinks I'd visited told me it was due to the fact that my father had kept me locked up for eight years of my life. Truth was, I didn't even remember most of it, certainly didn't remember him. They'd also said that was selective memory, a way for my brain to protect me from the trauma.

I'd long ago stopped paying attention to how other people wanted to diagnose me. I survived, which was the most important thing. In fact, it was the one thing I'd clung to all these years. I was a survivor. I'd been born into hell and somehow—with no help from those who'd created me—I had survived.

Oddly enough, these past few days had helped significantly. Being here, in this house, I'd never felt safer in my life. The chaos was manageable.

Having the opportunity to spend time with Everly had helped tremendously. I felt safe with her and I still wasn't sure why that was. She gave me purpose, perhaps.

My thoughts drifted back to the other night, Everly laid out on the dining room table like a feast. In that single moment, nothing had intruded. I'd been there with them. With Ian and Isaac. The way Ian had given me directives ... I needed more of that.

However, I wasn't stupid. Something had changed in the past few days, and I figured Ian and Isaac had dug up the news stories on me, figured out what had happened, why I sought solitude as a refuge. They didn't quite treat me with kid gloves, but it was damn close. I needed to knock down that wall, to let them in. They were the only ones who'd come close to giving me what I needed. And honestly, aside from Everly, they were the only ones who'd proven with their actions that they cared about my well-being and were willing to help me move forward instead of back.

It damn sure hadn't been that bastard Roger.

I forced myself to sit still when I was tempted to press up against the wall, to cower from the demons I knew weren't there. He'd brought them back tenfold, dredged up bits and pieces of memories that were better left buried. I didn't know what Roger had done to Danny the Dickhead, but I knew it wasn't good. It was a wonder the man was still breathing. Didn't mean he wanted to be. I knew all too well the pain that bastard could administer.

Then again, if he'd inflicted even a fraction of the pain on Heaven's ex that he had me, there'd be nightmares to follow. They would come after the body healed. Everly had witnessed them, but she never forced me to talk. Because I didn't want her to worry, I'd started reducing the amount of time I slept. I figured if I was still functioning, I was doing an okay job.

A knock sounded on my door. I immediately looked over at the clock, then to the window. The sun was just starting to turn the sky from black to gray, it would soon turn pink as the earth continued to spin.

"Come in."

Isaac stuck his head in, scanned the room. The bed was still made. I was sitting on top of the blankets. He frowned, obviously realizing I hadn't been to sleep.

"Want to get an early start on the run? Maybe add some distance?"

"Yes, Sir." I hopped off the bed, grabbed my running shoes.

"When we get back, we're going to talk," he said simply.

"Yes, Sir," I said by rote. Everyone seemed to want to talk to me.

"See you in five?"

"Yes, Sir."

I was out of my room and standing on the back porch in under three minutes. Ian and Isaac joined me shortly after.

And as we'd done for the past three mornings, we took off down the street. I'd learned which route they took and had forced myself to keep their pace, although I was almost positive they'd slowed a bit, coming closer to my time.

My head cleared as my feet pounded the pavement. I focused on my breathing, the wind on my face, my thoughts drifting.

After the neighbors had found me in the attic, I'd gone to live with a nice couple, though I'd heard rumors that I was going to end up getting stuck in some shithole with the scum of the earth supervising my every need. That hadn't been the case. And while I didn't open up to them, I had grown attached. Tom, my foster father, had inspired my desire for running. He'd been big into marathons, invited me to train with him. Since they homeschooled me, I'd never had the chance to join the track team, but Tom had told me all of his stories.

On the day I turned eighteen, I had thanked them for taking care of me, then set off into the world on my own. My instincts had been relatively decent, though there was no denying I'd made a few stupid choices in my life. Looking at Roger had been one of them.

Before I knew it, we were back at the house, having added two miles and an additional fifteen minutes to the run. We stepped into the house to the smell of bacon and eggs, Everly and Heaven in the kitchen, laughing about something as they worked.

"Breakfast in ten," Everly told us. "Might want to hurry through those showers."

I nodded, looking forward to a few minutes to myself.

"Actually," Isaac said, motioning toward me, "you pick up where they're leaving off. We'll be back in twenty."

While it should've seemed strange, I watched with interest as Isaac walked right over, scooped Heaven up over his shoulder, as Ian did the same with Everly.

They were switching. Though it didn't shock me completely, I couldn't deny the surprise. I could tell Isaac and Ian had deep affection for Everly, but they'd kept to the same dynamic since we'd arrived.

Was the switch signaling some sort of change?

I made my way to the stove, began working to finish breakfast, all the while thinking that the events that transpired in the next few minutes would either strengthen this bond or shatter it altogether.

"Twenty minutes," I muttered.

That was how long I had before I learned whether my life changed once again.

For better or worse.

ISAAC

HEAVEN DRUMMED HER FISTS ON MY BACK, giggling as I hauled her down the hall to the guest room she'd taken over. She kept it up until I deposited her in the bathroom, setting her little butt right on the counter.

"What are we doing in here?" she asked, giggling.

"Showering. What else?"

She grinned. "So, is this … you know … normal for people like you?"

I narrowed my eyes. "People like me?"

"Dominants," she said, drawing out the word.

"I don't think there's a game plan. Do you have a problem with this?"

Her eyes locked on my face and for a moment I thought she was going to back out. Funny, I couldn't decide if I was hoping she would or not.

Then her face grew serious for a moment. "Is Everly okay with this?"

"She doesn't get to make that decision."

That didn't seem to appease her.

I sighed. "Look—"

"No." She held up her hand, smiled. "I'm sorry. I'm ruining the fun. And that's what this is, right? Fun?" Her smile grew wider. "Show me some fun, you big, bad Dom."

Since she was feeling feisty, I figured now was a good time to show her just how much I enjoyed spunky little submissives.

If I were being completely honest, I'd been waiting for this. For Ian to ask for a switch, that was. And it had been his request that had gotten us to this point. He had reminded me of how we'd envisioned this to go, two submissives we could share between us when the urge arose. Initially, I'd considered refusing him, but I'd seen the need in my twin's eyes, knew he was hoping for time with Everly.

So, here we were.

I silenced Heaven's giggle with my mouth, earning a moan in response. She leaned into me, slid her arms up my sweaty chest. I didn't let go until she was panting.

"Time to get you wet," I mumbled as I slid my lips down her neck. "Very, very wet."

Gripping the hem of her T-shirt, I lifted it up and over her head, tossing it to the floor. Before she could sigh, I had my fingers in the waistband of her shorts and her panties, tugging until she used her hands to push up enough I could work them down her legs. They joined the T-shirt.

I dipped two fingers into her slit, watched her pretty green eyes glaze over.

"You're already wet. Excited?"

"Intrigued," she moaned.

I lowered myself to my knees, forced her legs wide, and licked her pussy.

"Oh, God…"

Yeah, I wanted to hear more of that.

I licked, sucked, teased, but never gave her exactly what she needed. I would make her come, but I would have her begging for it by the time I was done with her.

I took a break, gave her a few seconds to catch her breath while I started the shower. Figuring her knees were a little weak, I lifted her easily, carried her into the shower with me. When she was on her feet, I smiled.

"You're a tease," she said on a shaky breath. "I'm still light-headed from that."

"I'll make good on it, I promise. All in due time."

I turned her so that the water poured over her, slicking her hair, her skin.

Without asking, she reached for the shampoo.

It was then I missed Everly most. Heaven was nothing like my sweet submissive. In fact, I didn't think this woman had a single submissive bone in her body.

Which got me thinking. How had Ian dealt with this? His need to dominate was as powerful as mine.

Then again, he'd likely overpowered her, seduced her into complying. He had a unique way about him, and I certainly hadn't heard Heaven complaining.

Heaven stared up at me as she soaped her hair with shampoo. And while she did that, I took the opportunity to tease her tits, squeezing, plucking her nipples, hanging on every moan and sigh that escaped her. Heaven thrust her chest forward as she rinsed the soap from her hair.

I stopped, earning a frown in response.

I grabbed the conditioner, slicked it into her hair before I handed her the body wash Ian had obviously stashed in here. While I was all for shower play, I had no desire to smell like flowers for the rest of the day.

"Wash me," I commanded.

"Bossy."

"You don't know the half of it."

Her hands were playful as they danced over me, paying close attention to my nipples, my balls. She teased my cock but stopped long before I was ready. That was when I decided to show her what I wanted from her.

"Knees."

Her eyes darkened, her lips parting. The woman had claimed she wasn't submissive, but she sure did submit nicely. When she wasn't being a brat, that was.

Heaven eased down to her knees.

"Suck me. But don't you dare make me come."

There was a little smirk on her lips. I made sure it disappeared as I pushed my cock past them. She gripped the base of my cock, keeping me from going too deep. I obliged, not wanting to hurt her. Her fingers were too small to circle me fully, but she made up for that as she worked me with her mouth and hand at the same time, twisting her fist in the perfect motion to have me groaning.

"You've got a sweet little mouth," I murmured, ensuring she heard the praise. "So soft."

I let her work me to the best of her abilities for a few minutes, then decided to take over. I wasn't close. Yet.

"Put your hands on my thighs."

With my cock still buried in her mouth, she dropped her hands to my thighs.

I slid my fingers into her hair, tightened my grip, and pushed forward, careful not to make her gag. Initially.

"Can you deep throat me?"

Her eyes widened, but she didn't confirm or deny.

"I won't hurt you, I promise."

She gave a jerky nod of her head. I pulled back, watching her lips curl around the head before I pushed in, deeper this time.

"Relax your throat," I ordered.

She did, allowing me to push in another inch.

I pulled back when I felt her throat working. I did this several more times, her eyes watering with each thrust.

"Such a sweet mouth," I mumbled.

Wanting to feel her pussy sheathe my cock, I helped her to her feet, shut off the water. I didn't even bother with towels before I picked her up and carried her to the bed, tossed her onto it, earning another giggle. She really was cute.

"Hands and knees," I commanded, retrieving a condom from the nightstand.

I rolled it on, then joined her on the bed, kneeling behind her.

She grinned back at me over her shoulder. The smile faltered, her mouth forming a perfect O when I plunged inside her.

"Isaac..." She whimpered, her pussy flexing, gripping me like a velvet vise. "Oh, God, yes."

Fisting her hair in my hand, I fucked her. Hard.

Heaven gave as good as she got. Her verbal commentary spurred me on, the way she cried out in pleasure, begging for me to fuck her harder, deeper.

She robbed my lungs of air, driving me closer to the edge with her little ass grinding back against me. I slicked my thumb with saliva, teased her asshole. She moaned but didn't pull away. And when I slammed into her one final time, burying my thumb in her ass, she screamed, pure pleasure ricocheting off the walls.

We fell into a heap on the bed. I was careful not to rush her, brushing her hair back from her face as I pressed my lips to hers. "Thank you."

"For what? Trading?" She was still panting. "I don't get this whole BDSM thing. But I can't deny, the sex is fantastic."

I stared up at the ceiling, missing Everly.

For whatever reason, this had seemed a good idea when Ian had mentioned it. Now, I wasn't quite so certain. While Heaven was an interesting woman, she didn't quite fit where we were trying to place her.

Or perhaps that was me. I hadn't gotten Ian's take on her yet.

Maybe that was a conversation that needed to happen sooner rather than later.

IAN

ALTHOUGH THEY WERE SIMILAR IN APPEARANCE, EVERLY and Heaven were very different. So very different.

And though Everly looked like a sweet, innocent sweetheart, beneath that perfect veneer was a feisty hellcat, a submissive who wanted a man to dominate her in every way. And I had longed for this moment, ached for it. Now that I had her all to myself, I wasn't sure I'd be able to let her go.

What I had wanted to do was carry her to my bedroom and settle her in my bed. Instead, I had fought my baser urges and carried her to the guest room she'd used once, tossing her on the bed, pretending this was all fun and games for me. She watched my every movement as I walked over to the dresser, pulled open the bottom drawer, retrieved a few of the items stored there.

With Everly, I had an advantage. Having played with her at the club, I knew her limits, could safely push her boundaries without fear of causing her harm. While her limits were few, she still had them. However, she did not have a problem with bondage, which was why she ended up gagged, ass up, facedown on the four-post bed, immobile with the help of a restraint that kept her wrists secured at her sides, tethered to the straps that circled her thighs.

"Be a good girl," I told her, smacking her cute little ass. "I'll be back after I shower."

I was true to my word, making quick work of washing up, rinsing, drying off. I returned to find her in the exact same position I'd left her in. Her face was turned to the side, her eyes on me as I entered the room.

"Do you know how much I've thought about this ass?" I asked, swatting it again.

She moaned softly, wiggled her butt as though that would get her more of what she craved.

"We never fucked you at the club. Know why that was?" I joined her on the bed, leaned over her, pressed my lips to her shoulder. "Because Isaac wanted you all to himself."

I knew I was putting everything on Isaac's shoulders, but I was still attempting to play my brother's game. Last thing I wanted was for him to know I'd only requested this switch because I couldn't stand to be away from Everly any longer.

"And while he wants to share you, he's not willing to share that moment with the whole club."

Her shoulders relaxed.

I trailed my tongue from the center of her shoulder blades, down her spine, pausing at the crack of her ass.

Because I could, I switched to my native language. " *We've been waiting for you, little fairy.*"

I teased her asshole with my tongue. She moaned and tried to thrust back, the restraints keeping her in place.

"As much as I want to take this cute little ass, we're going to have to stretch you first." I took the toy, opened it, then lubed it generously.

I dipped two fingers into her pussy as I worked the plug into her ass. She moaned around the gag, her body rocking forward, back as her excitement built.

"Imagine what Isaac's going to say when he learns that you're wearing this plug today. I can almost promise you'll be fucked a couple of times. Is that what you need, little fairy? To have a big cock fill that little pussy?"

She tried to wiggle against my fingers still buried deep in her cunt, but I pulled back, refusing to give her the pleasure she sought. A muffled groan sounded, making me smile.

"Your pussy'll be so tight with that toy in your ass. And while you're wearing it, you'll wear a skirt, no panties."

I gripped my dick, stroked roughly, then reached for the condom I'd tossed on the bed earlier. While I wanted to forego the latex, to feel the wet heat of her pussy slide over my cock, that was an unspoken rule with me and Isaac. Everly didn't belong to me, therefore protection was unavoidable. If and when the day ever came that Everly got pregnant—something she and Isaac would have to figure out on their own—it wouldn't be by me. Isaac deserved that honor.

The thought had pain lancing my insides. My twin had gotten to her first, forcing me to take a step back. We'd fantasized about how our lives would play out, and I knew Isaac was under the impression this was the path we should take. While I wanted to rebel against it, to claim Everly as mine, too, I knew that would cause a rift between us. As much as I was coming to care for Everly, there was nothing I wouldn't do for my brother. Nothing.

So, for now, I would take what I could get.

"Squeeze my fingers," I ordered.

Everly's pussy tightened around my fingers. Goddamn, she was so fucking perfect. The easy way she submitted... It wasn't a game for her. This was what she needed, as much as I needed to dominate her.

I pulled my fingers out, sucked her sweet juices off them before gripping her hips and guiding my cock into the tight sheath of her body. I didn't slam into her, taking my time. The plug in her ass made her impossibly tight, her small body adding to the pressure. But as soon as I was lodged to the hilt inside her, the tight leash on my restraint snapped.

Everly moaned around the gag as I fucked her. I wasn't gentle, but I knew she didn't want gentle. Her hands flexed, fisted with every punishing thrust. I alternated between slow and deep, then fast and shallow. I paused long enough to flip the release on the gag. It fell from her mouth and a litany of pleas followed.

They were music to my ears as I drove into her again and again, using her sweet little body to drive us both to the precipice.

"Master Ian... Oh, God. Please..."

"Please what?"

"Harder."

I slammed into her, holding back just enough to ensure I didn't bruise her.

"I'm... Master Ian? May I come? Please. Please, may I come?"

"Aye," I growled.

Her pussy squeezed my cock like a fist, milking me dry.

I pulled out, leaned over her, planting kisses over her shoulders, her neck even as I worked the restraints free from her wrists.

"Thank you, Master Ian," she whispered, her body soft beneath me.

"Thank *you*, little fairy." I lowered my voice, kissed her neck one last time. "I'm not even sure you realize how much we need you."

How much *I* needed her.

Not that I was going to admit as much.
Not to her. Not to Isaac. Not to anyone.

Thirteen

Everly

ALTHOUGH I'D JUST SPENT THE LAST TWENTY minutes being fucked within an inch of my life by his twin, Isaac took my hand the second I joined him in the dining room. He pulled me into his lap, his arm wrapped over me possessively. I snuggled against him, wondering when he might figure out I had a plug in my ass.

"She's wearing something special for you," Ian informed Isaac when he came into the room.

Well, that hadn't taken long.

Isaac nuzzled my neck. "Is that right?"

"Yes, my Liege." I opened my mouth when he spoon-fed me oatmeal.

"Something special?" Heaven asked, glancing between the four of us.

"Tell her, little fairy," Ian ordered.

I loved that he called me that. He'd done so almost since the beginning. And I really loved it when he said it in Irish, with that lilt, it felt even more intimate. And while Ian and I hadn't had much time together, I couldn't deny the short time we'd had was something I was now hoping would become a frequent occurrence.

I smiled, hoped my cheeks weren't as red as they felt. "A butt plug."

Heaven giggled. "In your ass?"

Dante snorted. "Self-explanatory, no?"

"I wouldn't laugh if I were you," Ian told Heaven. "I've got an extra if you'd like to try one on for size."

Heaven's eyes shot to mine, widening as though the idea was horrific. "Uh … no, thanks. Totally not my thing."

"I've got a few errands to run today," Ian informed us, as though Heaven's comment had no bearing on anything.

It had me glancing between the two of them. For whatever reason, I'd thought they had gotten closer in recent days. Based on their body language, that didn't seem to be the case. Heaven seemed distant, almost.

"And I've got some phone calls to make," Isaac chimed in. "Then I'll be out for a bit." He pulled my hair back. "You want to go with me?"

I didn't bother to ask where. It didn't matter. "Yes, my Liege."

"Tonight," Ian continued as though we hadn't interrupted, "I want Heaven to cook, Everly to clean. Isaac and I need some time with Dante."

"It would be our pleasure," I told him politely.

I glanced over at Dante. He was eating as though he wasn't even in the same room. I'd seen him do this a few times, turning into a recluse, blocking me out even though I could tell it pained him to do so. I still didn't know much about his childhood, aside from the fact it had been traumatic. When I'd tried to talk to him, he'd always told me he didn't want to subject me to that. So, I had given him his space, ensuring he knew I was there whenever he needed me.

"I need to catch up on my homework for the week," Heaven told Ian. "It's due on Sunday and I'm usually done earlier in the week."

"Anything you need?"

"No. Just some peace and quiet."

"You'll have most of the afternoon to yourself."

She nodded, focused on her food. There was definitely a detachment there. One that hadn't been there prior to the switch Ian and Isaac had pulled.

"I'd like you to spend some time with Dante," Isaac told me before looking over at Dante. "I know you'll need some space, but I think you need her, too."

Their eyes met, held. I watched, wondering if they were having a silent conversation I wasn't privy to. Dante finally nodded. "Thank you, Sir. I'd like to spend some time with her."

My heart turned over. I hated that Dante wanted to keep himself closed off, but I understood it. Or I tried to. So those moments I could spend with him were ones I looked forward to. Cherished even.

Once we were finished with breakfast, I took dish duty while Heaven went up to the attic to do schoolwork. Dante disappeared into his room while Isaac and Ian headed for the basement. I hummed while I worked, realizing how content I was being here. Looked as though I'd settled into this routine nicely.

So much so, I dreaded going back to work. If I still had a job when this was over, that was. As it was, my boss wasn't too pleased when I told her I'd needed to take a week of vacation due to a family emergency. Luckily, I was one of those who rarely took time off, so she hadn't been able to hold that over my head. Then again, it wouldn't surprise me if I went back to find she'd replaced me. Baristas were plentiful, and with proper training and a decent amount of dedication, it wasn't all that difficult for someone to fill the position.

After wiping down the counters and the table, I went to Dante's room, knocked on the door.

With Heaven, he usually called out for her to come in, but with me, he'd always opened the door, just as he did now. I stepped inside, realized that was the first time I'd been in that room. It was huge. Probably twice the size of the room I'd started out in. While it was nice, it didn't feel like Dante.

For the first time since we'd arrived, I suddenly missed home. Only for Dante, though. Then I thought about the man who'd attacked me... I wasn't sure I'd be able to go back there.

Forcing the negative thoughts away, I peered up at Dante's handsome face. "When's the last time you slept?"

He shrugged. "Couple hours. Yesterday, I think. It's all jumbled together right now."

"Then we'll take a nap," I told him. I motioned for the bed. "May I?"

"Of course."

I pulled back the blankets and the sheet, then crawled in, careful not to flash him when I did. He joined me, pulling the blankets up, ensuring I was tucked in although it was him I was worried about.

I curled up against his side, my head on his chest. In a bold and daring move, I slid my hand beneath his T-shirt, wanting to feel his warmth. He settled his hand over mine, the T-shirt between us.

"Are you doing okay?" I whispered.

"Actually, yeah." He sighed. "Better than I've been in a while."

"It's not hard to be here?"

"It's comforting." He reached over, turned off the lamp. The room darkened thanks to the curtains over the windows. "How about you? How are you holding up?"

I smiled to myself. "I'm good. Really good."

He was quiet for a few minutes and I hoped he'd fallen asleep, but his breathing hadn't slowed, so I knew his mind was whirling.

"Does it bother you what I did the other night?"

His words were so soft, almost pained. I lifted my head, looked in his eyes.

"In the dining room?"

He nodded.

"No. I enjoyed it. Immensely."

"Me, too," he said, his eyes shifting away.

I turned his cheek, forcing his gaze to meet mine. "Nothing's changed about how I feel," I told him. "Nothing could ever change that."

He swallowed and I took a huge chance, leaning in, pressing my lips to his. He relaxed, his mouth melding to mine, his tongue sliding over my bottom lip, then dipping inside. I met his tongue with mine. It was the first kiss we'd shared that hadn't been instigated. This time it felt sweeter, far more intimate. And when Dante pulled me over him, I moved without hesitation, straddling his hips, letting the kiss ignite as his hands slipped beneath my shirt.

"Skin to skin," he whispered, his request surprising but not at all disappointing.

I let him pull off my shirt, unhook my bra before he gripped the back of his shirt and tugged. I leaned in, gave in to his kiss.

I'd actually dreamed about this from time to time, imagining what it would feel like to be with Dante. Sure, he'd become my best friend over the years, but there was a connection we shared, one based on love and desire. Though neither of us had ever acted on it, the feelings had never subsided.

Now that we were giving in to it, I wasn't sure I'd be able to stop.

"Dante ... touch me," I moaned. "Please, touch me."

His big, warm hands caressed my back. Like feathers over my skin, light and gentle. Always cherishing. I wanted to be close to him, as close as we could possibly be. But I needed this to be his idea. I didn't want him to think I was taking advantage. I knew how he felt about me. He knew how I felt about him, but we'd always fought it.

This felt right.

The door opened and before Dante could throw me off him, I cupped his cheek. "Don't stop."

I'd sensed him, knew Isaac had come into the room. I'd suspected he would after he'd instructed me to spend time with Dante. It had been a directive, and though he hadn't elaborated, he hadn't needed to. No one needed to order me to be with Dante. This was merely an excuse to act on it.

Isaac didn't say a word. He simply walked to the chair in the corner and sat.

As though his presence was the approval Dante needed, he took the reins, his hands roaming more firmly, cupping my ass, squeezing.

"Naked," Dante mumbled. "I want you naked."

I rolled off him and he followed, our mouths resuming their exploration as he pushed my skirt down my hips.

"Everly…" His kiss was harder, more controlled, as though he knew exactly what he wanted, and he'd been given instructions to take it.

I moaned, my head tipping back when his fingers grazed my clit. Despite Ian's exquisite fucking from earlier, I was still primed and ready to go.

"You're so wet," he whispered against my lips.

I whimpered, wanting him to take his pleasure from my body. Whatever he wanted, needed, that was what I was willing to give. Everything.

Dante trailed kisses across my chest, between my breasts, lower. He shouldered my legs apart, then lapped at me with that skilled tongue. Every so often he would nudge the plug that was still lodged inside me, ratcheting up my desire. He drove me up, up, but didn't let me go over. He did it again and again, driving me mad, insane with need.

I could feel Isaac watching us and it fanned the flames, made me hotter.

Dante paused long enough to shuck his shorts and roll on a condom before settling over me once more. He cupped my face, stared into my eyes. And when he entered me slowly, I felt tears forming. This man, so sweet, so gentle. So perfect. What I felt for him was intense, but we'd both known we had needed more. Now that we had more, had Isaac, I felt as though I could give him all of me.

He groaned, a strangled sound. I saw the torment in his gaze, knew he was holding back.

"You're what I want," I assured him. "What I need. Love me, Dante."

Dante remained where he was, settled deep inside me. "You're so tight, so wet."

The bed shifted and I realized Isaac had joined us, laid out, fully dressed beside us. Absently, I reached for his hand. He twined his fingers with mine, but he moved toward Dante, reaching for him, pulling him close until their mouths melded together.

And that was a sight. These two ridiculously hot men kissing... I couldn't look away.

"Fuck her," Isaac commanded, his words so low I could barely hear them. "I want to watch, Dante." Isaac kissed him again, dragging a strangled groan from Dante. "I need this as much as you do."

Though it was obviously meant to reassure Dante, I got the feeling it was the truth. Isaac wasn't the sort to show his emotions, but I'd sensed his need for Dante. They hadn't pursued anything, from what I knew, but it was only a matter of time.

Dante's hips retreated, then pushed forward, his attention returning to me. It was then I saw him, the clouds in his eyes dissipating. The man I'd come to love in our own way was there with me, deep inside me.

He took my other hand, threaded our fingers together as he began a rhythmic bump and grind, his movements in perfect time with my body. As he drove me higher, my back bowed, changing the angle, my body taking him deeper. He groaned, then let himself go, driving into me, his breath warm on my flesh as he buried his face in my neck.

"Dante ... God, yes. You feel so good." Better than good. It was more than I expected, everything I needed.

He released my hand, his arms sliding under me, holding me to him as he took from me all that I'd always wanted to give him. I released Isaac's hand, giving myself to Dante, holding on to him as he pushed me right to the precipice.

My body tensed, the electricity building in my core, radiating outward until I could no longer control it.

"I'm coming, Dante... Oh, God..." I shattered.

Dante let me ride out my orgasm before he slammed into me again and again. This time I waited him out, allowing the sensations to build once more. When he let go, I did, too.

Suddenly his warmth was gone, and I felt the chill deep in my bones. His absence bothered me, even as he disappeared into the bathroom. I stared at the empty space, willing him to come back, not wanting him to leave me, to put distance between us.

When he returned, he crawled into the bed, spooned behind me, and held me. Isaac kissed my lips before slipping out of the room.

The next three hours—before I slipped out of the house with Isaac for the afternoon—I spent in Dante's arms, deep in a sated, dreamless sleep.

Heaven

HOMEWORK SUCKED.

Well, technically, it was schoolwork that, since I took online classes, was done at home.

Still, it sucked.

But it was done for the week and just in time for me to cook dinner. The house was quiet, had been since everyone vacated a few hours ago. I hadn't seen Dante since he'd gone to his room right after breakfast, hoped he was getting some rest.

With my headphones still in, I danced around the kitchen, enjoying the solitude as I worked. I made baked chicken with mashed potatoes and green peas. Taking into account Everly was vegetarian, I baked her a potato, added some broccoli I steamed in the microwave, and tossed on some melted cheddar. For some reason, the girl loved that dish.

I set the chicken on the stove, grabbing the plates so I could dish it up. I turned, squealed, jerking my earphones from my ears. There, watching me from a safe distance, was Ian, Everly, and Isaac. All three with amused smirks on their faces.

Thanks to my headphones, I hadn't heard them come home.

"What? I like to listen to music while I cook."

"It's true," Everly agreed. "She does. She also likes to dance."

"Go get settled," I told them, pointing toward the dining room. "I'll bring it along in a second."

Dante appeared, his eyes scanning the room. He glanced at me, over to the other three, then back. "You were dancing, weren't you?"

"I was," I snipped.

He laughed, then grabbed drinks and went into the dining room with the others.

I smiled to myself, enjoying the fact that I'd made them all smile. It was my goal in life.

Not to mention, it made me feel a bit better about the situation. While I had enjoyed what had happened with Isaac earlier, it weirded me out. Probably because I was more of a one-man woman, and this situation was growing more intense with every passing minute.

Not that I had to participate. I knew that I could easily tell them no and they'd respect my decision. But part of me was curious, I figured. Which meant the only person I had to blame was myself.

However, I had every intention of easing out, allowing the four of them to do what they needed to do. That way, when I told them I was going to stay with my sister, perhaps they'd be too distracted to care.

"All right," I said, joining them at the table. "What did everyone do today?"

"Slept," Dante said simply.

"You needed it," I told him. "I'm glad you did. And everyone else?"

"Do you want a recap of what I did to you in the bathroom?" Isaac quipped.

My eyes shot up to his face. "You made a joke. That's the first time you've made a joke."

He rolled his eyes. "You want that recap?"

"Not necessary," I told him. "They've all got vivid imaginations. I'm sure they can figure it out."

"We went to Chatter PR," Everly said after taking her first bite of potato. "Why is it that your potatoes are always better than mine?"

I grinned. "That little pat of love I add." I swallowed down mashed potatoes. "What's Chatter PR?"

"A public relations company," she explained.

I turned my attention to Isaac. "You work there?"

"Not exactly," Ian supplied. "We work in their personal protection division. They've got plenty of others."

"Yeah, they do," Everly agreed. "They've also got all the Doms from Dichotomy working there."

"Not all," Isaac corrected.

"A few subs, too," Ian noted.

"True. Quite a few," Everly agreed.

"What did you do there?" I asked Everly, keeping the conversation moving while we all ate.

She blushed, then looked over at Isaac.

"No, no," I said quickly. "I don't need those details, either."

Isaac and Ian laughed.

"What did you do?" Ian asked me.

"I finished my work for the week, called my boss, begged her not to fire me. She assured me my job was safe and secure and would be waiting for me on Saturday."

"Saturday?" Ian and Isaac shared a look.

"What?" I glanced between them, then sighed. "This can't go on forever. While I get that I can't go home, I also can't give up my job. I don't want to."

"Eager to get out of here?" Ian asked.

"Actually…" I let the word drag out. "I … um … I think it's best if I go stay with my sister."

All eyes turned to me. Their abrupt movements had me dropping my fork.

"Is that a decision you made because of what's going on here?"

I wasn't sure if I was supposed to read something into that. Not wanting to brush it off, nor did I want to tackle that beast right now, I nodded. "I think it's best."

"For who?" Everly asked.

I honestly didn't want to go into this with such a large audience, so I shrugged it off. "Can we all talk about something else, please?"

No one said anything for a few minutes and the silence began strangling me.

"So, I cooked, Everly's going to clean, and you boys are going to go downstairs and do what boys do," I said, looking from one to the other. "While you do that, I was wondering if Everly and I could have a pillow fight naked. You know, to keep ourselves busy."

Everly laughed, Isaac smirked, and Ian groaned.

Still, the tension was there, tightening its deathly grip.

An hour later, Everly and I were up to our neck in warm water. Turned out, Isaac had a jacuzzi tub in his bathroom, and since it wasn't quite warm outside, she'd suggested we hang out there. I was not about to say no to an opportunity such as that.

"Okay, so I'm going to get personal," I warned her.

"You've never warned me before," she teased.

"True. But I need to know about this … butt plug thing."

Everly's face turned a pretty shade of pink.

"Are you still wearing it?"

She shook her head. "No. Thank God."

"Does it hurt … you know … to wear it?"

"Not really, no. It's uncomfortable at first."

I frowned, let my hand float on the churning water. "I mean, I get what it's for. To stretch … uh … that part." Now my face was turning pink. "So I take it you've had anal sex."

"I have." She said it so easily, as though I wasn't talking about an intimate act.

"Does it hurt?"

"Let's just say it's intense. But I do like it. Under the right conditions."

"You're not all that sweet and innocent," I told her, pointing right at her.

"Far from it."

"But you wouldn't know it by looking at you."

"Maybe that's part of the appeal," she said.

"I could see it. Guys get all hot for the sweet girl who's dirty in the bedroom."

"Now I have a question for you."

I grinned. "Hit me."

"Have you ever been with a woman?"

Wow. That wasn't what I expected her to ask.

"I actually have. Sort of."

"It's either all or nothing, no?"

"Well … it was a long time ago. I was dating this guy and we were hanging out with his best friend and his best friend's girlfriend. We were making out side by side. Things heated up. There was some experimenting that took place. Just when things started to really get hot, her boyfriend got all possessive, put a stop to it."

"That sucks."

"Yeah. What about you?"

"No. I haven't."

"Ever thought about it?"

177

"I might've entertained the idea once or twice."

I flicked water her direction. "You are just a tiny bundle of surprises, aren't you?"

Her answer was a beautiful grin.

Fourteen

Dante

I KNEW WHEN THEY MENTIONED WANTING TO talk to me that it was going to be intense.

Still, I made the trek down the stairs without hesitation. If they wanted the brutal details of the worst time of my life, I would give them to them. As much as I remembered, anyway.

When I arrived in the basement, Ian and Isaac were sitting on the leather sofas, chatting. They didn't get quiet as I approached, which I took to mean they weren't talking about me. Then again, they were speaking in what I assumed was Irish, so it wouldn't have mattered. I had no idea what they were saying.

I stopped between them, not sure what to do next.

Ian said something, and I caught one word in English, my gaze shooting to him.

"That's correct. I instructed you to kneel," he said, pointing to the floor near his feet.

The deep, rich tone had that strange tingling sensation dancing down my spine. Obedient and eager, I lowered myself before him.

"I know you think we brought you down here so we can interrogate you some more. You're right. That's my plan. Then again, that's always my plan. Do you have a problem with that?"

"No, Sir."

"While I have every intention of getting to know you on every level, I will tell you that you're not obligated to share anything you don't want to share when it comes to your childhood. I won't lie. We're curious by nature, dug up the information. Whether accurate or not, we got a glimpse into what happened. But we didn't do it to invade your privacy."

I didn't say a word, not quite sure I could agree with that.

"Did you fill out a limit list at Inferno?"

"No, Sir. They don't require that information."

"So, how does a Dominant know what you're willing to do and not do?"

I thought it was a rhetorical question, but when Ian didn't continue, I realized he was waiting for me to respond.

"I don't know, Sir."

"They don't," he said, as though my response hadn't mattered. "The issue I'm having is that we want to play with you."

His hand slid into my hair, then slowly tilted my head back. He stared down at me, his eyes intense.

"I can't very well play with you without knowing your boundaries. And if you even try to lie and say you don't have any, I'll kick your ass right out of my house."

"I have them, Sir."

He nodded, his eyes still locked with mine. His voice was softer when he spoke again. "We want to play with you, Dante. We want to give you what you need. It's taken a tremendous amount of restraint to have you here this week and not be able to do that."

I swallowed, fought the emotion that slammed into my chest.

"Have you ever had a Dom want more from you than your body?" Isaac asked.

Ian released my hair and I lowered my head once more. "No, Sir."

"Then it's safe to say you've never had two Doms who want that."

My chest felt as though someone was blowing up a balloon inside it. "No, Sir."

"In order for that to come to fruition, we have to know what you need. *Everything* you need."

I focused on breathing, hating myself for wanting this so much.

"I saw you with Everly," Isaac continued. "You wanted her, but you didn't know how to take what you wanted."

"That's not true, Sir."

"No?"

"No, Sir."

"Then tell me what happened."

"I needed you," I said softly.

"Me?"

"Yes, Sir. I needed you with me. *Wanted* you with me." Knowing I had to get this out, I took a deep breath and surrendered to it. "I won't deny I want her. I've always wanted her. Being with Everly … it transcended anything I'd ever known. But it wasn't until you came in, gave me your permission, that I could actually take it."

"You want absolute domination," Ian mumbled.

Even though it wasn't a question, I answered. "Yes, Sir." My voice trembled when the next words came out. "I want to be a humble servant, to give my whole self to my Master. Or Masters. I want someone I can trust to take but not break me in the process. I'm willing to give consent to having no consent. It's what I crave."

They were both quiet, and though my blood pounded in my ears, I didn't look up, wasn't sure I could handle seeing their faces. Most people didn't understand what I needed. Hell, some submissives didn't even understand it. But I knew when I found the Dominant who could handle me, he wouldn't need a long, drawn-out explanation.

"He raped you."

It was Ian's voice, full of anger and torment, that had me lifting my gaze to his. "Yes, Sir. He did. But he didn't break me."

His eyes locked on mine. There was no pity there, like I'd expected. Just a need to understand.

"We don't want to hurt you," he said softly, as though it pained him to think that it was possible.

"You won't."

"How can you be so sure?" Isaac asked.

I looked at him. "Because I trust you."

Isaac got to his feet, his eyes never leaving my face. "I want a limit list by morning. Filled out completely, no blank spaces. If it's there by the time I come out for our run"—he swallowed, his eyes narrowing—"then you'll know what it's like to be owned by this Dom."

With that parting shot, he turned and left the basement.

I remained where I was, kneeling beside Ian, my heart in my fucking throat.

"Once he claims you," Ian said softly, "he won't let you go. He doesn't do that lightly. In fact, until you, he's never taken a male submissive."

My heart was beating so loud I was sure Ian could hear it.

"Nor have I." His hand slid into my hair again. This time, he wasn't gentle when he jerked my head back. His voice was a rough growl when he spoke. "And for the first time in my life, I want that."

He released me, got to his feet. "Follow."

I got to my feet, fell into step behind him. He took a stack of papers off his desk, handed them to me.

"We're going out at seven in the morning," he said quickly.

"I'll have it completed, Sir."

He nodded, turned, stopped, keeping his back to me. "Have you been up to the library?"

"No, Sir."

"Will you?"

I opted for the truth. "Not unless you make me."

"Understood. And you can rest assured, we will *never* make you do something you don't want to do. Good night."

"Good night, Sir."

With the limit list in my hands, I went to my room, settled on the bed, and got to work.

ISAAC

Friday, May 31, 2019

I WAS AWAKE EARLY, BUT I STAYED in bed, held on to Everly as she slept soundly beside me. Dawn broke as I lay there, and still I didn't move until six forty-five for the sole reason that I wanted to ensure Dante had the time he needed to complete that limit list.

I wasn't sure when it happened, or even how, but I'd come to need what he was willing to give, seemingly as much as he needed what we could give him.

My brother would be the first to say I was driven by pure emotion. I doubted I'd be able to provide a reasonable enough counter to convince a grand jury. However, I would say my decisions were slightly more calculated, partially fueled by emotion. More so, I'd admit to having wanted something for so long that, the moment it was in my hands, I wasn't willing to let it go.

After all, God created the heavens and the Earth in six days, rested on the seventh. Who was to say I couldn't fall in love in that amount of time?

No one.

No one who mattered, anyway.

Without waking Everly, I tucked the blankets around her, then slipped out of the room, my running shoes in hand. When I got to the kitchen, Dante was the first thing I saw, stretching on the back porch. I did enjoy waking up to seeing him like that.

I walked over to the island, saw the stack of papers laid neatly. I picked them up, scanned through the pages covered in neat, block letters. He'd filled out everything, including lengthy explanations that he'd continued on the backs of the pages. Not a single line had been missed.

Ian appeared, his keen gaze zeroing in on the stack of papers.

I nodded. "Some light reading for later."

Ian looked as relieved as I felt.

"Five miles," I told them as I stepped outside. "Got to save some of my energy for later."

My brother coughed to cover his laugh, then broke out into a jog toward the street.

I forced my mind to blank for the run. Everything faded into the background, Everly, Dante, the asshole who'd hurt those I had come to care about. I let it drift away like mist, taking this time as my own.

It wasn't until a few minutes into the run that I'd realized Heaven hadn't been included in my list of people I cared about. I thought back to her mentioning she was going to stay with her sister. For some reason, I felt that was a good idea. Then again, I wasn't sure how Ian felt about that. Again, I had yet to ask him, to pursue the details of whatever was going on between them. However, I was in tune with my twin, and had there been something there, I would've recognized it. I didn't. As far as I could tell, Ian was indulging and that was all.

By the time I got back to the house, I was ready for a shower and food, but not necessarily in that order.

The kitchen was still empty when we returned, the girls likely still asleep. The three of us grabbed water bottles, then sat on the barstools and counters as we cooled down.

"The maid service comes by today," I reminded Ian. "Figured we could get out of here for a bit. Run them by Dante's." I glanced over at him. "In case you need anything from there."

Dante didn't respond immediately, but I saw the question in his eyes, waited for it.

"How long's this going to last?"

I knew he wasn't talking about the relationships that were building.

"As long as it has to," Ian said, not looking at him. "I'm not letting any of you go back there until this guy is no longer a threat."

"What about Heaven?" he prompted. "She wants to go to her sister's."

Ian shrugged. "Probably a good idea that she does."

Well, that told me more than I probably would've gotten out of my brother. He was willing to let her leave, which meant there was no attachment.

Dante broke eye contact with Ian, pinned his gaze on the counter. "I got fired yesterday."

"Fuck, man," Ian breathed out. "I'm sorry."

"Yeah."

I had to bite my tongue, remembering the argument I'd had with Ian. Asking Dante and Everly to move in here permanently would likely come across as abrupt, not thought out. It wasn't true, but I could see where he was coming from. The issue was, I was certain about them. More so than I'd been about anything in my life. I couldn't say the same for Heaven because … well, because she wasn't what I was looking for.

"I can get another pretty easily," Dante said. "Just need time to go look."

"No," I said. The single word snapped out had drawn Ian's gaze. He was glaring at me, but I shrugged it off.

I hopped off the counter. "I want you here. With us. And if that's the way it's going to work, you won't work. Not if I have a say in the matter."

185

Not wanting to hear Ian's rebuttal, I turned and left the room, making my way to my bedroom. I opened the door, noticed Everly still tucked in sound asleep. It would be so easy to wake her, to slide into the bed, sink deep inside her, and lose myself for a few minutes, but I wanted her to rest up. I'd taken a lot from her these past couple of days, and since I didn't see that slowing anytime in the near future, sleep was what she needed most.

I hurried through the shower, dressed, then headed back to the kitchen. It was empty, so I made a pot of coffee, grabbed a cup and Dante's limit list, then headed down to the basement.

Bypassing my desk, I sat on the sofa, got lost in reading. I skimmed it first, focusing on Dante's hard limits. All the ones that matched my own hard limits had been marked: asphyxiation, breath control, bestiality, and so on. The ones I'd expected based on the trauma he'd experienced: cages, cells, closets. I wasn't into that, anyway, but I was glad to know he'd been honest. There were a few I hadn't expected but would respect because he had elaborated with reasons. That generally wasn't how it worked, but I appreciated his candor all the same.

On the other hand, I noticed he had marked anything to do with bondage as a nonissue. I had to trust him. That was the only way this would work.

He'd gone so far as to rank them from zero to five for those he didn't consider a hard limit, five being the most desirable. I went back through the list three times, rereading his notes, and it all told the same story in elaborate detail. Dante wanted to serve and please. How some Dom hadn't come along and realized the gift he was, I would never know. Then again, he'd been targeted by some fucker using BDSM as his excuse to harm.

Footsteps sounded on the stairs, drawing my attention. I expected to see Ian, but my brother wasn't joining me. It was Dante, his steps somewhat lighter than they'd been in recent days. He moved with purpose, coming to stand before me. He knelt without direction.

"May I speak candidly, Sir?"

"Please."

He kept his eyes down. "I would never want to come between you and your brother. If I have, I wish to leave. I understand the fear for my safety, and I can promise, I'll do everything in my power not to get into a situation I can't get myself out of."

"You haven't come between us," I told him firmly. "No one will ever come between me and Ian. If there was a chance, that person would not be welcomed in our lives. We have a difference of opinion on certain matters. I respect his view, he respects mine. And as is human nature, we butt heads from time to time.

"Look at me, Dante." I waited for him to obey. "I meant what I said earlier. I won't take it back because Ian disagrees."

"I don't disagree, damn it."

My brother strolled down the stairs, heading right for us, hands on his hips, exasperation on his brow.

"Give us a few minutes. Please prepare something for breakfast."

"Yes, Sir."

"Master," I corrected at the same time Ian said it.

I sighed. "Anything but Sir. I don't care for Master, either, but if that's how you see us, we'll accept it from you. But only you."

"It would be my honor, Masters."

The strange sensation that filled me remained even as Dante headed upstairs to start breakfast.

Ian paced the floor. "Look. I get it. I do. I'm a fucking goner, too, damn it. The thought of him or Everly leaving … it makes me want to punch something."

"What about Heaven?"

Ian's gaze slammed into me. "What about her?"

"You're not broken up that she wants to leave."

He shrugged. "Heaven's not…"

"What we're looking for?" I filled in.

"She's not," he agreed. "She's fun and I honestly like her, but I don't see it going anywhere. Plus, I think she's intimidated by it all."

That made sense. Those who didn't understand or, more importantly, didn't feel the need for submission, would be.

"But Everly and Dante," Ian continued, "we can't hold them here. Don't want to. I would lay down my life for them. That's not something I've ever felt for anyone but you. If they want to be here, I'll worship the fucking ground they walk on for the rest of my days. But that feeling, the need, doesn't make it so."

He resumed pacing, his footsteps heavy.

His voice was sturdy when he spoke again. "Six days, six weeks, six months. It doesn't make any difference to me. It is what it is. Relaying that information to them could be tricky. Some things require a bit more finesse."

"And some things require truth," I told him.

"Yes. I agree. But they suspect this is only about their protection. If I'm being honest, it's never been only about that. Far more. But that doesn't change the fact they're not safe at home. Yeah, they can leave. Go stay with family, friends, a hotel. They're still in a vulnerable position. Can we just slow it down a bit? Let it play out for a few more days?" He faced me. "Can you do that for me?"

I hated when he played that damn card. "Of course I will."

"Thank you." He brushed his hand over his hair. "Now can we go upstairs, have some breakfast, and enjoy the rest of our time off? I have nothing on my agenda for today." He glanced up at the ceiling. "Nothing except showing Dante and Everly exactly what we want from them. Heaven's more than welcome to participate. Or not. I don't care either way."

Well, when he put it that way...

Fifteen

Everly

THERE WAS TENSION IN THE AIR AND a lot of it.

I felt it the moment I walked into the kitchen to find Ian and Isaac sitting at the island, Dante leaning against the counter. They quieted as soon as I approached, all eyes slipping in my direction.

"Good morning," I greeted.

"Good morning, fairy princess," Isaac replied, his beautiful green gaze sliding toward me.

Before I could pass him on my way to the refrigerator, Isaac reached for me, pulling me to him. His lips pressed softly to mine, making me smile. It had been a disappointment to wake and find the bed empty. Then again, when I'd realized how late it was, I hadn't been able to hold a grudge.

"I made biscuits," Dante said when I opened the refrigerator.

He knew I loved his biscuits. "A man after my own heart," I teased.

"That heart belongs to me," Isaac stated, his tone almost teasing but not quite.

It warmed me. "My heart is most definitely yours, my Liege."

Ian's hard gaze was pinned on me, and for a second, I thought I saw something there. Longing. Need. I wasn't sure, but a response filled me. While I'd respected the distance he'd been keeping, I didn't want that. I also didn't know how to tell him as much.

Because that was a conversation better left for later, I focused my attention on buttering two biscuits and being extra generous with strawberry jam. When I turned around, I noticed all three men were still watching me.

"What?"

"You really do look like a fairy princess," Ian said with a smirk.

"Whatever." I grinned, letting his words warm me. "So, what's on the agenda today?"

"This morning belongs to you," Isaac said. "This afternoon and evening, you belong to us." His eyes shifted from me to Dante. "And you do, too."

"It would be my pleasure, Master," Dante offered, his voice lower, more sensual than usual.

My head snapped as though it was held on by rubber bands. Master? When had that happened?

That was when I noticed Dante. It was as though his entire being had transformed, from the inside out, he seemed to glow. Master. Huh. He'd finally found what he was looking for. That warmed me more than I expected, my heart seeming to swell in my chest.

I bit into my biscuit. And to think, it only took one stupid asshole to set the whole thing in motion.

"So, I have a request." Heaven's voice preceded her into the room.

"Good morning," Ian said firmly. "How about you start with that?"

"Good morning." She grinned, at the same time rolling her eyes, a move that would've gotten a submissive punishment.

I glanced at Ian then Isaac. Neither man called her on it. In fact, neither seemed to care.

"What's your request?" Ian asked as she sauntered over to the biscuits.

She turned, propped against the counter. "Would it be possible for me to get a mani/pedi today? I know that sounds like a diva, but…" She studied her fingernails.

"I'm in," I blurted, figuring solidarity couldn't hurt. And I was so on board that train.

"Of course. Find a place nearby," Ian answered, though his response seemed directed more at me. "I'll take you."

"Good." Isaac pushed to his feet, picked up a stack of papers. "Some enlightening reading material while you wait."

"What are you going to do while we're gone?" I asked, simply to give him a hard time.

His gaze swung over to Dante. "I've got a submissive to deal with."

The promise in those words was enough to get me hot and he wasn't even talking about me.

Two hours later, I was relaxing in a big leather recliner, my feet in bubbling water while a woman with skilled hands kneaded my arches, another rubbing oil into my hand and some wicked machine working up and down my back.

"What's going on with Dante?"

I looked over to see Heaven staring at me, her head resting on the back of the chair. She looked as blissed out as I felt.

"I think they've claimed him," I said, keeping my voice low, not wanting Ian to hear me.

"That's a good thing, right?"

"He seems extremely pleased."

"He does, huh?" Heaven sighed. "I've never seen a situation like that. You know. With them and Dante. And you, for that matter."

She didn't have to explain for me to know she was referring to the dynamic at Ian and Isaac's.

"Me, neither," I admitted.

"No, but you're part of that world."

That world meaning BDSM, I knew.

"You're familiar with the ins and outs. I'm lost."

"You seem to be handling yourself well."

Her eyes met mine again. Her face sobered. "It's fun. Especially after all I went through with Danny, but Everly ... the more I think about it, the weirder I feel. I'm much more suited to being with one man. But not Danny. I need a man who'll put me first always."

For whatever reason, that warmed me. For as long as I'd known Heaven, she'd been a slave to Danny and not in the fun, fetish way. He had treated her like shit time and time again, and she was always going back for more. The thought of her moving past him made me feel better. And though she wasn't interested in the dynamic that Dante and I were, perhaps it had given her more perspective.

"I really do have to leave. I don't care to stay with my sister, but I think it's important. For all of us."

I glanced over at Ian. "I get it." I met her gaze again. "I just want you to be safe."

"Oh, trust me. That's high on my list of things to do. What that guy did to Danny..." Her eyes dropped to her feet. "I talked to him, by the way. Checked on him. He's fucked up. And not just physically."

I could only imagine.

"I'm not looking to go back to him, but I care about his well-being. Call me an idiot or whatever."

"You're not an idiot," I assured her. "You're a good friend."

I looked down at my foot, realizing the woman had stopped, her full attention on our conversation. When she caught me eyeing her, she looked away.

"And just think, being free of him will allow Prince Charming to make his move. Have you talked to him lately?"

Her eyes widened. "No. He hasn't come into the store in a while."

"Well, the next time he does, perhaps you should ask him out."

"Me? Really?"

"Why not? Women are allowed to ask men out, you know."

"I know, but..."

"But nothing," I picked up. "You're single. And provided he is, what's stopping you? You could play the pretty princess to his Prince Charming. Have some fun." I lowered my voice. "Perhaps you've picked up a thing or two during your time with all of us."

Heaven laughed, a sound so loud it had Ian looking up from the papers he'd been reading.

I smiled, waved. "We're being good, I promise."

He shook his head, had that exasperated look on his face, then went back to reading.

Heaven motioned toward me, waving her hand in a circle as though encompassing my face. "This whole thing ... the sweet, innocent look you've got going ... it's a façade."

I winked at her. I could be naughty when I wanted.

"So what do you think Isaac and Dante are doing?"

I noticed the woman working on Heaven's feet look up, waiting for a response.

"Hopefully really dirty things."

Heaven laughed again. "Yeah. You keep that up. I can see punishment in your very near future."

I sighed, relaxed. "A girl can only hope."

IAN

WHILE THE GIRLS WERE FINISHING UP INSIDE, I stepped outside to return a call to my boss.

"Hey, Ransom. Checking in. What's up?"

"So, I did some digging on that guy Isaac was telling me about."

"Why aren't you calling Isaac?"

"I did. He's not answering. Figured I'd try you. Got your fucking voicemail and was about to tell you both to go to hell."

I laughed. Irritating the man was so much fun. Considering he was an instigating bastard, it made it doubly so.

"Anyway. This guy Roger Cherlish... His real name's Vernon Hathaway."

"Seriously?"

"Yeah. I know. Thirty-four years old, though his current ID shows him to be twenty-eight. Dumb ass does *not* look twenty-eight. Born and raised in Chicago, belonged to a plethora of fetish clubs over the years under numerous aliases. Most of which he was kicked out of. The guy's got a long list of priors, some of them violent crimes."

"Rape?"

"More than one, actually. And while I'm following you on that, it's not the worst of it. Attempted murder is on that list."

"How's he walking free?"

"Daddy's got a lot of money. And by a lot, I mean he makes Trent Ramsey look like a gutter rat. Appears dear old Dad spares no expense to bail his little boy out of hot spots. Called a friend of mine, had him chat up a few people who know him..." Ransom exhaled. "It gets worse."

"How?"

"When you follow the breadcrumbs, he hasn't been after Dante for three years."

"What do you mean? Dante said that's when he met him."

194

"And it probably was, but Vernon actually met Dante a long damn time ago. Back before Dante was sprung from that hellhole his father kept him caged in."

I relaxed my grip when I realized I was about to crush my cell phone. "Please don't tell me this is going where I think it's going?"

"It is." Ransom's usually playful tone disappeared completely. "He tried to buy Dante from Dante's father when Dante was ten years old. A partial payment actually exchanged hands. I'm thinking Daddy Dearest backed out at the last minute, likely what prompted the attempted murder a couple of years after that. Right about the time Dante was moved into the system."

"Holy fuck."

"Not the worst of it," Ransom warned.

"Fuck, Bishop. I don't know if I can handle any more of this shit."

"Vernon Hathaway has been a person of interest in two ongoing investigations. Both underage boys, still missing."

"Okay, yeah. That's bad. And I hope they fry this fucker, but if he's into kids, what's his fascination with Dante now?"

"Got me. Unless it's an ego thing. He wanted Dante, couldn't have him. Found an opportunity and intends to get what he believes should rightfully belong to him."

I growled.

"I've got a call in to a detective buddy of mine with Chicago PD. I'm gonna get his take on this. Once I hear back, I'll give you a shout."

"All right. Thanks, man."

"Take care of him. He can't go home, Ian. It won't be safe until this guy's locked up or dead."

At the moment, dead sounded like the best option.

When I got home, I pinned Isaac down in the basement, relayed the information Ransom had shared.

"We have to tell Dante," my brother stated.

"I agree." There was no way around it. He deserved to know what was going on.

"And the girls?" Isaac asked.

"I want to say that's up to Dante, but since this guy's attacked Everly and put Heaven's ex in the hospital, I think they deserve to know."

"I still think it's up to him. We don't know how much he's shared. It's his story to tell."

"Agreed." I nodded toward the door. "Let's sit him down."

Isaac got to his feet. "All right. But I need a drink."

"You and me both, brother."

While Isaac drowned his frustrations in two fingers of scotch, I found Dante sitting at the small desk in the guest room.

He glanced at me over his shoulder. "What's up?"

"Let's sit outside."

Wary blue eyes scanned my face. I'd been told I would make a mean poker player, and I only hoped the mask remained in place.

"I put in a call to my boss, asked for his help in identifying this Cherlish guy. Took a little doing, but he found him. Or rather he found Vernon Hathaway."

With every detail I revealed, I saw Dante retreat, slowly slipping away from us. It pissed me off, but I couldn't blame him, either. I remembered the hard hands of my father as a child. The bastard was mean, but nothing compared to Dante's father, a man who would lock his own son in the attic and consider selling him to some pedophile ... bastard hadn't deserved to have children. Hell, the bastard hadn't deserved to breathe.

"Do you know where he is?" Dante asked.

"No," I told him. "But we're still looking. I'm sure he's stalking your house. He knows you and the girls disappeared, but he won't know where."

"So what do we do now?

NICOLE EDWARDS

My brother's eyes shot up to my face beneath his lashes. I knew what he wanted, but now was not the time to approach that subject. It would come in time.

"I know what I've got planned," Isaac said, setting his glass on the table. "And it doesn't involve memories or pain or any of this bullshit." His hand fisted, released.

"Do the girls know?" Dante's eyes shifted from my face to Isaac's.

"Nay," I assured him. "It's your story to tell. If and when … the situation changes … you can decide what to share with them."

"Thank you, Master."

I walked over to him, tipped back his head, and stared down into his handsome face. "You're safe with us."

His eyes implored me, the hope that was there strong enough to steal my breath.

"We won't let that bastard touch you again. Understood?"

There was a breathless quality to his voice this time. "Yes, Master."

I offered a wicked smile, wanting to divert his thoughts. Remove this pain from his past. At least for a little while.

"We're going to scene this afternoon," I explained to Dante as I stepped away, heading toward the door.

Isaac pulled out a folded sheet of paper, passed it over to Dante.

"When you're ready, we'll be waiting."

"Yes, Masters."

I headed inside, ready and eager for something to shift the mood around this place.

And I knew exactly where to find it.

Sixteen

Dante

WHEN IAN AND ISAAC WENT IN THE house, I opened the thin sheet of paper, smiled down at the tidy handwriting as I read the instructions.

PRETTY RICH BOY COMES HOME TO FIND TWO SASSY LITTLE MAIDS IN THE HOUSE.
HE DECIDES TO HAVE A PARTY.
JUST THE THREE OF THEM.

In order for this to play out in any way, I knew the girls had to be in on it. Luckily, no trips to the attic were necessary to locate them. They were sitting in one of the other guest rooms, on the bed, grinning as they relaxed against the pillows.

I smiled when Everly invited me in.

"What's up, handsome?" Heaven asked, grinning.

"We've been summoned."

Everly knew exactly what that meant, but Heaven's confusion was almost amusing. Her attention darted between us.

"What's that mean?" she asked, her pitch a little higher than before. "Summoned?"

"It means we're going to … play."

"Oh." Her eyes widened, but she didn't look happy.

"Come on," Everly urged. "Consider it a going-away party. Some fun memories to reflect on when you're having long, drawn-out conversations with your sister."

Heaven relaxed, even smiled as her eyes bounced back and forth between the two of us. "Okay, yes. I'll give it a shot. What do we do?"

I passed over the note, waited for them both to read it. Everly's breath caught, her eyes glittering with excitement.

A knock sounded behind me. I turned as Ian stepped into the room carrying two flat white boxes, both adorned with a wide red ribbon. "These just came."

He set them on the bed, grinned, but didn't say anything more.

As though the woman had never received a gift in her life, Heaven was up on her knees, staring at the boxes as though they were the most precious things in the world.

"Open 'em," I said, nodding. I figured I needed to know what I was walking into, right?

Heaven tore into the box that had a sterling silver H dangling from the ribbon.

"Oh … uh … these are maids' outfits."

"Yeah?" Everly giggled. "You see a lot of maids wearing skirts that don't cover their ass?"

"In porn, sure." She laughed, the sound musical.

"I'll leave you to it," I told them with a wink. "This pretty rich boy's got to get into character."

"I can't wait," Everly said softly, meeting my gaze.

While they giggled and cooed over the outfits, I made the trek to the other side of the house. Ian and Isaac were nowhere in sight, just as I'd expected. They hadn't laid out how they would work into the equation, but I figured that was going to be the interesting part.

But something told me all of our wicked fantasies were about to play out.

THEIR *Fairy* PRINCESS

I decided on a shower. I'd already taken one that morning, but I needed another. The information Ian had given me had left a coat of filth on my skin. I fought back the memories of Roger, the vile things he'd done to me. In my nightmares, I often saw his hands, only they weren't human in my dreams. They were demonic: thick red skin, long, pointed nails. Definitely the stuff of nightmares. But here, in the bright light of day, I knew he wasn't part of me, not in any way, and I damn sure wouldn't let him intrude now.

It took a minute to clear my head, but the warm water managed to wash the fog from my brain. I replaced those evil memories with thoughts of how this would play out.

I pulled on a pair of shorts, a T-shirt, opted to go without shoes. I wasn't quite sure what a rich boy's wardrobe looked like, but I figured that didn't matter a whole lot in this scenario.

I opened my bedroom door so I could hear the girls when they came in. When I heard Everly's lyrical laugh, I went to the hallway, watched as they moved around the living room, chatting away. Everly was right. I seriously doubted those outfits were anything a maid worth her salt would wear. The halter accentuated Everly's beautiful breasts, while the teeny-tiny skirt barely covered her cute little ass. Her midriff was bare, and I suddenly wished Ian and Isaac would find a way to have her wear something similar on a daily basis.

The thought made me smile.

Heaven danced around the room, teasing the tops of the furniture with a feather duster, though I knew she wouldn't find a speck of dirt. The maids who actually knew how to clean had come and gone, efficiently covering every inch of this place earlier that morning. But the girls were doing a good job of setting the scene.

I went to the refrigerator, grabbed a bottle of water while they continued the ruse in the other room.

"Who are these people, anyway?" Heaven asked, still chattering away.

Everly turned. "I don't know, but have you seen the son?"

"Who is he?"

I fought the urge to laugh, realizing they were seriously in character, chatting about the pretend rich boy.

"Don't know, but he's hot." The dreamy look on Everly's face had me believing she based that on her true feelings. It warmed me inside.

"Well, well, well." I propped my shoulder against the wall, eyed them with heated interest as I turned the water bottle cap between my fingers. "What have we here?"

"We just need a few more minutes, sir," Heaven said, almost dismissively, before she looked over, paused. Her eyes sparked with heat and interest.

"Don't mind me," I told them, walking into the living room and flopping down on the sofa, ensuring they saw me ogling them. Granted, my attention was more focused on Everly, but in an effort to set the scene, I included Heaven every now and again. I happened to enjoy role-playing. Mainly because it allowed me to get out of my own head for a while. Gave me a chance to explore the world in ways I'd never done before.

Everly went with the shy, innocent demeanor, something a lot of people assumed about her.

Granted, she looked the part, was incredibly sweet, but there was a hellcat underneath the facade, one who knew what she wanted and didn't care who knew. She was secure in her own skin, knew her self-worth. I appreciated that about her.

Heaven, on the other hand, had self-doubts cast on her by that asshole of an ex-boyfriend. I'd watched the guy belittle her with words disguised as jokes. She often let them roll off, but I'd seen how they hurt her. A few times, I'd wanted to punch the guy, but it hadn't been my place. I wondered, as I sat there, why I'd ever thought that. Heaven was my friend. She deserved people to take care of her.

Everly moved around the room, stopped directly in front of me to lean over the coffee table, gave it a slow swipe with the feather duster. My eyes locked on her ass, peeking out from beneath that skirt.

I reached up, allowed my hand to brush the back of her thigh. Rather than play the role of shock and dismay, she tossed her hair over her shoulder, gave me a heated look.

"You're a naughty boy, aren't you?" Her voice was low, seductive.

"Don't forget lonely," I teased, continuing to eye her exposed skin.

"Aww. You poor thing. What's a boy to do left all alone in this big house?"

I smirked. "I can think of a few things."

"Yeah?" She stood, walked past, her leg brushing mine. "It has been a long day."

Heaven, dusting a high shelf on the entertainment center, stared back at us.

"What about you?" I asked her.

"What about me?" Her words were whisper-soft, hesitant, not in tune with her character.

"You need a little relaxation time?"

She grinned, her lashes fluttering. "What did you have in mind?"

I nodded toward the backyard. "I've got a pool. Maybe you'd like to get … wet."

Everly played coy. "We didn't bring swimsuits."

"No clothing allowed," I told them.

Heaven walked around behind the sofa, her nail grazing my shoulder. "Are you suggesting we get naked?"

I gave a casual shrug. "Up to you."

In a bold move that I'd come to expect from Everly, she came over, forced the foot I had propped on my knee to the floor before she straddled my legs.

"What's in it for us?"

"I can think of a few things," I said, smirking up at her, all that silky hair falling like a curtain around us.

Her hands slid over my chest, her lips hovering just above mine. More hands glided over my chest as Heaven stood behind me.

"What do you think?" Everly looked up at Heaven.

"I wouldn't mind getting wet," she teased, her lips brushing my ear.

Yeah, these two feisty women could pull off this whole seductive maid thing.

And I was about to see just how far they'd be willing to take it.

Heaven

WHEN DANTE FIRST SHOWED US THE NOTE, I'd thought they were joking. Pretty rich boy. Maids. Who thought up this stuff? Other than porn writers?

However, based on the seduction routine taking place right now, I could tell they weren't joking.

Nope. Not even a little.

The gleam in Everly's eyes had told me that my sweet, innocent friend was excited to see how this played out. Initially, I'd considered hiding out in my room, but Everly had a way of persuading me to do things I wouldn't normally do. And this was certainly at the top of that not-in-a-million-years-would-I-ever-do-that list.

Yet here I was.

Since I had an out in sight—I was leaving tomorrow—I couldn't help but give in to that secret inner urge to indulge.

THEIR *Fairy* PRINCESS

While we'd dressed, Everly had given me suggestions, telling me to enjoy it. It was make-believe after all. We didn't have to be our usual selves; we could be anyone we wanted to be. Since I'd never done anything of this nature, I had followed her lead. The instant I saw the heated look on Dante's face, I knew this was a role I wanted to explore. After all, how often did a girl get to step into someone else's skin to play out someone else's fantasies?

I grinned. Probably quite often in this house.

Dante got to his feet, Everly sliding her arm through his as she stared up at him dreamily. That wasn't an act, I knew.

I fell into step, leaving the feather duster behind.

Practically molding herself to Dante's side, Everly smiled up at him. "I might need a little help getting out of this uniform."

Not missing a beat, he peered over at me. "Perhaps you could help her with that."

Breath lodged in my throat. I might not be versed in this sexy, wicked world of theirs, but I wasn't naïve, either. I knew what he was hinting at.

"Only if you watch," I told him, sliding my hand over his forearm.

"It would be my pleasure."

Funny, he was pulling off this role quite well. Almost as though he'd been born for it. Maybe every guy had a fantasy of seeing two women touching one another.

Dante stepped away, taking a seat, his eyes never leaving us. We were standing on the patio, the sun beating down overhead. It was broad daylight, and though the backyard felt private, I knew anyone could watch if they were determined enough.

Since Everly had taken the lead thus far, I decided it was my turn to flex my acting chops. I walked around behind her, slowly sliding her hair over one shoulder, letting my fingernail graze her neck. She tilted her head to the side as I reached for the tie on the halter.

"Take your time," Dante instructed, his voice an octave deeper than usual.

I fluttered my lashes, following his rules. I worked the knot free, trailed my fingers down to the clasp on her back. I stepped in close, my hips pressing to her butt as I flipped the catch open. Rather than let the fabric fall to the floor, I reached around, holding it to her breasts, cupping them in the process. Her skin was so soft, a stark contrast to what I was used to.

Everly leaned back against me, her hands covering mine, urging me to tease. The whole point was to give Dante a show, so we did. I slid my hands over Everly's breasts, releasing the fabric and allowing her warm skin to fill my hands. She inhaled sharply, her desire apparent. I continued the same treatment down her hips, moving to the zipper on the back of the skirt. I slid it down, allowed the black silk to flutter down her legs and pool at her feet. She stood there in all her naked glory and I could see the approval in Dante's eyes.

"Your turn," Everly rasped, turning in my arms. She glanced at my mouth briefly, then walked around me, a seduction playing out in broad daylight.

I didn't bother hiding my reaction to having her hands on me. I'd thought about it plenty of times. I wasn't a prude. And though Danny never understood my sexual desires, I knew that wasn't the case here. They wouldn't ostracize me for it. In fact, they would embrace it. Me.

"God, you're beautiful," Everly whispered, her words only for me.

Her praise warmed me from the inside out. When her arms came around me, her soft hands cupping my naked breasts, my knees wobbled only slightly.

Yeah. This was happening. Not because someone was directing it, either. It was happening because somewhere deep down, Everly and I wanted it to happen.

I didn't have to see them to know Ian and Isaac were watching. I could feel their eyes on us, taking it all in, seeing how it would play out. They were the puppeteers, putting this in motion, but it was our desires that would shape the role. It was a high I'd never experienced, one I'd never even considered.

And while nothing would convince me that this was something I could enjoy day in and day out, in this moment I was able to indulge myself, to let loose.

My skirt fluttered to the concrete and I looked up at Dante. He was watching us, his eyes slowly raking over Everly from head to toe. His attraction to her was potent. In fact, all the males in this house were quite transparent when it came to Everly. And while I didn't want their attention, per se, I did find myself craving someone's. My thoughts drifted to Prince Charming, as I'd come to refer to the man who'd graced the bookstore a few times. Truth was, I didn't know his name, but I'd been lusting after the guy for quite some time. He was shy, though. As I tried to picture him in this scenario, I smiled.

Everly cleared her throat, yanking me out of the fantasy.

"I think it's your turn, Mr. Novak," I told Dante, taking Everly's hand and walking toward him.

He got to his feet as we approached. I took his front, Everly his back. We worked slowly, efficiently to get him out of the T-shirt. I allowed my hands to glide over his hot, smooth skin. Over his well-defined pecs, the rippling lines of his abs. He was beautiful. I'd always thought so. Slightly damaged but still beautiful. Inside and out.

Since I knew where his true interest lay, I eased myself out of the scenario, allowed Everly to take over from there. As she crouched before him to work his shorts down his legs, Dante's eyes lasered in on her, hot, fierce.

But Everly didn't tease him, choosing to casually brush her hand over his long, hard length before standing tall once more.

"I think it's time to cool off," he said softly, leaning toward Everly, his mouth inches from hers, their bodies swaying as though gravity was drawing them together.

"I couldn't agree more," she whispered.

He took our hands, padded over to the pool, then led the way down the steps. The other day, we'd come out here, laughing, splashing. Friends enjoying an afternoon in the water. This time, we were lovers. A slow seduction born from role-playing set up by two wicked Doms.

My gaze scanned the back windows of the house, pausing on the two men standing in the kitchen, observing as it all played out. I wondered if this was how they'd envisioned it going or if they'd had something else in mind.

Knowing they would change the course if and when they saw fit, I decided to let it play out until then.

Everly dipped beneath the water, slicking her hair back when she surfaced. Dante reached for her then, pulling Everly into him as he waded into deeper water. His eyes were hot, focused on her mouth. I was awestruck by the sight of them. Even as Everly dipped beneath the water again, surfacing moments later. Before she could take one full breath, his mouth slowly covered hers. The kiss was soft, sweet, but the underlying passion was unmistakable.

Dante pulled back, his thumb brushing over her cheek as their eyes locked. "You're beautiful, Everly."

Yeah, I longed for the day a man said that to me. And meant it.

While there was a hint of envy coursing through me, I wasn't bothered by it. In fact, I was glad to see these two coming together. They'd been fighting it for so long. And after everything they'd endured, I figured they deserved it.

Just when I thought they would separate, Dante's hand cupped her butt, jerking her to him as though he couldn't resist any longer.

The kiss ignited, a passionate blaze that the water had no chance of dousing. Dante held Everly's body in that moment, but there was another part of her that Dante held even if he would never understand it. A part of Everly that belonged only to him. As a friend, a lover. It didn't matter. He was special to her in so many ways, and this moment, this opportunity they had to explore was far past due.

So while they made out, I settled for admiring them. Happy for my friends.

And secretly hopeful that I'd find my own happily ever after one day.

$\mathcal{S}$eventeen

ISAAC

"No mistaking their chemistry," Ian mumbled from where he stood beside me.

"Or how much they care about one another."

"Aye."

Hands in my pockets, I stared out the window into the sparkling blue pool, observing the two submissives who'd embraced the scene better than I'd expected.

I should've known. Everly was one of the few submissives I'd ever wanted for more than a single scene. At the club, it never mattered what we asked of her—within her limits, of course—she was always willing and eager to oblige. It wasn't an act on her part. I'd seen it with some submissives. They were more than willing to pretend they'd go as far as a Dom wanted, but when it came down to it, they balked, tried to top from the bottom.

Not my sweet fairy princess. She was the real deal, which likely helped to explain the powerful feelings I'd developed for her.

"He's opening up to her," I mentioned.

"Finally. I wonder just how long they've been playing this game."

"Too long."

"We haven't been fair to him. We've held back."

I could hear the disappointment in my twin's voice, felt his regret. "Maybe. But now that we know, we can give him everything he needs."

Ian chuckled. "Right now, I think he needs to have Everly bouncing up and down on him."

It hadn't surprised me that Everly and Dante had focused on one another. Even Heaven had recognized the passion they shared. I'd seen the moment she accepted it, stepped back to allow them to explore. Quite frankly, I was surprised she was participating. But not at all disappointed. In this particular scene, the more the merrier.

I grinned at Ian's crude remark. "I'm certainly looking forward to watching."

"Think we should go out there?"

I shook my head. "We'll wait for them to come inside. Dante won't take her out there."

"No?" Ian looked over at me.

I kept my focus on the three of them. "No. He wants us with him. Needs our verbal instruction. Our permission."

Dante understood us on some level, the same as we understood him.

"Everly told Heaven to consider this a going-away party. I'm curious to see just how far this party will go."

By that, I knew Ian meant he was hoping to see the two women together. No doubt it would be a delicious encounter to witness. More so because I didn't think Everly would ever consider it with anyone else.

"They'll explore. And it won't require our intervention."

I'd watched them undressing one another. There was interest there. An almost innocent allure. They wanted to explore, and here, they knew they could pursue it without repercussion.

"If this ... turns into something more—"

"No if. It will. It already has," I told Ian.

"Fine. *When* this turns into more, how do you see that working?"

By that, I knew my brother was referring to the fact that we'd never considered taking a male submissive. Certainly not one who needed his space.

"It'll work itself out," I told him.

I wanted Everly with every ounce of my being. Her whole heart, not only pieces of it. However, I knew her heart was big enough for me to share with Ian and Dante. Beyond love and affection, her soul had connected with mine. It belonged to me and me alone. I would cherish that, ensure that she knew it, too.

"I do enjoy watching his hands on Everly," Ian muttered. "The way he touches her, as though she's a gift."

It was the way Dante saw everything, I figured. He had all the reason in the world to have built hatred around his heart, to have used the anger at what had been done to him to do harm to others. But he hadn't. Beneath all the wounds, there was a pure soul that needed what we could give him. And I had no doubt, it would take all three of us to keep him whole.

"Care to predict where they'll go from here?" Ian inquired, his tone lighter.

"Living room," I said without having to think about it. "They're exhibitionists. They want us to watch."

Especially my fairy princess. She wanted me with her, even if I wasn't right there.

"Thoughts on dinner?"

"Chinese. We'll let them eat when they come in."

"Ah, naked dining in the living room. I like how your mind works."

I chuckled, turned to him. "It works exactly like yours does."

"That it does."

Ian sauntered off to place the food order, but I remained where I was, observing. I was a voyeur by nature, and this was the playground I'd always dreamed of having, never truly believing I would find it. There'd been no coaxing on my part. Or Ian's. This had come together on its own and I intended to do everything in my power to ensure it remained intact.

Everly turned in Dante's arms, her back to his chest and I could feel her. She knew I was here even if she couldn't see me. This was as much for me as it was for them. Tonight, I would have her all to myself, and even if my brother didn't agree with it, I intended to show her exactly what she meant to me.

An hour later, the food was delivered. A few minutes after that, the frolicking threesome came inside. While we remained out of sight for the moment, I could see everything they were doing. Heard Heaven's excitement that there was food. As a way of encouraging the outcome, we'd put it in the living room, hoping they'd follow the lead.

"Feeding us, Mr. Novak?" Everly teased, curling into the sofa, a carton of food in her hand, chopsticks her method of both eating and animating her conversation.

"Have to ensure you have the energy to"—he smirked—"keep up with me."

I admired the blush that heightened his color. Dante was a spectacular man, there was no doubt about that. And I was falling. Hard.

"Oh, I don't think that'll be a problem," Heaven rasped.

As they sat there, eating and talking, I watched Dante. He was relaxed, smiling, something I hadn't seen much from him. Yeah, Ian was right, we hadn't been fair to him. However, there'd been too many missing pieces and the last thing I ever wanted to do was inflict pain when there was the potential to avoid it. Had I taken him without knowing his history, I would've done more harm than good.

Heaven bounced to her feet, taking their discarded cartons to the kitchen. Rather than set them out of the way, she disposed of them appropriately, ensuring the kitchen was clean before she joined them once more.

"Come here," Dante told her when she returned.

"I took care of cleaning up, Mr. Novak. Wouldn't want you to get in any trouble."

And there was our cue.

"Trouble?" he laughed. "What makes you think I'd get in any trouble?" He motioned around the room, pulling off the arrogant rich boy persona to a T. "I'm the king of this castle."

Ian stepped into the room. "Is that right?"

As though she'd really been busted by some authority figure, Everly squealed, covering her nakedness with her arms.

Heaven tried to slip behind Dante, her eyes wary as she watched Ian walk toward them.

"Who is he?" Heaven whispered loudly, speaking to Dante.

I joined my brother, keeping my hands in the pockets of my slacks and scoping out the scene.

"Who are you?" Heaven asked, her eyes darting over to me.

"You want to tell them, Dante?" I prompted. "Or should I?"

His eyes glazed. "They're my Masters."

Heaven pulled back from him, glaring. "Your what? Who says stuff like that?"

God, she was cute.

"I think the more important question is, who are you?" Ian asked. "And what exactly are you doing naked in my living room?"

"We... We were ... uh..." Everly played the demure virgin. "We were working, Sir. Uh ... then we took a break."

"Working?" Ian glanced back at me before returning his attention to her. "Are you whores?"

"As if," Heaven snapped. "We're maids. We were cleaning."

I raised my eyebrows. "Cleaning what?"

Everly's eyes cut to the pile of clothes on the floor. "We should ... uh ... probably be going."

"Are you finished with the job?" Ian asked.

"No, Sir. Not yet. But we can finish," she said in a hurry, putting one foot on the floor as though she was going to make a beeline for her clothes.

I removed the temptation for her, kicking them out of the way.

"Since you're keen on being naked, perhaps you should finish the job like that."

She got to her feet, not quite sure how to cover herself completely. Her arms crossed over herself once, twice, then she gave up and dropped them to her sides. With her cute little chin tipped up, she walked over to the feather duster, picked it up.

I took the spot she had vacated on the sofa while Ian walked around, gripped Heaven's arm, and gave her a gentle nudge. "Go on. Pretend we're not even here."

Dante moved to the center cushion, sitting stiffly between us, his hands covering his erection.

"Decided to have a party while we were gone, huh?" Ian asked him.

"No, Master. It was... We were..."

I kept my eyes on Everly. "Does your employer know you offer naked cleaning services?"

She swallowed hard. "We don't, Sir. We... This is the first time."

"Is that so? And we're the lucky ones to watch you work?"

"Yes, Sir."

"Well, I'd like to see what I'm paying for." I motioned toward a lower shelf. "I think you missed a spot."

Her cheeks turned a perfect rosy pink. "Yes, Sir."

"Slowly," I instructed.

In a sassy move, Everly bent at the waist, spread her legs and took a generous amount of time to swipe the imaginary dust from the bottom shelf, her pretty pussy on full display.

"Very nice," Ian crooned. "And you? Care to show us what we're spending our money on?"

Heaven covered her breasts with her arm. "Actually, Sir. I… It's not really in my job description."

"Neither is seducing our property," I bit out.

Her eyes widened. "Your property?" She frowned. "How can you let them call you that?" Her eyes shot back to mine. "I can't believe you could degrade him like that."

I shifted, crossed one ankle over my knee. "Degrade? How is that degrading?"

"You don't … *own* him. No one can own him."

"But we do," Ian said simply, as though no explanation was necessary. "And since we're paying for this … extra service … perhaps you should do your job thoroughly."

"I'm sorry, Sir," Heaven said. "I'm not sure I understand."

Ian raked his gaze over Dante. "He looks like a dirty boy to me." His eyes returned to them. "Perhaps you can use your talents to clean him up."

Everly swallowed hard, her nipples puckered. "If that's what you'd like, Sir."

She was trying to remain in role, but she craved this part, wanted us to take the reins.

"It's exactly what we want," I assured her, speaking nothing but the truth.

Everly

FROM THE INSTANT THEY STEPPED INTO THE room, my blood started a heavy churn in my veins, heat pooling between my thighs. I'd enjoyed the role-playing so far, loved making out with Dante in the pool, but this … *this* was what I'd been hoping for all along.

"What are you waiting for?" Ian snapped. "Move the table out of the way."

"Yes, Sir," I said timidly, sticking to the role.

215

I hurried over and, with Heaven's help, moved the heavy coffee table to the far side of the room.

Isaac tossed one of the throw pillows toward the middle of the room. "Lie down," he commanded Dante. "On your back."

Dante's dark eyes were glazed over, his chiseled features reflecting the enjoyment he was getting from this scene.

"You," Ian snapped at Heaven. "Start with his cock."

"I'm sorry, what?" she asked, haughtily. "That is most certainly *not* in my job description."

"It wasn't a request."

Her eyes widened, but she moved toward Dante.

"No. Stay on that side. I want to watch every move you make, see every flick of your tongue."

Heaven glared at him but didn't say a word.

"You," Isaac spoke directly to me. "You can straddle his face."

I feigned affront, taking in a sharp breath as though I couldn't believe he'd ask for something like that.

"Again, not a request," Ian stated, his tone dark, commanding.

"Yes, Sir." I hurried over, stood above Dante's head.

"Facing us," Isaac added.

I turned toward them, my feet on either side of Dante's head. Lowering myself to my knees, I straddled his face. His warm breath tickled my sensitive flesh. I didn't expect him to move, so I tried to hide my reaction when his hands slid up over my thighs, widening my knees as he lifted his head and licked me.

My head fell back, the sensation overriding my thoughts.

"What are you waiting for?" Ian barked at Heaven. "His cock."

While Dante licked and teased me, Heaven took his cock into her mouth. She was hesitant, and I knew that had nothing to do with role-playing. This would be stepping over a line in their friendship, and it was obvious Heaven was considering that. She obviously came to terms with it, because, within seconds, she was paying careful attention to his cock, her soft moans a verbal acknowledgment of her approval.

Ian and Isaac remained silent for long minutes. I fought the building tension, not wanting to come without permission. Since I'd played with them numerous times, I knew that was a requirement for them. Coming without their consent would most definitely result in punishment. The thought of Isaac spanking me, like he'd done numerous times in the past, nearly sent me over the edge.

"Looks to me like the maids have missed their calling," Ian muttered crudely, laughing.

Heaven's head shot up, her hand fisting Dante's cock.

"Stop one more time and you'll be eating pussy rather than sucking dick."

Her mouth opened, closed, before she took Dante in her mouth once more as though the idea of the former was beyond conception.

"Perhaps she's seeking a little pleasure of her own," Isaac mused, his tone cool, unaffected by the erotic scene in front of him.

"Good point," Ian agreed. He tossed a condom toward her. "Put it on him, then climb on."

Heaven lifted her head slowly. Her eyes scanned Dante's prone form, her attention snagged by what he was doing between my thighs. When she lifted her head to look at me, I saw the curiosity, but there was something else. Doubt. Uncertainty. We'd pushed her today. Having never been in this position, she wasn't sure whether she wanted to proceed.

"It's okay," I told her, pretending I was still in character. I held out my hand to her. When she took it, I tugged her closer. Kissed her. Softly, soothingly. "You can stop this at any time."

She pulled back, stared in my eyes. "I know."

I nodded, comforted by her acknowledgement.

When she went to work rolling the condom on Dante, I glanced over at Isaac, saw his nod of approval.

"Reverse cowgirl," Ian commanded before Heaven could straddle Dante's hips.

From where I was, I got a front row view of Dante's cock sliding inside her. They both moaned as she sank down on him, his tongue pausing for a moment.

Ian was on his feet, walking around to stand in front of Heaven. He unbuttoned his slacks, lowered the zipper, then freed his huge cock.

"Let's see how you do with two at once," he mumbled, his hand gentle as it slid into her hair.

I glanced over at Isaac. He crooked his finger at me, signaling me over. I didn't hesitate. He was already freeing his cock. "Sit on me. Facing them."

I turned, my pussy clenching with anticipation. I wanted to feel him inside me. No, I'd go so far as to say it was pure need that drove me. I mounted him, sank down. His arms came around me, pulling me back against him. He held me in place, making it impossible to move. Then he rocked his hips, driving his cock impossibly deep inside me.

"Watch them, fairy princess."

His accent was thicker than before, the sexy lilt of Ireland drifting off his tongue. It spiked my lust. His hand dipped between my legs, his thumb skillfully teasing my clit while I watched Dante, Heaven, and Ian.

Dante was sitting up, his arms wrapped around Heaven as she rode him, her mouth wrapped around Ian's cock. They were double-teaming her, and she was moaning softly, her beautiful body owned by them. I could feel their pleasure, see the way both men cared for her while still taking all they needed.

My body tightened, my pussy clenching as my orgasm crested, shattering me without my consent. Or Isaac's.

"Ahh, fairy princess," Isaac rumbled in my ear. "You know what that means."

"Yes, my Liege. I deserve your punishment."

"And you'll get it." His voice was a dark promise. "But first you'll come for me again."

He drove me to orgasm three more times, my body vibrating, an almost painful lethargy taking over. It was more than I could handle, but he didn't seem to care.

"One more time, love. This time I'll be right there with you."

His thumb circled my sensitive clit, his cock filling me, stretching me as I lifted and lowered, eager to feel his release.

"Sweet girl, swallow me," Ian barked as his body jerked.

Heaven stilled momentarily, swallowing his cum.

When Ian pulled out of her mouth, he brushed his knuckles down her cheek. "Now take yours."

He tucked his cock away, his attention never wavering as Heaven repositioned, facing Dante. He lay back at her urging. His arms circled her, their mouths crushing together. Dante fucked her, driving up into her in a rhythm that matched Isaac's. I watched, entranced.

"Come for me, fairy princess," Isaac growled in my ear. "Right fucking now."

He slammed up into me, the force so powerful it triggered another release that drained me completely.

With me limp in his arms, Isaac got to his feet, carried me down the hall to his bedroom. Rather than dump me on the bed, as I'd hoped, he carried me into the bathroom. We showered together, his hands working over me, making me sigh in contentment. When he was finished cleaning us both, he dried me off, then himself.

"Are you tired?"

"Yes, my Liege."

"Well, then, once we've taken care of your punishment, you shall sleep."

My nipples perked up at the reminder. Although Isaac wasn't the sort of Dom who focused much on punishment, he would certainly dish it out when it was warranted. And based on experience, I knew he would not go easy on me simply because I was tired.

"On the bed," he said, smacking my ass gently. "Face down, ass up."

"Yes, my Liege."

I heard him opening a drawer, closing it, even as I crawled up into his enormous bed, pressed my chest to the fluffy comforter, leaving my ass in the air. Would he use a paddle? Or his hand? He'd used both on me before and was never consistent.

Something cool trickled down the crack of my ass and I flinched, then settled. It was lubricant and I knew exactly what my devious Dom was doing. Not only was he going to spank me, he was going to stretch my ass for his own pleasure.

"This one's bigger than the last," he said. He could've been talking about the weather, not warning me that the butt plug was going to cause me discomfort.

"Thank you, my Liege."

I sucked in a breath when he teased my asshole with his fingers, pushing in deep, slow. He scissored his fingers before pulling them out. The pressure from the plug was intense, but I forced myself to relax, wanting to please him.

When he had it inserted, he smacked my ass, making me yelp.

I heard footsteps, followed by water in the bathroom. A moment later, he returned.

"Now, for your punishment, fairy princess."

He was silent for a moment.

"Please, my Liege. Please punish me for coming without permission."

He squeezed my butt cheek in approval.

The smack that landed a second later made me scream. The leather paddle stung more than I'd expected, heat blooming instantly. Another landed a second after that, this time on the other cheek. He hadn't told me how many I'd earned, but when we passed five, I knew I would be crying before it was over.

I understood punishment, appreciated it even. It wasn't meant to feel good, and it didn't, but I would endure because I had earned it.

When he landed the eleventh blow, I sobbed in earnest, but I didn't beg him to stop. On fifteen, my ass felt as though it was blistered, the pain more intense than anything I'd ever felt.

But when Isaac climbed into bed with me, pulling me into his arms, I went willingly, holding on to him even as tears continued to streak down my face. They weren't from the pain at that point. They were emotions draining out me, the things I bottled up without knowing. He'd informed me of that one time and I had never thought about it that way. But it made sense.

"Sleep, fairy princess. I'll wake you in a bit."

"My Liege?" I mumbled, exhaustion pulling me under.

"What, love?"

"I love you," I whispered, then gave myself over to sleep.

Eighteen

IAN

As we stood in the shower, Heaven leaned back against me. I soaped her hair, rinsed it, never moving from where I was. I kissed her neck as I filled my hands with body wash, then coated every inch of her with the sweet-smelling stuff she liked.

While I was sated enough to sleep, I'd figured it was more important to spend time with Heaven. Not because I needed it but because she had just indulged in a rather intense scene. Processing the emotions it might've unlocked was as important as the scene itself.

She turned in my arms and I couldn't resist kissing her, cupping her smooth face, enjoying the way her soft hands slid over my back.

"Why don't you get dressed," I murmured. "I'll finish up here, then we'll grab something to eat."

"Oh, thank God," she groaned. "I'm starving."

I laughed as she trotted out, snatching a towel.

"I didn't eat nearly enough earlier and ... well, I need to get my strength back."

I rinsed my hair, opened my eyes, and realized she was staring at me as she patted the moisture from her hair.

"What?" I asked, turning to face the spray and wash my face.

"Nothing. I just like looking at you."

She made me smile. The sweet tenor of her voice, her chipper attitude. Had I not been head over heels for Everly, perhaps I could've come to care about Heaven. Thankfully, I didn't get the impression she was developing feelings for any of us. Quite the opposite, actually. I'd felt her detachment the entire time she'd been here. And sure, she was willingly exploring her own sexuality, but doing so without consequence. Based on what she'd told me of the douchebag ex-boyfriend, that had never been an option before.

I shut off the water, grabbed a towel, and stared off into space.

"If you don't hurry, I'm going to eat without you."

I pulled myself out of my thoughts and smiled. "Go on. I'll be there in a minute."

"If you insist," she said in a singsong voice. "But I'm going to cook if that's all right."

"It's fine."

She blew me a kiss, again making me laugh before she danced out of the room.

I took my time getting dressed. When I stepped out into the hallway, I heard a scream come from Isaac's room. A loud smack and another scream followed. I smiled. My brother was dishing out the punishment. One thing he didn't tolerate was coming without permission. That, and he knew it was one of the easiest restrictions for a dutiful submissive to break.

Figuring they would join us when they were finished, I headed to the kitchen. Heaven was moving around, grabbing things from the refrigerator and pantry.

"I'm making pork chops and potatoes au gratin," she announced. "It'll be a little while."

"I'm going to check on Dante," I told her.

Her face flushed as she muttered, "Good idea."

She turned away quickly.

"Uh-uh. Don't try to hide from me. What's on your mind?" I stepped around the island, stopped her frantic movements by taking her wrists, holding them still.

"Nothing."

"Your cheeks are pink. I don't think that's nothing."

She shrugged.

"Talk to me."

Her eyes met mine, her glare cute. She didn't like that I was bulldogging her about this.

"Fine," Heaven said with a temperamental huff. "I'm embarrassed, okay?"

"First of all, there's nothing to be embarrassed about." I lowered my voice. "You were beautiful."

More color highlighted her cheeks.

"Why are you embarrassed?"

She glanced around us, probably ensuring we didn't have an audience. "I'm embarrassed because I had sex with my friend. And I enjoyed it."

"Enjoyed what?" I stood tall, took a step back, and leaned against the counter.

"All of it." She suddenly found the floor fascinating.

"Look at me, Heaven. Talk to me. What did you enjoy about it?"

"All of it. The role-playing … I liked being able to escape from my own head. Be someone else for a little while. The frisky maid." She smiled shyly.

"Do you regret participating?"

"You mean do I regret fucking Dante?"

"Yes. How was it? Fucking Dante while I had my cock in your mouth?"

She flushed, looked away instantly. Goddamn, she was cute.

"I liked it."

"And when Everly kissed you? Tried to pull you back from the edge?"

I hadn't missed that part, the way Everly took charge, giving Heaven the assurance that she could put a stop to it whenever she wanted.

"I didn't know what to expect going into it. But … I can certainly see the appeal."

"You know you don't have to be in the lifestyle to enjoy role-playing," I told her. "It'll spice up any vanilla relationship."

"I've never met a man who's interested in stuff like that."

"But you will," I encouraged.

"That's my plan, anyway."

I stepped forward, took her hands, separated them, then held them to my chest. "Heaven, you're a beautiful woman. Inside and out. There's a man out there who can dedicate himself to you fully. And when you meet him, you'll know."

"I kinda wish it could be you," she said softly.

I shook my head. "No you don't."

Heaven's grin was slow and genuine. "You're right. I don't. I see what's going on here, and though it's been fun, it's not for me. I mean, being with Isaac… That was … weird. Good weird, maybe, but still weird."

"It's all relative," I told her. "For us, it's normal."

"Why didn't you watch us? When I was with Isaac?"

"I don't want to watch you with my brother."

"Why not?"

This was a little more difficult to explain. "It's not the voyeuristic aspect I enjoy when it comes to my brother. I don't need to see my submissive with Isaac. I get off knowing she's with him. That he's indulging in what belongs to me. That he's giving her pleasure and she's taking it, giving it in return."

"Is it the same for him? When you're with Everly?"

"Yes."

I could see the next question already forming, knew what was coming, still I waited for it.

"Do you … do you like being with Everly?"

She held my gaze, as though my answer was important.

"Very much," I admitted.

"Why?"

I'd known that was coming, too.

She must've taken my pause as a refusal to answer, because she cupped my face, held me there, making me grin stupidly.

She returned my smile. "Why do you enjoy it? We're friends. You can tell me."

I was surprised by her forwardness but not at all disappointed. "Because I love her."

Heaven's hands fell to her sides, her surprise glittering in her eyes.

"You love her?"

"With everything that I am."

I had no idea why I was revealing this side of myself to Heaven. Perhaps I needed someone to know because I'd been holding it in for so long.

"Does she know?"

I shook my head.

"Does Isaac know?"

"No."

"Why not?"

"Because she belongs to Isaac."

"But you want her to belong to you?"

"Not just me," I admitted. "To both of us."

It was true and not something Isaac and I had ever considered. My brother'd always envisioned us having two submissives, sharing them between us, but only one holding our hearts.

It had been a perfect plan.

One that had failed miserably when we'd met Everly.

Heaven took a step back, crossed her arms over her chest. She appeared to be tossing this information around in her head, trying to figure out what to do with it.

"What did you do with her? The last time you were with her?"

"I restrained her," I relayed. "Slipped the plug in her ass, thinking about the day that plug would be my dick. I fucked her. Hard."

"You don't have any issues being blunt, do you?"

"Why should I? It's who I am. I'm not ashamed of what I want."

She nodded as though that made sense. "What about Dante?"

Her abrupt subject change caught me off guard. "What about him?"

"During the scene, he said you were his Master. Is that true?"

"Yes."

"Do you want him?"

"Yes." I wasn't going to deny it.

"Do you want to fuck him?"

"Yes."

"Seriously, no filter at all. Right to the point."

I laughed, pulled her to me, and cradled her head against my chest. "You're something else, Heaven. I'm glad you've stayed. Glad I met you."

She pushed against me, then stared up in my face, smiled sweetly. "Well, I can tell you, if you ever want to invite me to dinner in the future, one of you guys can do the cooking."

"I'll be sure to remember that."

She was grinning, extremely proud of herself.

"I'm going to check on Dante," I told her. "Take your time. I'll be a while."

"Don't have too much fun."

I shook my head, chuckled. "No promises."

Leaving Heaven to cook, I headed toward the guest suite. I rapped on Dante's door, then opened it. He was reclined on the bed, his hair wet from his shower.

"We really need to redecorate this room," I told him. "It doesn't feel like you."

I moved with purpose toward him, not hiding the reason I was there.

"But I know what does feel like you."

He stared up at me, complete surrender on his face. "What's that, Master?"

"You." I placed one knee on the bed, moved over him, my lips hovering over his. "You feel like you."

His breaths were shallow, faster than a second ago.

"Kiss me, Dante."

He lifted his head, meeting my mouth with his. I sucked in a breath. My need for him had been building, my leash on it ready to snap. Now that I'd succumbed to the realization that I had to have him, there would be no stopping this.

He moaned softly when my tongue met his. I rolled onto my back, taking him with me, crushing his warm body against mine. While our tongues danced, seeking, searching, I lifted his T-shirt, breaking apart only long enough to force it over his head.

My hands itched to touch, roaming over his skin, feeling the flex of his muscles, his warmth, his strength. I slid my hands into the waistband of his shorts, cupping his ass as I forced the fabric down. I wanted to feel him, and I wanted him to know what my intentions were.

And while I was eager for him, I had absolutely no intentions of rushing. I was going to take my time learning every inch of his delectable body.

With my tongue.

Dante

THE GLEAM IN IAN'S EYES HAD BEEN present from the second he stepped through the door. I knew what he wanted, could feel his need coming off him in waves.

Me.

That was what he wanted.

Not simply sex, not to take from me without giving back.

I didn't know how I knew that, but I did. He wasn't like most men. Ian and Isaac were controlled, patient. And while they were quite open about their sexual preferences, their erotic desires, it wasn't just a way for them to quench their thirst.

The way Ian's hands squeezed my ass, grinding his thigh against my cock, I felt him slowing things down. His kiss was nirvana. And while he gave me the illusion I was in control, I knew better. Then again, he knew that was what I needed. The illusion. I had no desire to be in control. Not with him, not with anyone. I wanted this, wanted his dominance.

He rolled us again. This time, when I was beneath him, he didn't hover over me. I felt his weight on me, but it wasn't crushing. It was safety, security. He didn't scare me, although I think somewhere deep down, he worried he might. I could've told him that wasn't going to happen. I'd been scared plenty in my life, could feel evil in people, had since I was little. There was no evil here.

His lips trailed down my jaw, my neck. I turned my head, giving him better access.

"I want you to lie there," he whispered roughly. "Lie there and enjoy what I'm doing. I want to taste you." He lifted his head, looked in my eyes. "And when I'm satisfied with that, I'm going to bury myself deep inside you, make you beg me to let you come."

"Please, Master," I whimpered, bowing my body toward him, inviting him to do just that.

"I want to hear you, Dante. I want the whole fucking house to hear you. I want there to be no question as to what you like. Understand me?"

"Yes, Master."

His lips grazed mine, slid over my chin, down my neck. I tilted my head back, moaning softly as his warm mouth trailed over my nerve endings. He took his time, never rushing. His tongue wandered over my shoulders, down one arm, all the way to my fingers, then back up before he did the same with the other. I didn't move but he did. Lifting my hands, sucking my fingers, one at a time, into his mouth. He tickled the crook of my arm with his tongue, licked over my bicep, then all the way to my nipple. He nipped me, causing me to cry out as brutal pleasure slammed into me.

"Let me hear you," he growled.

As his mouth continued its delicious assault, I grew louder, more desperate. He was driving me fucking wild, insane with need. His warm breath fanned the swollen head of my cock seconds before he licked me, making my body twitch. When he took me in his mouth, it took everything in me not to reach for him, to hold him there.

"Master ... oh, fuck..." I threw my head back, my hips lifting, trying to take more than he was giving.

He chuckled, a sexy sound that danced down my spine.

Ian took me all the way to the root, the head of my cock spearing the back of his throat, but he didn't remain there for long. A vicious tease that had my insides quaking.

Kneeling between my legs, Ian took my hand, curled my fist over my cock.

"Stroke slowly," he ordered before his lips trailed the inside of my thigh, lower.

I lay there, completely blissed out as adrenaline pumped through me, my cock rock hard, throbbing. I swiped my thumb over the sensitive crest, hissed, never looking away as his lips moved down my leg, over my knee, my shin, my foot. He sucked my second toe into his mouth, and I could've come right then and there. I'd never in my life had this sort of attention. He didn't miss an inch of me, teasing, tormenting, his eyes hot as they caressed my face, watching.

NICOLE EDWARDS

I ensured he heard me, verbalizing the pleasure he drew out of me one second at a time, just as he'd instructed. As promised, he took his time. When he asked me to roll over, I knew he wasn't finished. He lay out over me, his weight draping me like a warm blanket. His lips grazed my neck, my shoulders.

"I want you, Dante. Do you even know how much?"

"No, Master."

He ground his hips against my ass, his lips continuing their delicious assault on my skin. "I want to feel you wrapped around me."

I thought for a moment he would take what he wanted, but he didn't. He merely trailed that skillful mouth over me again. My shoulders, the backs of my arms, my fingers once more, covering every inch he hadn't yet explored. He teased his tongue down my spine and I moaned, the pleasure intense. I hadn't realized how erotic this could be.

He bit my ass cheek. I cried out, pleasure assaulting me again and again. He spread my cheeks, licked downward, over my asshole, teasing momentarily before continuing down to my thigh.

"Master … it feels so good. Like nothing I've ever felt. Please don't stop," I pleaded.

"Never," he growled. "I'll never get enough of you."

The promise in those words had my chest filling with emotion. I'd longed to hear those words from someone. Anyone.

Once again kneeling between my thighs, he bent my knee, licked my ankle, the arch of my foot, once more taking a toe in his mouth. He performed the same action on the other leg. By the time he was done, I was a panting mess, boneless and aching at the same time.

He leaned over me. I watched as he retrieved a condom and lube from the nightstand. They hadn't been there when I first arrived, because I had searched every inch of the room, checking for cameras. I hadn't expected them, but it was still something I found myself doing. There hadn't been any. Ian and Isaac weren't trying to invade my privacy, something I'd rarely had throughout my life. Not until I had my own house. Still, it was something I checked daily. Good thing, too. Not long after Roger had raped me the first time, I'd found a camera installed in my bedroom. For a solid week after, I'd slept in the living room. When he asked me where I'd been, I knew he hadn't been talking about the club. He'd been watching me, and it creeped me out.

"Once we have your test results, we won't be using these," Ian rumbled. "I'll want you bare."

I nodded, fear slithering inside me. I hadn't been tested since Roger had…

"Here with me, Dante," Ian growled into my ear. "Don't you leave me right now."

He slid his hand over mine, twined our fingers as he pressed his lips over my shoulder.

"No one is here but us," he rambled. "You and me. I don't want anyone else here. Understand?"

"Yes, Master. I understand." I cleared the evil thoughts from my head, focused only on him.

"Turn over," he ordered.

Hesitantly, I rolled onto my back, confused.

He positioned himself over me once more, twined both hands with mine, kissed me.

"Who am I?" he asked, his voice rough.

"My Master."

"*Who* am I?"

Confused, I met his gaze. "Ian. My Master."

"Who are you giving yourself to right now?"

"You," I whispered. "I'm giving myself to you, Master."

"Then don't leave me." His eyes were hard, as though he could sense the evil that filled my head like a black, oily film.

"I won't," I assured him.

He kissed me, deep and long. Soft, gentle, still the hunger was building, the need overwhelming.

When he pulled back, I watched him. He knelt between my legs, rolled the condom on, his attention never leaving me. He took his time and I realized it was to give me the chance to use my safe word if I needed to.

"Green, Master," I said on a rough whisper. "So fucking green."

He nodded, as though he'd needed to know that.

When he stroked himself, I started to turn over, but he stopped me with a firm hand on my thigh.

I stared up at him, my confusion evident.

"I'm going to look in your eyes when I take you."

I swallowed hard. I'd never been with a man like that. They'd always taken what they wanted and the easiest way to do that was from behind, not rough but mean. It had started when I was young, the men my father would allow up to see me in the attic.

"Dante!" Ian growled, his tone hard.

I snapped open my eyes, not realizing I'd shut them.

"Look at me," he said, his voice softer as he leaned over me. "Don't leave me again. Do you understand?"

I nodded, felt the emotion building.

Ian shifted one of my legs back, toward my chest. Then the other. He kissed me throughout, his lips firm yet gentle. I could feel his hunger, his need. He was holding back. For me.

I was breathing hard but not from fear. My desire for him was too great. Potent. Overwhelming. When he pushed inside me, I cried out as the pleasure swamped me. There was no pain.

He lay out over me, twining our fingers again as he rocked into me.

"Stay here with me, Dante. Look at me."

I kept my eyes on his face, saw the intent in his gaze. He wanted to give me pleasure, not take.

When I tried to look away, he used his free hand to hold my jaw.

"You feel so fucking good," he growled. "Tight, hot." His eyes snapped on mine. "Perfect."

His pace never changed, the perfect rhythm to have me begging and pleading. Just a little more.

"Say my name," he ordered.

"Master."

He nipped my lower lip. "Not *who* I am. Say. My. Name."

"Ian," I whispered harshly.

"Hold on to me." There were more words, Irish words whispered in that rough brogue that drove me wild.

With my arms wreathing his neck, Ian pumped his hips, driving into me, the pleasure building as strongly as the pressure in my chest, the emotion I couldn't hold back. I buried my face in his neck, moaning softly, saying his name over and over as he took us both to the edge, held us there.

"Oh, fuck…" I groaned, the sound tormented only because it was too much, overwhelming with its intensity. "Master … please … I'm—fuck, I'm going to come."

"Come for me," he growled, his words vibrating over my skin.

His arm slid beneath my back, holding me to him as he drove into me again and again. I couldn't have let go if I'd wanted, my arms secured around him as my body, strung tight, threatened to shatter.

"Come for me," he urged, his voice a broken whisper. Again, more words in Irish, these spoken with reverence.

His hips drove forward again and again, his grunts and groans the music I moved by until I couldn't hold on any longer.

"Oh, fuck!" I cried out, my muscles locking as my cock pulsed between us.

Ian drove into me once more, growled low in his throat, his arm tightening around me as he came. His body jerked and twitched, never letting me go until I relaxed beneath him.

And then, when Ian could've easily slipped out of the room, he didn't. He kissed me. Softly, sweetly. It lasted as long as the foreplay, or it felt like it, anyway.

"I want something from you tonight," he said softly, pulling back, staring down into my face.

"Anything, Master."

His eyes searched mine. "I want you in my bed."

I sucked in air, almost told him I couldn't.

"Thirty minutes," he said before I could refuse. "That's all I ask. Thirty minutes. I want to hold you for that long. Then you can come back here. I won't push for more, but I need this." Once more with the Irish words.

"What does that mean?" I asked, still trying to come up with a way to refuse.

He smiled softly. "The literal translation is my heart's beloved."

My breath left my body in a rush.

"Thirty minutes. That's all I ask. For now."

I nodded, unable to deny him anything he asked of me.

"Thank you." He smiled, tacked on something else in that delectable brogue.

I raised my eyebrows.

"My pet," he said with a chuckle, then dipped his head, kissed me softly before climbing out of bed. "I'm sure dinner's ready. Get dressed. Join us."

"Yes, Master," I said, sighing.

It was then I realized there was a smile on my face.

That, too, was a first.

Nineteen

Heaven

W<small>HILE</small> I <small>COOKED</small>, I <small>USUALLY LISTENED TO</small> music, took the opportunity to relax.

That hadn't been the case tonight.

Sure, it had been a thought, right up until I heard the sounds coming from Dante's bedroom. The soft grunts, moans. That had been the music I had worked to this evening. And as I did, I had let the images form. I'd never seen two men make love, but it was a fantasy that burned hot when I thought about Ian and Dante.

And though I'd had sex with both men—something I certainly wouldn't brag about to my friends—I felt no jealousy that they were together. In fact, I was glad they'd finally given in. I might not have been the most perceptive person in the world, but I'd noticed the way Ian and Isaac had been keeping their distance from Dante.

Lucky for them, that didn't seem to be the case anymore.

Funny, so much had happened in the week we'd been in this house. Most of it transpiring between the four of them, but I could admit, the experience had changed me, too. Not that I was any closer to thinking this lifestyle was my thing. Nope. Still a one-man woman right here. But I liked that they respected that and still extended the offer to include me. But there was a bigger dynamic at play here, one that I was intruding on. I could sense my presence was like a brick wall resurrected on the freeway. Completely out of place and doing nothing except hindering progress.

What was more interesting? I had accepted it without disappointment. I think that was a turning point for me, a bit of growth on my part.

I was frying the last pork chop when Ian returned.

I glanced over, smiled. His hair was mussed, his eyes hooded. He looked sated, relaxed.

"Two minutes," I told him. I had taken my time, especially after I realized what was going on in Dante's bedroom.

Ian walked over, put his arms around me, held me to him. I hugged him back, inhaling his scent. He smelled like Dante and sex mixed with his unique, delicious scent.

"The things I mentioned earlier," he said softly. "Let's keep that between us."

Things being his feelings for Everly, I knew.

I nodded as he released me. "Of course."

"Thanks."

He disappeared toward his bedroom and I finished the food.

Dante appeared. He looked similar to how Ian had. Satisfied, relaxed.

"Hi," I greeted. "Hungry?"

"Starving."

His eyes searched my face, as though he expected me to say something. I realized then I needed to. The last thing I wanted was for him to wonder.

"About earlier … I really don't want things to be weird between us."

"They're not weird," he said, though I got the impression he wasn't being exactly truthful.

"Good." I took his hand, tugged him toward the kitchen. "Now, you get drinks. I'll get food."

"Yes, ma'am."

Ian returned a few minutes later.

"Are Isaac and Everly joining us?" I asked as I brought in two plates piled with food.

"No," Ian said. "I checked on them. Everly's asleep already."

I smiled knowingly. Good sex could take it out of a girl.

"I'll put theirs in the refrigerator. They can heat it up later."

Ian nodded.

"Were you born in Ireland?" Dante asked, surprising us both because it was rare he talked unless prompted.

Ian turned his full attention on Dante. "Aye."

"How long have you been in the US?"

"My father moved us here when we were sixteen," he said conversationally. "He came here for work. Corporate type."

"Is he still here?"

Ian shook his head, took a pull from the beer I'd brought him.

"No. He went back after we graduated."

"And you stayed?"

"Aye. Isaac didn't want to go back. Couldn't really blame him. So, we settled in here. Started doing some security work, bought this house. Made a go at our own security company, gave it up after a few years."

"Didn't like it?" I asked.

"Didn't like the politics that came along with owning a business, schmoozing people in an effort to get business. Not really my thing. Prefer someone else handle that. We stick to the protection part."

"What about your mother?" I asked.

"Let's just say she preferred the pub."

"Alcoholic?"

Ian leaned back, took a swig of his beer. "Men."

He didn't elaborate.

"You work in security now," Dante said. "Local gigs?"

"Not usually, no. A lot of what we've been assigned to are in LA and New York."

"Long-term assignments?"

It wasn't until that question that I understood what Ian was saying. They travelled. Were gone a lot.

"Yeah," he replied to Dante. "Usually two or three weeks. Sometimes a couple of months at a time."

The thought of a relationship having to endure that sort of distance… I was suddenly not hungry anymore.

"Problem?" Ian asked, frowning.

"Nope," I lied.

His eyes hardened instantly, a look I hadn't yet seen on his face.

"I might put up with a lot of things." He held my gaze in his without force. "But I don't tolerate lies or avoidance." He took a drink. "One more time. What's on your mind?"

"Nothing," I said, exasperation in my tone.

After depositing my plate in the sink, I took off for the guest room, ignoring him when he called after me.

I should've known he would follow. The man didn't know the meaning of personal space.

He stood in the doorway, arms crossed, his full attention on me.

"Would you mind?" I snapped. "I'd like to get some sleep. I'll need it at my sister's. Kids and all."

"I do mind." He stepped into the room, closed the door.

"Ian, I'm not interested in your games right now." I started to get on the bed, but he stopped me, his arm banding around my middle, lifting me off the ground. "Put me down, dammit."

"Something you haven't had a chance to explore yet," he said, depositing me on my feet. "Kneel."

I gave him a go-to-hell glare. "I've seen more than enough, thank you very much."

"Kneel." His voice was so low, so deep it sent chills down my spine.

For a second, I had to wonder if he even remembered who I was.

"Go to hell," I rasped, hoping he didn't singe me with the anger in his eyes.

Ian stepped forward, his hand shooting out. I flinched, expecting a blow, but he didn't hit me. In fact, his hand was almost gentle as it curled around the back of my neck. He was so close I was forced to crane my neck to look at him.

"I told you, I don't tolerate lies or avoidance. Not even from my friends. You've done both in less than two minutes." His gaze searched my face. "And I'm going to be clear on one thing. I will *never* hit you. Not out of anger."

I frowned. "What does that mean?"

His smile was vicious but not quite mean. "I'm quite intrigued by the idea of turning your little ass red."

I inhaled sharply. "You want to spank me?"

"Right now?" He leaned closer. "More than anything."

"Because I walked off?" I huffed a laugh. "That's just stupid."

"No, what's stupid is you avoiding the conversation. Something I said bothered you. Rather than talking it out, you stormed off. *That's* stupid."

I tried to form words but couldn't.

Ian released me, took my arm, and led me over to the bed.

240

"Bend over," he ordered, his clipped words telling me he was serious.

"If I don't?"

He took a step back. "Then I'll walk out. All forgotten."

It sounded to me as though he was leaving this in my hands. While I'd been taken aback by his high-handed behavior, I had to give him credit. That whole domination thing was quite hot. It did strange things to me.

"If you want to see what punishment feels like, Heaven, bend over the bed. If not…" He motioned to the door to the guest room.

"You're throwing me out?"

With a resigned sigh, I turned and bent over the bed.

I could hear him breathing behind me. He didn't move for the longest time. I thought for a second he was going to talk it out.

He didn't.

No, the big, bad Dom was going to hold true to his word, and my ass was going to hurt before this was over.

He took a deep breath, exhaled. "Strip."

I turned my head, glanced his way. "What?"

"Don't make me tell you again."

He moved then, taking a seat behind me.

I pushed off the bed, turned away, looked back. Did it several times before I huffed again but proceeded to strip. Before I could turn back to the bed, he patted his knees. "Over here."

I walked toward him, never more aware of how naked I was.

"Bend over my lap."

I wanted to ask him if he was serious, but I knew he was. The look on his face was fierce.

"Count for me."

I didn't quite understand, but then he smacked my ass with his hand and it didn't matter. I sucked in air. That hadn't been a playful swat. My ass stung.

"I can't hear you," he growled.

"One," I bit out, realizing *that* was what he'd meant by count.

He spanked me again, this time his hand moving slightly, not in the same spot but just as painful as the first.

"Two," I snarled.

Again.

"Three."

We made it all the way to seven before I sobbed, tears leaking from my eyes. The pain was intense, but I didn't try to move away.

His hand smoothed over me a second before he landed another.

"Eight," I cried, the dam breaking, emotion flooding out of me. Anger, embarrassment, remorse. Not just from this encounter, but from everything I'd been holding in for the past few months. Danny, his infidelity. It was all there, coalescing into a storm that ripped through me.

Just when I thought Ian would spank me again, he pulled me up, settled me on his lap, and wrapped his arms around me. I held on to him, not willing to talk or look at him, but I held on, burying my face in his neck and openly sobbing against him.

His hands were warm, gentle as they slid over my back. He held me just as tightly.

We remained like that for several minutes. Long enough for the tears to stop.

"Look at me, Heaven."

I didn't want to, but I managed to pull back, look in his face.

"Thank you," he whispered.

"For what?"

"Indulging me."

"If my ass didn't burn, I'd say you're welcome."

He grinned. "Believe it or not, it's the tears I was going for."

"You wanted to make me cry?"

"I wanted you to let it out. I can tell you hold everything in. You need to find a way to decompress."

His big hands cupped my head, brushing my hair back from my face before settling on both sides of my neck. His thumbs brushed over my jaw. "I'm going to miss you, but I hope you'll keep in touch when you're gone."

"Me, too," I said, realizing it was true.

ISAAC

I HAD LAIN IN THE DARK WHILE Everly slept, letting the minutes tick by while listening to her breathing, thinking about the three words she'd said before she succumbed to exhaustion.

That had been hours ago.

My brain was racing, making it impossible to relax. On top of that, my heart was beating hard, like I'd just returned from a jog, but it wasn't physical exertion that was causing it. No, the credit for that went to those three little words my fairy princess had whispered before she had drifted off. I couldn't stop replaying them in my head, relishing the peace that had settled over me.

At some point, I had drifted off, waking when she shifted, moving closer. I dragged my fingers over her soft skin, pressing my lips to her forehead.

When she tipped her head, I knew she was awake, but she didn't move, just held on. I kissed her nose, her cheek, then trailed down to her lips. Her hand curled against my face, her fingers whisper-soft against my skin.

"Say it again, fairy princess. I need to hear it."

Her lips brushed mine. "I love you. I'm not ashamed to admit it. I don't—"

I pressed two fingers against her lips. "I love you, *mo grá*. Have since the first day I met you."

"What does that mean?" she asked, moving closer.

"My love," I whispered, took her mouth with mine.

243

Everly sighed, rolling to her back as I encouraged her with my body.

An urgency ignited, my need to have her, to claim her. To possess her. What started as a gentle mating of mouths turned frantic. Everly cried out when I nipped her neck, sucking her skin, drowning in her scent. She did that to me. Made me wild, desperate. And it was a need I couldn't control, one that overpowered me, made me a slave to my own desire.

I took her hands, lifted them over her head with one hand on her wrists and crushed my mouth to hers. She writhed beneath me, her leg curling around my thigh, trying to tug me closer. I ground my hips, then angled my cock at her entrance and drove into her.

"My Liege!" Her back bowed.

I impaled her again, watched her lovely face as she gave herself over to me. She was the most beautiful creature I'd ever seen.

"Keep your hands there," I ordered, pushing up to my knees.

I jerked her hips toward me, impaled her on my cock, loving the way she came apart before me. I wasn't gentle, punishing thrusts of my hips driving us both higher. I rode her for what felt like hours, never giving her enough to send her over. I slid my arms behind her knees, bent her in half, and drove into her deeper than I'd ever been, staring down into her face. Her eyes were closed, head tipped back as she cried out my name over and over again. Never did she ask to come, nor did she give in to it. My sweet fairy princess had heeded the lesson, staying right there with me.

I couldn't get enough, fucking her hard, fast, sweat beading on our skin, her pussy hot and slick around me as I slammed my hips forward, paused, retreated. Again and again.

"Everly, I want you to come for me, love," I growled, dropping her legs when I shot to the precipice, hanging by a thread. "Hold on to me."

It was a plea more than an order, and she obliged me, crushing her mouth to mine as we came together in a conflagration of light and heat and love. I crumbled on top of her, knowing I was crushing her but unable to move. Her arms stayed around me, her hands sliding into my hair, nails tickling my scalp.

I lifted my head enough to stare into her eyes. "I'm never letting you go."

She smiled, so sweet. "I don't want you to."

Rolling onto my back, I brought her with me, my cock still deep inside her, still hard. My need for her never abated; it only grew stronger with every passing second.

Expecting her to sleep, I wrapped her in my arms, listening to the rasp of my own breath. When her pussy flexed, tightening around me, I had to smile.

"Little minx," I muttered, tugging her hair until she lifted her head. "You want more."

Everly pushed up, her hands on my chest, eyes bright. "I'll never get enough."

"Take all you want. All you need."

Grinding her hips forward and back, Everly rode me, never looking away. I cupped her breasts, pinched her nipples. Her soft sighs were music we made love by, the way I'd intended the first time. I teased her clit with my thumb, her mouth falling open as my sweet fairy princess took her pleasure from me. When I stopped, she pouted but took over herself, her back bowed, fingers teasing her clit while she rode me.

Our eyes met and I knew she was close.

"Please, my Liege," she whispered so softly, so sweetly. "May I come?"

"All over my cock," I told her, my voice harder than I'd intended, my restraint kicking in. I wanted to fuck her hard and fast, to chase my own release, but I wanted this more. To see her slide over the edge into oblivion without my help.

Seconds ticked by, my focus only on her as she tipped over that razor-sharp edge into bliss, my name falling from her lips. This time, when she collapsed on me, I held her in my arms, kissed the top of her head, and urged her to sleep.

Several hours later, I was up, ready for the morning run. By the time I made it to the kitchen, Dante and Ian were already outside waiting. Without speaking, the three of us took off, enjoying the solitude that came along with what had become a nice routine for us.

When we left the house, I noticed a black Jeep Cherokee parked two doors down. I wasn't familiar with it. And though I didn't track my neighbors' vehicles, I was very perceptive. Since that particular neighbor was prone to having overnight guests, I attributed it to that, not thinking about it again.

That would be the first of many mistakes in the coming days.

Twenty

Everly

Sunday, June 2, 2019

"HOW IS IT THAT YOU MANAGE TO beat me every time?" I asked Heaven as she took out my last piece on the board.

Though she'd said she was going to her sister's yesterday, her plans had changed when one of Honor's kids had gotten sick. She'd asked Heaven to delay a day or two. When she'd mentioned it to Ian, he'd told her to stay as long as she needed.

"Checkers is my jam," she said, something akin to sweet innocence in her voice.

"I can see that. I still think you cheat."

She laughed.

We'd been up in the attic for the better part of the afternoon, chilling, playing checkers, chatting, and reading. Nothing overly heavy, neither of us looking to move too much. Just a relaxing Sunday at home.

The thought had me stilling. This wasn't my home even if I was here for an undetermined amount of time. I'd probably do well to remember that.

"I don't know about you, but I'm starting to go stir-crazy in this house," Heaven said, her voice low, her eyes moving to the door.

I sighed, leaned back against the recliner at my back. "Me, too."

My butt had fallen asleep halfway through the last game and I rubbed at it to wake it up. Hardwood did not make a great chair when playing checkers.

"Don't you just want to go grab a coffee or something? Maybe see a movie?"

"Yep. I do."

"Instead, we're staring at the walls all day, every day. It's been a week," she whined.

"Eight days, actually," I said teasingly.

"Okay, *longer* than a week." Heaven turned so she could lie flat on the floor, staring up at the ceiling. "My boss was cool about yesterday, but I *have* to go back to work tomorrow." She turned her head toward me, peeking around the table leg. "If I don't, they *will* fire me."

"I've probably lost my job already," I admitted. "Dee told me she understood, but I could tell she didn't mean it. I mean, it's not that hard to find someone to take my place."

"Whatever." Heaven looked at the ceiling again. "You're a great barista. Not just anyone can walk in off the street and do that."

That was Heaven for you, always propping up someone else's self-esteem when she was the first to be hard on herself.

"Thank you," I told her. "Even if it's not true."

"It is," she insisted, glaring at me.

I laughed. "I'm kidding. But seriously."

"Don't get me wrong," Heaven said. "It's been an amazing week, despite the circumstances of why we're here."

"Have you talked to your sister?"

"Yeah. She called this morning, said the coast was clear. I told her I'd be there as soon as I could. She asked where I was. Told her we were staying with a friend."

"She's just worried." Heaven's sister was overprotective of her. It was nice to see, considering I had no one who was worried about me anymore. My own parents lived fifteen minutes from Dante's, but they'd long ago disowned me. I had let them, honestly. They'd never understood me. Not the real me.

"Yeah, probably. She'll get over it."

"I told Isaac I loved him," I said, eyes on the checkerboard in front of me.

Heaven popped up, her eyes wide. "Oh, my God. Do you?"

I laughed. "I wouldn't have said it if I didn't."

Her smile was sheepish. "I knew that. Wow. That's… Please tell me it's great."

"It is." My smile was so wide my cheeks hurt. "He said he loves me, too."

Heaven's mouth dropped open. "What does that mean?"

We stared at each other, then both burst into a fit of laughter.

"You know what I mean," she rasped between giggles. "I know what it *means*, but … what does it mean?"

More laughter.

I heard footsteps on the stairs, glanced back over my shoulder to see Ian. He was watching us closely. "What's so funny?"

"Just girl stuff," Heaven said before spurting into more giggles.

Of course, they were contagious, and I ended up flopping over onto my side.

"What brings you this way?" Heaven asked when she'd sobered somewhat.

Ian's eyes darkened. "I actually came to tell you that Isaac said he could take you to your sister's. Whenever you're ready."

She popped up so quickly I inhaled. "Really?"

Wow. I honestly hadn't realized she'd been that eager to leave.

"Aye."

I glanced at Ian. Admittedly, that Irish thing did it for me in so many ways.

Heaven's eyes shot to me. "It's okay, right? That I'm leaving?"

I pushed to my feet. "Of course it is. I know you need to get back to work. Just remember, you can't go home until they tell you the coast is clear."

"Oh, don't you worry. After what that asshole did to Danny, I won't go anywhere near it."

"What about your car?"

"Shit." Heaven's gaze shot to Ian's.

"Ask Isaac to take you by there. He can follow you to your sister's."

Heaven actually clapped, as though that was the best news she'd heard all month.

She grabbed me then, threw her arms around my neck. "I'll see you soon, right? When this is over, you and Dante'll be back home?"

"That's the plan." Though I didn't really know what the plan was at this point.

Heaven squeezed me once, then released me before hugging Ian. "Thank you again for everything. I really appreciate it. I had fun."

"You promised to grace us with your presence," he said.

"As long as I don't have to cook."

"Right."

Then she was gone, out the door, down the steps. Ian and I stood there, staring after her for the longest time. My body warmed at his nearness, though I wasn't sure why he was there other than to get Heaven.

"I've always loved this room," he said absently, walking over to one of the bookshelves.

"I do, too." I walked over to the recliner, sat on the edge of the cushion, waiting to see if this was going somewhere.

"You know what would make me love it more?" he asked, turning slowly to face me.

I waited, knowing he would tell me.

"Your mouth on my cock."

Heat swam through me, making my fingers tingle. I swallowed hard, met his emerald-green gaze.

Some people might consider his request crude, but my desire to pleasure him was so great, it was the best opportunity I'd been presented with lately. I couldn't explain the ache I had for him, the need that had yet to be sated. I'd tried to figure out a way to broach the subject, to see if there was the option of spending more time with him, but the timing never seemed to be right.

He was clearly waiting for me to say something, his black eyebrow lifting.

"It would be my pleasure, Sir."

He crooked his finger, a silent order for me to come to him.

"Bring a pillow."

I snagged one of the throw pillows from the recliner, dropped on the floor at his feet.

Ian leaned over, kissed me. It was a gentle kiss, unexpected and it took hold of my heart and twisted. I wanted to spend the rest of the day right here, in his arms, his lips locked on mine. Unfortunately, he stopped too soon for my liking.

"Strip," he murmured against my mouth. "Do it slowly. Let me watch you."

I was almost certain that was a plea in his tone.

"Yes, Sir."

I stepped back, slowly discarded my T-shirt and shorts, placing each piece on the checkerboard after I peeled it off. My bra and panties followed. All the while, his hot gaze raked over me, moving sensually as though he was memorizing me for later.

God, how had this distance come between us? I couldn't help but wonder if Heaven had been the reason Ian and I had yet to connect. But then I would think about the distance he kept with her. None of it made sense.

"Beautiful." He patted the edge of the desk.

Slightly confused about the direction this was taking, I hesitated a second before walking over to the desk and scooting up onto it. My butt squeaked on the shiny wood, my eyes shooting to the cushion he'd had me place on the floor. I lifted my gaze to his, saw the heat there.

"Lie back," he ordered.

I did.

"Grab your ankles. Hold on to them and spread your legs."

I did this, too, my body trembling with excitement as my most intimate parts were opened for his perusal.

His fingers slid through my slick folds. "Such a pretty pussy."

I moaned low in my throat. "Thank you, Sir."

Ian took his time, making me wait as he stared at my pussy, using his fingers to make me melt. He rubbed my clit, pushed one finger inside me, pulled it out. Over and over, not nearly enough attention on any one spot to get me going, but enough to make me yearn.

"No plug."

"No, Sir. I'm to wear it three hours a day. One hour at a time."

"Did you meet your quota yet today?"

"No, Sir. I'm going to wear it before dinner."

He looked up at my face. "Good girl."

His fingers teased me again, making me sigh.

"I have to say, I haven't had nearly enough time with you since you got here."

At least we were on the same page there. "I agree, Sir."

His eyes met mine, held, and there was so much emotion reflecting back I wasn't sure what to make of it.

"I thought you were spending time with Heaven," I said on a heavy exhale when he pushed a finger inside me.

"Not as much as you'd think."

"May I ask why not?"

His eyes lingered on my face, but he didn't answer, instead redirecting. "I think you deserve a reward."

I gasped for air when he bent over and licked me.

"Don't drop your ankles. No matter what. Understood?"

My voice quivered. "Yes, Sir."

Ian proved exactly how skilled he was with his tongue. Skilled and sadistic, driving me out of my head but never giving me the chance to come. When he stopped abruptly, I was panting and moaning.

He, of course, was smiling. "Kneel."

I climbed down onto trembling legs while he freed his cock. With one hand on my head, he guided himself into my mouth, held me there. His eyes were locked on me as he fucked my mouth. I sucked, licked, but he controlled my movements, all the while maintaining that eye contact, as though he was trying to relay his feelings that way.

"Tilt your head back."

I did.

He angled his cock, pushed down into my mouth, all the way to my throat. I breathed through my nose, fought my gag reflex. I knew Ian loved this part. It was the only intimate act I'd performed on him at the club. Only him. Isaac never let me touch him, but they both always ensured I came.

"Swallow," he said when he pushed in again.

I swallowed, knowing it would make my throat tighten around him.

"Good girl," he whispered, pulling out, pushing in again.

He used my mouth for long minutes, his breaths becoming raspy. All the while, he stared at me as though he wanted to say something. No words ever came. When he pulled out the last time, he reached for my arm, tugged me to my feet, then ordered me to kneel on the recliner.

While he was ripping open a condom, I crawled into the chair, grabbing the headrest with both hands seconds before I felt him moving behind me, his warm hand curling over my hip, urging me toward him. I bent forward and a second later, he plunged inside me.

There was a litany of words in Irish, but I knew none of their meaning. However, his body was speaking to mine in a language of its own. I cried out with every punishing thrust, not caring who heard me as he fucked me relentlessly.

I was soaring, and a breath from going over before I stopped myself.

"Good girl. Don't come yet."

Gripping my hips, he drove into me, filling me with purpose. It was exquisite and exactly what I'd come to love about him. And Ian was right, we hadn't spent nearly enough time together. I wanted more of it, but I wasn't even sure how to go about asking for it. Not without hurting Isaac in the process.

I whimpered. "Please, Sir. May I please come?"

"Not yet," he grunted, driving into me again and again, his fingertips digging into my hips as he held me in place.

It was intoxicating.

Ian never held back with me. He took what I freely gave him. I would likely have fingertip bruises on my sensitive flesh, but it would only remind me of how thoroughly he fucked me.

He grunted, groaned, his fingertips digging in deeper.

"Ah, little fairy. Such a sweet little pussy."

I moaned, suddenly terrified that I would come without permission. It was so easy to do, but when he spoke like that, it was like his finger was on the trigger.

He jerked me back, driving in deep, making me scream with the pleasure that threatened to earn me punishment in the very near future.

"Such a good girl," he groaned. "Come for me, little fairy. Come all over my cock."

With his permission, I gave myself over, screaming his name as I rocketed into the ether.

He wasn't far behind, slamming into me again and again until his hips thrust forward one last time before he came on a long, strangled growl.

"Thank you, little fairy," he whispered as he leaned over me.

I turned my head, met his lips with mine. "Definitely my pleasure, Sir."

He grinned, just like Ian always grinned.

Dante

NEVER THOUGHT I'D BE SITTING IN THE kitchen, listening to erotic screams sounding from above, but that was exactly where I found myself.

As I downed a sandwich at the kitchen island, I could hear Everly crying out, begging Ian to let her come. His answering grunts seemed to echo through the room.

I found myself smiling and I wasn't even sure why.

For the past two nights, Ian had instructed me to be in his bed for thirty minutes each night. I'd followed through, pushing past the anxiety. Admittedly, it wasn't as difficult as I'd thought it would be. Just the two of us in the dark. It wasn't even awkward when Ian had pulled me in close, falling asleep with his arms around me. I might've almost fallen asleep last night.

Although I wouldn't admit it to anyone.

Oddly enough, I'd slept soundly both nights after those events. Back in my own bed, alone, all the lights off. Dreamless sleep, too. No nightmares, no memories of hell invading.

A crescendo of cries came from upstairs, drawing my eyes toward the stairway leading up. It didn't sound to me like Everly had any problems being handled by the opposite twin.

In truth, I'd always thought Everly had a thing for both of them. However, since we'd gotten here, it seemed she'd spent the majority of her time with Isaac. Then again, I'd thought Ian and Heaven were going at it like rabbits, but I'd learned that hadn't been the case. Heaven and Ian had slept separately every night, even after the erotic encounters the five of us had endured.

My phone vibrated on the counter. After nearly dropping my glass, I set it down, snatched up the phone.

The Devil: *You can't avoid me forever. Remember that.*

I'd been getting the texts throughout the day and night for the past week, ever since we'd come to Ian and Isaac's. I hadn't bothered to tell anyone about them, and I never responded, not giving Roger—or whatever the fuck his name was—the pleasure of hearing from me.

I figured I needed to get a new phone number. And I would, once I went home.

While we couldn't stay here forever, I wasn't making a big deal about wanting to leave, either. I wasn't a prisoner, knew I could go whenever I wanted, with or without Ian's or Isaac's permission, but I'd realized I wasn't here anymore because it was for my safety.

I was here because I didn't want to be anywhere else.

Eight days ago, I'd been coming home from work, ready to fall into bed, fearing whatever hell I might encounter if and when the devil showed his face. Now I woke up, breathing easy, no exhaustion from watching the shadowy corners of the room all night and day. No, I didn't have a job anymore, but I could find something. I wasn't above any job, didn't care if I needed three to make ends meet. I would take care of myself. Had been since the day I turned eighteen.

I turned on the barstool when Ian and Everly came downstairs. He patted her on the butt, sent her to her room to shower and rest. A second later, he joined me in the kitchen.

"Isaac took Heaven to her sister's," he said simply. "Not sure if you knew it or not."

"Yeah. She came to tell me goodbye."

Ian's eyes instantly dropped to the phone I'd left out. I reached for it, but he beat me to it. My eyes met his.

He held it out. "Unlock it."

Without hesitating, I typed in the passcode. He could see every number, would likely not need me to give it to him again. I honestly didn't care. I had nothing to hide from anyone, certainly not the two men who had somehow given my life meaning.

"The devil." He grunted.

I dropped my head.

"For fuck's sake," Ian hissed. "Dante, look at me."

I jerked my head up at the vehemence in his tone. He was squeezing the phone in his big fist.

"Why didn't you tell us he was texting you?"

"I didn't think it mattered, Master." It wasn't an argument, a simple statement.

Ian took a deep breath, let it out, stared at the phone screen. "Son of a bitch." His eyes lifted, met mine again. "That bastard is vicious. Is this how he's always treated you?"

"Yes, Master." Only that was nothing compared to some of the shit he'd said or done during the time I'd known him.

Ian was still reading, and my tension was rising. I'd never deleted the text thread, so it went back for … however long the phone would go for the past few years. I tried to think about the things he might find.

"Oh, shit." I jumped to my feet, swallowed hard. "Please, Master. Please don't … I don't want you…"

Ian's eyes lifted, the emerald green filled with anguish. He'd read it.

I could feel my heart breaking. I didn't want him to know about the evil that I'd lived through. And Roger had always enjoyed reliving those moments in text, describing in horrid detail all the ways he had hurt me. My Masters knew some of it, things I hadn't even known, such as Roger/Vernon trying to buy me. That had been news to me, but not surprising. However, until now, I didn't think they'd fully understood the magnitude of the man's evil.

"He—" Ian inhaled deeply, his molars grinding.

"Please, Master." My voice was guttural, but it didn't stop Ian from reading more.

"Christ Almighty." When Ian looked up, he was breathing hard. The anguish had turned to rage.

I didn't know what to say, what to do.

"I'll understand if you want me to go," I whispered, my heart aching.

"What?" His shocked expression had me stilling. "You're not going anywhere. Not if my opinion means two shits to you."

"It does," I said quickly. "I don't… I don't want to go." I glanced at the phone. "But—"

I inhaled, exhaled fast and shallow, choking back the bile that always rose when I thought about what had happened. The memories had been buried. Right up until Roger/Vernon had decided to tell me, a couple of years back, in horrific detail the things that had been done to me. Not at the club. But when I was a child. Not only did he tell me, he sent it via text, again in email, as though he got off on reliving it, seeing it through my eyes.

"Tomorrow, I'm taking you to the doctor," Ian said firmly. "Let's get some tests done."

I nodded. "I've had them done. Every three months. Last one was right after…"

"And…?"

"God was looking after me in one area," I said harshly. "I have no STDs, and I'm HIV negative." I nodded toward the phone. "I can pull them up. Show you."

Ian frowned. "I believe you."

"I'm sorry you had to read that."

"You're sorry?" Ian barked. "That fucker…" He exhaled with a rough growl. "You have nothing to apologize for."

He looked at me, and I swore there were tears in his eyes. It pained me to know I'd hurt him like that. I didn't want to think about how Isaac would take the news when Ian told him.

"Do you remember it?" Ian asked, control masking his features.

"I didn't. Not until…" I nodded toward the phone. "He had installed a camera in my father's attic. Told me in an email. Said he was so angry when he learned my father was … let's just say my old man was making a lot of money off me."

"Which explains why Vernon wanted to buy you," Ian mused, his eyes dropping to the island. "So those other men couldn't have you."

"Yeah." I'd thought about that, too. And it wasn't because Roger wanted to save me. No, he simply preferred to be the only one to hurt me.

"How did Roger … Vernon … whatever the fuck. How did he approach you at Inferno?"

I clasped my hands in front of me. "I'd been a member for about a week, had gone several times but never ended up playing with anyone. A couple of females offered, but I politely declined. I was starting to think they didn't want me there. I decided on that Friday night, if I didn't meet anyone who interested me, I wasn't coming back. That night he approached when I was sitting in the community room by myself."

"How did he know you were there?"

"He followed me." I shrugged. "Not sure how long he'd been tracking me, but he eventually told me he had always kept his eye on me. I guess he got a membership there after I started going." I swallowed, continued. "He came across as a nice guy, never mentioned he was a Sadist. Asked if I enjoyed pony play. Told him I wasn't really interested. He urged me to give it a shot, to let him show me how enjoyable it could be." I kept my eyes on my hands. "It wasn't bad. He smacked me a couple of times with a crop, never asked for sex. I thought perhaps it could get interesting if I gave it a shot. So, I met him the next night. We spent the evening talking, then he suggested I try the spanking bench.

"Again, not terrible. I didn't care much for it, but he seemed to know what he was doing. Asked me to meet him the next weekend. I agreed. Showed up on Friday night, he was waiting for me. Said he already had a room reserved for us. It was a private room." I looked up at Ian. "At Inferno, their private rooms don't have safety protocols. No viewing windows. I didn't even know that was a thing until Everly was telling me about Dichotomy." I exhaled my frustration. "He locked us into the room and that night ... he was different. Meaner, I guess. He said he'd thought about me all week and couldn't stop. It made me feel good, I guess. He was telling me he wanted me. I'd needed to be wanted."

"You kept going back?"

I nodded. "I craved the attention."

"Did he insist on sex?"

"Yes."

"Did he force you?"

"Yes. But he said it was role-playing. That he wanted me to be the innocent victim. I didn't think anything of it at the time. He was rough. I didn't care for it, but when I told him as much, he would praise me for playing the role. The first time I didn't meet him, he showed up at my house. Everly didn't live there yet. He played the wounded role, said I was hurting him, and he didn't want to lose me. Begged me to go back to the club. I told him I'd give him another chance."

"Nothing changed?"

"Oh, it did. For one weekend. He toned it down, focused on me a little. He told me I was too naive, that he needed to train me. Said it was his ultimate goal in life to show me what it meant to be owned by someone. Him. He would drag me naked around the club on my hands and knees, offering me to other Doms for the right price. He had no takers. None that were willing to pay him, anyway."

"Thank Christ for that," Ian muttered.

"I think that pissed him off, that no one wanted what he did. His temper only grew from there and he took it out on me. If I didn't show up at the club, he would come to my house. One time he went to my job, told me he would make my life a living hell if I didn't come back. By then, Everly was living with me and I didn't want him going to the house, so I went back to the club again and again.

"He learned about Everly somehow, threatened to hurt her. He even showed up at the house one night. Everly was already in bed. He raped me in the living room, told me if I didn't do what he wanted, she would soon learn what it was like. I told him not to come back, that I would only do it if we could meet at the club. He agreed.

"I hated him, but I wasn't willing to risk Everly. Then Heaven moved in and I think that tipped him over the edge. He started accusing me of fucking them. His anger intensified; his threats became more violent. Then back in March, I went to the club. I talked to the manager, told him I was canceling my membership. He asked me why. I told him I didn't feel safe. He brushed it off, called me a pussy. Before I could get out of there, Roger arrived. I decided to stand up to him."

The memory of that night had my hands shaking.

Ian's arms came around me from behind, holding me together. I hadn't been aware he'd moved, but I was grateful for the comfort he offered. I gripped his forearms, clung to them. His strength was the only thing I had in that moment.

"Finish the story," Ian rasped, his chin resting on my head.

I nodded. "We went to a room for privacy. He locked us in. I told him I was leaving the club, that I didn't want this anymore. And I guess…" I inhaled, exhaled, felt light-headed.

"Breathe," Ian whispered near my ear, his arms still securely around me. "You're safe."

I shuddered. "He must've drugged me. The next thing I knew, I was chained to a bed. Not at the club. It was an apartment. Turned out it wasn't too far from my house. Anyway. I woke up and I hurt. Everywhere." I swallowed back the emotion that churned. "I needed a hospital. He had beaten and raped me. Repeatedly. While I was unconscious."

"Holy fuck," Ian hissed, his arms tightening around me. He didn't let go and I held on to him.

"I heard him talking on the phone. I don't know who it was, but he was pissed when he hung up. Ended up unchaining me. Told me if I went to the cops, he'd come after Everly and Heaven. Said he would be in touch."

"That was three months ago?"

"Yes. I didn't hear from him for a while. Then I got a few text messages. I always messaged back, told him I was busy. I didn't want him hurting them, but I refused to see him again. I had gone to the doctor once I'd healed, gotten tested. Being in the clear felt like a new beginning and I didn't want to risk that. Then he texted me a couple of nights before he attacked Everly. I told him I was busy. He didn't respond. I thought nothing of it, hoping he'd found someone else who interested him." I sighed. "Clearly I was wrong."

So fucking wrong.

Twenty-One

IAN

WHEN DANTE ASKED IF HE COULD BE alone, I couldn't deny him.

That story had taken a hell of a lot out of him. Out of me, too.

And while I would've held him for the rest of the day and all through the night, I knew that wasn't what Dante needed. The man thrived on having his own space, being able to make his own decisions, process his emotions in his way. It had been taken from him for so long, I understood.

Isaac had returned to the house and I'd filled him in on the details. He'd had the same reaction I did. Sympathy for the hell Dante had been through and rage directed at the bastard who deserved to burn in hell for what he'd done.

"Have you heard back from Ransom?" Isaac asked when we slipped down to the basement while Everly cooked dinner.

"No."

"Maybe you should call him again," he suggested, his attention on his computer.

It wouldn't matter, I knew. I didn't need to hear from Ransom, to even know if Ransom's buddy had come through with information. It wouldn't matter. Not with this guy. Vernon Hathaway had more money than God, had gotten away with this since he was a goddamn teenager.

No way was he going to stop.

And it wasn't like we had proof. Aside from them possibly tying back the attack on Heaven's ex to the guy, the police would be fucking useless.

"What about the texts?" Isaac prompted. "Can those be used against him?"

"Perhaps. If Dante testified, made his hell public. And with the money backing him, it's not like Hathaway'll have a public defender. Bastard probably won't see any jail time."

No, America's beloved justice system wasn't what they needed. It had failed Dante before, Ian had no intention of sitting back and watching it fail him again.

"Don't even think about it," Isaac warned, lifting his head. "We're not going that route."

I didn't respond.

"Ian." Isaac's eyes shot up to the stairs, then back to me. He proceeded to enlighten me in our native tongue. "*There's no turning back if you do this. They'll own you ... us ... forever. They're the whole reason Dad brought us to America, to get us out of that life before it was too late.*"

I did know that. Our father hadn't been a corporate type like I'd told Dante and Heaven, hadn't come to the US for a job. He'd gotten us out of Ireland because he didn't want the Irish mob to get their hands on us. We'd been riding a fine line up to that point.

"You promised me."

I glared at Isaac. Damn him.

"We'll take care of this ourselves," Isaac said, back to English. "We can keep him safe. For a little while longer."

I nodded. "Fine. We've got another week before we'll be shipped out on some job." I pushed to my feet. "But if we don't have him by then, I'm making that call."

Isaac stared at me. "It won't come to that."

"Dinner's ready!" Everly called from upstairs.

My brother and I shared another look, then tabled the argument for later.

265

After dinner, Everly talked us into getting into the pool. We indulged her while Dante slipped back into his room. I couldn't stop thinking about him and I knew Isaac was having the same problem. The man was haunted by the demons of his past, and this bastard had tormented him for too fucking long. How anyone hadn't stepped in to stop it, I would never know.

"Why are you so gloomy?" Everly asked, throwing her arms around me as she straddled my back.

The move surprised me. Up to this point, whenever Isaac was around, she tended to gravitate toward him. Admittedly, I enjoyed her touching me.

I gripped her forearms, held tight. "Just thinking."

"Perhaps I could distract you," she whispered against my ear.

"You think so?"

"I am naked, you know."

"So am I."

"I know." She nipped my earlobe.

"While you two play, I've got something to take care of," Isaac said, clearly distracted.

I waved him off, my full attention on the sweet girl who was evidently trying to seduce me.

With Everly securely wrapped around me, I waded out to the deep end, stopping at the point I knew she couldn't stand without going under.

"What are you doing?" she asked, kissing my neck.

"Come around so I can see your pretty face."

She used my body like a jungle gym, shifting around and wrapping her arms and legs tightly around me.

"That's better."

"I know what would be better than this," she murmured, her lips grazing mine.

"Feisty tonight, huh?"

She grinned.

"I've got an idea."

Her eyebrows lifted. "What's that?"

Sliding my hand between her legs, I teased her pussy with my fingers.

"Mmm. That feels good."

"Now, if you want me to keep that up, I want you to tell me which scene you've enjoyed most at the club."

"With you and Isaac?"

I could hear the teasing in her tone, but I nipped her lip anyway.

She giggled. "Okay. Let me think." Her eyes widened. "It was that time you and Isaac made me sit in the chair in the dungeon. All eyes were on me and there was no way I couldn't notice because the two of you were keeping your distance."

I remembered exactly the moment she was referring to.

"Then Isaac produced a vibrator."

"Two," I corrected.

"Right. Two. One thin one and a bigger one. You passed the bigger one over to me, told me to tease my clit until you said I could stop."

God, she'd been sweet that night, and though it had been a relatively innocent scene, it had drawn quite the audience.

I leaned in, kissed her neck, making her sigh.

"So I did."

I pressed my thumb against her clit. "Here?"

Everly gasped. "Yes. Oh, God, that feels good. Don't stop."

"I won't. As long as you keep talking."

"I … uh… Where was I? Oh, yeah. Vibrator on my clit. So I did that for a few minutes. Apparently, I was a little too good at it because … well, because I came." She lifted her head, stared into my eyes. "It wasn't until that night that I realized how serious Isaac took that rule. Like *serious* serious."

"He definitely does."

"Could've warned me."

267

I pushed my finger inside her pussy, felt it clamp around me. "Keep talking."

She moaned softly. "Since I hadn't thought anything of it, I... Ian ... that feels so good." Another moan, then she was back on topic. "I inadvertently earned punishment that night. But then Isaac surprised me. Told me you were going to dish out my punishment."

I added another finger inside her. I wasn't sure if Everly realized it or not, but she was fucking my fingers, lifting and lowering on them in the water.

She continued her story, pausing for breathy moans. "You made me go over to the spanking bench. Face down, ass up. I did. You didn't come over for a few minutes and I was starting to think that was my punishment. Being on display for the club. Nope. It wasn't." She ground her hips down, trying to take my fingers deeper. "You finally came over, brought the vibrator with you. Settled it against my clit and told me to hold it there, but I wasn't allowed to come. Since I already had, I figured that wasn't a problem."

She sighed when I added a third finger.

"Part of me had hoped ... oh, God, yes ... hoped you'd take me that night. Right there in front of everyone."

That was news to me, and her declaration had me pulling back, staring into her eyes. "Did you?"

Everly met my gaze head on, held it. "I did. Of course, you know that didn't happen. So, there I was, on the spanking bench, a vibrator on my clit, expecting to get a spanking but hoping to get fucked."

Those crass words coming out of her sweet, innocent mouth had my cock hardening. The fact that she was getting off retelling this story didn't hurt, either.

"Next thing I know, a vibrator's being pushed into my ass."

Her pussy clenched around my fingers.

Her voice was raspy with desire when she continued. "While I'd been hoping to feel your cock inside me, you fucked my ass with a toy."

"Did you enjoy it?"

She moaned softly, grinding against my hand. "Yes. More than I thought I would."

"Did you come?"

"Yes." She smiled sweetly. "But I asked permission first."

Everly kissed me, grinding against my hand. I teased her clit with my thumb, fucked her with my fingers. She was panting.

"One of these days," I whispered against her mouth, "my cock's going to be in your ass."

She inhaled sharply. "I know."

"Do you want that?"

"Yes."

I moved over to the wall, leaned against it, and bent my knees, shifting so that she was sitting on my thigh, her legs floating out to the side, her back across my arm.

"What are you doing?" she asked.

"Close your eyes. Lean your head back."

She did, her head bobbing on the water, ears submerged, face above. Her hair floated out around her.

I drove two fingers into her pussy, fucked her ruthlessly as I watched. She moaned, begged, her nipples puckering, stomach muscles flexing.

"May I have permission?"

"For what?" I growled, drilling my fingers into her.

"To come … oh, God. Please, Ian, please let me come."

"You may," I groaned seconds before she splintered in my arms.

I held on to her, keeping her face above water as she went limp in my arms. I pulled her into me, chuckling as I kissed her neck.

"Feel better?" I asked as she draped her arms around me.

"So much better."

I held her there for a few minutes, giving her time to recuperate. All the while, I secretly relished those moments I got to spend with her. I wasn't sure why'd I'd gotten so damn lucky that day, but I wasn't going to ruin it by thinking about it too much.

When Everly lifted her head, she was smiling.

"You do know you're going to return the favor," I told her.

"When?"

"That's for me to know and you to find out."

"You're going to surprise me?"

"Perhaps I will."

Everly leaned in, her lips hovering over mine, her voice but a rasp when she said, "Surprise me now, Ian."

She shifted, her legs coming around my hips, her arms wreathing my neck. I wanted to tell her no, to maintain control of this situation. I was the Dom, for fuck's sake.

"I'll beg if you'd like me to," she whispered, her mouth still close to mine. "I'll do anything you ask of me. Anytime. Anywhere."

I got the feeling she was telling me something. Something vitally important. But I could hardly think beyond the fact that she was in my arms and we were alone, out here beneath the stars.

Not like we hadn't been alone before. Hell, I'd just recently had her in the library.

But this felt different.

Everly pulled back, met my gaze. "I've missed you."

Her words tore at my heart, had my arms banding more tightly around her. I wanted to carry her into the house, deposit her on my bed, spend the next few hours buried deep inside her. Then I wanted to wake up with her in my arms and do it all again.

It wasn't an option, not with our current circumstances, but it was a great fantasy.

"Take me inside you," I breathed against her ear as I pulled her closer.

Her hand dipped into the water, sliding between our bodies before fisting around me. It was the work of a moment before she guided me home, her body shifting as she eased down on my cock.

For a few breathless moments, I remained like that, buried to the hilt inside her blistering warmth, content to hold her, to breathe in her delectable scent.

But then I was moving, positioning myself with my back to the wall in the shallower middle section of the pool. Sliding my palms up her spine, I curled my fingers around her shoulders, dipped her back and drove my hips forward, slamming in deep. Using the wall of the pool against my shoulder blades, I braced my thighs and fucked her as she leaned back, braced in my arms. Her breasts bounced with every punishing thrust. I could do nothing but stare at her as I lost myself in her body. Everly was so fucking beautiful as she gave herself over to me, offering up her body for my pleasure. But there was more to this and I felt that connection, the slow knitting of two souls.

Although I'd thought all this time that she belonged solely to Isaac, I had my first glimmer of hope as our bodies were joined in that moment.

"Hold on to me," I urged.

Everly instantly sat up, her arms ringing my neck, her ankles pressing into my lower back. I gripped her hips and jerked her into me, thrusting forward, impaling her on my cock again and again. The heat between us was so great, I was surprised not to see steam coming off the water.

"Ian … I need to come. Please…" Her eyes opened, met mine. "Come inside me when I do."

Oh, fuck.

I hadn't expected that. Her soft plea was more than I could handle. A dark, rumbling growl escaped as I slammed into her, jerking her down again. My release tore up through my shaft, erupting inside her, triggering the most beautiful cry I'd ever heard come from her.

It was in that moment that I knew there would be no other woman for me. Not for as long as I lived.

The question was: how did I tell Isaac?

Or better yet, could I?

Twenty-Two

Everly

Tuesday, June 4, 2019

BY THE TIME TUESDAY NIGHT ROLLED AROUND, stir-crazy was no longer the right way to describe what I was feeling. And I was making sure everyone knew it, too. I'd even texted Heaven to let her know I was climbing the walls. Although she wasn't locked inside, she didn't seem to be faring any better being at her sister's. But she seemed happy, so I figured she could deal with my complaining.

"Go get dressed," Ian ordered when he walked into the living room.

"For what?"

He turned slowly, eyes intense. "It wasn't a request. It simply requires you to follow directions."

Realizing I'd overstepped, I clamped my lips together as he disappeared toward his bedroom.

"Get dressed," Isaac noted, stepping into the room.

I got to my feet, started toward his bedroom. "Where are we going? I'm not sure what I should wear."

He started toward me, motioned to the hallway.

"Okay, okay. I'll go get dressed."

"Too late for that."

"What do you mean too late?"

His eyes narrowed.

"Not that way," he said when I paused at the guest room door.

"But my clothes…"

He pointed to his bedroom. I pouted, then walked inside. He didn't bother to shut the door behind him.

"Strip, then lie down. On your back."

When I didn't move, his eyes turned to slits.

It wasn't that I didn't want to follow directions, but I was a bit surprised by the fact we were obviously going somewhere, yet I didn't know where.

"Don't make me tell you again."

"Yes, my Liege," I said, accepting my fate.

He disappeared into his bathroom while I tugged off my shirt and shorts. I propped up on the pillow, spread my legs, resisted the urge to tease myself. I happened to enjoy the way his eyes heated when I did.

However, I'd already overstepped. Twice. No sense making it worse for myself.

"Five."

I sobered instantly. "Of course, my Liege."

Standing at the end of the bed, Isaac reached up, grabbed my ankle, then pulled. My weight was no match against his strength. He had me down at the end of the bed, staring up at him.

Isaac placed my feet flat on the footboard, knees up.

"Spread them."

I dropped my knees, giving him an up close and intimate view of my privates.

That was when I noticed we weren't the only ones in the room. I glanced over to see Dante standing in the doorway.

"She's earned some punishment," Isaac explained, glancing back over his shoulder. "Why don't you come over here for a minute."

"Of course, Master."

"I was thinking the vibrating egg would be enough, but I think she needs to be primed first. Eat her pussy, but don't let her come."

"It would be my pleasure, Master." Dante smiled at me.

When his head dipped down, I watched. When his tongue slid through the folds of my pussy, I gasped. And kept right on gasping as he used that wicked tongue to drive me higher and higher until I thought I would shatter. I wasn't sure how he knew, but he stopped just short of an orgasm, making me groan in disappointment.

Dante was still smiling when he leaned over, kissed me softly. "You're welcome."

Figuring it wouldn't do me any good to call him a tease, I snapped my lips together.

"Now you can go get dressed."

"May I ask where we're going, Master?"

"Dichotomy." He smiled over at Dante. "No training required. Nothing fancy. I have something for you to wear when we get there."

"Yes, Master."

Dante winked at me before slipping out of the room.

I dropped my head back on the bed. The fact that Dante had kindly asked the question and received an easy answer was not lost on me. Clearly my cabin fever was tripping me up.

I felt something press against my pussy. It slipped inside with ease, then something pressed against my clit. I peeked down my body.

"May I ask what that is, my Liege?"

He grinned, hooked something to it, then forced me to lift my butt.

"It's a Venus butterfly with a G-spot extension."

Although I'd been around quite a few toys, I didn't have any experience with this particular one. However, I was smart enough to know this was not going to be a pleasurable evening.

Isaac worked to get it in place, hooked something, then reached under my butt again, pulled something toward him, clipped it.

Whatever it was, it felt like a G-string, a tiny strip of floss in my crack.

"You'll wear this until we get home." He reached for my hand, helped me to my feet. "Any discomfort?"

"No, my Liege."

Isaac was smiling at me and I couldn't figure out why. Then it happened. A slight tingle between my legs that turned into a full-blown earthquake, making my thighs tremble as the vibration on my clit and against my G-spot nearly had me dropping to the floor.

He grabbed my arm, held me up. "Wearing it isn't the punishment, fairy princess. The vibration is."

It stopped suddenly and I was able to catch my breath.

"However, I think I'll let Ian handle the controls this evening," he explained, stepping up close and tilting my head back. His voice was soft, his eyes, too.

"I'm looking forward to whatever you have in mind, my Liege," I whispered, meaning every word.

It had been some time since I'd scened with them at the club, and if it meant getting out of the house, I was more than willing to endure just about anything.

"Now, you've earned five swats. You can take them now. Or if you prefer to have them when we return, you'll get five additional."

"I'd like to choose later, if that's all right with you, my Liege."

He smirked, his pretty eyes twinkling. "Perfectly fine with me. I do love turning that cute little ass red." He planted one more kiss on my lips. "Now go get dressed. Something casual. I'll have something for you to wear there."

"Yes, my Liege."

I hurried out of the room, went right for my closet. I opted for a skirt because of the contraption I was currently sporting. I managed to get dressed, brush my teeth, my hair, and pull on my shoes.

That's when the vibration started.

And it didn't stop.

My knees wobbled and I stumbled in the hallway, using the wall to keep myself upright.

"Problem?" Isaac asked, walking past me on the way to the living room.

"Oh, God," I moaned.

He chuckled.

Chuckled.

This was going to be a long... *Oh, God, oh, God, oh, God...*

...Night.

ISAAC

"WELL, THIS IS QUITE THE TREAT."

I shook the proffered hand, moved in for a back-slapping hug. "Good to see you, too. Talon, I'd like to introduce you to our pets."

Talon's gray eyes trailed over Everly first. "I think we've met."

"You have. Everly's a member."

"Ah. Training class."

Her eyes lowered respectfully.

"And this is Dante."

He didn't greet Talon, but Dante had already bowed his head respectfully. I was quite impressed. Then again, Everly had given him a quick rundown of some of the protocols of the club on the way here.

"Where's that mischievous brother of yours?" Talon asked.

"He's around here somewhere."

"You planning to scene tonight?"

"We are. Ian reserved a room for him and Everly."

"Perhaps I'll have to check it out."

"You should. She enjoys being watched."

"In that case, I'll definitely be there. I'll even bring a few friends." He smacked my shoulder. "I've got rounds to make, but I'll see you up there."

When Talon strolled off, I guided Everly and Dante through the dungeon, pausing every so often so they could watch one of the scenes. Ian joined us while we were observing a particularly intense spanking scene. He came to stand behind Everly, his hands curling over her shoulders. He'd been thrilled when I'd given him the controller, letting him know he was in charge of it tonight. I'd also warned him that she would earn punishment if she came without permission. He assured me he'd personally take care of it should the opportunity present itself.

It was then I'd seen the glint in my brother's eyes. Perhaps it had been there before, and I'd missed it. He was enjoying spending time with Everly since Heaven had left. In fact, I'd go so far as to say he was relieved to have the opportunity. I honestly hadn't expected it. And while I wasn't sure how to process it all yet, I was glad to see they were enjoying their time together.

For the next half hour, Ian and I took them around, introduced Dante to the club's Masters, let them watch scenes. After taking them up to the main floor, hydrating them, it was time to get the room we'd reserved. I could see the sparkle in Everly's eyes. She was excited, even though she had no idea what Ian had in store for her.

As we crossed the second floor, a couple of Doms glanced her way, eyeing her appreciatively. It certainly hadn't been the first time tonight, including quite the interest from a few Doms I knew she had played with in the past. And while I wasn't jealous that they'd had the pleasure of being with her in the past, nor did I care that they were watching her now, I was going to ensure they knew she was spoken for the next time we came.

"Right this way," Ian said, motioning into the room.

"Everly, kneel," I instructed.

I placed a hand on Dante's back, looked to my brother. He nodded.

"You and I … we're going to have our own scene. Somewhere a little more private."

"It would be my pleasure, Master," Dante said softly.

"We'll have a good time without you. Won't we, my little fairy?"

"Yes, Master Ian," she replied eagerly.

"We'll meet you at the bar in one hour," I told Ian as I pulled the door closed.

I walked across the second floor to another door that was closed with a sign that read: RESERVED BY ISAAC STOKES. NO VIEWING OR INTERRUPTIONS ALLOWED.

I flipped on the lights, signaled for Dante to precede me into the room.

"You're probably wondering why I've separated you."

"It might've crossed my mind, Master."

I closed the door, ensured the viewing window was closed appropriately.

"While the club monitors will check in at their discretion, I've asked for complete privacy otherwise." I walked around Dante. "My objective tonight is to show you proper protocol in a club. To give you the full experience in a safe environment. While I don't have a problem with Everly witnessing this, I wanted you and me to have this time alone. What questions do you have for me?"

"It's not so much a question, Master."

"Speak candidly, Dante. That's the only way this'll work."

His eyes lifted, met mine. "I know you're bothered by my past."

I held up a hand. "First of all, yes, I am bothered by your past. You never should've been subjected to that. Not as an adult and certainly not as a child." I stepped in, maintained eye contact, my voice dropping an octave. "I'm bothered because I want to kill the bastard who dared touch you. Every one of them, including that poor excuse for a man who fathered you. I, however, am not bothered by *you*. But I feel it's important you experience a scene without observation, interference, or interruption by anyone. That includes Everly and Ian. This is between me and you. Only us."

"Thank you, Master."

"For what?"

"For not treating me like blown glass, for not thinking I'll fall apart. I'm stronger than I look."

I gripped his jaw. "You're the strongest man I've ever met, Dante. Both your physical strength and your will. No man measures up to that."

His chin wobbled for a second, but he recovered, swallowed hard.

I took a step back. "Tonight, I'm going to be asking your color often. If at any time you want me to stop, either red or stop will work. If at any time I don't think you're in the right headspace, I will quit, understand?"

"Yes, Master."

"If you'd like me to relay the scene to you prior, I will. Until you're comfortable with me."

He shook his head vehemently. "No, Master. Please. I trust you. I want this." He swallowed again, his eyes imploring me. "I trust you."

"Then I'm trusting you to know your limits. Red or stop. Either one. At any time. Nothing I'll do tonight is a hard limit. Whether or not that'll change after we're through is something you and I will work on. Understand?"

"Yes, Master."

I walked over to the table, retrieved the envelope I'd had delivered there earlier. I tore through the flap, flipped open the paper, and skimmed the words. I glanced at the sheets behind it, then turned and took them to Dante.

"These are the blood test results. Yours, mine, Ian's, and Everly's. They're all clear."

There were tears in his eyes, but right before my eyes, he willed them back. "Thank you, Master."

I took them when he passed them back, leaned in, and kissed him. "Going forward, I won't be using protection with you unless you have a problem with that."

"No, Master, I don't have a problem."

After returning the papers to the table, I retrieved the blindfold.

"This is about trust tonight. You tell me you trust me. I'm asking you to prove it."

He glanced at the blindfold. "It would be my pleasure, Master."

I swallowed down the emotion that clogged my throat. When I told him he was the strongest man I'd ever known, I wasn't blowing smoke up his ass. To know what he'd been through *and* to have his trust ... that was humbling.

"I want you to strip, then we'll get you restrained. After that, I'll place the blindfold on you."

"Yes, Master."

As I moved over to the leather sling I'd had set up prior to our arrival, Dante stripped off his leather shorts, placed them on the stool by the door.

I patted the sling.

"Sit, then recline."

Once he did, I assisted him in getting his feet in the leather cuffs that hung from the top. They would keep his legs up and spread wide, leaving him fully available to me in every way. Once his feet were secured, I moved around to his head.

"Left arm."

Dante raised it above his head, allowing me to use the padded cuffs hooked to the chains that connected to the top bar.

"Other arm." I positioned it, fastened the cuff, then placed a leather-covered pillow beneath his head to keep him propped forward.

I walked around, ran my hands over the restraints on his wrists and feet, ensured everything was secure and that there was no risk of him being injured by the equipment. Once I was satisfied, I took the blindfold I'd tucked into my pocket, then placed it over his eyes.

"Color?"

"Green, Master."

"Very well. We'll get started."

His breathing had already increased, but it didn't seem to be out of fear. More so anticipation, which I definitely approved of. I wanted him eager.

I started with his cock first, letting my fingers brush over it.

"You are not permitted to come until I specifically give you permission. Do not ask. It will not be granted. And if you do come without permission, I will punish you when we get home."

"Yes, Master."

Using a small amount of lube, I slicked his cock, then slid a silicone ring on, stretching it around his balls and ensuring it was in place. It would make his cock more sensitive for what I had in mind for him. In addition, there was a prostate massager attached, which would help with stimulation throughout. I lubed it generously, then pressed it against his asshole.

"This toy is something I purchased specifically for you," I informed him. "It's brand new. For the record, I would never put a used toy inside you."

He inhaled sharply, moaned as I pushed it in as far as it would go. To give him something to think about, I clicked it on, left it on the lowest setting.

"How does that feel?"

"Good, Master." He gasped.

I smiled even though he couldn't see me. I wasn't quiet as I prepared the next toy. I wanted him to hear me, to be expecting something but not knowing what. I turned on the violet wand, placed my finger near the tip to allow the electricity to arc to my skin. I happened to know quite a few submissives who thoroughly enjoyed this particular instrument. Used correctly, it could and would provide a sensual experience unlike any other.

I didn't provide commentary as I brought the wand over, using the single glass electrode with a curved tip. I started on Dante's forearm, ensuring the skin wasn't super sensitive to the stimulation.

He moaned softly as I allowed the electrical current to glide over his skin.

"Color?"

"Green, Master."

I continued, sliding up his arm, down his chest, teasing his sides, then sliding down to his groin.

"Too much or too little?"

"I could use more, Master."

I clicked it up a notch, went over a spot I'd already touched. "Now?"

He moaned. "Better, Master."

I continued, moving back up to his nipples, circling them with the arcing current of electricity. He hissed, moaned. Not wanting to overstimulate any one area, I moved back down, making a detour around his cock. I would save that for last. However, I did take the opportunity to increase the speed on the prostate vibrator.

"Oh, fuck," he moaned softly.

I continued with the current, covering every inch of his body. Once I'd gone down both sides, both arms, both legs, and his torso, I moved to stand between his legs. I reconnected the current on his ass cheek, moving it up the back of his thigh, then angled toward his cock. The closer I got, the more he moaned, his body tightening, his cock throbbing. The cock ring was doing its job, making him more sensitive as it kept all the blood where it belonged.

I moved back to his thigh, and when he settled, I dragged the current along the underside of his cock.

"Fuck … oh, fuck…"

"Do not come," I commanded, teasing him relentlessly and pulling back right before he would've hit the point of no return.

He was panting when I turned off the electricity, set the wand to the side.

"Color?"

"Green, Master," he said between breaths.

Then we were a go for the next part.

A part I was particularly looking forward to.

Dante

THE PLEASURE WAS INTENSE.
Overwhelming.
I never wanted it to end.

284

Even as I lay in the leather sling, unable to move and plunged into complete darkness, I felt more alive than I'd ever felt before. Absolutely no fear, only anticipation, excitement. Tremendous desire.

Trust wasn't something that came easily for me, but I trusted Isaac. Not only would he not hurt me or push me to a dark place, he would care for me.

I'd never had that before, and I found I craved it like a drug.

I heard him move but had no idea what he was doing. Whatever he'd used on me had been stimulating, tickling over my skin, making the hairs on my body stand on end. The noise had been familiar, like an electric current or something, but I wasn't sure what it was.

Now I could feel him close, standing near my head. I waited, trying to ignore the vibrator currently making it difficult to focus on anything except for the pleasure in my ass.

Warm breath fanned my mouth and my head dipped back slightly. When Isaac's lips moved over mine, his tongue plunging inside, I wanted to grab hold of him and never let go. Instead, I turned my head, giving him better access. He kissed me, long and hard, urgent thrusts of his tongue against mine. I wasn't ready for him to stop when he pulled back. I could hear him breathing as hard as I was.

I relaxed my head back on the pillow, followed the sound of him moving around the stand. The vibrator in my ass slowed, ratcheting up my nerves as I waited for what was to come.

Something warm dripped onto my stomach, just above my navel. Another drop landed, then another. It took a moment for my nerve endings to realize the heat. By then I was moaning as more liquid dripped down on me. A line of warmth went up my stomach, my chest. Heat splashed on my nipple and I moaned low in my throat. My cock throbbed.

"Color?"

"Green, Master."

Isaac chuckled and I realized how urgent that sounded.

I suspected he was using wax of some sort because it cooled quickly, making my skin feel tight. When he dripped it on my other nipple, there was more of it. The exquisite pleasure/pain had me trying to arch my back, groaning as electric sparks ignited in the base of my spine. My cock was so fucking hard.

I breathed through it, thinking about colors in order to weaken the urge to come.

Something cool and wet covered my chest before it was wiped over me. The sensation was intense, my skin still warm from the liquid.

I lay there, breathing roughly as I waited, listening for any signal of what was coming.

Either he was trying to be silent or the blood pounding in my ears drowned any noise out, because I didn't know Isaac had moved until the warm liquid trickled over my cock.

"Fuck!" I jumped, hissed.

"Color?"

"Green! Oh, God!"

More liquid landed, tickling my balls with warmth. The vibrator increased and I cried out.

"Master! Oh, fuck." It took everything in me to hold back. My chest was heaving, lungs burning. My senses were overwhelmed and yet I still wanted more.

As though he knew, Isaac didn't stop. He poured the liquid over the insides of my thighs, then the sensitive head of my dick.

I fought the tears that threatened, the sensations brutal but amazing at the same time.

"Do not come," Isaac barked.

"I won't, Master." I jerked at the restraints, trying to distract myself. I was close, too close. "Oh, fuck."

And then it all stopped.

The heat, the vibrations. It disappeared completely, giving me a brief reprieve.

The room was eerily silent without the hum from the vibrator.

I hissed when the cool rag was dragged over my cock. The cock ring was removed, blood flowing in a painful rush. The vibrator was removed next. It gave me a moment to pull myself together, but I prayed our hour wasn't up. I wasn't ready for it to be over. I needed more.

Isaac returned beside my head. He leaned over and once again his lips met mine. I sighed into his mouth. He kept it slow this time, gentle. It made my insides quiver, my need for him intensifying.

When he pulled back, he reached for my left wrist. I thought he was going to release me, but he didn't. His hand curled around my wrist. It was slick with oil or something as he began massaging me. He worked his way down my arm, taking his time, enhancing my pleasure as he worked. I couldn't see him, but that didn't matter.

"Color?"

"Green ... Master," I said softly, emotion building in my chest.

He massaged my neck, my collar bones. Pecs, stomach, thigh. Then down my shin, even my foot. He disappeared, returning near my head again, working his way from my right wrist down to my right foot. I was boneless by the time he finished.

I heard his footsteps move to the back of the room, then return by my head. Once more he kissed me. Slow, reverent. My chest was rising and falling rapidly from the emotion that was threatening to explode. I'd never had any man treat me with such care the way Isaac and Ian had. Both had ensured my pleasure when I was with them, even beyond their own.

I'd never considered that was an objective when it came to Domination and submission, but I was learning more and more every day. What I thought I knew becoming obsolete.

As Isaac kissed me, I felt the blindfold loosen, then slip off. I didn't open my eyes until he pulled his mouth from mine. I had to blink a few times to adjust to the overhead lights.

He walked around to stand between my legs, and I thought he was finished.

His eyes were intense when they met mine. He retrieved something from a small table I couldn't see beneath me. It was a bottle of lubricant. He squirted it into his palms, then fisted my cock.

My eyes threatened to roll back in my head. It was warm as he stroked me. He took extra care, not rushing as he brought me closer and closer to orgasm with the glide of his hands over my cock. He added more lubricant twice, making me groan as the pleasure intensified.

I was starting to think he was going to get me off with his hand, then his fingers slid between my ass cheeks, pushed inside me. I locked my eyes with his, a silent plea. I wanted—no, *needed*—to feel him inside me. I wanted to be one with him. It would be the perfect end to the most intensely amazing scene I'd ever done.

"Color?"

"Green, Master."

"Is there something you want?"

"Yes, Master."

His eyes remained locked with mine, emerald green merging with navy blue. "Tell me."

"I need to feel you inside me, Master."

"Need? Not want?" He smiled, but his eyes were hotter.

"Yes, Master."

Isaac added another finger, pushing in deep, teasing my prostate as he worked me open. I dropped my head back, tried to focus on anything other than coming. It was too much, but not enough at the same time. His hands disappeared and I watched as he walked to the other side of the room.

Water came on, stayed on for a few seconds. When it went off, he returned. Isaac did something that tilted the sling, raising my head slightly. He returned to his spot between my legs, his eyes locking with mine as he freed his cock. There was no fumbling, no preamble. I felt the pressure as he pushed in deep. His eyes turned dark, his face strained, as though the pleasure was as great for him as it was for me.

I couldn't look away. He put his hands on the sling, pulled it toward him, using the momentum to thrust and retreat. He fucked me thoroughly, maintaining the same steady pace that had my breath halting in my lungs.

"Color?" There was a gruffness to his voice this time.

"Green, Master," I said on a raspy breath. "So fucking green."

He smirked and I saw the change as it happened, but he reined it in, slowed before he could speed up, braced himself before he could drive into me.

"Please, don't," I whimpered. "Please don't hold back, Master. I need you."

"You don't know what you're asking for, Dante."

"I'm asking for you, Isaac. *All* of you."

He inhaled sharply, jerked the sling toward him, impaling me. I cried out his name, followed by a plethora of pleas. I fought to keep my eyes open, not wanting to miss a second, although the pleasure was overwhelming me, tingling at the base of my spine, electric sparks igniting.

I held out and I was doing a damn fine job until he fisted my cock, then stroked in time with his thrusts, driving into me, pulling back. Again and again, faster, harder, deeper. So fucking deep.

I groaned.

And I knew right then that he needed me to come without permission. How I knew, I wasn't sure, but it was imperative that I did. He needed the control that came along with it, because I could see in his eyes that he thought he was losing it.

I threw my head back and roared, coming in a rush of blinding light that had every muscle flexing.

Seconds later, Isaac drove into me, impossibly deep, and erupted.

Once again, complete silence descended, our harsh breathing the only sound. I turned my head when he walked to the back of the room. I could hear him cleaning himself up. He returned with a warm, wet towel. Cleaned my cock, my ass, gently, thoroughly.

Air was scarce, my body weak as he released the restraint on my ankle. He rested that leg on his shoulder as he freed the other, then lowered them to the floor before unhooking my wrists. He massaged them briefly, then came to stand in front of me.

This time when he kissed me, he cupped my face, a move that made my heart ache in my chest. This man ... I was falling for him. Hard and fast. Something that I'd never thought would happen. Not in my lifetime.

When he pulled back, he slid his thumbs over my cheeks, stared in my eyes. "When we get home, you've earned punishment. I want you to go to your room, take a shower. When you're finished, I want you to kneel in the center of your bedroom until I come for you. Don't bother getting dressed."

"Yes, Master, it would be my pleasure."

He smirked. This time it was wicked and sexy. "We'll see about that."

And I knew we most definitely would.

Twenty-Three

Everly

THE SECOND WE PULLED DOWN IAN AND Isaac's driveway, I knew something was wrong.

Not because I could see it or sense it. Because Ian and Isaac could.

The garage door opened slowly, but Isaac didn't pull the Escalade inside. He left it out, turned off the engine.

"I'll go in the front. You take the back," Ian commanded. He glanced over his shoulder at us. "Dante, you get in the driver's seat. If at any time you feel either of you are in danger, I want you to leave. The police station isn't far from here. Go directly there, understand?"

"Yes, Master," he said firmly before opening his door.

Isaac didn't look back at us, his entire focus on the house. Dante climbed into the driver's seat, locked the doors when they closed. He turned the engine over, flipped the radio off.

"What's going on?" I asked, keeping my voice barely above a whisper.

"I don't know."

I glanced out all the windows, trying to see what had set them off. It took a minute, but I finally saw it. There was a red light flashing at the top eave over the garage. It was small, but they'd obviously known what to look for.

Minutes felt like hours, my heart pounding like a bass drum. Finally, Ian appeared, walking over to the driver's side.

"Pull it in the garage," he told Dante when he rolled the window down.

Ian waited while Dante parked, shut off the engine. The garage door was down before he allowed us out.

"Please tell me what's going on," I begged.

"Just stay quiet. Not a word," he snapped, motioning for us to go inside.

When I walked in, all the lights were blazing, every corner lit up like the face of the sun. Nothing looked out of place, just how we'd left it.

Dante started toward his room, but Isaac stopped him with a hand on his chest. "No."

I watched the staring contest that ensued.

I wasn't surprised when Dante didn't back down, his voice low when he asked, "What did he do?"

Isaac merely shook his head.

Dante tried to move forward. Isaac held him back.

"You don't need to see it. Neither of you do." He pointed across the house. "You'll sleep in one of those rooms tonight."

"Isaac." Dante's voice was clipped, angry.

Isaac got right in his face. "Don't."

"I have to."

I could feel the pain and anger coming off them both, knew whatever had happened was bad. Isaac was rattled, not to mention extremely pissed, and Dante seemed to know something I didn't.

"While you two hash it out," Ian growled, "I'm going to sweep the rooms."

Sweep the rooms?

I raised my eyebrows, glanced over at Ian. Then it dawned on me because, you know, I'd seen enough crime TV over the years. He was checking for bugs.

Holy crap.

Finally, Isaac backed down, stepping aside so Dante could go past.

I followed, pushed forward when Isaac tried to hold me back.

I could smell paint fumes when I stepped inside. I stared at the destruction. Every single thing in the room was destroyed. The bedding and mattress were shredded, doors ripped off the hinges. The furniture looked as though someone had taken an axe to it. Holes dotted all the walls except one.

That one, still intact, had a message painted in red:

YOU BELONG TO ME. ALWAYS HAVE. NO ONE WILL TAKE YOU AWAY. IT'S TIME TO COME HOME, DANTE. FOR EVERY DAY YOU DON'T...

Below the letters were five pictures, all taken here, in the backyard. Me, Heaven, Dante, Isaac, and Ian. In that order. Large steak knives had been driven into four of them, right between the eyes.

Dante was breathing hard, his chest rising and falling. I'd never seen him so angry. It pained me that anyone would do this to him.

I stared at the wall and that's when I saw the smaller message. There was an arrow pointed toward the picture of me. Beside it: SHE'LL BE THE FIRST TO DIE.

"Oh, my God," I gasped, stumbled back.

Isaac grabbed me, pulled me into his arms, and held me, his hands curling protectively over my head as I fisted his shirt and sobbed.

I walked with him when he led me out of the room. He guided me over to a barstool, held me as I composed myself. I couldn't seem to let go of him, not sure why.

"We need to call the police," I suggested.

"There's nothing they can do," Isaac said softly. "But it'll be taken care of."

Nothing they could do? Someone had broken in. Those were ... death threats. Surely they could do something. Find the asshole. Put him behind bars. Anything.

I heard footsteps, then Ian's voice. "Fifteen in the bedrooms alone."

I pulled back from Isaac. "Fifteen what?"

"Cameras. There were two in Dante's room. We took them down before we let you in the house."

"Are they all gone?"

"Yeah."

"I thought you set the alarm?"

Ian, obviously hearing my distress, walked over, hugged me against him, kissed the top of my head.

"We did," Isaac responded. "He bypassed it somehow."

"But there's another alarm," I stated. "The light on the house."

"Yeah. It's on a separate circuit. Detects any motion. It doesn't send a signal, though."

"I called Ransom," Ian said. "Asked him to come by. I don't trust my equipment alone. Need him to sweep again, make sure I didn't miss anything."

Isaac nodded. "When he gets here, I want you to go to our room."

I shook my head. "No. Please. I ... I want to be with you."

He must've heard the terror I had tried to disguise. I didn't want to fall apart, but this was terrifying. Especially for Dante.

Isaac pulled me into him again. This time I wasn't sure I could ever let go. I was trembling, petrified. Not only for myself but for all of us. This guy ... he was batshit crazy. He'd attacked me once, got into Isaac's. What would stop him from coming back, killing us all in our sleep?

I sobbed.

"I won't let anything happen to you," Isaac whispered in my ear, then gripped my shoulders and shifted me back. "I need to check the weapons. Don't move from this spot."

When he turned, I noticed the black pistol tucked into the back of his pants. He was a bodyguard, so that came with the territory, right? I hadn't seen any weapons since we got here, so I could only assume they had them locked up.

"Don't move," Ian said, following his twin.

When Isaac and Ian headed down to the basement, I remained where I was, my gaze scanning the kitchen, wondering if the asshole was out there watching us. Dante hadn't come out of the room, and I was tempted to check on him but scared to at the same time. I knew he needed to process, but he needed us, too. It was always a difficult decision when it came to overstepping with Dante. I didn't know who this guy was, what he wanted from Dante, but it wasn't a lover's jealousy that had driven him to destroy that room. No, it was insanity.

Ian and Isaac returned a few minutes later. They both headed straight for Dante's room, then brought him back out. It looked as though they'd had to force him, but they were gentle at least.

"Take Everly to the living room," Isaac instructed. "Turn on the TV. Settle. And don't move. Under any circumstance, understand?"

Dante's voice shook when he said, "Yes, Master."

Dante took my hand, tugged me toward the living room. When he went to sit at one end, I sat beside him, getting as close as I could.

We remained just like that when Ransom Bishop knocked on the door.

IAN

I GREETED RANSOM AT THE DOOR. "THANKS for coming, man."

"I brought backup," he said before stepping through the doorway and into the foyer.

Behind him was Zeke Lautner. A few steps beyond, Liam Murphy stood sentry, their keen gazes scanning the street before they stepped into the house.

I shook Zeke's hand, then clasped the hand of my fellow Irishman, pulling Liam into me and slapping him on the back. It was good to see him, though I wasn't fond of the circumstances.

"Let's see the damage," Ransom said, his tone flat and even, a no-nonsense guy when it came to business.

With a wave of my hand, I directed them toward Dante's wing of the house. I pulled up the rear when Isaac appeared and led the way.

All three men were silent as they took it in, walking through the bedroom, the bathroom. Ransom went into the closet, glanced around.

"Let me see your computers," Zeke said, his deep voice booming. "I'll do a quick scan, ensure he didn't plant something there."

"Sure thing," I replied. "They're in the basement."

He gave a backhanded wave, signaling he would find the way.

"He's lost it," Ransom mused, staring at the destruction.

"Yeah," I agreed, nodding toward the pictures. "Those were all taken here. He's definitely been watching the house. Not sure the last time, though. Heaven's been gone for a few days, but he doesn't seem to know that."

"She safe?" Ransom asked.

I nodded. "At her sister's. Probably wouldn't hurt to put a man on her house, though. Keep an eye out."

Ransom nodded.

"Probably tracking Dante's GPS," Liam said. "Could've hacked all their phones."

I'd already thought about that. Too little, too late, but whatever.

"We needed to gut the room anyway," Isaac said, the venom in the words only slightly masked.

"Upgrade the security," Ransom said, not bothering to ask what we currently had. Since the bastard had overridden it, it didn't matter.

"Could you do a second sweep for me?" I asked Ransom. "Need to ensure I didn't overlook something."

Liam was the one who grinned. "I brought some new toys. Won't miss anything."

"How's Dante holding up?" Ransom asked when Isaac took Liam through the rest of the house.

"He's pissed." I glanced toward him when we went back to the kitchen. "Can't blame him."

"No." Ransom thrust his hands in his pockets. "Good thing you're in town."

I'd thought about that at least a dozen times since we walked through the door. I didn't want to think what might've happened if they'd been alone when this happened. Or worse, if that sick bastard had come in while they were asleep.

"Any reason you didn't call the cops?" Ransom asked, his dark eyes pinning me in place.

He missed nothing, I knew.

"Don't need their help," I said simply.

"Because you're relying on mine, correct? *Only* mine?"

"For now," I said quietly, holding his stare. I wasn't above reaching out for help if necessary. Not when it came to their safety.

"I don't want any blood on your hands, Ian."

"Don't have to worry about that." That much was true. I would call in the ghosts who passed in the night before I would risk that.

"Need more eyes here?" he offered.

"Nay. Got it covered."

"That's what I'm worried about." He glanced toward the living room. "The girls know what's going on?"

I shook my head. "Everly saw the room, but no, Dante hasn't told them his story." I was hoping he would, but it wasn't my place to push him. Not yet, anyway.

"I'll put someone on the other girl's house."

I nodded.

We turned toward the basement stairs when Zeke came stomping up them. He glanced my way, gave a slight shake of his head. "Nothing. I even scanned the network. Found the back door he came in through the security system. Plugged it. He's not too savvy, but he's got some knowledge." He smirked. "Can't say the same for you. Quite talented."

"All Isaac," I assured him.

"Perhaps he needs to come work for me."

"Perhaps not." I couldn't see my brother jockeying a desk for the rest of his life. He'd go insane.

Zeke smirked again. "Figured as much."

For the next half hour, the five of us moved through the house, going through every room, closet, and bathroom several more times to ensure we hadn't missed anything. By the time I watched them walk out the front door, I felt better. No way we'd missed anything.

It was only a small comfort, considering.

"I'll get someone in to redecorate," Isaac noted, pouring his favored whiskey into a glass.

"Yeah. I'll tear out the Sheetrock in the morning, toss the rest."

Footsteps sounded, drawing my attention. Dante appeared, hands in his pockets, his face expressionless save for the glint of anger in his blue eyes.

"You all right?" I asked, squeezing his shoulder when he came closer.

"I need to be part of this."

Yeah, I had a feeling he was going to say that. Dante was damaged from years of abuse, but he wasn't going to risk those he loved.

"I'll agree to that," Isaac told him. "Once you tell Everly what happened."

Dante's head shot up. "All of it?"

"Yes." He sipped his drink. "She loves you. Don't you think she deserves to know what she's risking?"

"And Heaven?"

Isaac shrugged. "She deserves to know, too. But that's up to you."

Dante's eyebrows lowered. "I won't let him hurt them."

I stood tall, glared at him. "And we won't let him hurt you. Ever again."

"It's a small price to pay," Dante mumbled.

"What did you say?" I got right up in his face, nose to nose.

Dante didn't flinch. "If that's what it takes…"

"Bullshit. You've tried that already. It's our turn to take care of the problem."

Dante's hardened gaze scanned my face before he finally nodded.

Isaac cleared his throat. "I need you to watch Everly. Dante and I have some unfinished business." He pinned Dante with a hard glare. "You. My bedroom. Shower first. Then do as I told you earlier."

Something softened in Dante's face seconds before he said, "Yes, Master."

When Dante was out of earshot, I turned to Isaac, thrust my hand through my hair. "This ends now," I growled. "I won't tolerate that bastard walking into my house…"

"I know." Isaac's voice was low, his tone understanding. He glanced at his watch. "It's early yet. Wait till morning to make the call."

I knew he was referring to the time in Dublin. It was two in the morning there, and while I knew a few people who'd be up, it could wait a few more hours.

"Aye."

Isaac nodded toward the bedrooms. "This won't take long."

"Yeah. I'll sit with her for a bit."

Isaac moved with purpose, disappearing while I joined Everly in the living room. When I went to sit beside her, the little fairy moved over easily.

"Stand up," I directed, keeping my voice low, just between the two of us.

She got to her feet, wary eyes scanning my face, probably wondering what I was up to.

"Remove the butterfly," I told her.

Clearly having figured out the contraption, Everly tucked her hands beneath her skirt, deftly removed the device, setting it on the coffee table behind her.

I patted my lap.

When she turned to sit, I grabbed her arm, shook my head. She stepped forward, straddled my legs.

Unable to resist, I slid my hand beneath her hair, pulled her mouth to mine. I wanted to feel her wrapped around me. I needed her to clear the evil out of my head. Otherwise, I wouldn't be able to sleep. Nor would she.

When the kiss ignited, I released her head, working to free my cock from my slacks. With minimal movement, I shoved them down my hips, adjusted Everly so she was hovering right where I wanted, then guided her down on my cock.

I groaned as her slick, warm pussy sheathed me.

It was then I realized I wasn't wearing a condom. And I hadn't worn one when we were in the pool the other night, either.

Holy shit.

It didn't matter because I knew she was on birth control, but I'd failed in that regard. I'd taken what ultimately didn't belong to me. My brother and I had agreed, this was how it would work. Now ... I wasn't sure I could ever go back to having a barrier between us.

Feeling the overwhelming glide of her sex along mine, I got lost in her. Lips and tongues glided together as she rode me, working us both into a frenzy. I practically ripped her shirt from her body, her bra following. I filled my hands with her pert tits, squeezing roughly, inhaling her sighs and moans.

"*A chroí...*" I held her hips, jerked her down on me. "Fuck..." I dropped my head back, let the pleasure consume me. Her lips brushed over my skin, whisper-soft in response to the soft bites she trailed.

She was everything I'd ever wanted, more than I deserved. And I wanted her with a passion I couldn't explain. The first thought in my head when I woke up, the last when I went to sleep. She was my heart, my nirvana, my absolute sanity, and in the short time I'd had her, she'd burrowed in deep. So fucking deep.

I wrapped my arm around her, jerked her to me, holding her still. "Fuck me," I growled in her ear.

Her hips swiveled, trying to give me everything I asked for, but unable to move enough to get there. With a low growl, I grabbed her ass with both hands, lifted her as I stood, then pinned her to the nearest wall before fucking her ruthlessly.

This woman ... my little fairy ... she was what I needed, and I was tired of pretending otherwise.

Her arms wreathed my neck as she held on tight, urging me on with soft pleas, desperate moans.

"Mine," I growled against her neck.

"Yours, Ian," she whispered.

Her acceptance snapped the thread holding me together. My movements became frantic. The overwhelming need to mate, to claim fueled my blood, had me slamming into her as I crushed her to the wall. I nipped her flesh, slightly aware of the bruises that would mar her skin. It only made me hotter.

Her lips pressed to my ear. "May I come?"

"Come for me, *a chroí.* Fuck yes."

Her pussy clamped down, milking my cock. My release slammed into me when she cried out my name again and again.

It was then I knew that I would never let her go. Never.

Twenty-Four

Everly

WHEN I WOKE UP THE NEXT MORNING, I took advantage of being alone for a little while.

After brushing my teeth, I showered, letting the warm water pelt over my skin for long minutes. I washed, shampooed, shaved, conditioned, then climbed out. I'd noticed all of my things had been moved into Isaac's bathroom. The necessities I'd brought with me, as well as a few things he must've picked up or ordered online.

My heart swelled, threatened to burst in my chest when I opened the closet door, saw all of my things hanging there. They hadn't been there last night before we left for the club, which meant sometime in the night or early morning, Isaac had moved them.

With trembling hands, I pulled on a T-shirt and shorts, my heart overflowing.

Until I thought about Ian. Our encounter last night. Something had changed between us, something I'd always thought was there. For whatever reason, he'd been holding back from me. I'd given it considerable thought lately. Tossed around the notion that Heaven had been the cause, the distraction. But nothing had ever arisen from their time together. So not Heaven.

It wasn't Dante because Ian had established a relationship with him from the beginning and they had something ... special. Between only them. The same as Isaac did with Dante.

Which left me with only one though. Whatever was holding Ian back pertained to Isaac. The question was, was it between the two of them, some issue they needed to address? Or did Ian think I only wanted Isaac on those terms? We hadn't discussed it. In fact, no one had ever given me the opportunity to tell them what I wanted. Hence the reason I was now taking every opportunity to show Ian, hoping against hope that they would figure it out.

I remembered the look in Ian's eyes last night when he'd fucked me in the living room. Truth was, the more time I spent with him, the more I realized how deep I was in all this.

I loved him.

Not puppy love, either. Not some crush that would dissipate over time. This was a passionate burn, an ache in my chest that would cause both pleasure and pain over time, but ultimately, it would endure. I could feel it. I just knew.

It was the exact same love I felt for Isaac. For Dante.

Yes. That was the only explanation I had. I was in love with three men. Three very different men and I loved them all equally.

A knock sounded on the door, jerking me out of my wayward thoughts. I looked over, swiped the tear on my cheek as Isaac stepped into the room.

"What's wrong?"

I smiled, knowing better than to tell him nothing. It would earn me punishment. Since I was already owed some from yesterday, tacking more on didn't seem to be a wise choice.

Isaac came to stand in front of me, staring down, his glittering green eyes intense.

I stared up at him, and before I could stop the words, they came tumbling out of my mouth. "I love you."

His expression didn't change, eyes still fierce, affection in every line around his eyes. "I know."

I made a sound, part laugh, part sob.

Isaac chuckled, urging me back on the bed as he crawled over me. His mouth feathered kisses over my lips.

"I love you, too." He shifted from English to Irish, the words flowing right over my head. "With all my heart," he whispered, clearing things up for me with the translation.

I threw my arms around his neck, buried my face there, and sobbed, the emotional release ripping through me. My heart felt too big for my chest, an ache growing there. The feeling wasn't painful. No, that wasn't the right way to describe it.

I wanted to tell Ian the same thing, but I wasn't sure I could. Not when Isaac looked at me the way he did. It was as though I was betraying him somehow, though we'd all gone into this with our eyes wide open. Or I thought we had, anyway.

It was in that moment I knew something would have to give.

I just needed time to figure out what.

ISAAC

By NOON, WE HAD A DUMPSTER BEING delivered and the guest room stripped down to the studs.

By three, a contractor was scheduled for later in the week, a designer already tasked with decorating the space with Dante in mind.

And by five, Everly was putting the final touches on dinner. Everyone seemed to be on edge, and I couldn't say I blamed them. We'd spent the entire day focusing on the destruction that bastard had wreaked, dealing with the havoc his threats had induced.

I wasn't willing to allow that evil to settle into the house any more than it already had, so I decided to take the reins.

When Dante appeared in the kitchen, I addressed both of our submissives.

"Tonight, you'll be eating dinner naked," I said in passing.

"If that pleases you, my Liege," Everly said sweetly, not blinking an eye.

"It'll please me very much," I told her.

"Of course, Master," Dante said, his shoulders still holding too much tension.

I joined Ian in the dining room, wanting to see his expression when the naked submissives arrived.

I wasn't disappointed, his eyes darkening with approval as they came in, set the plated food on the table before taking their seats.

"Well, this is a nice surprise," Ian noted, his eyes raking over Everly when I pulled her into my lap rather than letting her sit in a chair.

"Good to see you didn't redden his ass too much," Ian noted, a glint of humor in his eyes as he glanced over at Dante.

"I don't think he'll forget that punishment for a while."

"Definitely not, Master," Dante grumbled.

I gave them a few minutes to eat, feeding Everly myself. The conversation moved to mundane things. Dante brought up the fact that Everly's birthday was in a few days, something we'd all started planning for. No one mentioned anything that had happened last night.

"I'd really like to thank Everly for continuing to feed us meat although she won't eat it herself," Ian said, keeping the mood light.

"I second that," I told her, lifting my glass in a toast.

"Well, as much as I don't like doing it, I love you guys more." She chuckled.

With that perfect segue, I decided to broach the subject I'd been pondering all day. "Speaking of love..." I said, drawing all eyes to me. "We would like the two of you to move in," I said, setting my glass on the table. "Permanently."

Everly looked at Dante. Dante looked at me. I knew it came as somewhat of a surprise, but it couldn't have blindsided them too much.

"If someone wants to raise an argument as to why they disagree, now's the time to do so." I stared at Dante, waited.

His eyes dilated and I noticed some of the tension ease out of his posture.

I glanced at Everly.

She had no verbal response, either.

"Since the day you got here, you haven't been merely houseguests," Ian said, taking the conversational baton. "And no, we're not prone to making rash decisions. We certainly aren't starting now."

Still nothing from either of them.

I looked directly at Dante. "Are you opposed to the idea?"

He set his fork down, wiped his mouth, sat up straight. "No, Master."

"You?" I asked Everly.

"No, my Liege." Her voice was soft, but I could hear the emotion churning.

She was showing more emotion than any of them, so I waited her out. A second later, she didn't disappoint. My fork clattered to my plate when Everly threw her arms around my neck, buried her face there.

I held her closer, pressed my lips to her cheek. "I love you, fairy princess."

"I love you, too, my Liege." She leaned forward, pressed her lips softly to mine.

Not allowing too much time to pass, I looked at Dante, waited until he met my gaze. "I love you, too."

His eyes widened. I had yet to reveal that to him, hadn't intended to do so in such a public forum the first time, but I didn't want to wait.

Dante swallowed hard. "May I … uh… May I be excused?"

"No."

His surprise was etched on his face.

"I'm not asking you to say it back," I told him. "I simply want you to know how I feel."

"I love you, Dante," Everly chimed in. "I hope you've always known that."

"I have," he said, meeting her gaze. "I love you, too." As he said the words, his eyes slid to mine. I knew he was including me, but he didn't address me directly. I would give him a pass because I fully intended to discuss this in detail later. Privately.

"Well, now that we've got that out of the way," Ian joked, "arrangements can be made."

"Arrangements?" Dante asked.

Ian's full attention shifted to him. "I'll schedule someone to clear out your house, bring all your things here."

Dante shook his head. "I'd like to do that myself."

"Not an option right now," I told him.

"Then we'll wait until it is," he said firmly.

I patted Everly's hip. "Would you please excuse us, fairy princess?"

"Of course, my Liege."

When she reached for the plates, I put my hand on her arm. "It can wait. Go on up to the library. Don't get dressed."

"Yes, my Liege." Everly quietly slipped out of the room, giving us the privacy I'd requested.

I tipped back the rest of my drink, set the empty glass on the table, then pushed to my feet.

"Basement, Dante," I said over my shoulder as I walked out.

Ian followed, as did Dante.

When we gathered in the seating area, I pointed to the center of the rug. "Kneel."

I took a seat on one sofa. Ian took the other.

"Now we can discuss this openly," I told him.

He lifted his gaze. "I don't want pity."

"Good," Ian said. "And we're not in the market for blatant defiance."

There was a hint of emotion in Dante's eyes. I figured that was what Ian was going for. Dante was obedient, he wanted to be, but that didn't make him emotionless. There were times when it was necessary for him to work through the issues, discuss what was bothering him.

Now was one of those times.

"Never mind," Dante said, dropping his gaze.

I glanced at Ian, nodded. He got to his feet, walked over to the storage closet.

When he returned, Dante hadn't moved. I stood, took the item from his hand while he went back.

"Hands and knees," I instructed. "Spread your knees wide, slide your arms beneath you, hands between your thighs. Shoulders and head on the floor."

Dante didn't so much as look at me before he positioned himself accordingly. This was the part he understood. For whatever reason, in all the years he'd endured, he had come to need this. In fact, I got the feeling it settled him, somehow, allowed him to release the emotions he kept bottled up.

I sat on my haunches near his ass, attached the spreader bar to each ankle. It would keep his legs wide. I then connected his wrists to the restraints on the center of the bar, clicked the locks in place.

I stood, admired him as he lay there, completely at our mercy, his balls dangling delightfully, his asshole on display. Despite the nature of our conversation, Dante had no way to disguise his arousal.

I took a seat, observed as Ian rolled over the machine we'd purchased specifically with Dante in mind. We'd made quite a few purchases in recent days, toys, tools, things we'd get a lot of use out of. Some pertained to disobedience, others pure pleasure.

This machine, however, would be used as a way to torment our submissive, to show him there was no reason for this blatant disregard for his own safety.

"Care to ask what our intentions are?" I taunted Dante while Ian set the fucking machine in place, adjusted the large dildo, lubed it liberally.

"No, Master," he said smartly.

"Well, then."

Ian remained in place as he turned the machine on, angled it toward Dante's ass. He made a few adjustments, clicked the remote so that the dildo moved toward Dante's ass. The machine was powerful enough to push past his body's natural resistance, gliding right into his asshole.

Dante didn't move, didn't grunt, groan. Not a sigh. Nothing.

Once Ian was satisfied with the setup, the depth of penetration, he returned to his seat. For a few minutes, we focused on the machine drilling slowly into Dante's ass. His cock had hardened, despite his refusal to make a sound.

I had a feeling this was about to get really interesting.

IAN

AT ISAAC'S NOD, I DECIDED TO TAKE over the conversation. More accurately, I was going to turn Dante's lack of concern into something he could no longer ignore.

"Do you enjoy having your ass fucked?"

"Yes, Master," he said through gritted teeth as the dildo slid out of his ass.

"Do you like that we're sitting here watching you being fucked by a machine?"

"Yes, Master."

I watched for a moment, waited for the dildo to penetrate him again. The movement was excruciatingly slow, probably driving Dante out of his mind right about now.

"Are you at all concerned about the threats that bastard made last night?"

"Of course I am," he growled.

I clicked the button, turning the machine up a notch. It moved faster, pushing in, retreating. Not fast enough to bring him to orgasm in the near future, but it was a start.

"Are you worried what he might do to Everly or Heaven?"

"Yes, Master."

I clicked the button, slowed it back down. Isaac got up, moved over to his desk, and sat down with a huff, clearly exasperated by the back and forth.

"What about yourself? Are you worried what he might do to you?"

"No, Master."

I stopped the machine when it was fully dislodged from his ass.

"You want to rethink that answer," I growled, ensuring he heard my disappointment.

"My only concern is for…" His words trailed off, his body relaxing as though he was too weak to hold himself up.

"Talk to us, Dante."

"I don't want anything to happen to any of you," he said quickly.

I turned on the machine, let it drill deep into him, retreat.

"You don't think, by putting yourself at risk, that you'd be affecting us also?"

"Yes. Of course I do."

I turned the machine up a notch.

"Go on."

He was silent for a moment, but I noticed his chest expanding, his breaths becoming choppier. Not from the fucking machine but from the emotion building inside him.

A minute passed, then another. When he said nothing more, I turned the machine back down.

"You can stay right there," I told him, pushing to my feet and nodding to Isaac. "Enjoy yourself, Dante."

I walked over to my desk, not saying anything to my brother. No way would I leave Dante alone, but I wasn't above turning my back to him for a bit, allowing him to think it through.

I opened my messenger window, typed in Isaac's name.

Ian: Suggestions?

Isaac: Did you make the call?

Ian: I did. Waiting for a call back. I also heard from Ransom this afternoon. He said he's got something he's working on.

Isaac: Did he elaborate?

I looked over at my brother, gave him a look that said, *what do you think?* I wasn't going to put the information in writing, though.

He nodded.

Isaac: I don't care how you handle this, but I want Dante here. I want him to want to be here. He needs to know how we feel. Needs to accept it. He's fighting because he's scared.

Ian: I know that.

Isaac: Then it's time you use those interrogation skills to get him to understand.

I lifted my head, nodded.

Isaac pushed to his feet, walked up the steps, and closed the basement door, sealing us down here together.

I took a deep breath, walked over to Dante. He was fighting it. All of it. The emotion, the pain the incident had caused him.

I remembered how Heaven had let go so beautifully when I had spanked her. It had drawn the emotion to the surface, given her the opportunity to let it all go. I went to the storage closet, retrieved a crop.

"We're going to try this one more time," I told Dante, sliding the flat leather end over his ass, then smacking him gently. "Do you understand?"

"Yes, Master." He sounded completely defeated.

I clicked the machine up several notches, watched as it penetrated him. It moved with intent now, enough to excite. Every time it drilled into him, I smacked his ass with the crop. I wasn't gentle, not hitting the same spot twice. I continued until he was whimpering.

"Do you want more?"

"Yes, Master," he panted.

I clicked the machine up another notch, smacked his ass harder. It took a few minutes before he was crying out, but it was a start. I doubled the taps, smacking him twice in rapid succession again and again until I could hear him sobbing. I didn't stop even when I turned the machine off, watched it retreat from his ass. I kept spanking him, listening to the emotion that escaped in deep, ragged breaths, his chest heaving, his shoulders shaking.

I paused, stripping off my own clothes before picking the crop up again.

"Do you need more? Or do you understand where I'm going with this?"

"I understand, Master," he gasped, choking on the emotion.

I used the key Isaac had left sitting by Dante's feet, freed him from the restraints. Before I gave him permission to move, I massaged his wrists and ankles, then took my seat on the sofa, commanding him to crawl over to me.

When he was kneeling between my thighs, I patted my chest. "Lay your head here."

He draped himself over me, resting his head on my chest. I ran my hands over him, enjoying his warmth, relishing the tears that continued to fall. He needed this, needed to let it out. When he settled somewhat, I ran my hands over his hair, soothing him.

"This isn't a game, Dante." When he tried to lift his head, I held it in place, then resumed brushing my hand over his hair when he stilled. "I'm talking about the relationship. All four of us. It's serious. As serious as it gets. Love shouldn't be taken lightly. And while I understand your need to protect everyone, I won't let you do it at your own expense. That's not how love works."

I cupped his cheek, lifted his head. When his eyes met mine, I held the stare for long seconds, willing him to see the emotion I wouldn't hold back from him. I didn't say the words immediately, wanting him to feel me. When his face softened, I grazed his cheek with my knuckles.

"I love you, Dante. I won't make excuses for it. I'm not going to pretend—not to you or myself—that it's not there."

I could hear my accent thickening, something that always happened when I was driven by pure emotion.

"I don't even care if you love me back," I told him. "The fact is, I love you. And I'll take care of you, protect you, keep you safe. Last night…" I blinked, swallowed past the lump forming in my throat. "I can handle the destruction. That's nothing. I've got plenty of money. Furniture, walls … all that shit can be replaced." I gripped his chin between my finger and thumb. "You can't. I won't let him touch you again. You can bet your life on that. He won't touch you." I stared hard, wanting him to see as well as hear the promise in my words. "I will kill him before I allow that to happen."

It was then that Dante broke. His face crumpled seconds before he buried it against my chest, sobbing uncontrollably. The man had years of torment and heartache built up. It pained me to hear it, but he had to let it out. If he ever wanted a true chance at happiness, he had to find a way to let it go.

"We won't let him win," I assured him, soothing him with my hands, roaming them over his back.

His head turned, his lips pressing against my chest. I knew what he was seeking. Comfort. Something he'd rarely gotten from sex.

My cock stirred as he trailed his lips lower.

"You can have what you need," I told him, sliding my fingers in his hair and holding his head still. "But I won't let you escape this, Dante."

He lifted his head, his eyes full of anguish and pain and need. "I don't want to run, Master. It's hard for me to say it, but…"

"Tell me."

"I love you." He inhaled sharply, as though it was painful to let the words out. "Not only you, but Isaac. Everly. All of you. With everything I am. It's just…"

"Difficult," I completed for him.

He gave a jerky nod. "Yes. It hurts. And it scares the shit out of me." He lowered his head, kissed my stomach. "It terrifies me. I've never felt this way before. I have a hard time saying it."

I forced his head up. "It's not always about sex."

His Adam's apple bobbed. "I know. But I need this."

"Need what?"

I thought for a second he wasn't going to answer, his eyes so tortured it broke my fucking heart.

"I need you to love me, to show me. To replace the evil with … love."

I fought to breathe even as he dropped his head, trailed his lips down my stomach, his tongue sliding over my cock before he took me in his mouth.

My head dropped back. I hissed, raising my hips and pushing deep into his throat while I kept my hand twined in his hair, holding him in place.

As I sat there, Dante worked me over with his mouth. I didn't stop him, didn't encourage him, either. I simply enjoyed the warmth of his mouth on me, the slick heat that enveloped me again and again. He never stopped, never asked for more, simply worshiped my cock with his mouth, his tongue, his throat. He never used his hands, only his lips and tongue. I couldn't take my eyes off him, the feeling so fucking perfect I wanted it to go on for days.

When the door to the basement opened, he didn't falter, continued as though it was his only job, to please me.

I looked up, saw Isaac coming toward us, Everly behind him. He stripped off his clothes as he came over, leaving them where they fell. When he dropped to the opposite sofa, I lifted Dante's head.

"Show him," I urged.

Dante nodded, kissed the head of my cock once, then crawled over to Isaac while I motioned Everly over.

"Knees," I ordered.

Her eyes were hot, her lips parted as she lowered herself between my thighs.

And when her soft, wet lips wrapped around my cock, I dropped my head back once more and moaned.

Dante

I CRAWLED OVER TO ISAAC, PEERED UP at him, and saw nothing but love in his eyes. His hand came out, cupping my cheek. I pressed against it, then kissed his palm.

"Let me show you, Master," I whispered.

"Show me. Show me how much you love me."

"I do," I assured him, pressing my lips to his wrist, then his stomach.

I poured everything into licking, sucking. I didn't rush, didn't want to hurry. I wasn't looking to get him off. I wanted this connection, for him to know that I was willing to take care of him the same way he was willing to take care of me.

Yeah, it was sexual, but it wasn't about the act. As far as I was concerned, there was no way to be closer to them right now and I was desperate to feel them. All of them.

Isaac's hand slid into my hair, gently, firmly, holding me in place as I laved his cock, taking it deep, licking along the vein, memorizing every inch.

Someone moved my legs and suddenly I was very aware of what was going on.

Everly was beneath me, on her back, her head between my legs as she took my cock into her mouth. Focus was no longer an option. I peered down my body, watching as she swallowed my cock. Isaac's hand remained in my hair, soothing as I stared at the beautiful woman whose luscious lips were wrapped around my rock-hard shaft.

"Enjoy it," Isaac whispered.

I'd never felt anything quite this intense. I couldn't count how many times I'd dreamed about having her sweet mouth on me. I inhaled, exhaled, prayed I didn't fall over.

When Isaac's fingers tightened in my hair, guiding my mouth back to his cock, I went willingly. He sighed, allowing me to take the reins, trusting me to take care of him.

Minutes passed before Isaac lifted my head, motioned me over to Ian. I swapped positions easily. I couldn't see behind me, but I heard Isaac crooning to Everly, directing her onto her knees, urging her to take more of his cock in her mouth.

I didn't know how much time passed, but Isaac was the one who made the next move. He ordered Everly to join him on the sofa, then instructed me to lick her pussy. Wanting to give her the same pleasure she'd given me, I went willingly, shifting her so that her pussy was in my face, her small body folded nearly in half on the sofa. I was aware of Isaac getting to his feet, but my full attention was on pleasuring Everly, letting her feel how much I cared for her.

I felt someone move behind me, swayed when the broad head of his cock pressed against my ass. The voice that sounded was Ian's, the grunt deep as he pushed in, retreated slowly. The leash on Ian's restraint snapped when he slammed into me. I cried out, unable to focus as he fucked me relentlessly, driving me straight to the edge before I knew what was happening.

"Master!" I screamed, unaware of the strangled moans coming from me as pleasure threatened to take me under. "Please!"

"No," he growled, bit my shoulder. "Do not come."

It was both heaven and hell, but I held back. Barely.

When he pulled out, I regained my focus, buried my face in Everly's pussy, licked, teased.

Right up until Isaac impaled me, his familiar grunt telling me who he was.

"Oh, fuck," I groaned against Everly's slick flesh.

Her soft fingers slid through my hair as she pulled me toward her, trying to get my tongue where she needed it. I wanted to help her, but it was pointless. I was overwhelmed, completely enraptured by the pleasure assaulting me.

I wasn't sure how it happened, but I passed the point of no return, swamped by the pleasure. Ian and Isaac took turns then. They both fucked me. Rough, hard, gentle. They alternated, mumbling things as I rested my chest on the sofa cushion, muttering incoherently, begging for more.

I wasn't sure who came first, Isaac or Ian, but I felt it cover my back. It wasn't long before the other filled my ass, then rolled me onto the floor, onto my back.

My head shot up off the floor, peering down my body when I felt a hot, wet mouth on my cock. Everly was there and she wasn't worshipping my cock any longer. No, she had an end goal, and it was to blow my head right off my shoulders.

It worked. Within minutes, I was begging my Masters to let me come. They gave their approval, and the next thing I knew, I was coming down Everly's sweet throat, before I dropped back to the floor in a heap.

"Your turn, fairy princess."

I was in a daze, unable to focus, but I could see Everly on the sofa, Isaac's tongue working her pussy while Ian observed from the other end. Everly erupted into soft mewls, which quickly graduated to desperate cries as she begged and pleaded and was finally granted permission to come.

The room grew silent. I knew I needed to get up, but it wasn't possible.

Finally, Ian gave me a hand, helped me to my feet, then smacked my tender ass.

"Go to Isaac's bathroom. Everly's waiting for you. She wants to shower with you."

"Yes, Master."

Before he let me walk off, he tipped my chin up. "I love you, Dante."

"I love you, too, Master," I whispered, the emotion so close to the surface I wasn't sure I would ever be able to bury it down deep again.

As I walked to Isaac's bathroom, I realized that had been Ian's intention all along.

Sneaky Dom.

Twenty-Five

Everly

Friday, June 7, 2019

"HAVING SECOND THOUGHTS?" ISAAC ASKED AS HE carried more of my clothes to the closet, hung them up.

I smiled over at him. "Not at all. You?"

"Not possible."

He carried two more loads of hangers before returning.

He tipped my head up, kissed my lips. "I've got some things to take care of. I'll send Dante in here to help you."

"Thank you, my Liege."

His eyes twinkled. "My pleasure, fairy princess."

We'd spent the majority of the day unpacking after the moving truck delivered everything from Dante's house. Evidently, Ian and Isaac had had a conversation with Dante, and somewhere in there he'd agreed to put the house on the market and let Isaac and Ian handle the rest. The moving truck had surprised us that morning. Well, not all of us. Apparently, the Doms were quite aware of what was going on. Heaven, too, because she'd texted to let me know she would be temporarily staying with her sister until she could find an apartment of her own.

"Hey," Dante said when he walked in.

I went up on my toes, kissed his lips when he walked over.

After grinning at the surprised look on his face, I went back to pulling things out of the box I was unpacking.

"What was that for?"

"What?"

"The kiss?"

I pretended to be offended. "You don't want me to kiss you?"

He chuckled. "I definitely didn't say that."

"Well, then. Can't I just kiss you because I want to?"

He laughed, rolled his eyes. "What can I help with?"

"Um." I looked around the room. "I've got two more boxes in the garage. After that, I think I'm finished."

"You travel light," he teased.

"Yeah, well. Can't acquire much on a barista's salary."

Dante dropped his butt onto the mattress. "What're you going to do about that, anyway?"

I shrugged. "I don't know. Dee fired me, but I expected no less. I'm sure I could beg for my job back, but I get the feeling Isaac doesn't want me to work. And while the idea of it is great, I can't sit around here like a diva all day long."

"We could take care of the house," he suggested.

I tucked the last of my shorts into the dresser drawer.

"We?"

"Yeah. You know, cleaning, cooking, yard work, taking care of the pool."

I smiled. "Grocery shopping. I could see that working. It's a big house and a massive yard."

We sat there for a moment. I could practically hear Dante's mind working, but he didn't speak for the longest time. I thought he was going to go get the boxes when he stood, took my hand, tugged me toward the door.

"Where're we going?"

"I need to tell you some things."

"Okay."

He started into the guest room at the same time Ian was walking toward us.

Dante stopped. "We're going to … talk."

"Sure. You seen Isaac?"

I nodded. "He said he had to take care of some things."

Ian nodded, turned, and headed in the opposite direction.

Dante pulled me into the room, gestured toward the bed.

"What's going on?" I asked, turning to face him.

"Can we sit?"

"Of course."

With no other options, I climbed onto the bed. Dante joined me, then tugged me into him, pulled me down onto the pillow. He spooned behind me, wrapped his arms tightly over me.

"What's wrong, Dante?"

"I need to tell you what happened to me."

I tried to turn, to face him, but he held me against him, not letting me move.

"I need it this way," he said, pressing his face into my hair. "Please."

The pain in his voice scared me, but I managed a nod, gripping his arm, holding him.

"I'm going to preface this by saying that I'm damaged, Everly, but I'm not broken. It's important that you understand that."

I wasn't sure what to say, so I remained quiet.

A few minutes later, I understood all too well. He told me about Roger/Vernon, what he'd done to him at the club, the abuse he'd endured, the threats that had been made against me and Heaven. That was horrific, but it didn't hold a candle to what he told me after. When Dante launched into the abuse he'd sustained at his father's hand, I started to cry.

"I didn't want to tell you," he whispered. "For this reason, Everly. The last thing I want to do is hurt you."

322

"You couldn't hurt me," I said on a jagged sob. "It just…
It breaks my heart that someone could do that to another person.
Much less you."

"I know, sweetheart. Which is why I couldn't tell you. I
knew you'd understand, but I also know that hearing it will take a
piece of you. I don't want that."

This time, I did turn in his arms, facing him, cupping his
face. "I *gave* that piece of me to you, Dante. A long time ago.
Because I love you."

"I know you do. And I cherish that." He brushed my hair
back from my face. "I love you, too. And that'll never change."

For some reason, I believed him.

Two hours later, I was sitting in the library, taking
advantage of the peace and quiet. It gave me time to think, to
process. I was sitting in the window, staring out at the backyard as
I'd been doing for the past hour. Replaying Dante's story again and
again, feeling my heart break over and over.

"You all right?"

I didn't turn to look at Ian, but I managed a nod.

"I will be," I assured him.

He came over, and in his true Dom fashion, he forced me
to look at him by picking me up, carrying me over to the recliner,
then sitting down and situating me on his lap.

Unable to resist his warmth, the security I found in his
arms, I held on, listening to the steady beat of his heart beneath
my ear. He didn't push me to talk, just hugged me to him, kissed
the top of my head.

We remained like that for long minutes until I knew I had
to get some of it out, fearful the evil would settle in somewhere
and break me into pieces.

"Ian?"

"Hmm?"

"How can someone do that to another person?"

"Which someone are we talking about?"

"Any of them. Dante's sick father, this asshole who thinks Dante's something he can own. I just don't get it."

"I don't, either, Everly."

I tilted my head back, stared at his neck. "Tell me about your family."

"What do you want to know?"

"Everything," I admitted.

He sighed. "They're back in Dublin. I hear from my father a couple times a year. On our birthday, Christmas. For the most part, we've separated from him by choice."

"Your choice? Or his?"

"Mutual." His hand brushed softly over my hair. "Before we came to the US, things were rocky between my father and me. Normal teenage stuff. I thought I knew everything; he insisted he did."

I chuckled. "I can see that."

He squeezed my thigh. "Since we were old enough to wreak havoc, Isaac stuck with me wherever I went, and I wanted it that way. We'd been best friends since the womb. I can't be away from him for long before I get antsy. Not many people know that, either."

"Your secret's safe with me," I whispered, sliding my hand over his chest, wanting to hear his stories.

"As was expected, we got caught up with the wrong crowd. Some ne'er-do-wells we had no business being around. As we got older, I got bolder. I could hold my own, started to build a reputation, one that garnered respect in our circles. Da knew it would only go downhill from there, so he uprooted us, brought us here to keep us away from the..."

I lifted my head. "The what?"

"The bad guys," he said on a slow exhale.

"The Irish mob?"

NICOLE EDWARDS

He chuckled. "Can't get anything past you, huh? Anyway. We got here, settled in. Not much changed. I was still wild, looking for something to get into. Ended up meeting a couple of bouncer types. Started doing a few odd jobs protecting some folks. They weren't the decent type, either.

"One day, while I was running an errand for these guys, Isaac got jumped. Bad stuff. They fucked him up, put him in the hospital. I knew at that point, the direction I was headed was only going to get him hurt if not killed. Luckily, I'd only skirted the circles. Wasn't too difficult to separate myself."

"You don't associate with them anymore?"

"I try to keep my distance."

"How'd you get interested in BDSM?"

I could feel his smile against my head. "You know Talon."

"Yes."

"We go way back. Met him shortly after we moved to the States. He was into the scene, introduced us. The rest, as they say, is history."

"And Liam?" I asked, referring to the guy who'd come over the other night after the vandalism.

"Same. Met him years ago. He's been here less time than we have, hit it off."

"Do you sit around and talk about home?"

"We have, sure."

I pressed my ear to his chest. "Thank you."

"For?"

"For clearing my head."

Ian kissed my forehead. "What Dante went through was pure hell. No one should've been subjected to that, much less survived. But he did. And he's strong. Stronger than most people even realize."

"Do you love him?"

"I do. It's sometimes difficult to explain."

"I feel the same way."

"Do you?"

325

I lifted my head again, met his gaze. "I do. Because that's how I feel, too. It's powerful, overwhelming even. Confusing at times. But it feels right. Like this was how things were supposed to play out."

"And how do you feel about me?"

His eyes were intense as they locked with mine. Neither of us had ventured down this path yet, but I felt it important that he know how I felt.

I kissed his chin. "I love you, Ian."

"That's what I needed to hear."

When he kissed me, it was sweet, warm. As though it was the only thing that was necessary in that moment. It didn't escalate, but it didn't end. Minutes rolled on with his mouth covering mine.

It was what I needed, what I hoped he needed as well.

ISAAC

WHILE EVERYONE WAS OFF DOING THEIR OWN thing, I pitched in for dinner.

I wasn't a cook by any means, didn't even pretend to be. Before Everly—and Heaven, when she'd been there—had taken over the nightly meals, Ian and I usually splurged on delivery, sometimes going out to grab a bite. I fell back on old habits, placed an order through one of the food apps, then sat back and waited while I flipped through channels on the television.

Dante appeared, his face sallow, his eyes red-rimmed and tired.

"You okay?"

His gaze cut to mine, surprise replacing the exhaustion. "I... Yeah."

"Did you sleep?"

Dante's hands dipped into his pockets. "For a bit." His eyes moved to the stairs. "After Everly slipped out."

I'd seen some progress in recent days, ever since we punished him the other night for hiding. It would take some time, perhaps even a few sessions with a shrink, before he was on his way to being healthy. But that was the end goal.

"How'd she take it?"

"Hard." A small smile tugged at the corners of his mouth. "She got mad. Said I wasn't allowed to keep shit from her ever again."

"I can hear her saying that."

"It makes me laugh to hear her curse."

The thought made me smile. Hell, anytime I thought about Everly, I smiled.

"Dinner'll be here shortly. Figured we'd relax tonight."

"Are we still on for tomorrow?"

He was referring to the birthday party we had planned for Everly. "Yes. I filled Heaven in, asked her to come over. She's on her way now. Said she wanted to spend the night. For safety reasons, it'll only be the five of us tomorrow. Once this is … resolved … we'll have an official party at the club."

"I think she'll like that."

She would. My fairy princess was a dirty girl underneath the sweet, innocent outer coating. She would definitely enjoy tomorrow, but the club party would be what she looked most forward to.

"Oh, I talked to Master Chaos," I told him. "He's the head Master of Dichotomy. Talked to him about you. He said you're more than welcome to join without undergoing the training class. I informed him you were spoken for by me and Ian and we weren't willing to share you with anyone else. Not now. Not ever."

His eyes widened. I'd been sitting on that information for a few days.

"That's… Thank you, Master."

"My pleasure. I talked to the designer. She assured me your room'll be completed by Monday. I told her anything else wasn't an option. If she couldn't deliver by then, we wouldn't need her services any longer."

His eyes went blank again, as they did anytime the incident was mentioned. I knew Dante felt responsible for what had happened, although no one saw this as his doing. No one except him.

"Also, Ian called in a favor. Turns out Vernon took a trip out of the country. There's a flag on his passport. We'll be notified once he's back in country. So for now, you can relax your guard a bit."

"I'll relax it when—"

"I know. I will, too."

The doorbell rang.

"I'll get it," I snapped when he turned to answer. "You go in the kitchen."

I grabbed the Ruger I'd tucked under the couch cushion, checked the chamber, then went to answer the door. Until this bastard was caught, it was a precaution Ian and I were both taking.

When Dante didn't move, I glared his way. "Kitchen. Now."

He turned and walked off, but not before exhaling heavily. It made me smile.

Heaven was the first to arrive, which of course had the effect we'd hoped for, turning Everly's glum mood around.

After dinner, the girls cleaned the kitchen, then went to one of the guest rooms to watch a movie. I'd offered the living room, but they politely declined. I got the feeling they were up to something, but I didn't know what.

I found out not too long after.

With Ian at my side, I barged into the room. Fast enough to have them both jumping, guilt splashed over their faces as Heaven quickly tucked her iPad under the blanket.

"What's going on in here?"

"Nothing," Heaven said quickly. "We were ... uh ... watching a movie."

"Yeah?" Ian walked over, reached under the blanket and pulled out the iPad.

He grinned over at me, held up the screen.

"Porn?" I pinned Everly with my stare. "You're sneaking around watching porn?"

"Yes, my Liege," Everly said, always the sweet, innocent one.

Ian hit play and the two men on screen continued their erotic encounter.

"Gay porn."

Ian hit pause. "What prompted this?"

Everly shrugged but her eyes quickly shot to Heaven.

Heaven wasn't quite so tight-lipped. "We were curious."

We? I found that interesting considering Everly was quite adept at watching man-on-man action. She'd witnessed it the other night when Ian and I had tag teamed Dante.

"Curious?" Ian prompted.

"Yeah." Heaven glared at Ian. "Is that all right with you?"

He glared right back. "Sassy mouth'll earn you punishment. How many would you like?"

Her face took on that sweet, serene look she'd been known to give him. "I won't apologize. My sweet friend and I were just curious what it was like. Since, you know, *I* haven't had the chance to see it up close and personal."

"Well, in that case"—Ian tapped the screen, clicked a few times, then passed it back over to Heaven—"why don't you watch something that makes *us* curious?"

"Two women?" she huffed.

"Exactly."

"That's for you to watch, not us."

"Really?"

I grinned, knowing exactly which direction my brother was headed.

Based on Everly's expression, she'd already caught on, too. Heaven seemed to be the only one out of the loop.

"What?" she asked, glancing between the three of us.

Everly bit her lip to keep from smiling.

Ian glanced over at me. "I think these dirty girls need a shower."

"I couldn't agree more." I crooked my finger at Everly. "Come on, fairy princess. Why don't we get the water warm?"

"Yes, my Liege."

Once I had her in the bathroom, I backed her up against the wall, crushed my mouth to hers.

"Do you want to see us together, my Liege?"

"Most definitely." I stared into her eyes. "But I don't think I'm the only one who wants the experience, am I?"

"No, my Liege."

I kissed her again, softer this time. "Your pace, love. As far as you're willing."

"It'll be my pleasure, my Liege."

I released her so she could start the shower water.

Heaven walked in, her gaze hot. I grinned at her. I was almost positive she blushed.

"What did you tell her?" I asked Ian when he joined me.

"Just gave her a few explicit details of what would definitely be a good early birthday present for Everly."

"Ah."

"Strip," Ian ordered. "Each other."

"Slowly," I added.

"Pretend we're not even here," Ian said.

"As if," Heaven retorted with a huff.

"I'm thinking she's been gone too long," I told my brother, ensuring Heaven heard me. "She forgets what punishment in this house looks like."

"I agree."

I'd already had the pleasure of watching them strip one another once. Outside by the pool. I was fairly certain I would never tire of it.

The only problem I saw was the fact that they were nervous. Too nervous. To the point, Heaven continued to giggle, and it was a trickle-down effect, causing Everly to do the same.

"I have an idea," I said, stepping over to Everly. "Turn off the water."

She did.

I pointed toward the bedroom.

"I think this is going to require some assistance."

"I like where your head's at," Ian told me, taking Heaven's hand and leading her back to the bedroom.

"On the bed, fairy princess."

"Yes, my Liege."

Everly climbed up onto the bed, but before she could crawl away, I put my arm around her waist, pulled her back against me, her back to my chest.

Ian positioned Heaven the same way on the opposite side of the bed. "I figure there's no reason I can't indulge a little. This is her early birthday present, is it not?"

Heaven nodded. "It definitely is."

I slid my hands beneath Everly's tight little T-shirt, lifted it higher, before pulling it over her head. She shook out her hair while I unhooked her bra, slid it off.

"Your turn," I told Ian as I reached around Everly and cupped her small tits in my hands.

She sighed, leaning back against me.

She was so fucking soft. I found I could never seem to touch her enough.

"Keep your eyes open, Everly. I want you to watch as he undresses her."

We both did.

"What do you think?" I asked my fairy princess.

"She's beautiful," she said on a soft moan.

Heaven was watching my hands as they moved over Everly's chest, cupping her, tweaking her nipples, making her moan.

I moved lower, unbuttoning her jean shorts, dipping my hand inside.

Everly moaned when I slid my finger along her slit.

"You're already wet. Because I'm touching you? Or because you're watching Heaven?"

"Both, my Liege."

She ground her pelvis against my hand.

Ian went a step further, pulling Heaven's shorts down her hips, then teasing her pussy while Everly and I watched them.

We worked them both into a frenzy but never gave them the nudge they needed to make it over. When I stepped back, I heard Everly's frustrated sigh.

"Now it's time for that shower."

They were both breathing hard when Ian walked them into the bathroom. A minute later, they were wet, their hair slicked back.

"Now, I know two dirty girls who need to get clean. The only rule is … you can't wash yourself."

They didn't need any more coaxing than that.

As though we weren't even in the room, Heaven took the lead, sliding her soapy hands over Everly's petite body. They got caught up in the moment, and when Heaven leaned in and kissed Everly, I knew they wouldn't care if we left the room or not.

Not that I was going to miss this.

Not for anything in the world.

IAN

Porn.

I found it amusing that the girls had been watching porn. More entertaining was the fact they'd tried to hide it.

However, it had been the perfect segue for the scene we were watching now.

When I'd suggested it, I'd expected Heaven to balk at the idea. I had no clue what she'd been up to in the days she'd been gone. But I'd been pleasantly surprised when she entertained the idea, more so when she'd agreed to take the reins.

And right now, watching Heaven sliding her slick hands all over Everly was quite the sight.

There was no denying a man did enjoy watching two hot women playing with one another. This wasn't much different, only it was significantly hotter. These two women wanted to touch, to taste, to explore.

They took their time, washing one another's hair, rinsing it. Adding in conditioner, letting it sit while they did another thorough cleansing, this time without soap. Their hands roamed, never lingering for long.

When they finished, I stepped out of the bathroom with Isaac, taking a seat in the bedroom while I waited for them to come in. They didn't take long. Nor did they let go of one another. The towels they'd used fell to the floor as Heaven crawled on the bed first.

I hadn't expected her to be quite so bold, but if I had to guess, she wasn't exactly new to the experience. Their kiss lingered, Everly sliding over Heaven, their breasts crushed together.

I glanced over at Isaac. "I think we might need to intervene again."

"I agree."

We were both on our feet.

It wasn't that the girls needed interference, but I had control issues. As far as I was concerned, it was my duty to be in charge.

"Come here, Heaven."

She turned her head, glanced up at me, and smiled. "Were we doing it wrong?"

She was breathless, enjoying herself clearly.

"Not at all."

When she made no effort to move, I reached for her, pulling her toward me with my hands under her arms. I lifted her, forcing her to sit with her back against me.

"Now spread those legs for me."

Heaven played coy, separating her knees, then locking them together. Over and over, teasing me relentlessly.

"I want that pretty pussy on display," I growled. "Right now."

Her legs fell open, a soft moan escaping as I ran my hands down her chest, her flat belly, then between her legs. I pulled her pussy lips open, flicked her clit.

She hummed her approval.

I watched with definite interest while Isaac positioned Everly the same, her pussy flowering open. He teased her, ensuring Heaven had the perfect view.

"I want to see your mouth on her pussy," I told Heaven.

"If it pleases ... Everly," she said with a giggle.

I met Everly's gaze. "What's the verdict, little fairy?"

"Yes, please," she whispered, her nipples puckering.

When Heaven got to her knees, moving toward Everly, I got on the bed with her, lying at her side.

"Lick her."

Heaven's tongue darted out, sliding over Everly's clit.

"You're a tease," I accused. "She needs more than that, don't you, Everly?"

"Yes, Master Ian. I need more."

Isaac helped Everly out, reclining her so she could position herself flat on the bed. He kneaded her breasts while Heaven feasted on her pussy. Little flicks of her tongue to start. As the seconds ticked by, she became more daring. The louder Everly's moans, the more effort Heaven put into it until she was squirming against the mattress.

"Please, my Liege," Everly pleaded.

"Please what?"

"I want to taste her."

Isaac stepped back and Everly took over, flipping Heaven onto her back, then crawling over her.

"Sixty-nine. Nice." I grinned.

I had to sit up to catch all the action as Everly buried her face in Heaven's pussy, grinding her own on Heaven's mouth. They were beautiful together. And though I insisted on inserting myself into the moment, they certainly didn't need my guidance.

Heaven went a step further, pushing two fingers into Everly's pussy, making her cry out. Not one to be left behind, Everly followed her lead.

They didn't need our permission here and I certainly didn't intend to give it, watching the erotic fantasy play out live before me as both women cried out in ecstasy as they drove each other over.

Out of breath and evidently sated, Everly fell to her side.

"Well, I'd say that was a good start."

Heaven glared at me. "A good start? That was freaking amazing."

Everly laughed. "I have to agree."

"Now that you're good and clean," Isaac told Everly as he reached for her, "I think it's time for bed. You've got a big day tomorrow."

"I do?" She was smiling brightly. "Good night, Heaven."

"Good night."

When they slipped out, I remained where I was, reclined on the bed beside Heaven.

She turned to face me, not at all bothered by her nudity. "So. How's it going?"

"Fine."

She smiled. "I mean with Everly. Anything new going on?"

"Such as?"

"Such as you admitting you love her?"

Pushing up to a sitting position, I shook my head. "Not going there with you."

"Oh, come on. I did what you wanted."

I laughed, getting to my feet. "I get the feeling you've been wanting that for some time now."

"Maybe. But still." She flipped on her stomach, watched me as I moved toward the door.

"Thanks for coming, by the way." I reached for the doorknob.

"Thanks for inviting me. I take it there's more of this in store for tomorrow?"

"Let's just say you'll need a good night's sleep if you expect to survive it."

She chuckled. "I've got a question for you."

I turned to give her my full attention, arched an eyebrow.

"Perhaps I could get a firsthand account of some man-on-man action? You know, since you got to live out your fantasy and all."

I considered it for a moment, smiled. "Give me a minute."

Her answering grin was wicked as she scissored her legs behind her, an obvious sign of anticipation.

Leaving her in the guest room, I slipped down the hall to the living room, stuck my head in. As expected, Dante was sitting on the sofa, his eyes glued to the television until he heard me clear my throat.

"Join me," I said, ensuring my tone was commanding.

He seemed surprised, but there was most definitely heat flashing in his blue eyes as he got to his feet.

NICOLE EDWARDS

I didn't expect him to question my intentions, and he didn't disappoint. Instead of questioning my motives, Dante stepped into the guest room when I motioned him in.

His eyes shot to Heaven, who was still naked on the bed, although she'd pulled a pillow into her lap, shielding her from our view.

"You want to watch, lose the pillow," I told her.

With another mischievous grin, she tossed it aside, revealing all those lovely curves.

Dante's eyes shot to my face.

"She's been a good girl," I explained. "A good girl who's curious to see two men together. Do you have an issue with that?"

Based on the hard ridge I could see tenting his shorts, I knew the answer, but he said, "Not at all, Master."

"Strip," I demanded.

While Dante made quick work of removing his shorts and T-shirt, I shed my own clothes, tossing them onto the floor.

Once we were both naked, I motioned to Heaven. "On your back. You want to watch, you have to participate."

To my surprise, she flopped back on the bed, her eyes on me the entire time.

"Grab the lube," I instructed Dante as I moved around to the side of the bed.

I gripped Heaven's arms, pulled her to the edge of the mattress, letting her head fall over the side before I guided my cock to her lips.

"Suck."

She did. Oh, how she did. Although I was hard as steel, I allowed it to go on for some time while I watched Dante watching me. I loved the way his eyes dilated, his cock bobbing freely, hard and eager.

"Join her on the bed," I told him, gripping my cock and pulling it from Heaven's mouth. "On your back, ass toward me."

Dante easily crawled onto the bed, getting into position. I took the lube from him, then instructed Heaven to straddle his face. Her eyes widened, her mouth falling open when Dante curled his arms around her thighs and pulled her down to his mouth.

Watching the pair of them, his mouth working between her split thighs, I lubed my cock generously, then joined them on the bed. Heaven's attention shifted to where my cock was aligning with Dante's ass as I shifted his knees back.

"Hold his legs for me," I encouraged.

Heaven placed her hands on his knees as she rocked on Dante's face.

I had to admit, the idea of her watching was quite potent. Enough so, I had to rein myself in as I pushed inside Dante, his asshole stretching around my girth. His soft moan was muffled by Heaven's pussy, but I heard it all the same.

Taking my time, I pushed in deep, retreated slowly, giving her the perfect view of me fucking him. Again, it was a heady predicament I found myself in, the rush threatening to make me come before I was ready. I managed to distract myself by stroking his cock, teasing his balls, listening to the heavy rasp of their breaths.

I lifted my gaze to Heaven's face. "You'll have to move aside if you want me to really fuck him."

As though the orgasm she'd had earlier was plenty to tide her over, Heaven instantly fell to her side, her eyes never moving from where I was intimately joined with Dante.

While she watched, Dante met my gaze as I leaned over him, planting my palms on each side of his head. He took over holding his knees, offering himself up to me. My hips jerked as I slammed into him, pleasure shooting up my spine.

I fucked him then, lost completely in his midnight gaze. At that moment, everything else fell away. The only thing that mattered was him. I never looked away, gauging his need. His breaths were rasping in and out of his lungs as his hands slid up my arms, back down. The emotional connection was what did me in.

"Come for me," I growled.

Without touching his cock, Dante's body grew taut. I drove in deeper, harder, faster, loving the way he took me, the pleasure I could see on his face. I didn't relent, giving all of myself with every erotic thrust.

"Come for me," I repeated.

"Oh, fuck…" He cried out my name and came, his cock spurting between us.

I lost it, taking all he was willing to give until the pleasure drown me, pulling me under. I erupted deep inside him, my head tilted back, his name said through gritted teeth.

It took a minute for us to catch our breaths and only then did I remember Heaven was in the room with us.

"Meet me in my shower," I instructed Dante. "I'll be there in just a minute."

He nodded, accepted my quick kiss, then rolled off the bed after I'd dislodged from his body.

"Was it good for you?" I teased Heaven as I snagged my clothes from the floor.

"That was … beautiful."

I shook my head, smiled. "Now get some sleep. I expect you to be on your absolute best behavior tomorrow."

"I will," she said in that chipper, if not somewhat awed, tone. "It's my present to Everly."

"I think she'll be extremely pleased."

In fact, considering what Isaac had in store for her, I knew she would be.

Twenty-Six

Dante

Saturday, June 8, 2019

WHEN I WOKE ON SATURDAY MORNING, I was surprised to find Ian and Isaac in the kitchen, waiting for me.

"Ready for a run?" Ian asked.

"Really?"

"I've got some extra eyes on the house, and we know Vernon's out of the country still. Figured you might need it considering you'll be unable to find much solitude today."

"I just need five minutes," I told them before darting back down the hall. I grabbed my running shoes, pulled them on, then met them at the back door.

With their help, I was able to get out of my head for a bit, enjoying the seven-mile run more than usual.

Once we were back at the house, the day was underway. Heaven was in the kitchen cooking breakfast, while Everly was ordered to sit this one out. It was her birthday after all.

I hurried through my shower, joined them in the dining room. Everly made every attempt to guess what the plan for the day was, but Isaac did a good job of throwing her off track.

While he kept her preoccupied, Ian and I went to the grocery store to pick up a few things Heaven had requested specifically for the birthday dinner she was cooking.

"I was thinking about something, Master," I told him as I pushed the cart down the aisle while Ian tossed things in it.

"What was that?"

"Isaac mentioned he'd prefer I stay at home. You know, in lieu of working."

"We both prefer that," he noted.

"Okay. Well, I was thinking it would be more cost-effective if you weren't paying for lawn service or the pool guy. The maids. I could handle that stuff. Me and Everly."

Ian paused, looked over at me. His eyes were serious when he spoke. "That's a lot of work."

"Well, I've kinda got a lot of time."

He smiled. "I know that. And I want you to have things to do."

"So do I. I can't sit around and mooch off of you."

He stepped in close, tilted my chin up. "First of all, if we want to take care of you, that's our business. Not yours."

"Yes, Master."

An old lady moved passed us, her eyes wide as she did.

Ian didn't acknowledge her in any way, never broke eye contact with me. I liked that it didn't bother him what other people thought.

"I'll have the conversation with Isaac tomorrow."

"Yes, Master."

He leaned in, pressed his lips to mine before stepping back. "Just so you know, we've got plenty of things that'll keep you busy. None of which include you cleaning bathtubs and toilets."

I smiled, thinking about what those could possibly be.

"The most important will be taking care of Everly when we're out of town." He grabbed two loaves of bread, set them in the cart. "We travel a lot. We're gone a lot."

"She'll be my top priority, Master."

"And you, hers."

"But I'd like you to consider it, Master. It would put me at ease to have chores to do."

341

"I know it would. We'll talk about it more. Right now, we just need to get back to the house before Everly has a coronary."

She was rather worked up, quite excited about what Isaac and Ian had in store for her. So I understood his distraction. In fact, I even managed to let thoughts of her push out all the others. There would be time to deal with reality later. Today was going to be special.

When we arrived back at the house, Isaac was already pouring a drink.

"Where's Everly?"

He nodded toward the living room.

I had to pause to observe the scene.

"Well, well, well," Ian said, setting the bags on the island and walking over to look at Everly. "Enjoying yourself, little fairy?"

Her eyes widened. Thanks to the gag in her mouth, she couldn't speak.

That didn't stop her from moaning as Heaven sat between her thighs, which were restrained to keep her ankles against her butt, knees wide, wielding one of those torture devices they called a vibrator. This one had a narrow handle, a wide, bulbous head and was being applied directly to Everly's clit.

"You want to come, don't you?" Ian taunted.

Everly nodded, the move causing the chain attached to the gag to tug on the clamps pinching Everly's nipples.

She moaned loudly, whimpered.

Isaac appeared. "If she does, she gets punished. Again."

"Again, huh? She's already earned punishment today. On her birthday of all days."

"Her ass is not only stuffed full, it's also a pretty shade of red," Isaac informed us, sipping his drink.

"Well, if this is what we get on *her* birthday, I can't fucking wait till it's ours." Ian chuckled, then went to the kitchen.

I followed, helping him unload the groceries while Everly continued to moan from the living room.

I smiled, a little disappointed that I'd have to wait until February before I got to see what they had in store for *my* birthday.

Everly

HE WAS KILLING ME SLOWLY.

Torturing me for the thrill of it.

And I loved every freaking second of it.

It wasn't lost on me that Isaac was being extremely strict today, dishing out punishment for every little infraction. He knew what it did to me. And he was getting extremely creative.

The spanking I'd gotten earlier had been nothing compared to the torture session with the magic wand he'd had Heaven use on me while I was gagged and restrained.

Now I was serving as their dinner dish.

While I'd heard about this practice, submissives being used as various pieces of furniture, I'd never experienced it. Yet here I was, on my twenty-fifth birthday, laid out on the dining room table while the four of them ate off of me.

Yep.

The food, a variety of finger foods, had been strategically placed over my naked body. As they ate, the spots they uncovered were subjected to the cool air, making my skin tingle, along with other parts of my body.

But they weren't only eating, they were teasing me in the process.

At the moment, Dante's fingers were buried in my pussy, skillfully brushing my G-spot while I was forced to endure. If I moved or made a sound, it would only add to my punishment.

"I'm quite impressed," Ian said conversationally. "Not only with the food—nice job, Heaven—but also with how well the birthday girl's holding up."

"I am, too," Isaac noted.

I knew that tone, knew something bad—translating to very, very good—was about to happen. I held myself as still as possible, holding my breath in anticipation.

Dante's fingers pulled out, pushed back in. He did it several times before vibrations erupted in my ass.

I whimpered, swallowing the sound a second too late.

"Uh-uh-uh," Isaac said. "What did I tell you?"

I wasn't supposed to answer him, so I didn't.

He smiled, a mischievous smirk that promised punishment for my transgressions. At this point, I wouldn't be sitting down for a week if he decided to spank me.

The vibrations stopped, but not Dante's fingers. He began fucking me faster, his fingers pushing in deep, driving me to distraction.

The plug in my ass came on again, making me whimper. It was an involuntary reaction to the stimuli. Not at all my fault! Then again, I was certain Isaac knew that, hence the reason he continued to do it.

When they finished their meal, Dante's fingers blessedly disappeared, and I thought I was in the clear for a few minutes at least.

Turned out not to be the case when Ian disappeared, only to return with a bottle of chocolate syrup. Rather than cover my body with it, he let the cold liquid drip onto my nipples.

"Heaven, you take one. Dante, the other. Clean her thoroughly."

I swallowed hard, trying to prepare myself.

It didn't help. Their warm mouths covering my nipples dragged a ragged moan from my chest.

Dante bit down gently and I damn near came from the sensation.

"I think you might need a little more," Ian offered.

Heaven and Dante lifted their heads, Ian added more of the chilled chocolate before they resumed feasting again.

344

I was so focused on their brutal torment, the mouth that descended on my pussy nearly had me bucking off the table. Strong hands held down my thighs as Isaac feasted on my pussy. He was relentless in his pursuit of my orgasm, so it was no wonder he achieved his goal.

When I came with a strangled cry ripped from my throat, it earned me a chuckle from Ian.

"You're a beautiful birthday girl," Ian whispered before leaning down and kissing me thoroughly.

I was panting and trembling, wondering if I would survive the rest of the evening, knowing deep down that it was hopeless. I was meant to enjoy this day, even if it felt like torture. The sweetest torture imaginable, of course.

"It's time for the next portion of our evening," Isaac said, holding out his hand.

I was still trembling when he helped me down from the table, and Isaac must have noticed because he brought my fingers to his mouth, brushed his lips over them, then pulled me into him.

"Are you enjoying your birthday, fairy princess?"

"Very much, my Liege." And that was the honest-to-God truth. I'd never felt more alive than I did that day. The attention they'd given me, even though it was mostly erotic in nature, was mind-blowing. Perhaps *because* it was erotic in nature. Not that I expected anything less from them. My twin Doms were experts in sexuality.

"Good. Because it's not over yet."

With my hand in his, Isaac led me out to the backyard. He stopped, placing his hand across my chest and holding me against him. There, standing beside the pool, Dante and Heaven, already naked, were in the process of undressing Ian. Hands, mouths, whatever it took to get the man down to his birthday suit.

Admittedly, I wished I was part of it, my lips tingling to feel Ian's skin.

The way they touched him, kissed, licked, sucked … all while Ian stood by, his eyes hooded as he observed. It was obvious he thoroughly enjoyed them as well.

Once naked, Ian directed Heaven into the water before he took the liberty to tease Dante. It was an impressive sight, watching Ian proficiently and seductively stroke his submissive. Yeah, I found the whole male-on-male interaction rather intriguing. This especially.

Long before Dante could get off, Ian motioned him toward the pool, then turned to me.

Isaac released me, nudging me toward the other object of my affection, the one I loved with another piece of my heart.

"Ah, little fairy. It's your turn," he said softly, reaching for my hand.

I grinned. "But I'm already naked."

"That you are."

He lifted me up, forcing me to wrap my legs around his waist. I all but glued myself to him as his lips found mine. I sighed, giving myself over to the kiss, eager to see what was in store for me next. Truth was, I would've been content with everything they'd given me already. But I knew these Doms, knew the best was yet to come.

"Happy birthday, little fairy," he whispered against my mouth.

"Thank you, my Alpha," I replied, purposely using the honorific I'd come up with for him but had yet to use.

His head snapped back, eyes locked with mine. There was so much heat there I thought for a second we would disintegrate. Lucky for us both, we didn't.

He set me on my feet, smiled. "Now do the honors for your Master, then join us."

I turned to Isaac, watching as he approached. The way his hot gaze raked over me had my skin tingling and my nipples pebbling. I wasn't sure I would ever get used to seeing that look on his face. It was so much more than appreciation for a female body. It was something powerful, all-consuming.

It was love and that was what made it so potent.

"May I undress you, my Liege?"

"Only if you take extra special care."

"Always and forever."

I took my time with Isaac. Though they were identical in appearance, Ian and Isaac were different in so many ways. They felt different, smelled different. Each had an intoxicating scent unique to him, despite having identical DNA. And each of them affected me differently. They had their own distinct brand of sex appeal.

When I tried to tease him the way he'd teased me, Isaac tilted my chin up and curled his other hand around my wandering wrist.

"Not yet, fairy princess. I promise, we'll have all the time in the world in a few hours. Just me and you."

"I'm looking forward to it, my Liege." I went up on my toes, pressed my lips to his. "In fact, that's the birthday present I'm looking forward to most."

His eyes warmed, his face softened, and he looked at me the way he always did, speaking directly to my heart.

"Some time for relaxation before the birthday surprise," he said, taking my hand and leading me to the swimming pool.

The water was warm, warmer than it usually was, and I wondered why but didn't have time to think about that because all four of them were surrounding me. Isaac remained at my back, supporting me with his chest and arms. Heaven took one of my feet, Dante the other. Ian took hold of my hand as they led me into deeper water. They had to turn, keeping Heaven on the shallowest side, which caused a few bouts of laughter to erupt, including from me.

That died away when Isaac instructed me to close my eyes. "Relax, love. Let us take care of you now."

Dante, holding my right foot, began massaging, starting with my toes, then my instep. He moved slowly, patiently, working his way up my leg, ensuring he soothed every muscle while keeping me secure in the water. When he stopped, Heaven picked up, doing the same with my left leg. I found it interesting the difference in their touch. Dante's fingers were bigger, stronger while Heaven's paid more attention to detail, smoothing my skin while massaging it.

There was nothing sexual about the massage, just deeply relaxing. My arms were next, and I knew it was Ian because Isaac remained behind me, his arms curled under mine, his fingertips lightly massaging my chest.

When I was once again boneless, Isaac moved back until I was laid out in the water, supported entirely by the people I loved.

Hands shifted, moved, supporting my back and my butt.

That was when it turned sexual. Soft hands—Heaven's for sure—caressed my breasts. Not teasing, massaging, but it was sensual in nature, heating my body from the inside. When she stopped, bigger hands, stronger hands—Ian's, I figured—took their place, grazing over my nipples, then moving over my stomach. I inhaled sharply when those skilled hands massaged the folds of my pussy. He teased my clit but not with intention of working me into a frenzy.

Then there were more hands, Dante's, I assumed, which began massaging my butt, kneading the flesh, teasing my cheeks apart, brushing against the plug still lodged inside me, keeping my nerve endings lit up like the surface of the sun.

I was drifting on a euphoric high when Isaac shifted me, pulling me into his arms.

"Better?"

"Perfect."

He smiled against my lips. "Not quite yet."

348

"No? There's more?"

"There is." He pressed his lips to mine, kissing me thoroughly as I wrapped my arms around him, holding tight as he carried me out of the pool and into the house.

We bypassed the kitchen, the living room, then moved down the hallway. I was thinking we were going to our room, but he surprised me, stopping in the guest room attached to his.

"I'll be back," he whispered. "But I promise, you'll enjoy this."

I stared up into his eyes, grinning when he lifted a blindfold, dangling it above me.

"I know I will, my Liege."

"This is sensual play," he said, as though I needed the explanation. "Which is why I'll also be using noise-cancelling headphones."

When he placed them over my ears, I couldn't see or hear, so I lay there, in the center of the bed, not moving.

Music started, soft in my ears. Soothing instrumentals, which helped me relax. I could smell something. It was sweet, fruity. I didn't know what or who, so I remained there, holding my breath as I waited for what was coming next.

Soft fingers moved over my foot. There was something warm. Oil, maybe? Yes. Massage oil.

And those were Heaven's hands.

I didn't know how long she worked, but it felt like hours as she massaged me from my toes to my neck on the front side, then had me turn over, careful to keep the headphones in place while she did the same with my back, down my legs, and once again to my feet.

I probably drifted off a couple of times from the overwhelming pleasure. Although the massage in the pool had been stimulating, this one had soothed, relaxed.

Heaven's hands caressed my calves one last time before disappearing altogether.

As I lay there, blissed out, I couldn't imagine anything that could've made this birthday better than it already was.

A few minutes later, I found out exactly what could be.

Twenty-Seven

ISAAC

"THANK YOU FOR COMING TODAY," IAN TOLD Heaven when she returned to the living room a solid hour after she'd gone in with Everly.

"You're very welcome. And thanks for inviting me." She smiled sweetly, grabbed the bag she'd brought with her. "I've called my sister, let her know I'm on the way."

Ian nodded. "Text me when you get there, so we know you're safe."

I offered her my thanks, gave her a hug before Dante did the same. While Ian walked her out to her car, Dante and I remained in the living room. I gripped the back of his neck, massaged the tension there.

"You doing all right?"

He nodded, eyes lowered. "It's been a long day."

"You've done well." I pulled him toward me, met his gaze briefly before pressing my lips to his.

The man sighed, relaxing in my hold as my tongue explored his. We were still like that when Ian returned. My brother cleared his throat, chuckled.

"We've got a birthday girl waiting for us."

That we did. And though I could've spent another half hour with my mouth fused to Dante's, I figured it was best not to keep her waiting.

With the two of them in tow, I led the way to the guest room, where I imagined my fairy princess was drifting off right about now. Once Dante was inside, he closed the door behind us as quietly as he could.

We wasted no time, the three of us discarding the shorts we'd donned after leaving the pool. Dante rolled on a condom and crawled onto the bed with Everly. He removed the headphones, set them aside, but left the blindfold intact.

"Happy Birthday, Everly."

"Thank you, Dante."

He lay on the bed, pulling Everly so that she was draped over his long, lean body. I took a moment to admire the two of them together. Dante took her mouth with his, kissing her as he ran his hands over all that smooth skin, still glistening from the oil Heaven had rubbed on to her.

Everly took what he offered, her hands sliding into his hair as the kiss heated, sweet and soft morphing into passionate until it was ablaze, Everly moving against him, trying to get closer. She'd endured rather well today, considering. I'd put her through the motions, keeping her suspended in a constant state of arousal, all in preparation for this.

I moved onto the bed, kneeling between Dante's legs, positioning Everly's so that she was straddling his hips.

She moaned softly, then sat up, reaching back for me.

I pressed my chest to her back, slid my hands around to cup her sweet tits, kneading them firmly. Slow and soft would come later. Right now, I wanted her on fire, eager.

"My Liege," she moaned, turning her head as though searching for my lips.

I kissed her hard, lifting her as Dante positioned his cock before guiding her down onto him.

Her sweet mouth broke from mine, a passionate cry escaping her lips. She pressed her hands to Dante's chest as he began rocking his hips, pushing in deeper.

"Dante…"

"I'm here, baby," he crooned, twining her fingers with his and urging her forward. "Right here."

I focused on them as Ian joined us, kneeling near Dante's head, his cock in his hand. He stroked himself, enjoying the show as much as I was.

From behind Everly, I squeezed her ass, kneading the smooth globes, letting her know what was coming. Our touch seemed to ignite her. She was trying to get more friction from Dante while mumbling incoherently. Dante pulled her down to him, crushed his mouth to hers, keeping her still while I took the opportunity to remove the plug. I tossed it onto the floor, then grabbed the lubricant and coated my cock.

"I want that sweet mouth on my cock, little fairy." Ian's voice was stern, demanding, his hand slipping under her chin, separating her from Dante so he could feed his cock past her lips. "Ah, that's it. Suck me."

His hand curled around the back of her head, holding her in place as he took charge, controlling the movements, flexing his hips forward, fucking her mouth while Dante fucked her pussy.

I knew this was a risk, me taking her like this. Here. With them. My need for her was irrational, had me losing control in a way nothing and no one ever had. But I wanted this for her, to give her the pleasure I knew she craved. I'd already warned my brother, told him to follow my lead without question. He had promised, ensuring me they would retreat if he saw the need for it.

I gripped Everly's hip, guided my cock right where I wanted it.

It took tremendous restraint not to drive myself into her, to sate the ever-growing desire that never seemed to abate, no matter how many times I took her.

Her sweet moans fueled me, growing louder as her tight ass squeezed my cock.

Ian pulled out of her mouth, stroked himself as she cried out. Not from pain. This was frantic, a desperate need that I understood because I felt it inside me.

"Please … my Liege … fuck me. Oh, God … fuck me."

I retreated, drove into her, harder this time, bottoming out, my hands gripping her hips firmly.

Knowing I would lose control soon enough, I nodded to Ian, signaling him to move. He guided Everly's mouth back to his cock as I fucked her, Dante using my momentum to drive deep into her cunt. I could feel his cock against mine, which in itself drove me fucking crazy. I loved feeling him like this, deep inside the woman we loved.

Minutes felt like hours, the erotic pain taking over, the need to dominate, to control so great I could hardly breathe. It was always like this with Everly.

I focused on her pleasure, remembering this wasn't about me. It was for her, only her. I fucked her, the combined grunts and groans echoing, her soft moans lingering in the room, until the air became too stifling, my body an inferno.

"Ian," I growled. "Go."

I wrapped my arms around Everly, pulling her back against my chest as my hips pumped, my cock driving into her ass even as Dante pulled out, rolled out from under her. When they were out of sight, nothing mattered. I ripped her blindfold off, held her tightly against me as her arms covered mine.

"My Liege … it's too good."

I growled in her ear, overcome by the insanity I only felt with her. I pushed her forward. She fell to the bed, propped up with her hands while my fingers dug into her hips, impaling her ass again and again as she writhed, moaned, took everything, begging for more. Her back bowed, hips lifted, that sweet ass rocking back, meeting every punishing thrust, and still I couldn't get enough. It would never be enough.

"Fuck…" I hissed the word, my body catching fire, burning out of control, and my release threatened to overtake me.

"My Liege, please … come inside me. Let me feel you come."

That did it. I drove into her once, twice. My body erupted, my cock pulsing as I spilled deep inside her ass.

As the air returned to my lungs, I came back to myself, knowing I had taken more than I'd given this time, and regret was a hot lump in my throat.

I pulled out, fell to my side, and pulled Everly to me. Her eyes were wild, her mouth tipped up in a smile, and still, I couldn't understand it.

"Thank you, my Liege," she whispered as she brushed her lips to mine. "This was the best birthday ever."

I wrapped my arms around her, pulled her face to my chest, and let the emotion churn, willing it to abate. The crazed feeling was still there, the desire to possess her, own her. It was overwhelming.

When she lifted her head, looked into my eyes, I knew she could see it, the storm of emotion that threatened to level me.

Everly's hands cupped my face. Her body shifted as she got closer, her lips pressing to mine. "I love you, Isaac. I love you with all that I am."

I wasn't sure how she knew I needed to hear it, but it soothed something inside me, had my breaths evening out.

"I'm not through with you yet," I warned her. "We'll shower. Then I'm going to take you slow, make love to you all fucking night long."

"I'm looking forward to it, my Liege."

It took effort, but I managed to get to my feet, lift her in my arms, and carry her into the room that was ours and ours alone. I padded into the bathroom, turned on the shower. Through sheer force of will, I soothed us both, cleaning the oil from her skin, washing us both, then carrying her to the bed that only she would sleep in with me.

Through it all, I never stopped touching her. My hands needed to be on her skin, to feel every breath she took, the blessed beat of her heart. I had no idea how I'd ever found this, the love that surpassed any and all others. She was my heart, my soul.

I kissed her for long minutes, covering her body with mine, knowing that I would lose the self-control I prided myself on when I slid deep inside her. But she wasn't scared of that, of me. My fairy princess knew what I needed the same way I knew what she needed. She was my perfect mate, the other half of my heart.

"Love me," she whispered, her lips trailing over my jaw as she held on to me.

I covered her body with mine, slid inside her soft heat with ease. Her legs wrapped around my hips, holding there, giving me free rein when the need to thrust into her, to claim her became too great.

Twining her fingers with mine, I pinned her hands to the bed, hovered over her as I thrust, deep and slow, rolling my hips, watching her eyes dilate, her lips part on every soft moan that escaped her. She begged for more, pleaded, but never pushed, giving all control over to me. She trusted me to take care of her.

And I would. Now and always.

Nothing and no one would ever come between us.

IAN

When I left Everly's room, I went to the kitchen, needing a minute to catch my breath. Dante followed, not saying a word, although I could hear a million questions rattling around in his head.

I grabbed the bottle of Irish whiskey my brother was so fond of, poured two fingers in a glass, then forced myself not to down it.

I turned, stark naked, standing in my kitchen and faced Dante.

"You're wondering what happened."

"Actually, I'm not, Master."

"No?" I cocked my head to the side. "You expected that?"

He laughed, and the sound actually released some of the tension inside me.

"I wouldn't exactly say that. But I guess, in a way, it didn't surprise me."

"Well, it surprised the hell out of me." I'd never seen my brother like that. Intense and … on the verge of losing control.

"I saw it before," Dante admitted. "At the club. During our scene."

"He was like that?"

"Well, no. Not quite like that, but I could see it in his eyes."

I took a long swig, let it burn all the way down.

"He loves her," Dante stated. "He won't hurt her."

"That's…" I shook my head. "That's not what I was thinking. I know he won't hurt her." I turned to pour another drink.

"What's wrong, Master?"

With my back to him, I sighed, hung my head. "I felt it."

"Felt what?"

"What he was feeling. So much love, he thought he would go insane with it. It was intense."

It was exactly the same feeling I got when I was with Everly. When I really allowed myself to have her the way I wanted, when I permitted myself to open up fully. I had yet to do that, always holding myself back in some way. Because it scared me, the thought of losing my shit, feeling so damn much for a woman. It was the reason I rationalized, talked it out. That way, I could relay my feelings without actually having to … feel them.

Warm hands trailed up my back. I found myself leaning into Dante.

I felt the same thing with him, and I'd probably shown him more of it because I didn't worry that he couldn't handle me.

He kissed my shoulder, his soft lips trailing over my skin. I set the glass down, turned to face him, then pulled him to me.

"I need you," I whispered, trailing my hands over the hard muscles in his back.

I loved the way he fit against me. Dante wasn't a big man, but he wasn't small, either. He was perfect.

When his eyes met mine, they were midnight blue and so full of knowledge it scared me a little.

"You're holding back," he whispered, evidently a mind reader.

"How so?"

"With Everly." His gaze never wavered. "I see it in your eyes. The way you look at her. The longing. Isaac doesn't know how you feel."

This mind reader was also perceptive.

I opted for honestly. Gripping his face in my hands, I locked my gaze with his. "Yes. I am. I have to."

"Why?"

"Because he's my brother. I... One of these days, I'll break. Won't be able to hold it in. Until then ... I just... Fuck, Dante. I need *you*. So fucking much. I think about you all the goddamn time. And that ... that's what scares me most."

"Why?"

"Why?" I dropped my hands. "That doesn't bother you? That I want you as much as her and her as much as you?"

His eyebrows shot downward. "No. Why should it?"

"Because it was supposed to be her *or* you. Not both. I never saw myself loving more than one. Is it even possible?"

"Yeah. It is. It's definitely possible."

I sucked in air, forced myself to calm down.

When he backed away, I dropped my head. "I need you tonight."

"Me?"

"Yes. In my bed." I lifted my head, held his stare. "All night. Can you give me that?"

"Yes, Master," he said softly. "I can give you anything."

"Anything?" I stepped toward him, backing him against the counter. Somehow, I managed to keep my hands to myself. "All of yourself? Can you give me that?"

"If you'll take it … of course I will."

My heart felt like it would explode. The pain was intense. I had to breathe through it, worried I was about to have a fucking heart attack at the age of thirty-one.

"But I need you to understand something."

I lifted my eyebrows, urging him to tell me.

"I love her."

"Everly?"

"And Isaac," he said, and I could tell it pained him to tell me this. "In a way that'll never make sense to anyone."

I wasn't sure what to say, so I kept my mouth shut.

"But what they have … it defies logic, reason," he whispered. "I'll never have that with any of you. Not because I don't think I'm worthy. More so because … I'm me."

"We'll see about that," I told him. I already knew that all of this defied logic. And though no one had broached the subject with Isaac, my brother would figure it out. In time.

"I hope you're not tired," I told him as we approached my bedroom.

He chuckled. "Not in the slightest."

I opened the door, stepped inside. Before the door was closed completely, I backed Dante against it, crushed my mouth to his. We were both naked, which made exploring him with my hands that much easier. And I did, my palms roaming over all that smooth, warm skin. His moans of pleasure spurred me on.

And though I knew I would never have his whole heart, I prayed I would have hers. Without it, I wasn't sure I would ever be complete.

By the time we stumbled over to the bed, we were both frantic, mouths moving together, hands searching, seeking.

As though he sensed what I needed, Dante took the reins. I wouldn't go so far as to say he was in control, but he was far more assertive than I'd ever seen him. Forcing me onto my back, he knelt between my legs, inhaling my cock into the warm haven of his mouth.

I cried out, hips jerking upward. He never slowed. He took his time, sucking, licking, driving me out of my fucking mind. I took the time to watch him. His shabby blond hair swayed as he bobbed his head, that chiseled jaw flexed as he took my cock deep into his throat. He was a beautiful man, in so many ways, and I felt incredibly lucky that I'd found him.

When I neared the brink, I slid my hand in his hair, tightened my grip. "Don't you dare make me come," I growled in warning. "I'll be deep in your ass when I do that."

He moaned, as though that was the best thing he'd heard all damn night.

Releasing his hair, I gripped his arms, jerked him up on the bed with me, and sealed my lips to his. I kissed him, losing myself in his warmth even as I rolled us so that he was beneath me. This was where I liked him most. Under me.

"Don't move," I bit out, pushing to my knees.

I reached for the nightstand, retrieved the lubricant I kept there.

And while he stared up at me with those bottomless blue eyes, I generously lubed my cock, applying some to his in the process. I stroked us both. His eyes glittered as they watched the movement of my hands.

"Spread your legs," I ordered, still stroking.

His feet shifted so they were flat on the bed.

"Knees to your chest."

Dante grabbed his knees, pulling them toward his chest, opening him to me.

My gaze dropped to his asshole as I leaned forward, guiding myself home.

We both drew in big gulps of air as I thrust inside him.

I took him, driving in hard and deep, rocking forward, back. Retreating. I relied on the control he willingly gave me, used it to drive us both higher and higher. I wasn't gentle, but I knew I didn't have to be. Dante knew what I needed, accepted it, offered his complete submission. And even when I thought I was out of control, I knew I wasn't. He would hold me together, keep me in one piece. Which meant I had to trust him.

The same way he trusted me.

"Dante." His name came out as a plea.

"Master! Please ... oh, fuck. Feels so good."

His head fell back, hand reaching for his cock. He jerked himself roughly while I hammered into him. His ass clamped down on me, milking my cock until the leash on my control threatened to snap.

"Come for me, Dante," I demanded.

His fist worked furiously over his cock, his breaths sawing in and out of his lungs. He was so fucking beautiful. My heart lodged in my throat as I watched him, willed him over the edge because I wanted to watch him come.

When he did, it was with a rough growl. The sight of his cum splashing onto his belly, his chest sent me over the edge. I slammed into him, let myself go.

And knew, above all else, this man's love would sustain me.

I didn't want to deny my feelings for Everly, but if I never found the nerve to address them, I had more than enough to make me happy.

Twenty-Eight

ISAAC

Tuesday, June 11, 2019

"Yeah. Thanks, Ransom. Tell Liam I appreciate him covering for us."

"Will do. He said he'd be happy to fill in for as long as you need him."

"We got a hit on the passport yesterday," I informed my boss. "Vernon Hathaway is back in Chicago, so I expect this to escalate soon."

"I do, too. I'm not too keen on Ian's idea, but I can't think of anything better at the moment."

"A trap's pretty much our only option." Aside from making a call to the dark side of the law, which I was hesitant to do. The Irish mob did not forget someone who owed them a favor, and if we called one in, we'd be on the hook for the rest of our lives.

"Doesn't mean it's a smart move," Ransom grumbled. "This bastard's not just crazy, he's mentally ill. I figure he has to know who you are by now."

I figured that, too.

"Plus, we've kept the local PD in the dark on this one. Not much they can do until we've got some sort of proof of what he's done. At that point, Dante would have to press charges."

Which I knew he wouldn't do. The man had his pride and I knew he wanted to put this all behind him. Couldn't say I blamed him, either.

On the other hand, I wanted Vernon Hathaway to get the punishment he deserved. And as far as I was concerned, the rest of his life in a prison cell wasn't even the half of it.

"Hit me up when you know what the plan is," Ransom said. "I gotta go."

"Thanks again."

I disconnected the call, leaned back in my chair, and glanced over at Ian's desk.

He'd spent most of yesterday out of the house, then this morning, he'd hightailed it as soon as he woke up. I wasn't an idiot. I knew there was something going on with him. Since the night of Everly's birthday, when I kicked him out of the room, he'd been acting different. Dante and Everly were walking on eggshells and it was all starting to piss me off.

Since I couldn't leave, I had to endure or at least find a way to smooth out the tensions in the house until Ian got his shit together.

When I stepped into the kitchen, I found it empty. A sound from Dante's wing of the house drew my attention, so I wandered that way, stood in the doorway, and watched as Everly helped Dante empty a box.

"Heaven called me this morning," Everly told him. "Prince Charming asked her out."

Dante laughed. "I'm assuming she knows his name by now?"

"Todd something or other. Anyway, he's taking her out on Friday."

"Does she know anything about him?"

"He's twenty-nine, works for a tech company, but she didn't say which one. Has his own house, a dog."

Dante spun to face her. "A dog?"

The longing on his face surprised me. Then again, it shouldn't have. I knew plenty about the man, but most of it was his past. I had yet to delve into his hopes and dreams though I wanted to.

"Yep. Golden retriever named Sam."

"How old?"

"Three, I think." Everly tucked a stack of comic books into the nightstand.

Dante sauntered across the room to the bathroom. Not wanting them to know I'd been eavesdropping, I slipped back to the kitchen, pulling my phone out of my pocket as I went.

Perhaps Dante needed a dog. Ian and I had never had a pet of our own, but I could see one thriving here. Between Everly and Dante, the thing would be spoiled.

The thought made me smile.

Two hours later, I found Dante and Everly sitting at the breakfast bar. They were finishing up their lunch. When I joined them, two sets of wary eyes turned toward me.

"Have you heard from Ian?" Everly asked, concern evident in her tone.

"He'll be back shortly." Though I didn't know that for sure. My brother wasn't answering his phone. It was clear to me he was pouting, but I had no idea why.

Well, that wasn't entirely true. I had the feeling it was thanks to my high-handed behavior on Everly's birthday. Try as I might, I couldn't quite understand why Ian would go off on me for that, but he'd done so for less.

"Should we check on him?" Dante asked, his gaze darting toward his phone

"I'll try to call him again," I told them. "When I come back, I want you two kneeling in the living room, waiting for me."

"Yes, my Liege," Everly said softly, a hint of confusion in her tone.

"Yes, Master." Dante was already placing his glass in the sink.

With a sigh, I headed out onto the back patio and dialed Ian's number.

"What's up?" he answered hotly.

"Any idea when you're coming home?"

"Why? You miss me?"

"Everly and Dante do," I told him.

"Did they say as much?"

"Ian, what the hell's going on with you?"

He grunted. "Nothing. I'll be back in an hour."

The call disconnected and I stared at my phone.

Yeah, something had to give.

And soon.

Everly

"I'VE COME UP WITH A LIST OF chores," Isaac said when he came into the living room after spending a few minutes on the back porch. "Dante mentioned the two of you wanting to take them over. Is this true?"

"Yes, my Liege," I said softly, keeping my eyes cast downward.

"There are a few things we'll continue to pay services for such as the lawn care and pool maintenance, although I don't mind decreasing the service and allowing the two of you to do them in between. While I appreciate your desire to help out, it's something we'll discuss from time to time because I don't want you to be my maid or my pool boy. At the same time, I want you to feel as though you contribute to the household. You're not a guest anymore. This is your house. Once we've settled the problem we're dealing with, you'll have the freedom to come and go as you please. Until it's resolved though..."

"I understand, Master," Dante said firmly.

Dante and I had already discussed chores. And I liked the idea of having something to keep me busy. More accurately, I greatly liked the idea of taking care of Isaac and Ian. That was important to me and I wasn't sure they understood that yet. I still felt as though this was a honeymoon period. I wanted to settle into a routine, to know what I needed to do every day in order to have a sense of accomplishment.

"The chores have been written out. By the end of the day, I want you to provide me with a detailed outline of when you'll be handling which ones. You can divvy up meals as well. Dante, you can handle dinner tonight."

"Of course, Master."

"When Ian returns, I think it would be wise for the two of you to spend some time in the pool. Swimsuits are necessary as I've got a few men stationed around the property now that Vernon has returned to the States."

"Yes, my Liege."

His hand grazed the top of my head and I sighed.

Some people didn't understand this aspect. They thought BDSM was strictly sexual in nature. That wasn't the case. Not for me. Not for Dante.

Sure, there was a sexual aspect, one that I craved. But I also looked forward to serving my Dominant. Pleasing him. That was my one goal, and honestly, I'd always wondered if I would ever find a man I could trust or love enough to pledge my submission to. I'd been lucky to find that with two, even if I didn't get to spend nearly enough time with Ian. And I didn't care what anyone else thought about it. I would be their humble servant in every way, for as long as it would please them.

The front door slammed, causing me to jump.

Isaac sighed. "Go get changed. We'll finish this discussion later."

While Dante went to his side of the house, I raced to Isaac's room, grabbed my swimsuit, then hurried to pull it on. I couldn't help but do so silently, trying to listen for whatever conversation might've been taking place between Ian and Isaac.

I had no idea what was going on, but I could tell there was a rift between them. Neither had said anything to me about it, but I hadn't really expected them to. It wasn't as though they were big on sharing details of ... well, of much of anything, really. Ian was all about interrogating other people, getting them to open up but very rarely free with his own emotions.

When I got outside, Dante was waiting for me, his face solemn.

"You know what that's about?" I asked him, jerking my chin toward the house.

"Family squabble," he said with a smirk.

"Really?"

"Just a guess."

"Did something happen?"

He shrugged.

With the sun warm on my shoulders, I waded down into the pool, grabbed one of the floats we'd added earlier in the week, put my arms across it while Dante did the same from the opposite side.

"What do you think it's about?"

Dante rested his head on his arms, looked at me. "You."

I frowned. "What? What did I do?"

"Nothing. And I think that's the problem."

Feeling defensive, I glared at him. "What does that mean? What have I *not* done that I was supposed to?"

"Nothing," he said firmly. "And that's the problem."

"Okay, PB, you're making absolutely no freaking sense here."

"I know. But that seems to be the trend."

"I was thinking it had to do with Heaven," I admitted. "Maybe Ian misses her."

"Nope. Definitely not the problem."

"So you don't think he loves her? That he was disappointed when she left?"

"No."

"You sound so sure of yourself."

"Because I am," he declared. "Ian does not love Heaven.

For whatever reason, that made me feel better.

It wasn't that I was necessarily insecure, but the thought of Ian loving someone else ... well, it bothered me.

"Do you love him?" Dante prompted.

"Who?"

"Ian."

I propped my chin on my arm. "Of course I do."

"The way you love Isaac?"

Okay, now I sensed he was fishing for something specific. I met his blue stare. "Yes."

"Heart, soul, and everything in between?"

"What are you getting at?"

He looked away. "It's just that ... well, you spend so much time with Isaac."

"Because I sleep in his bed?"

He was silent for a minute and I thought he was going to drop the subject.

He didn't.

"Back before I met them," he began, "when you'd talk about them, I got the impression you were interested in both of them."

"I am."

"Equally."

I floated for a minute, thinking back on when I'd first met Ian and Isaac. "The first time I played with them at the club," I explained. "It was during submissive training class. I was attracted to both of them. But there was something in Isaac's eyes that captivated me, drew me to him. I felt a connection."

"But you kept your distance."

"I did." God, I remembered how anxious they'd made me. "You would've done the same thing in my place. They were larger than life when I met them. Submissives at the club practically throw themselves at their feet, worship the ground they walk on. I figured they had more than enough to fill their time. And you know me, I'm not the sort who can let emotion in without embracing it. And with them, I knew I would lose a piece of myself anytime I was with them, so I tried to avoid them as much as I could. But if they asked me to play, I couldn't say no. Didn't want to."

"Do you think any of this would've happened if...?"

He didn't finish, but he didn't have to. He was referring to that man attacking me, and I knew he had a hard time thinking about it.

"I do." I turned my head, locked my eyes with his. "I'd been invited to Zeke's that day and I was going there no matter what. I knew they would be there, and I'd been hoping for a chance to see them outside the club. I think it would've progressed from there."

"I do, too."

"What about you? When did you know?"

"The instant my eyes met Ian's in front of my house. I knew right then that I could trust him, felt the pull. My inner submissive connected with him." He grinned. "I sound corny, huh?"

"No." I grinned. "You sound like a man in love."

"I am, but not just with Ian."

Though he didn't elaborate, I hoped he was including me in the sentiment. Dante and I had a connection all our own. The few times I'd been with him had been amazing, and though I secretly wished for more, I didn't feel it was my place to pursue him. The dynamic had shifted once we'd become involved with Ian and Isaac.

For the next half hour, we floated in the pool, the warm breeze floating over my skin, rustling the trees.

"Time to come in," Isaac called from the patio. "I'd bet money neither one of you thought about sunscreen."

I lifted my head, smiled, but it disappeared as soon as I saw Isaac's face.

Though his tone was light, his eyes told a different story. He was worried.

The question was: about who?

Twenty-Nine

Dante

Friday, June 14, 2019

THE HOUSE WAS TOO QUIET.

Had been for the past few days. Ian wasn't talking about whatever was on his mind, and no one was asking, either. Certainly not me. I didn't know what had happened to prompt his attitude, but deep down, I knew exactly what it was about.

Now he was withdrawn, brooding. Acting more like Isaac than himself.

Every now and then, I would catch him looking at Everly with a pained expression on his face. One I couldn't interpret. I knew he felt something for her. He had admitted as much. But from the looks of it, his feelings for her were coming to the surface and he wasn't all that happy about it.

Having wanted someone to talk to, I'd reached out to Heaven via text. Turned out, Ian had admitted to her he had feelings for Everly, too. It seemed everyone was in the know except Isaac.

A knock sounded on my door. I knew instantly who it was, so I knew a response wasn't necessary.

I had already put the footrest on the recliner down and was sliding to the floor on my knees when I heard footsteps moving toward me, through my bedroom, and into the small living area I used to watch television.

It was a position I'd gotten used to being in as of late. One I'd personally requested. When Ian and Isaac were around, I wanted to kneel at their feet, to feel their presence, to comfort them in some small way. Since their preference seemed to be to have Everly sitting beside them, it worked for us.

As had become the routine, Ian walked over and sat in the recliner. I rested my head against his knee and his hand moved to my head, fingers combing through my hair.

"I'm sorry," he said softly.

I didn't respond. Didn't need to.

"I didn't mean for this to happen."

I knew that was true. I also knew that if he would address the situation with Isaac, they could come to some sort of resolution. I truly believed Isaac was blind to the fact his twin was in love with the same woman he was.

"Do you mind if I ask you something?"

Ian grunted.

"You and Isaac … you've wanted a submissive, right?"

"Two," he said, his tone clipped.

I lifted my head, watched him.

He sighed. "As you can see by the way we designed the house, Isaac and I always intended to have two submissives. One for each of us. Before we were in the lifestyle, it was your run-of-the-mill relationship. He would have a wife. I would have one, too. However, we'd intended to live together. It was never a question. That morphed into submissives. One for each of us. Only we intended to share them on occasion. From a sexual perspective only. One to love, cherish, give our hearts to. The other would be for fun, to incite the kink we've always been drawn to."

Well, hell. That explained why Isaac wasn't seeing this through his brother's eyes. He expected Ian to spend time with Everly but not to fall in love with her. Epic fail on their part, clearly.

We sat like that for a long time, the silence as comforting as the sound of his breathing. When he spoke, the abrupt tone startled me.

"Who am I?"

I peered up at him. "My Master and—"

He growled. "Who, Dante? *Who* am I?"

His outburst confused me, rendering me motionless, unable to speak.

Ian's lips pressed together, his head tipped back. "I want to be more than that to you."

There was an unfamiliar plea in his tone. It caused my heart to ache.

"Tell me," he groaned. "Who am I to you?"

I pressed my forehead to his knee and went with the truth. "My rescuer, my defender, the man who saved me from myself."

"Look at me, Dante," he commanded.

I lifted my head, met his tormented gaze.

His breaths came faster now, his eyes shifting over my face, studying me. Whatever had prompted this ... I think it was spur of the moment. The pain he was battling, it was building, and this was his way of releasing the pressure.

He didn't have to ask me again. I knew what he needed.

"The man I love," I whispered, the admission falling from my lips easily. "My Master."

He didn't speak, so I continued. "And I am your humble servant. Not only do you have my submission, you have my heart."

"And you have mine." He squeezed his eyes shut. "I need you, Dante."

He didn't have to say anything more than that. We both knew I would give him whatever he needed, whenever he needed it. Considering he hadn't asked anything of me since the night of Everly's birthday, I'd been hoping he would come for me. He might not see it that way, but I found significant comfort in his presence.

I lifted my head, met his gaze. "May I take care of you, Master?"

"Please." The single word was full of anguish, pain, but there was something lurking just beneath the surface. I had to believe it was relief, maybe even acceptance.

I pushed to my feet, stripped off my clothes. I could feel his eyes on me, hot as they raked over my skin. His gaze trailed me even when I went to my knees between his thighs. He was wearing athletic shorts, which he pushed down his hips. His cock was hard, and my mouth watered with the need to taste him, my heart aching with the need to soothe him in the only way I knew how.

Without using my hands, I took him in my mouth, caressed him with my tongue. I didn't rush, nor did he. As the minutes ticked by, his breaths remained slow, even, his hands moving into my hair. He was gentle, allowing me to give him pleasure, to worship his cock.

"Your mouth's perfect," he muttered, a low rumble of pleasure in his throat. "I could sit here all night. Let you suck me. Feel those sweet fucking lips on me."

He growled, as though he needed an outlet for the pleasure.

I hummed low in my throat, letting him know I was more than willing.

Several minutes passed before Ian widened his legs. "Lick my balls."

My cock throbbed in response to the command. I focused on his balls, licking them thoroughly as he growled low in his throat, his hand fisting his cock leisurely, his head tipped back, eyes closed.

"Take care of me, *mo grá*. Sit on my cock. Let me have you."

My breath halted in my chest, the need in his voice something I longed to hear, probably because it was so rare.

I managed to get to my feet, walked over to the dresser, retrieved the lubricant, returned. He was watching me now, as I lowered myself to my knees once more. I used the lube to coat him, stroke him. His breaths became more labored as I fisted him, preparing his cock for my ass.

"Tired of waiting." He groaned, gripped my hand, stilled it.

I felt the hum of energy vibrating under his skin.

"Come up here," he groaned. "Sit on my cock."

When I stood, Ian shifted in the chair, his hips sliding lower. His hands reached for me when I turned around. He assisted me, my leg muscles straining as he guided his cock into my ass. The blunt head pushed inside, slipping past the tight ring of muscles, making me grunt, my head falling back as I lowered all the way onto him. When I was fully seated, impaled by him, his cock filling me, stretching me, I was prepared to move when Ian's arms came around me, pulling me to him, my back against his chest.

"Don't move." He nipped my earlobe. "Just let me feel you for a minute."

His hips bucked ever so lightly, gradual nudges, pushing him in deeper than I thought possible. I breathed through the ache that was building, the desire to have him fuck me. When the chair began to gently rock, I turned my head toward him, moaned softly, urging him to continue.

"You feel so good," he whispered on a raspy breath. "Tell me you love me."

"I love you, Ian. With all that I am." I purposely used his name, wanting him to know I was talking to him. Not only as my Master, my savior, and the lifeline I'd come to think of him as, but as the man I'd fallen hard and fast for.

He continued to rock for long minutes, making my body hum, my cock throbbing. When he took me in hand, stroking firmly, I tipped my head back against his shoulder, letting him hear my pleasure.

A soft rumble sounded in his chest as he impaled me. I could feel his muscles coiling, knew the beast was waking. He'd held back with me before, but I knew it was in there and I knew one day it would come out. He would claim me, and though I doubted he would believe me, I was counting down until that day. When he unleashed, took from me exactly what he needed, all that I was willing to give. Only then would I know he truly understood just what I felt for him.

His hand curled under my chin, tipping my head back. His lips covered mine and he groaned, the sound almost feral.

"I'm going to take you, Dante."

"I'm yours to take, Master."

He said nothing, but I felt it. The tether holding him together snapped as hard hands curled around my arms, pushing me off him. One second I was on my feet, the next I was on my knees, chest flat on the recliner.

"Fuck," he cried out as he dropped down behind me, grabbed my ass, separated my cheeks, and drove into me.

The pain was brutal but exquisite at the same time. This was what I wanted. His unrestrained lust, all that he'd held back since that first night we were together.

I wanted it.

Wanted *him*.

And I prayed he wanted me enough to finally take all that I needed him to have.

IAN

MY CONTROL SHATTERED.

Completely obliterated by my overwhelming need for this man.

In that moment, I was reduced to nothing more than an animal desperate to mate, a beast eager to claim what rightfully belonged to him.

Gripping Dante's shoulders, I plowed into him, driving as deep as I could over and over, unable to stop. The beast was free, taking in an attempt to quench the thirst that would never be quenched. The hunger was intense, driving me into him deeper, harder. I pummeled him, wanting to hear him scream for me. I'd always been gentle, cognizant of all he'd been through. Deep down, I knew I wasn't being true to myself or to him.

And right here, right now, I intended to show him.

"Turn over," I growled, jerking out of him.

Before he could move, I was dragging him to the floor, flipping him onto his back, hefting his legs over my arms, and slamming into him again. Every punishing thrust rocked his body forward. His grunts were the fuel that kept me going, driving me deeper until I feared I would hurt him but couldn't seem to control myself. My entire body burned, every muscle rigid as I ruthlessly plunged my cock into his ass.

I lifted his legs up straight, held them with my hands, my only goal to sate the urge that was out of control, desperation overwhelming me.

Dante took everything I gave him, didn't whimper when I bent him in half and drilled my cock down into him. He willingly gave up all control and I feasted on it, absorbing it into my skin as I took and took. He would be sore tomorrow, but I didn't care. I needed him. His love, his submission, his ultimate surrender.

My muscles strained, burned as I impaled him over and over.

"Tell me," I roared, knowing he could hear the rage in my voice, the words ripped from my throat.

"I give … myself to … you, Master." Every other word was punctuated by a rough grunt brought on by my thrusts. "I'm yours … to have … to use."

"To love," I snapped. "You're mine to love."

"Always."

"Fuck!" I came on a vicious groan, my throat raw from the sound.

I didn't pull out, held myself inside him, dropping his legs.

"Make yourself come," I ordered, leaning over him.

His hand gripped his cock, jerking roughly. I met his eyes, willing him to surrender to it, to me.

"Master…" He panted, his ass milking my cock.

"Come for me, Dante," I demanded.

His head dropped back against the rug with a thud, his body jerking as his cock erupted, spurting all over his chest.

Still buried deep inside him, I leaned forward, lapped up his cum with my tongue, the adrenaline waning, leaving me drained but not quite sated. I fell over him, dislodging from his ass. I rolled, taking him with me as I buried my face in his neck and let the emotion break free.

Dante's arms slid around my head, holding tight. My lungs heaved, air never quite filling them as the ache inside me wouldn't subside.

We remained like that for minutes. Maybe hours. I couldn't move, didn't want to, and Dante knew what I needed.

Him.

In that moment, he was the center of my world and I didn't want it any other way. I didn't want to think about the pain my own betrayal had caused, the constant ache in my chest. Loving someone so much … I never thought it could hurt, but it did.

"You love her," Dante whispered.

I forced him off me, rolled so that I stared down into his face. "And it's fucking killing me."

His eyes were wide, surprised by the savageness in my tone. I was, too.

"It wasn't in the plan. It's not how Isaac saw it playing out."

Dante's hands curled around my arms, squeezed.

I looked down at him. "But it happened," I admitted. "I fell in love. Not just with one submissive but two. You and Everly."

That was the realization I'd come to. I fucking loved Everly and Dante. She was my heart, he was the heartbeat that kept me going. Only them. As much as I wanted someone of my own, to live out the fantasy Isaac and I had planned so perfectly, it would never happen because *they* had happened.

My chest heaved again, the pain lancing through me.

Though I could admit it to myself, no one would understand the depth of what I felt for her. Not even Everly. I had never told her. That day when she'd told me she loved me had been life-altering. However, I needed more than the words. I needed her. To feel her, taste her, touch her. To hold her in the dark of night, to wake with her soft warmth next to me. And not just every now and again. Every. Single. Fucking. Day.

That was what I needed.

That could never happen because Isaac wouldn't understand. It wasn't in the plan and my brother followed the road maps, always had, always would. He'd been so excited to map out our destiny. And truth be told, he'd had Everly first. He'd fallen first. More importantly, he'd told her first. Therefore, in his eyes, she belonged to him.

And throughout all of this, as I sat back and watched the two of them grow closer, their bond strengthen, I'd still held out hope that the tide would shift, that I'd be included. That I could have her, too.

Perhaps the worst part was Dante. I loved him to the depths of my soul, but I felt as though I kept him on the perimeter. Not on purpose, because he certainly wasn't my second choice. I wanted him the same as I wanted Everly. Loved him the same. But his needs were unique and in order to give him that, I had to keep my distance. I was failing miserably in that department, too. I was asking too much of him, expecting more than he had to give.

Yet, like tonight, he was always willing.

So fucking willing.

"I love you, Dante," I whispered into the dark room.

I had to hope that over time, it would eventually be enough.

For all of us.

Thirty

ISAAC

Sunday, June 16, 2019

I SAT AT MY DESK, THE ONLY light coming from my laptop screen, casting a soft glow over me and pitching shadows through the rest of the basement.

I'd been down here for a couple of hours, seeking solitude, trying to figure out what the fuck had happened. The weekend had gone by, slowly, miserably. Everly had spent most of her time in the library, Dante in his bedroom, while Ian had buried himself in work, claiming to be solidifying a lead that could very well take down Vernon Hathaway once and for all.

I hadn't asked what it was, leaving him to it because I recognized his need for distraction. Not once had he mentioned what was bothering him, nor did I ask. I'd tried it already, gotten his wrath in response. Which I took to mean he didn't want to discuss it.

That bothered me, and being that I hated to see my brother in pain, I'd decided to do a little detective work of my own.

My phone buzzed and I glanced at the screen.

Heaven: Hey, big guy! How's it going?
Isaac: Good. You?
Heaven: Better than good. I went on a date last night.
Isaac: With Prince Charming?"
Heaven: LOL How'd you know?

Isaac: I have my ways.

Heaven: Eavesdropping on Dante and Everly, I see. So, what's up? How's everyone? How's Ian?

Isaac: He won't talk to me.

I didn't know why I was admitting something so personal to a woman I'd spent so little time with, but for the moment, she was the only person I figured would tell me something.

Heaven: Have you tried talking to him?

Isaac: No. Not really.

Heaven: That's your first mistake. If you stop long enough, look hard enough, you'll see what's been there all along. Questions won't even be necessary.

Isaac: Which is?

She sent back a smiley face emoticon and I sighed.

Figuring that was all she was going to give me, I set my phone down, dropped my head back on the chair, and tried to figure out the fucking riddle that had caused such an uproar in my house.

When my phone buzzed again, I glanced at it, frowned.

Heaven: Everly.

What the hell was she talking about? Was she asking if Everly was all right? Or had she meant to text her?

Isaac: She's fine.

Heaven: Not even a little, but I can see how you'd think that.

Isaac: What are you talking about?

A minute passed as I stared at the screen, watching the three dots that danced as she typed.

Heaven: You love her to distraction. She completes you in a way you never expected. That's what people say when they fall ass over tea kettle, right? Well, it's true. But not only for you, Isaac. It's true for Ian. He loves her, too. Exactly the same way you do. Only you can't see that, and he's tried to pretend it's not true. But it's there. Has been all along. If you stop and think about it, it makes perfect sense. That the two of you would fall so hard, so fast for the same woman. After all, you're two halves of one whole.

My gaze shifted to the top of the stairs.

Was that true?

Heaven: I enjoyed the time I was there, Isaac. And though I enjoyed getting a glimpse of the dynamic, I realized something. Not everyone's cut out for that. But Everly and Dante are. And they love you both. Equally. Do you get what I'm saying? Everything you and Ian have ever needed is right there with you. You only have to open your eyes a little wider, see past your own heart.

The one thing I admired about Heaven was that she always told it like it was. I didn't suspect she was sugarcoating it to make me feel better. That wasn't her nature.

Isaac: If you ever need anything, Heaven...

Heaven: I know. Same goes. Now quit playing on your phone. It's your move on the chessboard, Isaac. Make it.

I set my phone down again, grinned. The woman and her fucking riddles.

I let the past couple of weeks play back in my mind. Not the scenes, the sex, the erotic encounters. I focused on the other moments. From my perspective, everything was exactly as it was meant to be. Or was it? Was I the only one who had everything I'd ever wanted? Everly. Dante. The fierceness I felt, the savage love that overwhelmed me when I was with them. Did Ian feel that, too? I knew what he felt for Dante because he hadn't hidden his feelings. Not from any of us.

So what was I missing?

Flashes of memories came back, moments I'd seen Ian watching Everly, pain and anguish in his eyes. I'd attributed that to fear, thinking he was worried about what the crazy, sadistic bastard had threatened to do to her. But that hadn't been it. Not entirely.

How had I missed it? If what Heaven said was true, how had I not seen it?

Ian was in love with Everly.

But that wasn't the only thing I'd missed.

I'd caught Everly looking at him the same way. When she thought no one was watching.

"Holy fuck." I dropped my head back, closed my eyes.

I had come between them. Kept her all to myself while we'd played some stupid game. Ian had played along. But why? Why hadn't he told me?

I heard a door open, close. Footsteps moved overhead. Too heavy to be Everly, which meant Ian was home. He had slipped out earlier, insisting he had something to take care of.

More like he'd been avoiding us.

I pushed to my feet, grabbed my phone, then made my way up the stairs. The house was silent, the only light on in the kitchen the accents over the cabinets.

Dante's door was closed, as usual, so I went to my bedroom. Everly was sitting in our bed, the television on. She sat up, smiled, but it wavered instantly.

"My Liege? Is everything okay?"

"No." I stared at her. "It's not."

She went up on her knees, concern etched across her beautiful face. "Is it that man?"

I shook my head, hating that she would instantly think that. "No, no. Not him. We've got people watching the house. You're safe here. So is Dante."

Her face relaxed somewhat.

Stepping toward her, I studied her face. "Have I been selfish?"

Her eyebrows lowered, as though she wasn't sure what I was talking about.

"With you. Have I been selfish?"

"Of course not."

"Have you talked to Ian?"

Her eyes lowered only slightly. "I... Not for a couple of days."

I tilted her chin up, recognized the pain there, silently urged her to explain.

"He's not talking to me," she whispered. "I think he blames me for something. Not sure what, though."

I prayed like hell she didn't really believe that, because even I knew that wasn't true.

When her eyes met mine again, I saw it. The anguish, the pain her acknowledgment brought with it.

"You love him."

Again, her eyes shifted from mine but quickly returned because she knew that was what I wanted, expected.

"Tell me," I ordered her, gripping her chin firmly.

Her eyes widened with shock and confusion.

"I've come between you and Ian," I acknowledged aloud. "I've kept you from him. Haven't given you the time you want with him."

Her silence was the only answer I needed.

I released her, paced to the other side of the room, tried to see where it had all gone wrong. At what point I'd become a selfish bastard, thinking only of myself.

"My Liege, I'm so sorry."

I walked back to the bed, cupped her face, pressed my lips to hers.

"What did I tell you about apologizing?"

Her small hands fisted in my shirt, holding me there. "I love you," she whispered fiercely, as though she thought for a second I wouldn't know that.

Dropping my forehead to hers, I smiled. "I know you do, fairy princess. But you love him, too. Need him as much as you need me."

A tear trickled down her cheek, but she hurried to wipe it away.

"You should've told me."

"I didn't want to hurt you." Her voice trembled, breaking something inside me.

I lifted my head, held her gaze. "You could never hurt me, Everly. And the last thing I would ever do is hurt you."

"You haven't," she declared.

"I have."

She shook her head, but I stilled it with my hands, smiled.

"But I can accept responsibility," I told her. "And I can make it right."

Tears glistened in her beautiful eyes.

"I didn't see it," I admitted. "I only saw what I expected to see."

"I don't understand."

"You won't. It's for me to discuss with Ian."

Her brow wrinkled, more confusion.

I smoothed the line away with my thumbs, kissed her forehead, then took a step back.

"I need you to do something for me, fairy princess."

"Anything, my Liege."

"Go to him. Tonight. Go to him and show him, tell him." I swallowed hard. "Love him."

Another tear fell, breaking my heart.

"I'm not going anywhere," I reassured her. "I'm right here. Always."

"But—"

I put two fingers over her lips. "No buts. There's nothing for you to think about here." I lowered my hand to cover her heart. "I love you, fairy princess. You know that here. It's not up for debate, either. And if I hadn't been so selfish, I would've seen that you have more than enough to give in return."

Forcing myself to release her, I took a step back.

"My Liege?"

I turned my back to her. "Go to him, Everly. Don't make me tell you again."

I thought she would leave, follow my instructions as she always did. When her soft hands slid up my back, moving around to my stomach as her arms encircled me, I sighed.

"I don't want you to be upset with me, my Liege."

I placed my hands over her arms. "I'm not."

I was upset with myself, but she didn't need to know that.

"Then why are you turning your back on me?"

I turned, wrapped her in my arms. "Do you want to go to him?" I asked.

She didn't lift her head, her arms squeezing me tightly. "Yes, my Liege. I do. And not because you instructed me. Because ... because I know it's where I'm supposed to be."

"That's something we can both agree on," I admitted. "Even if I've been too blind to see it."

Her eyes lifted, imploring me without words. She needed my reassurance as much as I needed her love.

"It's what I need as much as you."

When that had become the truth, I wasn't sure.

Perhaps it had been the case all along.

And they weren't the only ones pretending otherwise.

Everly

WALKING AWAY FROM ISAAC SHOULD'VE BEEN HARD but it wasn't.

I trusted him, knew he wouldn't lie to me. Initially, I'd thought he was pushing me away to punish me. Deep down, I knew he wouldn't do that. It wasn't in his nature.

That was what he'd said in the very beginning. That I would always know where I stood with him. He hadn't gone back on his word, even now as he urged me to go to Ian.

Ian.

My heart squeezed as it always did when I thought about him.

These past few days had been hell. I knew he was ignoring me, though he wasn't rude about it. When it came to Ian, his moods were pretty simple, and I'd never seen him so withdrawn. That was Isaac's forte. Ian was the one who opened up, was quick to smile, and had a plethora of questions. He hadn't been himself these past few days.

I made my way to the opposite end of the hall, paused outside his bedroom with my hand fisted, ready to knock. Before I could work up the nerve, the door opened.

His eyes, so beautiful despite the misery I could see churning there, settled on me.

"May I come in?"

He glanced down the hall briefly before stepping out of the way.

"Is something wrong?" he asked when he turned to face me.

"Everything's wrong," I told him truthfully. "You know it. I know it. Isaac knows it."

"Did he send you in here?"

"No. I came because this is where I want to be." I swallowed hard. "Where I *need* to be."

Ian didn't move, didn't speak.

I could see his disbelief, knew it would take more than that to convince him that here, with him, was the only place I wanted to be right now.

A minute passed, then another.

"I love you," I told him simply.

"Do you?" he asked, skepticism dripping from his words.

I ignored his reaction. I didn't blame him for asking that, for thinking I was trying to soothe him.

I wasn't.

"Truth is," I began, "the short time Heaven was here, I was jealous of her. It's not an emotion I'm familiar with. One I know isn't appropriate. I have no claim to you, despite what my heart has wanted all along. Those moments I got to spend with you…" I swallowed hard. "I cherished that time, wished it wasn't all I was given, but I loved you enough to accept it. To trust you were following your own heart."

His lips formed a hard line, as though he was holding back whatever rebuttal he had.

"And I know I'm overstepping here," I continued. "You're in pain, that much is obvious. You won't talk to me. Most of the time you won't even look at me. I've done something, but for the life of me, I can't figure out what. But you owe it to me to tell me. Give me a chance to fix it.

"At the club. Back when this first began, you and Isaac scared me. No. Not the right word. Terrified is better. I knew what would happen. From that first night we played together, I fell a little bit in love. With both of you. It wasn't right or fair. Not to the two Dominants who were training me. I kept telling myself I was confusing lust with love. That it was normal, and I needed to put distance between us. So I did. As much as I could. But there was no way I could deny either of you. So when you requested I scene with you, I gladly accepted, pretending it was a role I was playing. Only it wasn't."

Ian's feet shifted, his hands sliding into his pockets, but still he didn't speak.

"The day that man attacked me, I'd been getting ready to go to Zeke's because I had been invited. Thought it would be a good thing to spend time with people outside of the club, see how they interacted, get a feel for the dynamic. I knew you and Isaac had been invited, looked forward to the chance to see you. When that man attacked me, my only thought was to go to Zeke's because I knew the people there, knew I would feel safe for a little while.

"Though I secretly wished for it, I didn't expect you and Isaac to care for me. I swear it. I hadn't been thinking at all, driven mostly by fear, pain. Then I felt it. While I knew any Dom at that party would've ensured no man hit me, they weren't going to care for me the way you both did. And yeah, I'd been a little in love with you both before then. But it was that night that I fell all the way."

I took a deep breath, willed myself not to fidget. I had to get this out. He needed to know the truth.

"When you invited Heaven to come back here, I was jealous. But not enough to put myself above her safety. She was my friend. She still is. And I'm versed enough in this lifestyle to understand it. I saw the interest in your eyes when you looked at her. There was chemistry there. I also knew it wasn't my place to interfere. And while I sat back, wishing like hell you would take me as your submissive, I kept my mouth shut. But my love for you didn't subside like I expected. It grew, intensified.

"Every now and then, I would catch you looking at me. I imagined that you had the same feelings for me that I had for you, but—"

"Stop talking."

His rough command shocked me into silence.

Ian didn't move, his hands still tucked in his pockets, his emerald eyes locked on my face.

"You didn't imagine it, Everly. But I thought I'd hidden it better. Tried to pretend it wasn't true because…" He exhaled deeply, looked away.

I held my breath, hoping he would elaborate, to tell me I wasn't an idiot for standing here, laying it all on the line for him.

When his gaze shifted back to my face, there was something else in his eyes, something deeper, warmer than I'd seen in recent days. "I love you. No matter how hard I tried to deny it, the feeling only grew stronger."

He took a step closer, stared down at me.

"It didn't take long to realize I was so far gone, so in love with you, there was no turning back."

His hand was warm and gentle when it curled over my cheek. I leaned into the touch, tears forming.

"No one will ever replace you."

While protocol dictated that I stand there, wait for his command, I couldn't hold back any longer. I threw my arms around his neck, buried my face there as the tears broke free. He lifted me, as though I weighed nothing. My legs wrapped around him securely and I held on, let the emotion I'd bottled up for the past few weeks loose.

His hand cupped the back of my head, his cheek pressing against mine, and in that moment, I'd never felt quite so complete. Whole for the first time since I'd walked into their house.

"I see the way you look at Isaac," Ian whispered.

I lifted my head, stared into his eyes, willed him to see it because it was there. I loved him as much as I loved Isaac.

A small smile tipped the corners of his mouth. "Yeah. Like that."

"It's always been there," I whispered.

"Fuck. What am I going to do with you?"

"Love me," I pleaded. "Not only with your body." I smiled, couldn't help myself. "Though I'd like that, too."

He moved then, closer to the bed. His strong arm banded around my back and I held on tightly as he lowered me to the mattress, his mouth settling over mine.

I was almost positive my body was glowing with the warmth that spread through me. Not lust. Love. Pure and primal, given freely, accepted and returned.

Ian's mouth was strong, firm, dominating mine with every stroke of his tongue. He wasn't rough or rushed, but it was different than before. As though everything he'd been holding back had been set free.

When he pulled back, stared down at me, I was overwhelmed by the emotion I saw there.

He rasped out a few words in Irish, the gruffly spoken words making my chest swell.

I could only stare as the words processed. I was familiar with them because Isaac called me that.

"It means—"

"Pulse of my heart," I filled in.

Ian smiled. "Aye."

They both called me that, and it was the way they said it that got to me.

Not simply the beautiful lilt of their Irish brogue, but as though it had come from their heart. More accurately, they sounded identical.

That was the moment I realized I was meant to belong to them both. They might've been two separate men, but they were one. And there was no way to love one without loving the other.

"Are you tired?"

"Not in the least, my Alpha."

He smiled and I knew right then that he was going to find a way to ensure I slept soundly that night.

IAN

THE MOMENT SHE STEPPED INTO MY ROOM, my heart had lodged in my throat.

I'd seen it in her eyes before she'd even started to talk.

Then, when the words came, I hadn't been able to stop her, needing to hear that she felt what I was feeling, had all along. At first, I'd tried to find the untruth, looked for the explanation that didn't fit. I was a skeptical man, I wouldn't deny that. There hadn't been any untruth in her gaze, and now, as Everly stared up at me, I could see everything I'd been wanting to see all along.

And while my love for her was powerful enough to steal my breath, there was something stronger than that. A primal heartbeat, a need to claim her in a way I had yet to do.

Her soft hands cupping my face held me in the present.

"My Alpha," she whispered, "I'm yours. Now. Forever."

The words I'd longed to hear.

I rattled off words in my native tongue, words I'd longed to get out. Then I smiled when her eyes clouded over, prepared to translate for her.

"I love you, too."

Evidently it wasn't necessary.

Crushing my mouth to hers, I hovered over her, my hands sliding under her back, over her shoulders. Our clothes were in the way, but I couldn't stop long enough to do anything about it. I didn't want to let her go, not for a second. The way she moved beneath me, her arms twined around my neck as our tongues searched, sought everything we'd denied ourselves, it stirred the beast.

My muscles coiled as I crushed her to me.

I needed to be inside her. Nothing between us.

With one arm beneath her back, I dragged her across the mattress, needing more room. It took tremendous effort, but I managed to drag my mouth from hers long enough to all but rip her clothes from her body. Her back arched when I took her nipple between my teeth. Her sweet cries, her perfect surrender fanned the flames and I knew this would have to wait.

It was all I could do to push my jeans down my hips before I settled between her thighs, aligned our bodies and drove my cock into the sweet heaven that was her pussy.

Everly cried out, the most beautiful sound I'd ever heard in my life.

My hips pumped furiously, thrusting into her again and again, taking what she offered without apology. It was as though I hadn't been able to fully breathe until that moment.

"Hold on to me, *mo grá*. Don't let go."

Her arms wreathed my neck, her head falling back, exposing the soft, smooth skin of her neck. I sucked and bit, knowing I would mark her but not caring. I pounded into her, robbing us both of all sense as I claimed her as mine.

She didn't ask permission to come, Everly simply fell over the edge, crying out my name again and again as her pussy milked me. I didn't stop, didn't falter, thrusting harder, deeper, faster. I would never be sated, I knew it then. I would never get enough of her. I could spend the rest of my days buried balls deep inside her and I'd still want more, need more.

I focused on making her come again. Those sweet cries were a drug swimming through my veins. An addiction I knew would never go away.

The out-of-control feeling consumed me, became more potent the longer I fucked her, unable to stop myself. I knew in that moment what Isaac felt. That night he'd sent me and Dante away … it was this. The absolute driving need to have her all to himself. Nothing compared to this. Nothing.

"One more," I growled. "Let it go, little fairy."

Everly's pussy contracted over my cock, her body trembling sweetly as her breaths rasped against my neck.

"I love you, Ian."

Her words, spoken directly in my ear, shattered me, split me entirely in two as I slammed into her, coming with such fury I thought my head would explode.

A few hours later, after drifting off into exhaustion, I woke, Everly still curled up against me, her thigh resting over mine, her arm over my chest as though I was her own personal body pillow.

The thought made me smile. I wanted to be her body pillow.

Hell, I wanted to be her everything.

That thought had me thinking about Isaac.

For the past three weeks, Everly had slept in his bed every night. He'd kept her close, the same way I was now. The thought of my brother sleeping alone bothered me on some level. It wasn't difficult to put myself in his shoes, to think of the nights when I would be alone in my bed without her.

Of course, I could convince Dante to sleep in my bed. He'd done it before, but I saw what it cost him when he did.

I wouldn't pretend to understand his need for solitude because I didn't share it. However, I also wouldn't pretend I didn't love him because of the man he'd become, stronger than any and all I'd ever met.

Dante would never become a regular fixture in my bed or Isaac's, although we would both welcome him at any time. Perhaps one day, the dynamic would shift, and he would get used to living with people, interacting day after day, accepting the love the three of us offered him.

Everly was the exact opposite of Dante. She wanted comfort, constant touching. The way she slept was proof, burrowed against my side as though this was the most comfortable place to be.

I glanced down at her, the moonlight slipping through the blinds, caressing her face from above. She was at peace, possibly more so than I'd seen her since she came here.

As carefully as I could, I shifted out from under her, then lifted her into my arms.

She stirred, her arms curling around my neck. "Where're we going?"

Complete and utter trust. That was what she gave us, and it humbled me.

"To bed," I told her.

She rubbed her cheek against my shoulder, smiled, her eyes never opening. "We were already *in* bed."

"I know."

Without explaining myself, I carried her down the hall to Isaac's bedroom, turned the knob, and pushed it open, holding her securely in my arms.

Just as I thought, Isaac wasn't asleep. He was propped up on a pillow, his television on but muted.

He sat up, worry dragging his brow down.

I shook my head, then walked over to the other side of the bed before easing Everly into it. He watched me closely. Without asking whether he was okay with it or not, I crawled in beside her, nudged her toward the center.

Isaac's eyes met mine and he knew the same as I did that this was the only way this would work. There was no separating our love for her, sharing it by way of rotation. When she was with him, I would feel the loss tremendously and vice versa.

Everly rolled to her side, curled up along Isaac's side, then reached back for me. She, too, knew this was the only way this played out.

She took my hand, tugged until I was pressed up against her back.

"I love you," she whispered.

We didn't need her to clarify who she was speaking to.

Both of us.

The way it had been since the beginning.

There was only one obstacle left for us to tackle where this situation was concerned.

Taking her at the same time, overcoming that driving need to possess. The beast was fierce, independent, and as far as I was concerned, would have to find a way to share.

This was exactly where we'd been meant to be all along.

Thirty-One

Dante

WHEN I WOKE UP ON MONDAY MORNING, showered, then sauntered into the kitchen, I was surprised to see Isaac working at the stove, Ian perched up on the counter, Everly straddling his lap.

She tipped back, smiled at me.

There was such pure elation there, I couldn't help but smile back as I took it all in.

"Something happened last night," I said aloud.

No one responded, but their silence was the only confirmation I needed. The dynamic had shifted there.

"I'm making omelets," Isaac announced. "What do you want in yours?"

I glanced over at him, about to remind him that I didn't eat eggs when he pointed toward a carton on the counter.

"Vegan eggs," Ian supplied. "Who even knew that shit existed?"

I laughed. I did, actually.

"Isaac looked it up," he told me. "Found all kinds of shit at Whole Foods."

"They love you, PB," Everly said in a singsong voice. "Ian even promised to make cookies."

"I most certainly did not," he said, leaning in and chuckling against her neck.

"Can't blame a girl for trying," she teased.

I watched the three of them. It would've been easy to explain away the light atmosphere as being related to whatever obstacle they'd overcome, but I got the feeling it was more than that. This wasn't about Ian giving in to the love he felt for Everly. That was inevitable even if he'd never realized it. I'd known all along, though it wasn't my place to point it out.

Isaac looked up, his eyes locked with mine.

"What's going on?" I asked, ensuring he knew what I was referring to.

He motioned toward the barstool with his elbow. "Have a seat."

"No." I wasn't intentionally disregarding a command, but I could see in his eyes he thought I was. "Tell me."

Ian moved, getting to his feet and holding Everly in his arms. "We'll give you two a minute."

"No," I said, more firmly this time. "I want to know what's going on."

Everly dropped her legs from around Ian's waist, waited until she was on her feet before turning to study me and Isaac. It was obvious she didn't know what was going on, but Isaac and Ian sure did.

"Tell me."

"A warrant's been issued for Vernon's arrest," Isaac said, plating the last omelet.

"A warrant?" I glanced at Ian, who nodded. "For what?"

"Conspiracy to commit murder," Ian relayed.

"Whose murder?"

"Your father's," Isaac said.

Everly gasped, her hand covering her mouth.

I knew he was dead, knew it hadn't been a pleasant way to die, but considering the hell he'd put me through, I had never found it in myself to give a shit.

"Who killed him?"

"Hathaway hired a hit man."

"They've got proof?"

"Yeah." Isaac nodded to the stool once more.

Realizing my legs were shaky, I managed to make my way over, drop onto it.

Everly was behind me in a second, her arms draped around my shoulders, holding me. I put my hands on her arms, clutched them tightly. I would never deny that her comfort always managed to settle me.

"But that's not all," Ian added, walking over to stand in front of me.

"What else could there be?"

"Vernon's gone to ground," Ian explained.

"Doesn't surprise me," I told him. "With his father's money, he'll likely stay hidden for as long as he wants to stay hidden."

"True," Isaac said, standing beside Ian. "But there's something Daddy's money won't be able to cover up."

I frowned, glancing between the two of them. "What? Just fucking tell me."

Their disapproval at my outburst was instant, both of them glaring at me. I could see their desire to punish for the transgression, just as easily as I saw them erase the idea instantly.

"Vernon's father … Thomas Hathaway…" Ian sighed, crossed his arms over his chest. "From the information that's been gathered, he's responsible for your mother's murder."

"Murder?" Hating myself for doing it, I released Everly, pushed her away from me. "What are you talking about? My mother abandoned me when I was a baby. Left me with *him*."

"Actually, she didn't," Isaac stated. "Your mother, at the age of sixteen, just months after you were born, was sold to Thomas Hathaway."

My mouth was dry, as though I'd swallowed sand. "Sold? By…? No." I shot to my feet. "That bastard *sold* her?" I glared at them, baffled. "For how much?"

"Ten thousand."

A scream formed in my throat, anger, bright and fierce, unable to escape as a roaring sounded in my ears. My father had sold my mother for a measly ten grand?

I was barely aware of Isaac approaching, strong arms banding around me. Instinct had me fighting him off, but he was stronger, more determined than I gave him credit for. He jerked me back against him, his steely arms banding around me, pinning my arms to my chest.

"I'm so fucking sorry," he murmured in my ear and I could hear the pain.

My breaths sawed in and out of my lungs as my legs weakened. He held me, never letting go as all the pain built and spewed out. Angry tears burned my eyes. Vicious sobs scoured my throat. How could he do that? To her? To me? How could God let that happen?

The next thing I knew, I was on the floor, Isaac still kneeling behind me, holding me, his strength the only thing safe in my entire world. I was vaguely aware of Everly crying, Ian soothing her with words.

"She didn't leave me."

"No," Isaac assured me. "She didn't leave you. The devil took her."

"And the devil's spawn tried to take me," I acknowledged aloud.

"Yes."

I sat there until the pain subsided, my breaths returned to normal. "I'm sorry, Master," I whispered, hoping he heard the sincerity in my tone.

Isaac pressed his lips to the top of my head. "Do not apologize. Not to me, not to anyone."

"I need to get up."

When he released me, I pushed to my feet, turned to Everly.

"Come here, sweetheart."

She ran into my arms and I held on tight as she shook, her tears soaking my shirt, but it didn't matter. When she settled, I didn't move, didn't release her, but I did turn my attention back to Isaac and Ian.

"How did you find this out?"

"Let's just say, there's quite a bit of support when it comes to friends and family."

I knew he was talking about *his* friends, *his* family because I didn't have any.

"They didn't do it for us," Isaac said, a slight edge in his tone as though he knew what I'd been thinking. "They did it for you because they know how important you are to us. That makes you family, Dante."

My heart felt as though it wobbled slightly, but I ignored it.

"Now what?" I asked, releasing Everly when she pulled back. "How do we find him?"

"*We* don't," Ian said firmly. "It's being taken care of."

He sounded so sure of himself, but he hadn't met Vernon. He didn't know the depth of his depravity. That man would not go down without a fight.

And though I prayed I never had to see him again …

There was no way I would get that lucky.

ISAAC

"No luck, Isaac." Ransom's disappointment echoed in my ear.

I'd spent the better part of the afternoon making calls, promising favors I feared I would one day be called on for in the hopes of finding Vernon and Thomas Hathaway.

"Something clearly spooked Daddy Dearest," Ransom explained. "When the police got there to serve the warrant, he was gone. They searched the house, took the wife into custody, but she denies knowing anything about it."

"They believe her?"

"If she's not telling the truth," Ransom said, "then she deserves a fucking award for her acting abilities."

"Shit."

"Exactly." He took a deep breath. "Look—"

"No," I snapped. "We're not discussing it again. I'm not using him as bait."

"I get it, Isaac, I do."

I sat up straight, gripped the phone hard enough to shatter it. "No. You don't get it, Bishop. You don't have a fucking clue."

Ransom growled. "You don't give me nearly enough credit. I do get it."

Not caring that I was unleashing my frustrations on a good friend, I seethed. "One day you might get lucky and fall in love, but until then, Bishop, don't even pretend to know how I feel."

Ransom was quiet for a moment, and when he spoke again, there was a restrained edge in his voice, something I'd never heard from him before. "Just because I haven't taken a submissive doesn't mean I don't…"

"Don't what?"

"Nothing. Forget it. We'll figure it out. But Isaac, I can't keep posting men outside your house. This is costing a fucking fortune. It doesn't matter that it's your fortune. I've got jobs to deal with, ones those men need to be assigned to. Not to mention, I need you and Ian out on one by the weekend. I can't put it off indefinitely. We're running out of time."

Feeling rightfully chastised, I fell back in my chair. "I'm sorry."

Ransom exhaled roughly. "Let's just find a way to settle this. I've got a few ideas of my own, but I figured I owed you the courtesy of running it by you first. And before you tell me you've got some ideas, I've talked to Liam. He warned me of what your options are."

"They're still options," I told him.

"No. That kind of debt … no. You want to spend the rest of your life waiting for the axe to fall, sure. You can call in the Irish mob, Isaac. You want to live happily ever after and not worry about Everly and Dante, you forget that shit once and for all."

He was right. But I wasn't going to give him the satisfaction of hearing me say so.

"I'm gonna take care of this," Ransom said, his tone steely. "I want you and your new family to sit tight. Together. Understand?"

I could read between the lines as well as anyone else. Ransom was ordering us to be one another's alibi.

"I understand."

"At the house," he clarified.

"I hear you."

"Cameras record things," Ransom added.

"I get it," I huffed.

"There doesn't have to be fireworks and drama, Isaac. It'll be handled quietly and efficiently while you … do whatever it is the four of you do."

"I'm not worried about what we're doing," I assured him. "What are *you* going to do?"

"Let's put it this way, you're not the only one with connections."

Before I could protest, the call disconnected. I slammed my phone on my desk.

"Problem?"

I snapped my head up, stared at Ian, who'd obviously been eavesdropping from where he sat on the stairs.

"Let me guess," Ian mused as he got to his feet and walked down the stairs. "Ransom wants us to make a sex tape."

I choked out a laugh. "He didn't exactly suggest that."

Ian smirked. "Maybe not. But he certainly wouldn't mind some time-stamped video as backup."

I rolled my eyes.

"Fine. You don't want to talk about it." He pointed toward the ceiling. "I'm going to spend some time with Everly. In the library."

"Why are you telling me this?"

His grin widened. "I was wondering if perhaps you'd want to join us."

Admittedly, I was still getting used to this new dynamic. While we hadn't discussed what was going on, Ian and I didn't necessarily need to. I knew the moment he'd carried Everly into my room two nights ago that everything we'd ever thought we wanted had merely been a romanticized role-playing exercise. There was no way to map out how things would go when it came to love. Everly was our case in point.

"I'd like that," I told him, realizing I really would. "I'll be up shortly. Fifteen minutes?"

"We won't wait for you," he said with a chuckle.

He moved with purpose, calling out to Everly when he got to the top of the stairs. I listened to the rumble of voices, and when they disappeared, I made my way upstairs and headed for Dante's room. At his request, I'd given him space, but that didn't stop me from worrying about him.

I rapped on the door, then let myself in.

He was sitting at the desk, and when his eyes met mine, he slowly but efficiently moved to kneel on the floor.

I took a seat on his bed. "I've decided to implement a few protocols."

"Of course, Master."

"Starting tonight, you are not allowed to go to bed without asking permission. If that means seeking us out, then you will do so. Once you've been given permission, you can come back here, strip, then kneel beside the bed until one of us comes in. Understood?"

"Yes, Master."

There was a hint of approval in his tone.

"Should you forget about either of those, you will be punished the following morning."

"Yes, Master."

"You might not completely understand this, but it's not as easy as it looks to make any and all decisions in a household. For instance, deciding what you can and will do next is not something I can manage. From here on out, it's your responsibility to ask permission for what you can and will do. Whether it's to take a swim or a leak, I don't care. I expect you to ask one of us for permission.

"Now, I don't mean when you're sitting down for dinner, that you should ask me if you can eat this or that. That's trivial. But I know you want this, Dante. I'm not oblivious. And in an effort to do right by you, I need your assistance in that matter. Does that make sense?"

"Absolutely, Master."

"The last one for now... Every Monday morning, when I'm not traveling, of course, I want you to come into my room at six o'clock. You will join me in the shower. Just me and you. Every Monday. No matter what. I don't care if you're pissed off or if I am. That's our time together. Understand?"

"It would be my pleasure, Master."

"Mine, too." I got to my feet. "And since today is Monday and we missed our shower, I'll expect you to make up for it tomorrow morning."

"Yes, Master."

"Stand," I instructed as I walked toward him.

Dante was on his feet, hands clasped behind his back, head dipped low.

I corrected that, tilting his chin up and pressing my lips to his gently, then holding his stare. "We'll be in the library for a while. Me, Ian, and Everly. While we're up there, I want you to spend some time thinking about what we'll be doing to her."

His eyes flashed with heat.

"You may get in your bed or the recliner, either one's fine. I expect you to be naked while you fantasize about it."

I waited, anticipating the question I could see burning in his eyes. I didn't have to wait long.

"May I touch myself, Master?"

"I expect it."

"May I have permission to come, Master?"

"Absolutely."

"Thank you, Master."

I kissed him again, then turned toward the door. "Just so you know, I'll be thinking about what you're doing while I'm with her, too."

Dante smiled and that tightness in my chest, the one that had been there since our conversation that morning, eased slightly.

Thirty-Two

Everly

THE HEAVY THUD OF FOOTSTEPS ON THE stairs had me looking up from where I was sitting at the small writing desk.

"What're you working on, little fairy?" Ian asked, his gaze zeroing in on the sketch pad laid out in front of me.

I smiled up at him. "I was just … doodling."

His eyebrows lifted as he reached for the pad, brought it closer. "This is a little more than doodling." He glanced around the pad at me. "In fact, it's rather impressive."

"Thank you, my Alpha."

He smiled, set it back down. "I didn't know you were an artist."

I laughed. "Oh, definitely not. But I enjoy drawing from time to time."

"What is it?" he asked, nodding toward the picture.

"Just an idea I had."

"For?"

I swallowed. I honestly hadn't expected him to see it. Anyone to, for that matter. I'd just been thinking about it since the three of us had started sleeping in the same bed together.

Realizing he was still waiting for an answer, I brushed my fingertips over the page. "I was redesigning the bedrooms. Trying to get a feel for what it would be like if the separation was no longer there."

"Separation?" He walked over to the recliner, took a seat, then patted his leg.

More than content to be close to him, I walked over, sat in his lap, and allowed him to put his arms around me.

"Well, right now there are four bedrooms, three of which aren't really being used anymore. I thought maybe we could put some of that space to better use."

He brushed my hair back from my shoulder, kissed my neck. "How so?"

"Well, for starters, we could merge three of the rooms into one. Isaac's and the two guest rooms. Add some closets, an entertainment area, bigger bathroom." I chuckled. "This is all hypothetical, of course."

He brushed his lips over my ear. "Of course."

It took effort to ignore the wicked things his mouth stirred inside me. "Then, I was thinking. What if Dante moved into yours and we found a way to connect it to ours. I know he needs his space, doesn't care to sleep with other people, but it would be nice to have him close by. But, you know, maybe we could convince him that the four of us could share a bathroom. More specifically, a shower."

"You've given it some serious thought." Ian's hands began to roam in time with his mouth.

When he nudged me to sit up, I did. He had me topless within seconds before pulling me back against him, big, warm hands cupping my breasts.

"I think we should do it," he said.

"You do?"

"Of course. I do have one suggestion."

"What's that?" I asked on a moan when he plucked my nipples.

"A bigger bed."

I giggled, but it was cut off by another moan. "A bigger bed ... okay."

"Since there's so much space," he mumbled, his lips gliding over my neck again, "maybe we add a playroom in there."

"Okay." At that point, I didn't care if he thought my ideas were stupid, I just didn't want him to stop what he was doing.

"Naked, little fairy. Now."

I unbuttoned my jean shorts, lifted my butt, and pushed them down my legs, never leaving his lap.

Ian's hands trailed down my belly, slipped down to my thighs before pushing my legs wide.

"Over my knees," he ordered.

I hooked my legs over his knees, leaned back against him.

He was looking down my body as his finger glided through my slit. I was wet and ready, but he didn't mention it. In fact, he teased me as though he didn't even notice.

Only, I knew he did, and this was merely sweet torture.

Between the roar of my own blood in my ears and the rasp of his mouth against my neck, I didn't hear Isaac join us.

"This is how you should welcome me anytime I come into a room, fairy princess."

I gasped as Ian pushed a finger inside me.

"It would be my pleasure, my Liege."

Isaac's grin was wicked, his eyes fierce as they focused on Ian's long, strong fingers sliding deep inside me.

I watched him, a little uncertain about what was happening. The one and only time I'd been with them at the same time, we'd been in the guest room. On my birthday, when they all three took me at the same time. That night, Isaac had ordered Dante and Ian out of the room. I knew why, but I'd never discussed it with him.

"Stop thinking so hard, little fairy," Ian whispered in my ear, a gruff, sexy sound that made my pussy clench around his fingers.

My attention shot up to Isaac when he removed his shirt, tossed it on the desk before easing down to his knees between our legs.

Ian's hand withdrew slowly as Isaac's head lowered.

I gasped when the warm, wet heat of his tongue caressed my clit.

"Suck," Ian ordered, dipping his fingers in my mouth. "See how sweet you taste."

I tried to buck my hips when Isaac sucked my clit between his lips, but Ian held me in place.

"Watch," Ian ordered.

My eyes locked on Isaac's head between my thighs. It was difficult to keep them open as pleasure assaulted me. His mouth, so hot, so perfect, drove me to distraction as he feasted. The almost perverse ebb and flow had me panting, desperate to reach the peak he was equally as desperate to keep me from.

"My Liege," I begged.

"Not yet, little fairy," Ian said.

This was new. The two of them working in tandem, as though one knew exactly what the other was thinking.

"We're just getting started," Isaac said.

Relief and disappointment flooded me when he got to his feet.

Ian nudged me up as Isaac took a seat in the other recliner, lowering his slacks as he did. He fisted his cock, hard and heavy in his hand, then beckoned me over with the crook of his finger.

"Put your mouth on me, fairy princess," Isaac crooned. "Let me feel those sweet lips on my cock."

I started to go to my knees, but Ian's gruff command had me pausing.

"Stay standing."

I bent at the waist, my hands on the arms of the chair holding me up as Isaac fed his cock into my mouth. His hands curved over my head, holding me there, guiding me as I took him deep, released him.

I heard movement, wasn't sure what Ian was doing. Didn't really care, either, as I focused on Isaac's beautiful cock, thick and hard and smooth as velvet, as it slid over my lips. His satisfied grunts and groans an erotic symphony that urged me to ignore the discomfort of the position I was in.

Ian, once again behind me, squeezed my ass, then lightly smacked it. A second later, he was probing my ass with his slick finger.

Lube. He'd gotten lube.

The thought made me smile, though it wasn't easy with Isaac's cock lodged almost in the back of my throat.

I moaned, pleasure beginning to hum inside me as Ian gently finger-fucked my ass while I continued to lick and lave Isaac's cock. Time seemed to stand still as the pleasure intensified.

I was slightly dazed when those wicked digits slid out and Isaac pulled his cock from my mouth before pulling me onto him. I stumbled, managed to get my knees on the sides of his thighs before he crushed his mouth to mine.

"Take me, fairy princess," he growled, the head of his cock pressing against the slick entrance of my pussy.

I lowered myself onto him, dropping my head back as the delicious friction ignited all my nerve endings.

Isaac pumped his hips as he pulled me flush against him, his mouth once again seeking mine.

It was then I realized what was happening.

Ian's hands gripping my ass, the thick head of his cock pressing against my anus. I could feel the unsteady tremble of his hands as he held me firmly in place, pushing his cock into me. The feeling was overwhelming, being stuffed full. I broke my mouth from Isaac's, stifled a cry as I willed my body to relax.

Isaac didn't say a word, nor did Ian, but there was a wealth of emotion I could sense in their hands, the way they touched me.

Ian began to move, fucking into me, the pace increasing as Isaac moved in tandem. They fell into a rhythm, giving me some relief as they alternated filling me. When Ian retreated, Isaac thrust forward.

"Oh, God..." It was more than I could take. The feeling unlike anything I'd ever experienced before.

The three of us ... together ... as one.

"My Liege ... my Alpha..."

"What is it, love? Tell us," they said in unison, their voices settling over me in stereo.

"More..." I pleaded, buried my face in Isaac's neck, and surrendered. "Everything."

Four hands then roamed over me as they fucked me relentlessly, impaling me again and again. The room warmed, the scent of sex filling the small space as their combined grunts, the punishing thrusts drove me straight toward the peak. I held on to the razor-sharp edge for as long as I could.

"Please ... my Liege ... my Alpha. Let me come. I need..."

"God, yes," they both snarled. "Come for us."

Air was driven from my lungs when they both slammed into me at the same time. I screamed, the orgasm battering me like a stormy sea crashing against rock.

I couldn't move, didn't want to. And I knew it wasn't necessary.

They would take care of me.

So I let them.

IAN

AFTER GETTING EVERLY SETTLED INTO BED, THEN heading to my bathroom for a quick shower, I met back up with Isaac in the kitchen. He was tossing together sandwiches, enough to feed an army. Since we were the only two eating meat, I knew we were the troops he had in mind.

"It's a good thing she likes to nap," I told him as I pulled two mugs out of the freezer, set them on the counter.

Isaac smiled. "She needs the rest."

I filled both mugs, tossed the bottle in the recycle bin. When I turned back, my brother was staring at me.

I didn't say anything, didn't have to. I knew what he was thinking, what he was feeling. That this was exactly as it was meant to be.

Honestly, the library had been a test. For me, for him. To see how it would go without risking being in Isaac's bed. I hadn't wanted to take the chance that we'd fuck things up where we slept.

"This is exactly as it was meant to be," Isaac said softly, passing over a plate.

"No truer words," I mumbled, taking the plate. "Back porch?"

"Yeah. Why not?"

He followed me out to the table, took a seat. The sun was setting, and because of the long days, night was already closing in while there was still light.

"Did you know she can draw?" I asked.

Isaac took a bite of his sandwich, shook his head.

"Quite impressive, actually." I smiled, thinking about what she'd drawn up. "And I think she's redesigning the house."

"Really?"

I nodded, took a gulp of my beer. "She wants Dante closer."

Isaac's eyebrows rose.

"She's got the idea we should turn three bedrooms into one, have Dante move into the fourth."

"That'd be one giant fucking room."

"Oh, don't worry. She's got plans for the bathroom. Probably be twice the size of yours and mine combined."

Isaac chuckled.

"I suggested she configure a bigger bed. And a playroom."

Again, I was testing the waters, wondering how my brother would react.

"And a bigger shower?" he asked.

I grinned. "That's her idea. Room for four, she said."

"Good." He took a drink, set his mug down. "I say we get a contractor over here ASAP."

As though he knew I was waiting for something more, Isaac set his sandwich down as soon as he picked it up.

"I'm not going to apologize," he stated, his attention on me. "But you don't need an apology. We all played this incorrectly. I was too selfish to see it. You tried to be the martyr." He sighed. "And Everly and Dante got caught in the middle."

I took a bite, chewed, tried to relax.

"We came up with the idea of sharing two women long before we ever thought those women might be submissives. Teenage fantasy. We never amended that fantasy and I don't figure it would've mattered. We hadn't figured Everly into it."

"True."

"It's different with her," he admitted.

"It is."

He lifted his mug, held it out.

I picked mine up.

"To the two submissives who restructured our lives the way they intended them to be."

I grinned, clinked my glass to his. "And to a new and improved sleeping quarters."

Isaac chuckled. "Thank God for a bigger bed. You can sleep on your side."

"With Everly," I added.

He laughed. "Every Tuesday, Thursday, and Sunday. The rest of the time, she's in my arms."

Knowing he was kidding, I laughed. "Not a chance."

We ate in silence for a little while, finishing off the sandwiches and downing the beer. I took the empty plates inside, brought out two more beers, poured them.

"I gave Dante some rules tonight."

"Yeah?"

"You should consider giving him a few. I think it'll help."

I nodded. "I agree. Structure. He needs it to feel settled."

Isaac turned to me. "He also needs to know that it's okay he's sleeping on his own. I think he worries it bothers us."

I blamed myself for that. I wanted Dante in my bed, but I knew from the few instances he'd been there that it wasn't comfortable for him. I couldn't pretend to understand, but I would accept it because I loved him.

"What are the rules?" I asked.

"Monday mornings he's to shower with me. No matter the situation. He has to ask for permission to go to his room. Not because I figure we'll tell him no."

"Because you want him to know we care how much he's hiding in there?"

"Yeah," Isaac agreed. "Exactly."

"Anything else?"

Isaac set his beer down, leaned back. "I explained how hard it is to command at all times, to decide what everyone else will do. I know they want that, Dante probably more than Everly. But it's not sustainable for us to direct his every move. He has to make the decisions on his own. Now he has to ask permission to do them."

"That could get interesting. We supposed to stand over him and give him permission to wash his body after he shampoos?"

Isaac laughed. "Hell no. I told him he can't ask which food to eat first. He understands."

"Then I'll divvy up the chores. Come up with some creative ways to spend his time."

"That'll be fun for you."

It would. I was a creative guy. I was sure they'd both enjoy what I had in store for them.

I stared out at the pool, the blue lights beneath the surface. "What'll we do when we're out of town?"

"It can't be helped," he said, clearly understanding the deeper meaning to the question.

"They'll have each other to look after. They've been doing it for a long time."

"I know. I just…" I didn't like the idea of being gone for a couple of months, not seeing them during that time.

"I think Ransom'll understand we can't take the longer assignments," Isaac said. "We'll tell him two weeks is the limit."

It was a start.

"And you never know, they may want to kick us out from time to time."

The thought made me smile. "You're probably right."

"There's no probably about it. I am. You'll see."

Isaac was correct about one thing.

Only time would tell.

Thirty-Three

Dante

I COULDN'T REMEMBER THE LAST TIME I'D woken with an alarm.

Before I'd come here, I hadn't slept enough to need one.

This morning, I was grateful I'd had the forethought. I managed to drag my ass into Isaac's room with only a minute to spare. There, on the big bed, were Isaac, Everly, and Ian, all sleeping soundly.

Not wanting to be creepy, I decided not to watch them sleep, choosing to get on the bed and kneel between Isaac's legs as he'd instructed. At first, I had wondered why he hadn't wanted me to simply kneel beside the bed. When he shifted as I settled, I realized it was because it would allow him to be notified of my presence.

His eyes were hooded as he glanced over at the clock, probably verifying I was on time. The clock read six on the dot, so I was doing fine.

He dropped his head back onto his pillow, ran his hand through his hair as he came awake slowly. I kept my eyes downcast, but I couldn't help but notice him. Aside from the shower he'd promised, I had no idea what his plan was for this weekly encounter, but I had looked forward to it all night. In fact, I'd gone over his instructions numerous times in my head, the anticipation building every time I did.

Isaac moved his right leg, bending his knee, then pushing the blankets down. My gaze locked on the hard cock he revealed.

He didn't touch himself, his eyes scanning my face as I fought the urge to lick my lips.

Isaac crooked his finger, a silent command that had me leaning over, taking his cock in my fist, then circling the head with my lips, licking him lightly. I could feel his eyes on me as I sucked him.

I was so caught up in it I never felt Ian move, didn't realize he was behind me until his big hands squeezed my ass, spreading my cheeks wide, his tongue pushing deep inside. I swallowed the groan that threatened to escape, not wanting to wake Everly, who was still sleeping.

Isaac moved back, propping himself up on pillows. I crawled forward, realizing he was giving Ian more room at the end of the bed.

Before I could lower my head to his cock again, Isaac pulled me toward him, his mouth meeting mine. The kiss was soft, but there was a flame flickering in the way his tongue pushed against mine. It wasn't going to remain soft for long.

While Isaac's tongue explored my mouth, Ian's tongue drove into my ass. Isaac finally guided my head back down, his cock filling my throat once more while Ian teased my ass with his thumb. He prodded me thoroughly, slick fingers replacing his thumb. Before I knew it, I was grinding back against the two fingers buried in my ass.

Isaac tossed something to Ian. I heard a cap flip open, felt the cool drizzle of lubricant slide in the crack of my ass. Two fingers became three as I panted, holding in the moans as I took Isaac's cock deeper into my throat. Up to that point, they'd given me the illusion of some control.

So when they stripped it from me in a sudden shift of bodies, I soared higher than I'd ever been. Isaac's hands covered my head, his fingers twining tightly in my hair as Ian drove his cock into my ass in one punishing thrust. My hands were pulled behind my back, held in Ian's strong, unrelenting grip. Overwhelmed by their physical assertion, I surrendered to the pleasure. Unable to move, I choked on Isaac's cock as he forcefully fucked my face while Ian pounded my ass.

It was pure bliss, the most intriguing high I'd ever experienced. Unable to ask permission, I came, my body jerking and twitching. Neither said anything, continued to drive me higher and higher.

Then they stopped.

Isaac's hands turned gentle. Ian's pace slowed. He released my hands. Isaac then massaged my shoulders, grinding his hips up as I sucked his cock. I wasn't sure which was more painful, the sweet way they teased me or the brutal flex of their control. Both had my heart pounding, my breaths rushing out on stifled moans. I was lost in a world of ecstasy far surpassing anything I'd ever felt when the icing on the proverbial erotic sundae opened her eyes, propped herself up on a pillow, and watched.

Ian and Isaac, aware that Everly was now witnessing what was happening, shifted once more, Isaac driving his cock deep in my throat, holding me there with his hands fixed roughly on my head while Ian drilled my ass again and again.

Not believing it possible, I came again, groaning around the cock lodged in my throat.

"Fuck," Ian hissed, slamming into me one final time, his cock pulsing in my ass.

Isaac groaned low in his throat, holding my head in place as he came down my throat.

When they released me, I fell to my side and smiled.

Everly's soft hands rubbed my shoulders as she leaned over and kissed my cheek. Ian disappeared first, slipping down the hall, probably to his shower.

I heard Isaac's shower water come on and sighed.

Isaac caught my gaze, snapped his fingers. I managed to roll to my feet, stumble toward the stall. My entire body was sated, my muscles lax.

"Come on, fairy princess," Isaac called out. "Join us."

"It would be my pleasure, my Liege," Everly said, her voice rough from sleep.

Naked and sexy, Everly joined me, coming up on her toes and kissing me so sweetly. I fell into the kiss, cupping her head, pulling her body flush with mine.

When she pulled back, she was smiling. I stood there, head still spinning while Everly turned one of the greatest mornings of my life into something I would never forget. Her soft hands soaped every inch of my body. She took her time, not teasing, simply touching. It was all I could do to remain on my feet.

Once we were clean, I had the presence of mind to grab a towel, drying her off, then myself. I expected to go back to my room, get dressed, and start the day.

Isaac had other ideas, pointing to the bed.

Everly crawled in first. I followed, curling up behind her as Isaac dragged the blankets over us.

"Sleep," he ordered.

For possibly the first time in my life, I drifted off, Everly in my arms, not once thinking I would rather be alone.

RANSOM

DARK THIRTY COULDN'T COME FAST ENOUGH.

As I sat in my living room, the light finally fading outside, I stared at the wall while finishing off the first of two shots of vodka I allowed myself each day.

I never needed more than that, and coming from an alcoholic father and a drug addict mother, I knew better than to tempt fate. Alcohol was a poison that could stir in the veins and become more important than the blood that flowed there. My parents had proven that long ago.

My cell phone, resting on my knee, buzzed with an incoming text.

I downed the other shot before picking it up.

Done.

That was all it said. All it needed to say. And it didn't require a response of any kind.

I exhaled, dropped my head back against the chair.

Some would've thought I could ignore the niggling at the back of my mind telling me I'd sinned again. They would've been wrong.

My reputation portrayed me as a man whose sole job in life was to stir up mischief. While I enjoyed that minor role I played, it was only a fraction of who I was.

Some thought I was little more than a sexual Sadist who got off on other people's pain. They were more accurate in that regard. I did enjoy it greatly.

However, those were pieces that came together, merging with my past, to form the whole.

And now…

Now my true colors were bleeding through with every passing day, the world I thought I'd left behind finding me, shackling me like one of the masochists I very much enjoyed making cry.

Soon, everyone would realize the instigator was merely my way of coping with the truth, the Sadist was only part of the darkness that lurked inside me, and my past …

My past had finally caught up.

ISAAC

THE KNOCK THAT SOUNDED ON MY DOOR at eleven o'clock at night had me grabbing my gun and slowly moving toward the entryway.

My brother was right behind me, both of us silent.

"It's Ransom," the deep voice bellowed from the other side. "Open the fucking door."

Frowning at Ian, I unlocked the deadbolt, opened the door before lowering my weapon.

"You could've called," Ian said before starting toward the living room.

"No, I couldn't," he countered causing my brother to stop short, pivot.

"Come in, then. You want a drink?"

"I'm not staying," Ransom announced as he stepped inside, not bothering to close the door.

I turned to face him, Ian stepping up beside me.

"I'm just here to let you know that I've reassigned the men."

Before Ian could ask, I put a hand on his arm, silencing him.

"Understood."

Ransom turned to walk out. "Oh, and I heard there's an interesting story on the news. Might want to check it out."

"Will do."

As quickly as he'd come, Ransom left.

Ian didn't say a word, leading the way down to the basement. He was on his computer, fingers flying over the keys. He stared at the screen a moment before turning the laptop toward me. I stood over his shoulder and read.

LOCAL WEALTHY BUSINESSMAN AND SON KILLED IN HOME INVASION.

I skimmed the article that announced the death of one Thomas Hathaway and his son, Vernon, both shot multiple times when thugs barged into their home. The wife, who had hidden in an upstairs closet, and the housekeeper and two others, were not harmed. According to investigators, a suspect was taken into custody, interrogated, and confessed.

"Holy shit," Ian groaned, his eyes hard.

Yeah. Holy shit was right.

There was no mention of the details Ransom had relayed, those relating to Dante's past. If I had to guess, they would never see the light of day. I hoped that was the case. As far as I was concerned, Dante had been through enough already.

There was only one way they'd gotten a suspect, though, much less someone to confess. It had been set up that way. A fall guy put in place, which wreaked of organized crime.

I glanced at Ian.

He instantly shook his head. "No. Wasn't me. I didn't make the call."

"I know." I held his gaze, waited for him to catch on.

It didn't take long.

"Fuck."

Yeah. That about summed it up.

The following morning, I slept in. Rare for me but sometimes necessary. However, I wasn't the only one.

When I cracked open my lids, glanced over, Ian stirred.

While I was still getting my bearings, he rolled toward Everly, pulled her against him, and snuggled her close to him. There might've been a smirk on his face, but I couldn't quite tell.

After using the restroom, I pulled on shorts, grabbed my running shoes, and headed for the bedroom door. Just in time to hear Everly's soft sigh as my twin woke her appropriately.

"You want to go for a run?" I asked Dante when I found him sitting on a barstool drinking orange juice.

He peered over at me, evidently confused by my offer.

"Okay. Shall I rephrase?" I stated, grinning. "You and me. Run. Five minutes."

"I would love to, Master." His eyes briefly darted toward the hallway to my bedroom.

I waited to hear the question, but it didn't come. I took that as a good sign. He trusted me to take care of him.

While he went to his room to get ready, I walked out on the back patio to stretch. The morning was underway, the birds chirping in the trees, a couple of bees already buzzing around a rosebush near the window. It looked no different although I wasn't sure why I figured it should. Perhaps it was because some of the evil lurking had been eliminated. I didn't know how or by whom, but those were questions I didn't need answers to. The only thing that mattered to me was that Dante did not have to worry about them anymore.

The door opened behind me. Dante stepped out.

I smiled over at him, then took a step closer. Cupping his face, I pressed my lips to his gently, held it for a few seconds simply so I could satisfy myself that he was good.

When I pulled back, he not only still looked confused, now he could add dazed to the mix.

"Let's get to it." I motioned toward the street.

"My pleasure, Master."

We hit the pavement at a jog. As we circled around the house via the side street, there was no longer a man stationed there, keeping an eye on the house. The others were gone as well, and Dante was as aware of his surroundings as I was. I noticed him glance over twice before he picked up his pace, a small smile on his lips.

I let him lead the way today. Keeping up with minimal effort but giving him the freedom that came with the weight being removed from his shoulders. I had every intention of discussing it with him, sharing a bit of information I'd uncovered, wanting to give him whatever closure I could, but I figured that could wait. He needed this as much as I did.

By the time we were back at the house, he was smiling, and it did something to me to see it. The storm clouds in his eyes, perhaps not completely gone, were certainly not as heavy.

"May I shower, Master?"

"Aye. I'll start breakfast."

I trailed him across the kitchen until he disappeared from view. Rather than take a shower of my own, I started a pot of coffee, pulled out whatever crap it was that made up those vegan eggs, snatched a couple of real ones, then went to work making scrambled egg sandwiches.

By the time Dante returned, I had the sandwiches plated, coffee poured, and was about to carry them out to the back patio.

"May I, Master?" Dante asked as he reached for them.

I smiled, took the coffee mugs, and allowed him to lead the way.

"You haven't asked any questions," I mentioned as he started in on his sandwich.

"I don't have any," he said softly, wiping his mouth with a napkin. "The guys are gone, which I take to mean all is well."

"It is," I assured him, sipping coffee.

His eyes lifted, met mine. "I trust you, Master. Questions aren't necessary when you know someone's going to take care of you."

I reached over, squeezed his hand. "I'll answer them if you ever have them. As best I can, anyway."

"I know you will."

I picked up my sandwich, took a bite, stared out at the yard. There wasn't a cloud in the sky today. Crystal clear and blue overhead, the breeze warm. These were the days I enjoyed sitting out here, in the shade. I tended to gravitate here when we weren't on the road. It offered peace, but until today, I hadn't realized how much.

Once we'd cleaned our plates, Dante asked to clear the table and do the dishes. He refilled my coffee before getting to work. I was still sitting there when he returned. Rather than take a chair, he came over and knelt at my feet.

I twined my fingers in his hair, and we sat like that for a long time. No words passed between us. None necessary.

When he finally spoke, his question didn't so much surprise me as it did make my heart ache for him.

"Master, would it be possible to find my mother?"

"I've already found her," I informed him. "I thought you might want to know."

"Where is she?"

Sliding my fingers through his hair, I stared at the pool, watching the specks of sunlight that danced across the water. "Your mother's body was never claimed. Her mother—your grandmother—died before she was a teenager and her father died shortly after you were born. He hadn't been well, and the alcohol abuse hadn't helped. I made a couple of calls. Turns out one of the local churches laid her to rest in a cemetery not far from where you were born."

"Can we go visit her?" His voice had a jagged edge to it, the pain he felt evident.

"Of course we can. Whenever you want."

"Thank you, Master."

"No thanks necessary," I whispered, finding comfort in the way he rested his head against my thigh. "You did get a contract on your house. List price, no conditions. The inspection's this week. If all goes well, you'll have the money in hand in thirty days."

He didn't say a word.

"Ian had the Camaro disposed of," I added.

"Thank you, Master. I never drove it."

I knew he hadn't because it only had a few miles on it. Ian had informed me the car had been purchased by Hathaway, given to Dante as a gift. He hadn't wanted it, but I couldn't blame him.

"I love you, Master."

I smiled, loving those words spoken so softly, so reverently, and without premeditation. While I'd gotten so many things wrong in my life, my expectations set in a manner that didn't allow for exceptions, I still found it amazing that Ian and I had ended up right where we were meant to be.

"I love you, too."

Thirty-Four

Everly

WHEN I STAGGERED INTO THE KITCHEN, STILL sleepy but extremely satisfied, I devoured the last bit of coffee in the pot before starting another.

While I sipped, I stared out the door, watching Isaac and Dante, not wanting to intrude. They were beautiful together. Dante kneeling beside Isaac was a sight that warmed my heart. I knew how much Dante had always hoped to find a love like this.

Neither of us would've ever predicted it would happen. In fact, we would've had a good laugh if someone told us we'd fall in love so quickly and so deeply. And with the same two men. We were nothing if not cynical. Hopeful, sure, but skeptical all the same.

"What are you doing, little fairy?"

I didn't turn away when Ian walked up behind me. "Just admiring them."

Ian planted a noisy kiss on my cheek before making his way to the refrigerator. "Scrambled egg sandwich?"

I turned toward him. "Only if I can cook."

He pivoted, narrowed his eyes as a smile tugged at his mouth. "Are you insinuating there's something wrong with my cooking?"

"No, my Alpha." I couldn't hide the amusement and he noticed.

"For that, you may cook breakfast naked."

I grinned. "It would be my pleasure, my Alpha."

"I just bet it would." Ian stole my coffee, downed what was left as he eyed me.

Since I was wearing only a T-shirt—one of Isaac's I'd pilfered—it didn't take long to strip. I tossed the T-shirt on the counter, then pranced over to the stove. I knew he watched me, loved that he did, so I put an extra bounce in my step.

They called me their fairy princess, had since the first night we scened together. Secretly, it pleased me greatly to hear it. I'd never been anyone's princess, hadn't expected to, but they both made me feel as though I was. Being loved and cherished, and knowing that I was, made all the difference in the world.

It even made cooking breakfast in the nude worthwhile.

"Well, isn't this a nice sight first thing in the morning," Isaac said from behind me.

I gave him a warm smile over my shoulder. "Would you like breakfast, my Liege?"

"Already had mine. But thank you."

There was something in his tone.

In fact, there was something in Ian's that had me turning slowly to stare at them both. They were different this morning, as though they weren't carrying the weight of the world on their shoulders. I couldn't believe I had missed it until then.

"What happened?" I asked, glancing between the two of them.

Ian's eyes raked over my upper body, the only part of me he could see because the island was blocking his view. "Well, if you'd like me to give you a play-by-play, I'll start at the point when your mouth—"

I choked on a laugh, held up my hand to stop him. "No. Not that. I know what happened when you woke me up, thank you very much." I cut my gaze to Isaac. "What's different? Something happened."

"All is well, fairy princess," he said, his tone reassuring. "That's all you need to know."

Considering Dante was still outside, by himself, I might add, I figured he wasn't simply referring to today being a good day.

I searched his eyes for any hint of concern but found nothing but relief. "Understood, my Liege." I smiled, then turned back to the stove.

"Just like that?" Isaac questioned from behind me. "No follow-ups?"

"None necessary," I told him. "I trust you both, infinitely. When you tell me all is well, then all is well."

"Such a sweet submissive," Ian teased. "Now where's my breakfast?"

I wiggled my butt at them. Sweet, my ass. I was anything but sweet, but I'd been blessed with the face of an angel, or so I'd heard repeatedly throughout my life. It worked well for me. Not that I'd ever used it to get what I wanted, but admittedly, I didn't mind seeing my twin Doms look at me as though I was a treasured gift. It made my heart swell, my love for them only grow.

"I have a contractor scheduled to come out tomorrow," Ian informed me when I passed over a plate with two pieces of toast and two eggs, scrambled.

I turned back to get mine, wondering what he and Isaac were working on now. Couldn't be Dante's room because that was finally complete. Granted, they'd gone with a relatively minimalist decor, something that didn't necessarily fit Dante any more than the previous decor had. Then again, Dante had never been much for decoration. The only things we'd had at his house were those Heaven and I had brought.

I had just settled my egg onto a piece of toast when Ian said, "I'd like you to work with him, get the new room designed."

I spun around so fast I nearly threw the spatula across the room. "What?"

They were both grinning at me.

"I'm looking forward to the redesign," Isaac noted.

"Really?"

"Really."

431

My heart swelled.

"However, I want to keep my room," Isaac said firmly.

My elation faltered.

"For Dante. The bathroom's bigger than Ian's," he explained. "So, you can simply flip your design, use the other end."

I let out a heavy breath, relieved.

"But remember, little fairy. You promised us a bigger bed."

I chuckled. I knew how much they wanted one. And while we slept in a king bed now, we definitely needed more space. I would never say it aloud, but my two Doms were bed hogs.

"Eat, little fairy," Ian said, pointing at my plate with his fork. "Then you can swim with Dante."

They would not hear any complaints from me.

Half an hour later, I was diving into the water from the second step. I swam over to Dante, surfaced in front of him.

"Good morning," I whispered, grabbing on to him to stay afloat.

"Good morning." His smile was wide, genuine.

"So what's the plan for the day?" I asked, and I could see he knew what I was referring to.

His arms tightened around me. "I was thinking perhaps we could go see a movie."

"Really?" I squeezed his neck.

"Just me and you."

"I would love that. But I get to pick the movie."

Dante laughed, such a beautiful sound my heart lodged in my throat.

"Not a chick flick," he insisted.

I puffed out my lower lip.

In a bold and daring move I didn't expect from him, he nipped it. Before he could release me, I kissed him. It was sweet and soft.

His arms tightened around me as he settled into the kiss.

"What was that for?" he whispered when we broke for air, his forehead pressing to mine.

I grinned. "Because I love you."

His eyes warmed. "I love you, too."

"I know. I'm irresistible."

He laughed again and I hoped it was a sound I would hear more of.

IAN

"Thanks, Ransom. Send us the itinerary."

"Will do. Your flight leaves at eight in the morning. Puts you in LA in time for rush hour."

"Great. Nothing I enjoy more. Appreciate it."

He chuckled. "Anything I can do for a friend."

The call disconnected, and when I set my phone on my desk, I noticed Isaac watching me.

"LA," I told him. "Some society princess is having a birthday bash this weekend. Needs extra security."

"Friend of Trent's?" he asked.

"Yep. He's trying to drum up business, offered to send a couple of guys out to watch over her."

"No threat?"

"Just some stalker. According to Ransom, he seems harmless, but he said not to underestimate him. Asked that we stick with her for a few days until he can get someone else assigned long-term."

Isaac nodded, his gaze sweeping toward the stairs.

"They're fine," I assured him.

From the moment Dante and Everly had left for the movies, Isaac had been on edge, although he was doing his damnedest to hide it. It wasn't working, but I gave him credit for trying.

I knew he would worry until they walked through the door. I could've told him he had nothing to worry about because I'd already done the research necessary to ensure all was as it should be. The article in the paper was true. The devil and his spawn had been taken care of. Dante did not have to look over his shoulder or worry about a crazed, sadistic bastard stalking him or those he cared about ever again.

Returning my attention to my computer, I finished up the list I'd been working on. Chores for Dante and Everly, at their request. It was lengthy and would keep them busy for the most part.

"He needs a new car," Isaac mentioned, drawing my attention toward him.

"I agree, but I don't think he'll feel the same."

The one thing I'd gotten from Dante was that he did not want to be anyone's charity case. It wasn't like I could go out and buy him a car and expect him to drive it. It would have to be more subtle than that and Isaac knew it, too. And while I wouldn't do that to him, I wasn't above using Everly's safety as a bargaining chip. It was how I'd convinced him to take the Escalade rather than his hunk of junk for their trip to the movies.

Perhaps he'd consider that. Taking the Escalade and we could buy something else. Maybe another just like it. I smiled at the thought. Manipulation at its finest.

Isaac's cell phone buzzed and we both stared at it.

He smiled. "They're on the way home. Want to know if they should pick up something for dinner."

"Pizza," I suggested.

Isaac relayed the message, then turned back to his computer.

"Who's the society princess?" he asked.

I rattled off the name, knowing he would want to do a search, find out as much information as he could. "Oh, and I talked to Triton about the surprise party for Everly. He jotted us down for two weeks from Saturday." I smirked over at him. "I'll work with Talon on the logistics."

Isaac grinned. "I've got some ideas on that."

"I'm sure you do. I'm thinking we'll have the submissives working the party."

"As furniture," he noted, still staring at his screen.

"Absolutely. I do get a kick out of that shit."

"So does Everly."

"Yeah, she does."

"Oh, and I got Dante a dog," Isaac said absently, as though that news wouldn't have my full attention.

"A dog?" I frowned. "What the hell are we—"

"Not we," he interjected. "Dante. I heard him talking to Everly. Apparently, he's always wanted one. Found a little guy at the pound looking for a home."

"What kind?"

He shrugged. "Some retriever mix, they said. He's getting snipped, then I can go pick him up." He peered over at me. "Thought I'd take Dante. Stop by the pet store on the way home."

"Wow." I huffed as I relaxed into my chair. "Already getting pets. Next thing you know, we'll have little feet running through this house."

He grinned. "One day. But I'm not in a rush for that."

Nor was I. We had all the time in the world. For now, I was quite content to enjoy the family we had.

Granted, I wasn't sure how I felt about the dog…

Then again, if it made Dante happy, who the hell was I to intervene?

ISAAC

Seven weeks later, Monday, August 5, 2019

I WOKE WHEN I FELT THE MATTRESS shift, but I didn't open my eyes right away.

It was the first morning I was waking up in my own bed after two weeks in New York. The past month and a half had been hectic, but the routine was proving to be good for all four of us. Being away was as difficult as I'd thought it would be, but we were working through it. FaceTime had certainly come in handy, allowing me to keep my eyes on my sexy submissives when I wasn't here to do so in person.

I cracked open my eyes, peeked at the sexy submissive kneeling between my thighs. His head was down, hands resting on his thighs, his body still.

Perfection.

That was the one word that came to mind when I looked at Dante. That wasn't to say he wasn't flawed. He was. Which, I figured, was what made him so perfect.

Everly, curled up at my side, stirred, her hand sliding over my chest, as though assuring herself I was still there.

I put my hand on hers, grazing her smooth skin until her thigh shifted over mine.

Ian cleared his throat as the bed moved again. "Are we having a party?"

"Was thinking about it," I mumbled, my eyes on Dante. "In fact, I'm thinking breakfast in bed."

As though he knew exactly what I was referring to, Dante's gaze shifted over to Everly.

"Something sweet?" I asked.

"Sweet sounds perfect, Master."

I shifted my attention to Everly, turning on my side while Ian positioned himself on her other side, gently nudging her onto her back.

She sighed, her legs falling open as Ian revealed her smooth curves, slowly pulling the sheet down her body.

"Good morning, fairy princess," I whispered, trailing my lips over her jaw, her throat.

"Good morning, my Liege." She bowed her back as I grazed my fingernail over one nipple, Ian doing the same to the other. "Good morning, my Alpha."

I reached over her head, pulled one of the restraints down, then positioned her wrist in the cuff and buckled it. She offered her other arm to Ian, her body coming awake as we secured her to the bed.

I had to admit, the design for the bed was rather impressive. The king bed we'd been sleeping in had been replaced by one roughly one and a half times its size, along with several inches longer, giving us plenty of room to sleep and to play. The restraint system Ian had installed was genius, too. And utilized quite frequently.

"Have you missed us?"

"Very much, my Liege."

I glanced at Dante as I tugged her knee toward me, Ian doing the same with the other.

"Wake her properly," I instructed.

"It would be my pleasure, Master."

Dante repositioned himself so that he was flat between her thighs, his big hands settling on her shins before slowly sliding up over her knees, the insides of her thighs. Using his thumbs, he held her pussy lips open, the tip of his tongue lapping along her slit.

For a few minutes, we remained like that. Me on one side, Ian on the other, both of us watching as Dante feasted on Everly's pussy, teasing her with soft licks and flicks of his skilled tongue. As the sun rose in the sky, so did the temperature in the room, the three of us focused on the woman who'd become the center of our world.

We were starting to come into our own where living together was concerned. Admittedly, being away from them was not something I was enjoying. Not sure I would ever get used to it either. The first trip we'd taken to watch over the LA debutante had been three days and at the time, it had felt like an eternity. Then we'd been home for two weeks, handling a few gigs locally, before another three-day trip. Again, it had been painfully long. Back for two more weeks and then we'd been off to New York. Two weeks away had been absolute hell. Which, perhaps, made waking up to this all the more sweeter.

"I think she'd like to return the favor," I told Dante. "Straddle her chest. Feed her your cock."

His eyes were heated as he did as instructed, carefully crawling up her body before hovering over her chest. He teased her lips with the swollen head before dipping it inside. While she focused on Dante, I crawled between her thighs, buried my face in her pussy. I made sure not to push her too close to the edge, wanting this to last a while. I'd missed them both and I had no desire to hurry this along.

Dante and Everly groaned in unison, their sweet sounds something I'd come to crave and certainly something I'd missed.

Not wanting to be selfish, I gave Ian a turn. He gladly took it, his tongue spearing Everly's pussy while she used that sweet tongue to drive Dante crazy.

"I think I'll take a shower now," I told them, getting to my feet. "Dante, join me."

"With pleasure, Master."

Although I could've spent a couple of hours feasting on my beautiful fairy princess, I'd missed my Monday morning showers with Dante, and I had no intention of missing this one. I knew Everly would be well taken care of in Ian's capable hands.

Dante was in the shower before me, the water heated when I joined him. He was on his knees, ass resting on his heels, something he was apt to do without suggestion or command. I'd come to expect it, enjoying the sight of him eagerly awaiting my attention, his eyes hot as they watched my every move. I took my time beneath the spray, stroking my cock firmly as he observed every firm caress of my hand.

I tapped the button that had all the heads spraying with water, warmth coming from every angle, filling the shower with steam. I stepped over to Dante, guided my cock into his mouth. He opened eagerly, his eyes closing as my cock tunneled past his lips, the water coming down over us both.

Slick and warm, I used his mouth for my own pleasure, taking what he offered in a way I knew he loved. My submissive had proven in the past month and a half that he wasn't telling us what we wanted to hear when it came to his complete surrender. He craved our domination, and in those moments when we took away all control, he looked more at peace than I'd ever seen him.

It had taken some time to get used to, his past never far from my mind. And while I would never quite understand how his desires had formed, I didn't question them, either. It all came down to trust. Since he'd proven to trust us with his care, I trusted him to know his limits.

Sliding my hands into his wet hair, I gripped firmly, tugging him up onto his knees while pushing my cock deep into his throat. I held him there for long seconds, released him. I repeated the movement again and again, my cock throbbing, pleasure blinding me, driving up my need.

I stepped to the side, my cock still buried in his throat as I dragged him by the hair. He moaned softly in approval. When I seated myself on the long bamboo bench that ran the length of the entire wall, I released him, pulled him in closer. I fucked his throat roughly, building the heat between us, igniting the flames.

Hand still fisted in his hair, I retrieved the lubricant someone had had the forethought to stash there. Ian, most likely.

I passed it over to Dante, pulling his mouth from my cock.

I didn't have to tell him what I needed. He knew.

There was confidence in his movements as he stroked my cock, preparing me to take his ass.

When he had me generously lubed, I jerked his head and he stilled his hands.

"Kiss the head," I ordered gruffly.

He leaned forward, pressed his smooth lips to the glistening tip, his eyes glazed with the same hunger burning inside me.

"It's your turn, sweet boy. Time for you to make us both come."

He lifted his head, met my gaze. "It would be my pleasure, Master."

Mine, too.

Most definitely mine, too.

Dante

I HAD MISSED THEM.

When they had left the first time since we had moved in, I hadn't known what to expect. Having Everly here had kept me sane. We had fallen into the routine we'd established when we had lived together before. While we alternated who would make each meal, we'd tended to our own chores and spent much of our spare time working with Bo, the retriever/mix Isaac had surprised me with. Needless to say, my dog was doing much better in terms of obeying.

Days had passed slowly, sometimes painfully so.

That had been a month and a half ago. I was getting used to it now, always looking forward to the day they would come home. More importantly, looking forward to moments like this one.

As I stood, turned, then eased down onto Isaac's cock, I worked to keep my entire body from trembling. The need was intense, overwhelming. The longer they were away, the more I craved them, the more desperate I became.

It seemed Isaac was always a bit rougher when he returned, and those were the times I relaxed most. He would take my control completely, asserting his dominance, proving he was the man who owned me, heart, body, and soul. I wasn't sure what it was about him, why I enjoyed the way he used me for his own pleasure, but I did.

"All the way," he growled.

I dropped down onto his cock, grunting as his thick shaft filled me abruptly.

"Keep going. Don't you dare fucking come," he bit out when I lifted and lowered again.

I worked his cock with my ass. Lifting, lowering, grinding against him until we were both groaning, the sounds drowning out the rain from the numerous jets spraying us from all directions.

Strong arms banded around me. Isaac moved, turning us both so he could straddle the bench. Leaning forward, feet on the tiled floor, I curled my fingers around the edges of the teakwood, held on when Isaac drove into me. Hard.

"Oh, fuck," I groaned, holding still as he rammed me again and again.

"Don't you dare come," he snapped. "This is my ass to use."

"Yours, Master," I confirmed, grunting and groaning as he fucked me harder and harder.

When his hips slammed into me one final time, his fingers digging into my hips, I felt his cock pulse. He came in a hot rush deep inside me before smacking my ass and ordering me to stay where I was.

Isaac went back beneath the spray. I heard the snap of the body wash, smelled the intoxicating scent. I wanted to watch him wash himself, but I didn't dare move, holding myself where he'd left me, still straddling the bench, my arms burning from the effort to keep me upright.

"Your turn. Wash yourself thoroughly," he commanded. "You've got three minutes."

He walked out of the shower, grabbed a towel. Before he could dry off, I was already lathering myself, his cum dripping from my ass.

I used the sprayer to rinse off, cognizant of the time I had. Three minutes wasn't enough, but I knew Isaac meant for me to fail at the task, likely already having my punishment lined up.

I didn't mind.

When I came out of the bathroom, Isaac was nowhere in sight, nor was Ian. Everly was still restrained to the bed by her wrists, smiling up at the ceiling.

"They said to tell you to kiss me when you came in here," Everly said, lifting her head enough to peer over at me.

"Did they really?" Last thing I needed was to compound the punishment.

"I think Isaac's exact words were for you to kiss me thoroughly, but I was not allowed to push for more."

I chuckled. I could actually hear him say that.

Not wanting to disappoint my Masters or Everly, I joined her on the enormous bed, crawling over her and straddling her hips.

She moaned softly when my lips touched hers.

Unable to resist, I fell into the kiss, covering her body with mine as I tucked my arms beneath her, bearing my weight on my forearms so as not to crush her. She was so soft, so warm.

"Where'd they go?" I whispered between kisses.

"They didn't say. Nor do I actually care right now." Her voice was rich with lust. "Kiss me, Dante, and don't stop. Please."

I couldn't resist her, even if I'd wanted to. I stroked her lips open with my tongue, dipped inside, and kissed her. Slowly, sweetly, relishing every second. At her request, I'd slept with her in my bed two nights last week and once on the living room sofa. Bo had slept at my side, regardless where I had rested my head. I knew Everly didn't want to be alone. And while I wanted to appease her, it wasn't easy because I needed my solitude, with the exception of my dog. I'd gotten used to having him with me and I was starting to believe he was his own form of therapy. Just having him there helped.

I had tried to figure out why that was, giving up long ago because nothing made sense. It had nothing to do with trust because I trusted all three of them with my life. They'd proven I could. However, I needed that separation for whatever reason.

I was still kissing Everly when Ian returned to the room. He was wearing shorts and nothing else.

"You're needed in the kitchen," he told me as he approached. "Neither of you is allowed to get dressed today. Understood?"

"Yes, my Alpha," Everly said when I crawled off of her.

"Of course, Master," I said with a smile.

Before I could stroll past him, Ian grabbed my arm, jerked me toward him, then pressed his mouth to mine.

"Good morning, Master," I whispered when he released me.

"That's better."

My thoughts exactly.

"Oh, and one more thing," he called out as I was walking into the hallway. "Keep some lube handy. In every room. You're going to need it today."

I grinned. "I'll be ready and waiting, Master."

In the kitchen, I found Isaac sitting on the counter, a bowl of cereal in his hands. At his feet, Bo was peering up at him hopefully. Good thing I'd taught the dog not to beg, otherwise, he likely would've been on the counter, lapping at the milk that was not his.

I held up a palm when Bo looked my way, silently signaling him to stay. He responded with a disappointed whimper but remained where he was.

It was then that Isaac's head lifted, and he swallowed.

"My cock needs your mouth," he said simply before resuming to eat his breakfast.

Without resistance or hesitance, I made my way over, with his help, managed to pull his shorts down his hips, then took his cock in my mouth. I worshipped him with my tongue while he ate, his attention seemingly on the cereal. His cock gave him away, hardening beneath my ministrations.

"Enough," he finally said.

I took a step back, then took his bowl when he passed it over. He hopped down, righted his shorts, then headed out of the room.

"May I have breakfast, Master?"

"You may."

He disappeared down the basement stairs.

I was left holding his cereal bowl, my cock hard and throbbing, a huge grin plastered across my face.

This was going to be a good day.

Everly

BEING WOKEN UP THIS WAY WAS ALWAYS a thrill.

Granted, it wasn't as often as I would've liked now that Ian and Isaac were back into a steady routine of work, but I knew I'd be treated to it for at least a few days. Longer if I was lucky.

"I'm considering keeping you there all day," Ian informed me when he crawled back onto the bed. "Ready for me to use anytime I want."

"I serve at your pleasure, my Alpha."

He smirked. "We'll see if you feel that way when the day is done."

Oh, I would. I knew that much. Didn't matter that I could see the wicked glint in his pretty eyes. My Masters were on a mission today, and I could only imagine what they had in store for me and Dante. They'd done this the last time they'd been gone. And that had only been for a few days. These past two weeks had been brutally long, so I could only imagine what they were up to now. At the time I'd thought it had been a treat for us, but I was starting to suspect it was as much for them.

"Tell me how much you missed me, little fairy," Ian ordered, his voice rough as he knelt between my legs, kissed my belly, then slowly glided up toward my chest, pausing long enough to bite each of my nipples.

"So much, my Alpha." I cried out, thrusting my chest forward, not wanting him to stop.

"Feisty this morning?"

It was a question he'd asked me before, one that was meant to find out my mood, my preference. Sure, there were times neither of them cared what I had in mind. I enjoyed those times, too. Loving them when they were sweet and when they were rough.

Then again, they'd been known to ask the question, find out my answer, and give me the opposite of what I hoped for. Either way, I was never disappointed.

As for this morning, I was definitely feeling feisty. Perhaps it was because I'd had all three of their mouths on me and I'd been left wanting. Whatever it was, I wasn't in the mood for sweet and gentle. Ultimately his decision, I still opted for the truth.

"Very feisty, my Alpha."

His green eyes heated as he leaned over me, his mouth inches above mine.

"I like my girl feisty," he whispered, leaning down and kissing me softly.

That sweetness lasted all of a second before he growled, crushing his lips to mine in a bruising kiss that had me squirming beneath him.

He pulled back, chuckled, then reached for something on the headboard. Since my arms were already secured, I knew exactly what he was doing, was in no position to resist. I moaned as he roughly secured my ankles to the restraints attached to the headboard. The way they were connected bent me nearly in half, my legs spread wide, ankles even with my head.

"That's more like it," he groaned, dipping his finger into my pussy. "Now you're mine to do with as I please."

"Always, my Alpha."

He smacked my ass hard.

I swallowed the cry of ecstasy.

"When I want you to talk, I'll tell you."

Looked as though I wasn't the only feisty one this morning.

"In fact, for the remainder of the day, I don't want to hear a peep out of you. I'll inform Isaac as well." His smiled turned savage. "I think I'll enjoy using you for a day without your input."

I grinned back at him. Considering I was always sweet to them—usually on purpose because I loved seeing the way they reacted to it—keeping me quiet wasn't necessarily a punishment. Just another form of control I gladly handed over.

Ian, kneeling near my ass, bent over and pressed his mouth to my pussy, devouring me like a starving man. Completely at his mercy, I wasn't able to get close enough, and he was torturing me, never giving me what I needed. When he lifted his head, he pushed two fingers in my pussy, then dipped his thumb into my ass. He fucked me like that, his eyes locked with mine. I swallowed my moans, trying not to make a sound, but it wasn't easy. The pleasure, although rough, was exquisite, my body greedy for more.

"Which shall I take this morning, little fairy? Your pussy or your ass?"

I didn't say a word. I would gladly give him whatever pleasured him, because I knew he would give me the same in return.

However, Ian didn't take either. Instead, he crawled off the bed and sauntered out of the room once more, leaving me alone with my thoughts. I remained like that for ten minutes before I heard footsteps approaching.

Ian returned, Dante with him. I didn't smile, watching them as Ian instructed Dante to get on the bed.

While Dante joined me, kneeling near my butt, Ian rummaged through a drawer in his nightstand. He produced a bottle of lubricant and a thin vibrator.

"Prepare her ass for my cock," Ian instructed. "Start by using your mouth. Then these." He tossed the items onto the bed. "I'll be back in ten minutes." His eyes shifted to mine, locked. "You are not permitted to come."

I nodded but remembered not to speak.

Obeying Ian's instructions not to say a word, I kept my mouth closed even as Dante leaned forward, rimmed my ass with his tongue.

This was an intimate act we'd never engaged in, and while I'd had him inside me, this felt significantly taboo. But it didn't seem weird the way I expected. Feeling his tongue on me, teasing, bringing those sensitive nerves to life was amazing. My breathing became labored, louder in the otherwise silent room. I had to wonder whether they had instructed him not to speak as well because he hadn't said anything since he came into the room.

Dante's fingers replaced his tongue as he lubed my asshole generously before he fucked me with the vibrator. It took everything in me not to make a sound. The sensation was overwhelming, my pussy growing wetter by the second as he gently worked my asshole with the toy.

"Time's up," Ian announced when he returned. "Hold the toy still."

He did, and I could feel the vibrations all the way to my throat.

I was panting, my eyes focused on the ceiling in an effort to distract myself. It wasn't working.

Ian addressed Dante. "Clean up in the bathroom, then have a seat in the living room. Do not touch yourself."

Dante didn't respond, confirming my suspicions that he'd been silenced as well.

"Such a pretty little ass." His eyes were heated when he climbed naked onto the bed, kneeling once again. "It's going to look even better stuffed with my cock."

I held his stare as he positioned himself, slowly pushing inside me, stretching the tight ring until pain ricocheted along every nerve ending. He filled me, held himself still as he burrowed as deep as he could go, giving my body a chance to relax and adjust to his girth.

Ian remained there as he reached up, grabbed the top of the headboard, bending my body to his will before he lifted his hips, slammed down into me. Again and again, he punished my ass with every brutal thrust. I tried to remain quiet but failed miserably. Grunts and groans escaping as he roughly fucked my ass, driving into me harder, deeper. He ignored my pussy, taking his own pleasure from me. Every time I made a sound, he drove into me harder, until he roared low in his throat, his hips stilling as he came deep inside me.

He was breathless when he pulled out. With one quick peck on my lips, he left me there, restrained to the bed, still achy, needy.

So fucking horny.

And when he walked out of the room once again, I resigned myself to my fate.

This was going to be one hell of a day.

Thirty-Six

IAN

WHILE OUR SUBMISSIVES HAD ALREADY CAUGHT ON to the plan, I had to admit, it wasn't as easy as we made it look.

For one, I wasn't fond of leaving Everly restrained to the bed. It wasn't good for circulation, which was why I had returned a few minutes after I'd fucked her sweet little ass. I released her ankles first, then her wrists. Before I helped her out of the bed, I massaged her thoroughly.

Without a word, as I'd instructed, Everly managed to get to her feet. She was unsteady as I led her to the huge bathroom and into the shower that took up almost half of the space. I washed her hair, conditioned it, then slowly soaped her up, ensuring I worked her into a frenzy along the way with the instruction she was not to come.

She would. In the very near future and probably more than she wanted to, but she wasn't aware of that yet and I wanted to keep it that way.

After drying her off and combing her hair, I took the time to do the same, then pulled on my shorts.

"Living room," I ordered, following her out of the bedroom and down the hall.

When she stepped into the room, she stopped abruptly, making me smile.

NICOLE EDWARDS

We'd done some rearranging while she was relaxing in the bedroom. Utilizing two padded tables I'd ordered online, we had configured our very own play space.

Dante, already laid out and secured to one of them, was watching the television, probably not enjoying all the stimulation he was currently undergoing. Between the porn playing on the television and the vibrating dildo in his ass, he was likely dangerously close to detonating.

Exactly how we wanted him.

"On your knees," Isaac instructed, patting the table.

Everly walked over, climbed on, ever so graceful as she positioned herself on her hands and knees.

Isaac pressed his hand to the center of her back, forcing her chest flat on the table.

"Keep your eyes on the television, fairy princess."

While she watched two men double-team another male, Isaac wrapped a strap over her back, securing her to the table. He did the same with her ankles, utilizing a spreader bar to keep her legs from closing.

Once he was satisfied with his work, I grabbed the large vibrator, securing straps around Everly's thighs to hold it in place. I settled it against her clit, positioning it so she couldn't move forward or back to get away from it.

I turned it on, then joined my brother on the sofa behind them. Bo, Dante's black and white Labrador retriever mix, was watching intensely, though the poor sap had no idea what was going on.

Aside from the dog being there, it was quite stimulating, I had to admit. Sitting there, watching them while they watched porn. I didn't need to see the screen. I had a live show right in front of me.

"I talked to Ransom," Isaac said conversationally.

"Yeah?"

"Told him we wanted the entire month of October off. Figured I'd give him some time to plan."

451

"For?" I glanced over at him.

"We're taking a vacation." Isaac began absently scratching Bo's neck, the dog relaxing toward him.

"Ah. I like the idea. Someplace special in mind?"

"Somewhere with some unique accommodations," he mused.

"Sounds like you have a place in mind."

"I do. Down in Texas." Isaac hit a button on the remote he was holding, causing the dildo in Dante's ass to retreat before pushing back in.

"Yeah? What's the name of it?"

"Alluring Indulgence Resort."

"Really? What accommodations do they have?"

Not wanting Everly to be left out, I turned up the speed on the vibrator.

"Spa, clubs, private villas, events for like-minded individuals."

"Sounds interesting."

"Trent recommended it. Which came as a surprise until he told me he was a silent investor."

That didn't surprise me.

"Invitation only," my brother added. "Got it yesterday. Made reservations for the first two weeks of October."

"What about the other two weeks?"

"I'm sure we can think of something to do."

I grinned, observing Everly as she attempted to grind against the vibrator.

"Pets," Isaac called out, "you both have permission to come."

I grinned when they both shifted their hips.

"However, once you do, I'll ensure you come at least ten times before I let you up from the table. So keep that in mind."

I laughed. While it sounded good and fine, I'd witnessed orgasm control before. And a submissive might enjoy the opportunity to get off, but when it was forced upon them, it wasn't so easy to deal with.

Everly was the first to break, her whimpers becoming more insistent as that vibrator pressed against her clit. Her hips shifted as she accepted the sweet release. On the heels of the first one, I ensured she got another. Then another.

Dante lasted longer than I expected, but the dildo, attached to the machine, began fucking him in earnest. Since he couldn't move, he was forced to endure the repeated penetration. Probably didn't help that there was a vibrator on this contraption, likely driving him insane with the sensation against his prostate.

True to his word, Isaac kept them there until tears streamed down their faces, their bodies lax on the table, completely drained from the stimulation.

"Hot tub," I suggested to Isaac.

"I think they'll enjoy that."

It only took a couple of minutes to get them untethered from the toys and the tables. Clearly in need of her, Isaac took over Everly's care, lifting her into his arms and carrying her out to the hot tub.

I helped Dante to his feet, supported him as I led the way, Bo trotting along beside us. The four of us got into the hot tub, Isaac keeping Everly in his lap while I held on to Dante, allowing his body to float. The dog opted to sit on the edge, head down, eyes on his master. He was usually right at Dante's side, never leaving him unless otherwise forced to.

Because it pleased me, I ran my hands over Dante's body, massaging him until he had relaxed completely. There was more in store for them, made obvious when Isaac roused Everly, instructing her to go inside and make lunch.

She didn't speak, merely smiled, her eyes still wild with pleasure.

I watched her cute little ass as she pranced toward the house. Evidently, the little fairy had been storing up her energy for our return.

"You think she can handle more?" I asked Isaac when my brother moved between Dante's legs, his hands sliding up his shins, his knees, the insides of his thighs.

"I think they both can," he said as he slowly stroked Dante's cock.

Though I wondered how it was even possible, I watched as our submissive hardened in Isaac's hands.

"We have been gone for a while," I said. I pinched one of Dante's nipples. "You missed us, didn't you?"

He nodded but didn't speak.

I pressed my lips to his neck, pulling him closer to me. "Such a good boy."

He hummed, clearly approving of the praise.

Isaac released his cock, shifted back to his seat.

"Why don't you go inside and help Everly. When it's ready, we'll eat on the patio. Bring a couple of pillows because we'll be feeding you both."

Eyes filled with anticipation, Dante climbed out of the water and headed toward the house, once again, Bo trotting at his side.

I smiled at my brother.

Damn glad we'd come up with this idea.

ISAAC

WE SPENT THE REMAINDER OF THE DAY tormenting Dante and Everly. After they had lunch, I joined Everly for a nap, waking her with my tongue between her legs.

I didn't let her come that time.

I learned not too much later that Ian had woken Dante in a similar fashion, refusing him an orgasm as well.

Dinner had been casual. I'd given them both a break, figuring they might as well take it because they would need it.

Afterward, Ian and I took a seat in the living room, my twin flipping through channels. There wasn't much on, so he settled for some cop show drama, waiting for Everly and Dante to finish cleaning the kitchen.

When they joined us in the living room, I motioned Everly to come to me while Dante took a seat on the sofa between me and Ian.

I patted my thigh. "Lie down. Head right here."

She glanced at Ian and Dante, then lay across our laps, her head on my thigh. I brushed her hair back, playing with it while we watched television.

"Don't be afraid to touch," I told Dante.

His hands moved over her back, rubbing softly, tickling her skin.

Nearly an hour passed while the three of us touched her, keeping it as innocent as three pairs of hands on one naked female could keep it. When the show went off and the news came on, Ian clicked off the television.

Not ready for bed yet, I lifted Everly's head using the hand I had fisted in her hair. She sighed as I pushed down my shorts. She didn't need instruction from that point, simply took my cock in her sweet little mouth.

Ian had his own ideas. Shifting so that his back was to the arm of the sofa, he spread Everly's legs wide, one foot on each side of him, watching while Dante dipped his fingers into her pussy.

While sex was an important aspect of our relationship, we'd never spent an entire day like this, and I had to admit, I was enjoying myself. We'd started this practice after our first out-of-town trip, elaborated on this one. I wouldn't mind implementing more of them, getting even more creative. After all, it was something to look forward to.

However, while pleasure was certainly on the menu, sex was the main course for the evening, and we weren't quite there yet. Right now, my goal was to get Everly relaxed and ready for bed.

"Stop," I ordered, lifting her head from my cock. "Kneel on the floor."

Everly slid off our laps, going to her knees. She looked between me and Ian, but it was Dante I wanted her to focus on.

"Using only your mouth, fairy princess, I want you to make him come."

Dante's eyes widened as Everly scooted between his legs.

Ian went to the bedroom while I ensured she followed my instructions.

She did.

And Dante was apparently worked up enough, it didn't take long before he was trembling.

"You have my permission to come. Right down her throat."

As though the thought was more than enough, Dante's hips thrust upward, his hand covering her head and holding her in place as he came down her throat. Everly took her time cleaning his cock before sitting up and waiting for more instruction.

I leaned over, kissed Dante. "Good night," I whispered. "We'll go for a run in the morning."

He looked at me and I could see the question in his eyes. I smiled, nodded, giving him permission to speak.

"Thank you, Master. For an amazing day."

"You're more than welcome."

I watched as he headed for his bedroom. Once the door closed, I stood, held out my hand to Everly.

"Now you're ours, fairy princess, for the rest of the evening. You may speak again."

Everly practically skipped to the bedroom, her energy clearly renewed.

"Ian drew you a bath," I told her, motioning toward the bathroom with my chin. "We'll join you."

"Thank you, my Liege."

I watched her little ass jiggle as she fluttered away. The woman amazed me. Made me feel things I'd never imagined. Being away from her … well, it was more difficult than I'd thought it would be, and I'd known it wouldn't be a walk in the park.

What I hadn't told Ian was that I had also discussed options with Ransom regarding travel. When I requested an entire month off, he didn't seem shocked, nor had he flinched when I mentioned that I would be taking that time to decide what we would be doing going forward. While I knew Dante and Everly were quite capable of taking care of themselves while we were away, it wasn't ideal. Not for any of us.

Turned out, I wasn't the only one who'd broached the subject with my boss. He'd already had the same conversation with Ian. My brother and I, once again, were on the same page.

Which brought me to our vacation in early October. My brother and I would be going to Alluring Indulgence Resort with Dante and Everly mostly for vacation, but we were also there to scope out the scene, and to present Trent with ideas for a resort right here in the heart of Chicago. Looked as though Mr. Ramsey wasn't slowing down anytime soon. He was now venturing into the resort business as well, though he would not be managing the day-to-day. Ian and I would, alongside Talon, who had agreed to come on and oversee the entire resort with the help of a few friends.

Needless to say, I was intrigued by the idea.

Figuring I'd wasted enough time, I wandered into the bathroom, stripped off my shorts, and climbed into the tub.

"Come here, fairy princess," I whispered to Everly, needing to hold her in my arms.

When she came to me, I pulled her in close, pressing my lips to hers, drifting in her sweet scent and the soft moans that escaped. Her pleasure was what I was after, while her love was what I cherished most. Raunchy sex and taboo encounters would always be a preference of mine. I wouldn't pretend otherwise. But this … holding her against me, feeling her soft skin, had become my ultimate desire. As usual, it would only last so long because that overwhelming urge to possess her would come to the forefront, but I'd come to accept that part of myself. As easily as I'd accepted that sharing her with my brother was the only way we could all be happy.

I turned her in my arms, relaxed while Ian lathered her skin with some sweet-smelling shit I would no doubt be wearing until I took another shower.

Once more, our little fairy princess relaxed, the sweet mewling sounds coming from her spurring my need to have her.

I passed her over to Ian so he could help her out of the tub. We took turns drying her before I carried her into our big bed, settled her on the pillows.

"I love you, Everly," I whispered, moving over her and claiming her lips once more. "With everything I am."

Her arms wreathed my neck, holding tightly as my heart threatened to explode. She never had to say the words and I would know exactly how she felt about me. Not need, want, desire, or lust. Deeper, far more complex than those basic human needs.

It was love in its purest, simplest form.

"Love me, fairy princess," I crooned as I pushed inside her.

The hot clamp of her pussy on my cock stole my breath. The sweet heaven of her body would never be enough for me.

"I love you, my Liege," she said softly, her lips near my ear. "Now and forever. Yours."

I buried my face in her neck, accepted all that she offered as I plunged inside her, keeping the beast at bay for as long as I could. When the mattress shifted, I forced myself to pause, to withdraw from her body. I rolled to my side, Ian moving between her thighs.

As I watched the love they communicated with both words and bodies, I felt something settle inside me. There was no jealousy or fear of losing her. She loved us equally, two people who were essentially one.

When Ian moved off of her, I reached for Everly, pulled her over me, pushed deep inside her wet pussy, guiding her hips, urging her to take all of me. She sat up, her hands on my chest as she rode me, her gaze only on mine. Minutes passed before Ian made his move, taking her from me, pulling her onto him, and immersing himself in her sweet warmth.

The next time, Everly was the one to make the move, alternating between us as though she couldn't get enough. Maybe she couldn't. I knew I was having difficulty letting her go each time.

The last time, when she draped herself over me, I drove up into her, held her there as I banded my arms around her.

Ian moved behind her, straddling my legs as he positioned her the way he wanted.

And this time, rather than take her ass, Ian's cock joined mine deep in her pussy, stretching her, making her cry out as she took both of us at the same time. It was all we could do to maintain it for several seconds before Ian pulled out. I fucked her roughly from beneath, retreated as he shoved deep inside her.

I held her to me, felt the control snap, then took her again, forcing her to look in my eyes as I gave her every piece of myself.

I didn't stop until she cried out, her pussy clamping down on me. I came, hard, fast, the breath rushing out of my lungs. Her body remained over mine as Ian picked up where I left off, driving deep inside her, coming on a roar as she cried out his name again and again.

When he fell onto the bed in a heap, Everly giggled.

I glanced over at her, shocked by the sound. "You find something funny, fairy princess?"

"Funny, no," she said, still giggling. "Amazing, yes." She turned her head, looking at me, then Ian, then up at the ceiling. "Please tell me we'll do that again."

"Not tonight we won't," Ian grumbled, making her laugh again.

Not tonight, no.

But we would do it again.

And again.

IAN

Thursday, October 31, 2019

"IT'S GOOD FOR THEM TO SEE HIGH protocol," I told Isaac as we moved around TJ Arlington's lavish home.

"I'd like to see his rules and rituals list," my brother mumbled. "Has to be ten pages long."

It was possible considering the lavish digs we were currently wandering and the over-the-top fetish party that was underway.

How we'd gotten an invite to this esteemed event, I would never know. Then again, I couldn't explain a lot of what had happened over the past year. Last October, we'd been assisting the submissive training class at Dichotomy. This year we were on TJ Arlington's guest list.

"At least the costumes aren't ridiculous," Isaac muttered.

"I heard someone mention they had a farm animal theme at one point," I told him as I watched a Dominant bend over to suck a piece of fish off a submissive's breast. It was all right, considering she was unattached, as was he, and she was technically filling in as a serving tray. The food was there for the taking. Evidently, she was, too.

"Can't do the farm animal thing. Don't care if it's only submissives dressing up."

When we'd received the invitation for the Halloween party, along with a note informing us that it was a costume party and the strict dress code had to be followed, we hadn't been sure whether we would accept or not. In the end, we'd been nudged in the direction of rubbing elbows with famous people.

Hence the reason Isaac and I were dressed as 1920s gangsters, complete with charcoal-gray three-piece suits, black wingtips, and fedoras. I had to admit, I was rather fond of the double-breasted striped suit jacket and the vest. Not a bad look if I did say so myself.

Everly and Dante hadn't been so lucky when it came to clothing options. Their costumes had been provided after we'd been required to send measurements to Mr. Arlington directly. Last week, their wardrobe had arrived in wrapped gift boxes. They might as well have been naked for all the fabric the outfits provided.

In some exotic play on the theme, someone had come up with the idea for the female submissives to be naked, save for a garter belt and sheer thigh-high hose. Nothing else. Everly's were light blue, but there was a range of pastel colors at the party. They also wore gold T-strap heels.

Dante, not to be left out of the sexy costume department, was wearing what equated to an erotic jockstrap. A single black band circled his hips with two thin black chains that connected to a pouch that barely covered the head of his dick. There was absolutely *nothing* left to the imagination, that was for damn sure.

Not that I was complaining. I certainly didn't mind watching my sexy submissives mingling in those outfits. In fact, I had every intention of making them wear them when we got back home. Perhaps while they were tending to their chores.

As we were weaving through the people milling about, I heard someone call my name. Isaac and I turned as Trent Ramsey sauntered over. I'd been introduced to his submissives, Clarissa and Troy, already, and along with Everly and Dante, they'd been relocated so they could all perform their duties, along with every other submissive brought this evening. Tonight, submissives were not allowed to mingle with the Dominants.

"Glad I caught up with you," he said, reaching out to shake my hand, then Isaac's. "Glad you could make it."

"I'd bet money you're the reason we got an invitation."

"I'm not top dog here tonight," he said, motioning toward a set of chairs not occupied.

In his mind, maybe.

I took a seat, set my whiskey on my knee, turning my attention to him. "What's up?"

"I never did ask what you thought." He motioned toward us with an unlit cigar he had between his fingers.

"About?"

He smirked. "Travis Walker."

Ah. Travis Walker, the owner of the exclusive fetish resort that had certainly taken the small town of Coyote Ridge by surprise many years ago. We'd spent two weeks there on a so-called vacation.

"I liked him," Isaac said, already knowing Trent's take on the man.

Trent had a fondness for Travis Walker, but due to his endeavors, there was a mild jealousy that he couldn't hide if he tried. I'd heard stories from Travis himself, regarding Trent's need to build something bigger and better than anything Travis or his brothers could come up with. Travis, very comfortable in his own skin and the life he'd built for himself, was not bothered by that, though Travis's husband did have a penchant for bringing it up.

"You would," Trent joked, grinned. "I do think we'll make Walker jealous by the time we're finished."

463

"Travis mentioned you'd say that," I told him, unable to hide my grin.

"Did he?"

"He did," Isaac confirmed.

"So, what do you think of the party?" Trent asked, changing the subject smoothly.

"I haven't been to one of these in a while."

"It's on my plan for the resort," he said. "I figure monthly would be ideal."

"Over-the-top? Like this?" I asked.

"Yes."

"I'm sure Talon will ensure that's handled," I told him, although I would be interested in seeing Talon's idea of over-the-top.

"Is he here?" Isaac asked, his eyes scanning the room.

"Yeah. Down in the dungeon, I think." Trent's attention focused on me. "You get a chance to visit it yet?"

I shook my head. Although everyone had boasted about how great TJ's dungeon was, I had no reason to venture that direction. "Something specific you want us to scope out when we're down there?"

"No. I'm quite content with my own dungeons."

I was quite fond of them myself, having visited the Dichotomy dungeon as recently as last week, when we took Dante and Everly to play.

Trent leaned forward, his eyes serious. "I did want to thank you both for taking on this endeavor. You know, helping out with the resort. I know it's out of your comfort zone, but I have complete faith that you'll both handle it exactly as it should be handled."

I nodded. "Thank you for giving us the opportunity."

"What do the pets think of the change?" he asked.

"We kept it a secret for as long as we could," I told him. "Figured they would hear about it soon enough, so we told them this morning."

"And…?" Trent glanced between us.

"They tried to pretend it wasn't a big deal that we would no longer be leaving them alone, but we could see it. They weren't any happier with us traveling than we were. They seemed content to know we'd be home every night."

"Good. I'm glad it's working out. Well"—Trent got to his feet—"I better make my rounds, check on my own pets. Clarissa was not at all keen on the idea of serving as a table this evening."

"Tell her she was the lucky one," Isaac noted. "Everly's a statue."

"That doesn't sound too bad," Trent said, clearly not understanding the problem.

"Oh, sorry." Isaac chuckled. "Did I forget to mention she's a statue in the water fountain? Had to slip off the hose and shoes, too."

Trent's grin was slow and wicked. "I'll have to check that out."

"You should. She's rather delightful." The deep voice had us all turning as Talon stepped up.

He was one of the few men I had to look up to. Him and Zeke Lautner, being that they were the same height, clocking in at six eight. I was pretty sure they ate small animals for meals considering they were probably as wide as they were tall, solid muscle. Granted, that was where the similarities ended. Talon had long black hair that hung well past his thick shoulders. His Native American heritage was prominent, his dark eyes usually shielded by a pair of dark glasses.

"Good to see you both," Talon said politely, nodding rather than offering a hand.

"The same. Did the dungeon check out?"

A faint smile turned up one corner of his mouth. "I found it rather pleasurable, yes."

With Talon, that could've meant practically anything.

"You didn't bring a pet along for the evening?"

Talon's dark brow lifted.

Yeah, it was a stupid question, I knew, but hey, couldn't blame a man for trying. Talon was known to play with the submissives at the club, both male and female. He had no preference. Most of them would come running back for more if he would have them, but that was the thing with Talon. He didn't mess with a submissive more than once. Unless, of course, it was one of the trainees. At that point, he would pitch in, but he didn't get involved. Ever.

"I don't know if there's one who could handle you," Trent joked, slapping him on the back before heading in the opposite direction.

Talon's gaze snagged on a tiny little thing making her way through the room. I trailed her with my eyes as she pushed her way through the throng of people.

"I'll be back," he rumbled before walking away.

I glanced at Isaac, who simply shrugged.

"Well, I guess we should enjoy this party," I told him.

"You're probably right." He smiled. "I think maybe we should go check out that fountain again."

I grinned, then started toward the other side of the house. "A really nice art piece."

"The nicest I think I've ever seen," Isaac noted.

"You thinking perhaps we should get one for the house?"

He chuckled, his gaze swinging from Everly as a statue, then over to Dante who was still serving food and drinks though practically naked. "This place is giving me quite a few ideas."

Yeah, now that he mentioned it, there was a lot of potential.

Always something to think about.

TALON

"I TOLD YOU, I NEED TO FIND my brother," the woman exclaimed, her low, raspy voice bordering on hysterical.

I had followed her from the moment she stormed through the house. Tiny little thing, no bigger than a minute. A bit on the thin side, with the longest, shiniest hair I'd ever seen. Before I could approach, a male in a tacky suit grabbed her arm, jerked her toward him.

"You can't be here," the little twit currently squeezing her arm insisted. "You don't have an invitation, nor are you wearing the appropriate attire."

I seethed, something dark and fierce uncurled inside me at the sight of him bruising her soft flesh.

On a good day, I wasn't the sort of man to stick my nose where it didn't belong, but I was compelled by some dark driving force to intervene.

"I'm not here for the party," the caramel-haired female insisted. "I told you, I'm looking for my brother."

"Not tonight, you're not," the male declared as he pulled her toward the front of the house.

"Hey," she hissed, trying to pry his fingers from her arms. "You're hurting me."

I stepped into the male's path, blocked his attempt to drag her away. Anger, hot and bright erupted and it took everything in me not to rip his head clean off his body.

"If you wouldn't mind," he huffed, trying to move around me. "She's not permitted to be here."

"I think she asked you to remove your hand." I kept my voice even, the deep bellow all I generally needed to get the desired result.

The male sighed, glared up at me. "I'm not here to argue with you, Talon. She can't be here. Master Arlington said—"

I nodded my chin toward his hand still gripping her arm. "Off."

He released her, then stepped back, his palms coming up in a sign of surrender. "Whatever. I've got to inform the security team. They won't be nearly as nice as I've been."

"Tell whoever you need to." Before he could walk off, I gripped his shoulder, my hand covering the entire shoulder joint, squeezing just enough to have his arm going numb. "Next time you think of being *nice* to her, I'll break your fingers. One by one." I leaned down to his level. "Then I'll feed them to you."

The male howled, his knees buckling as my fingers dug deeper into the nerves.

"Okay. Yes. I won't touch her again."

I released him, my eyes shifting to the female. More specifically the way she was rubbing her arm.

The bullshit excuse for security stormed off in a huff, but I was more interested in the big brown eyes peering up at me.

"Are you okay?" I took her wrist, gently raised her arm and studied the red marks the bastard had left. Perhaps I should break his fingers anyway.

Her eyes locked on the spot where my skin touched hers, but she didn't pull away. When she peered up at me, those beautiful dark eyes were calmer.

"Yes. I'm fine. Look," she said softly. "I really am sorry. I'm not trying to crash the party. I just need to find my brother."

I motioned her out of the direct path of the other guests. "Who's your brother?"

"Ransom Bishop."

"He's not here," I told her.

Her eyes widened and a glimmer of fear replaced the determination. "He's not? He said he'd be here."

I motioned toward the front door. "Left about an hour ago. Said he had to take care of something."

Her hand covered her mouth. "Oh, God."

Releasing the wrist I'd inadvertently been running my thumb over, I motioned for her to step toward the hallway. No sense causing a scene.

Footsteps erupted behind me. With my body blocking her from view, I glanced over my shoulder.

"Hey. She can't be here."

The new arrival was glaring up at me as though he just might have the mind to take matters into his own hands should I not abide by his declaration. He attempted to look around me to locate the female. As though it was my sole position in life, I didn't move, keeping her sheltered between my body and the corner, my back to the room.

I turned my attention back to the female while I continued to speak to the male who was making a feeble attempt at passing himself off as security. "She's here. And she's not leaving until I say she's leaving. Understand?"

She craned her neck, staring up at me, but I didn't detect any fear in those pretty brown eyes.

"Look, man," the male muttered. "I'm not some submissive you can boss around. I'm TJ Arlington's second-in-command."

"Ah." I smirked, never taking my attention off the female. "Well, why don't you find me the top dog then. Perhaps he'll have a bit more respect for Mr. Arlington's guests."

"She's not a guest," he argued.

"Maybe not. But I am." I spared him one quick glance over my shoulder. "Consider her my plus one. Interrupt me again, you won't walk out of here under your own steam."

He swallowed, clearly detecting the sincerity of my threat. I didn't bother waiting for him to walk away before I peered back at the female.

"What's your name?" I asked, my voice softer than before.

"Braelyn," she whispered, still looking up at me. "Braelyn Bishop."

I nodded as I stood tall, still keeping her protected from the room. "I'm Talon."

As though she'd heard my name before, her eyes flared slightly before settling.

I took one step back, giving her room to breathe, but I kept her shielded in the corner.

"Did you try calling him?"

"Yeah." She took a deep breath, exhaled slowly. "Several times. But he does this on occasion. Ignores my calls when he's too busy."

"Talon?"

The familiar voice had me turning to see TJ Arlington strolling my way.

A foreign need to defend had me standing taller, maxing out my full six feet eight inches, broadening my stance as I turned my back on the female. Didn't matter that I knew TJ wasn't a real threat. The beast inside me panted, paced, readied for a fight and I'd never felt it as fiercely as I did at that moment.

"Relax, big guy," TJ joked. "I just wanted to let you know you've got access to any place in my home." He motioned down the hall. "There's a library and an office that way. Guest rooms upstairs. I've informed my boys to keep clear."

I offered a nod of thanks.

Without waiting for more, TJ turned and walked off, greeting another guest.

"Why don't I try calling him," I told Braelyn when I turned back, gestured for her to head down the hallway. "Perhaps we should check out the library."

She smiled, obviously hearing the amusement in my tone. I would never understand why someone had a library in their home. I had bookshelves full of books in my house, but they weren't in the library, it was simply a room. In my house.

Perhaps that was too pretentious for me.

When we stepped into the room, I retrieved my phone, pulled up Ransom's contact info and dialed. A minute later, I was leaving a message for him to return my call.

"Does he usually avoid your calls, too?" Braelyn asked, her cute little ass leaning against the wall, arms crossed over her chest.

"No. Never."

"Shit," she bit out seconds before she began pacing the ridiculous room.

NICOLE EDWARDS

The ceilings were roughly twenty feet tall, some awkward mural of what could've passed for Greek mythology painted across it. The walls were lined with dark wood shelving, all filled to overflowing with books. The bulk of which I was almost certain cost more than a small country. One bookshelf was dedicated to TJ Arlington and his wealth of publications revolving around romantic BDSM fiction.

I doubted Braelyn would've been able to tell me the color of the shelves, her attention directed to the overpriced gold rug covering a majority of the floor.

"Why don't you tell me what's going on," I suggested. "Perhaps I can help."

When she stopped her midnight marathon, Braelyn turned to look at me. This time, when those beautiful eyes met mine, they were flooded with tears.

It was then, that very moment in time, when I realized exactly where I was meant to be.

Acknowledgments

Of course, I have to thank my wonderfully patient husband who puts up with me every single day. If it wasn't for him and his belief that I could (and can) do this, I wouldn't be writing this today. He has been my backbone, my rock, the very reason I continue to believe in myself. I love you for that, babe.

I also have to thank my street team – Naughty (and nice) Girls – Your unwavering support is something I will never take for granted.

I can't forget my copyeditor, Amy at Blue Otter Editing. Thank goodness I've got you to catch all my punctuation, grammar, and tense errors.

Nicole Nation 2.0 for the constant support and love. You've been there for me from almost the beginning. This group of ladies has kept me going for so long, I'm not sure I'd know what to do without them.

And, of course, YOU, the reader. Your emails, messages, posts, comments, tweets… they mean more to me than you can imagine. I thrive on hearing from you, knowing that my characters and my stories have touched you in some way keeps me going. I've been known to shed a tear or two when reading an email because you simply bring so much joy to my life with your support. I thank you for that.

About Nicole Edwards

New York Times and *USA Today* bestselling author Nicole Edwards lives in the suburbs of Austin, Texas with her husband and their youngest of three children. The two older ones have flown the coup, while the youngest is in high school. When Nicole is not writing about sexy alpha males and sassy, independent women, she can often be found with a book in hand or attempting to keep the dogs happy. You can find her hanging out on social media and interacting with her readers - even when she's supposed to be writing.

Want to see some fun stuff related to Nicole's books, you can find extras on her website. Or how about what's coming next? Find more at: www.NicoleEdwardsAuthor.com

If you're interested in keeping up to date on any new releases and preorders, you can sign up for Nicole's notification newsletter. This only goes out when she's got important information to share.

Want a simple, fast way to get updates on new releases? Sign up for text messaging. If you are in the U.S. simply text NICOLE to 64600 or sign up on her website. She promises not to spam your phone. This is just her way of letting you know what's happening because Nicole knows you're busy, but if you're anything like her, you always have your phone on you.

You can also find Nicole here:

Twitter: @NicoleEAuthor

Facebook: /Author.Nicole.Edwards

Instagram: NicoleEdwardsAuthor

By Nicole Edwards

Alluring Indulgence Series
Kaleb
Zane
Travis
Holidays with the Walker Brothers
Ethan
Braydon
Sawyer
Brendon

Walkers of Coyote Ridge Series
Curtis
Jared
Hard to Hold
Hard to Handle
Beau
Rex
A Coyote Ridge Christmas
Mack

Austin Arrows Series
The SEASON: Rush
The SEASON: Kaufman

Club Destiny Series
Conviction
Temptation
Addicted
Seduction
Infatuation
Captivated
Devotion
Perception
Entrusted
Adored
Distraction

STANDALONE NOVELS
Unhinged Trilogy
A Million Tiny Pieces
Inked on Paper
Bad Reputation
Bad Business

NAUGHTY HOLIDAY EDITIONS
2015
2016

www.ingramcontent.com/pod-product-compliance
Lightning Source LLC
Chambersburg PA
CBHW070828260626

47170CB00007B/2301